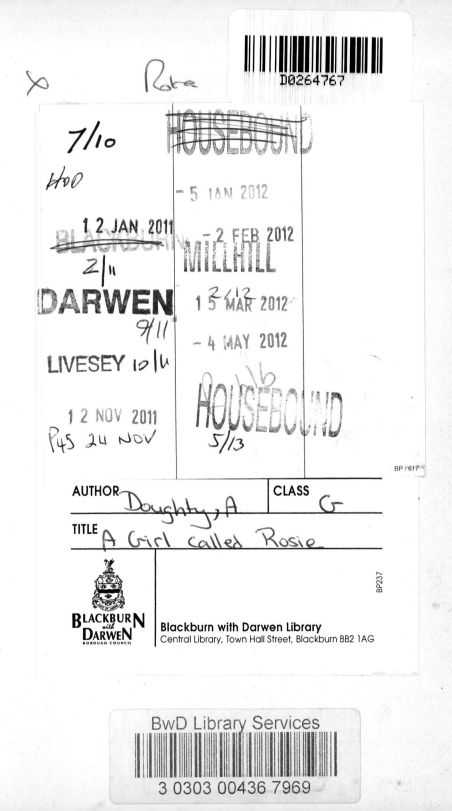

A GIRL CALLED ROSIE

A GIRL CALLED ROSIE

Anne Doughty

Severn House Large Print
London & New York

This first large print edition published 2009
in Great Britain and the USA by
SEVERN HOUSE PUBLISHERS LTD of
9-15 High Street, Sutton, Surrey, SM1 1DF.
First world regular print edition published 2008 by
Severn House Publishers Ltd., London and New York.

British Library Cataloguing in Publication Data

Doughty, Anne, 1939-
  A girl called Rosie. - Large print ed.
  1. Grandparent and child - Fiction 2. Vacations - Ireland -
  Kerry - Fiction 3. Ireland - Social conditions - Fiction
  4. Domestic fiction 5. Large type books
  I. Title
  823.9'2[F]

ISBN-13: 978-0-7278-7776-5

Printed and bound in Great Britain by
MPG Books Ltd, Bodmin, Cornwall.

In Remembrance
Mackie Spratt
of
Woodview and Mullabane
County Armagh

Do-it-yourself car builder and storyteller
April 1921 – April 2007

Acknowledgements

The 1920s have an image of gaiety. Books, films and magazines are full of bright young things tripping around in short skirts, daringly smoking cigarettes in long holders, dancing new dances, driving in fast cars and listening to the wireless or gramophone on sunshine picnics.

I am grateful to my many friends in libraries and archives for producing the alternative view. Whatever personal joys there were, life was not easy for most people. Jobs were scarce, the Depression had arrived and was a standing threat.

In Ireland, newly partitioned, the years of the First World War had been extended by the Anglo-Irish War and then the Civil War within the newly-formed Irish Free State. In both parts of Ireland the economy was in difficulties, emigration was high and bitterness and old feuds were rife.

I have had much help for this novel from friends and family, who have offered me fragments of their own memories, and by complete strangers who have gone to great lengths to provide me with details of road engines, Lagondas and Bentleys, motor and motorcycle racing and rose breeding. If I have failed to use all their material it is simply because they were so very generous.

Some readers may be familiar with Rosie Hamilton's family from previous novels of mine, but each individual novel stands alone. What Rosie knows about her family is what she is told or finds out. Like most people, there are things she doesn't know, stories that have been forgotten, people who have moved away.

Finishing this novel in May 2007, I am struck by how very far away Rosie's world now seems, but also by the fact that the long years of bitterness into which she was born are at last in the process of becoming history.

Anne Doughty
Belfast
May, 2007

One

Even in high summer the interior of the grocer's shop was always cool. Little sunlight penetrated beyond the windows that looked out over the wide thoroughfare where once linen merchants had come to buy webs of cloth. Now, time and circumstances having changed, the only sign of life was a baker's cart, its deliveries complete, moving through the empty space, idly observed by a couple of small boys playing marbles in the heavy dust of an unusually dry and warm June.

The boxes and tins that decorated the two small windows on either side of the open door, a couple of advertisements for soap and tea, their colours faded to strange muted shades of red and blue, their curled-up edges yellowed by age, were the only signs that this two-storey dwelling was any different from its neighbours. The adjoining grey terraced houses marched up the hill, their doors also standing wide, their half-curtained windows reflecting the unremitting sunlight.

Henry Loney kept the back door of his shop propped open with a brick. What cool air their might be in the deep shadow of the yard behind

9

flowed down a narrow passageway where sides of bacon hung against the wall in woven nets, boxes of butter piled beneath.

He lifted his eyes from the account he had just added up and ran them across the shapely figure of the slim, dark-haired girl who stood waiting in the small space between the wooden counter and the towers of cardboard boxes stacked against the wall of what had once been his grandmother's parlour.

'Ye've a brave list the day, Rosie,' he said, as he stuck his pencil behind his ear, turned away from his account book and gave his attention to the shelves behind him.

Rosie brushed back her dark hair from her perspiring forehead and followed his practised movements with wide dark eyes. Now he'd added up the cost of her mother's groceries, he'd want to know all the news from the long, low farmhouse at the foot of the winding lane leading down to Richhill Station. She dreaded the weekly inquisitions but they were not to be avoided. Gossip was Henry's favourite pastime.

'Yes, there's a bit extra. Billy's coming home this afternoon.'

'Ach, is he now? Yer ma'll be glad to see him,' he replied, as he placed packets of tea and sugar on the counter. 'Ye'll want to know how he's doing down there in Enniskillen. Far better pay in the police than what he was doin' afore.'

She watched as he reached up for more packets and boxes, his bald head tipped back towards her. Henry was her uncle, one of her mother's brothers, a part of her everyday life, but she'd

10

never liked him, even when she was a little girl and he sometimes gave her chocolate.

She'd liked him even less since the day he'd found her alone in the kitchen at home, slipped his arm round her waist and moved his hand up towards her breast. From that day onwards she'd avoided him when he visited the farm and kept well out of reach in the shop if he came round the counter on the pretext of helping her get a good grip on her well-filled shopping bags.

'Are ye all well down at the farm?' he asked, turning back towards her, a polished brass scoop full of porridge oats poised over an open paper bag. He readjusted the scales, weighed out lentils and barley and enquired about her father and mother, her brothers and sisters.

'Yes, indeed, all just as usual,' she replied, making an effort not to sound as weary as she felt.

It was the same every Saturday morning. After she'd done the jobs her mother lined up for her, washing the kitchen floor, cleaning the stove, feeding the hens, she was always glad to get out of the house. Even if the weather was bad, she didn't mind. She enjoyed the walk up the lane. There were always birds in the hedgerows; the buds, or leaves, or blossom, depending on the season; friends or neighbours to wave to as she passed. What she did mind was Henry and his endless questions and having to be sure to say the right thing.

At almost sixteen, Rosie Hamilton had no illusions at all about her mother. Martha had a sharp tongue and was easily annoyed. A chance word, a harmless remark and you'd get an outburst of fury or a clip round the ear. Often, her anger was unpredictable. One minute she was talking about some piece of news picked up from a neighbour and the next she was shouting, berating her in her thin, hard voice for something she had done or not done. It made little difference which it was once she got started.

Apart from absence and saying as little as possible, Rosie had never found any real defence against her mother's tirades. There was no surer way of provoking her than to fail to remember exactly what Henry, or any of her mother's other relatives, had said to her, and what she had said in reply, for the questions and comments of neighbours and friends, and particularly of Rosie's aunts and uncles, were a matter of great significance to Martha Hamilton.

On her return from any errand to the village, from school, or even from a walk with her friend, Lizzie Mackay, Rosie knew she would be questioned as to who she'd met and what they'd said.

'Did he ask ye how I was? Did ye tell him I was in Armagh yesterday? Did ye tell him Charlie has bought a motorcycle? What did he say? An' what did you say to that?'

'Joe well?' Henry continued, a small half smile crossing his well-rounded face as he wrapped Sunlight soap in thick brown wrapping paper. 'Still complainin'?'

Rosie knew better than to agree. Her Uncle Joe, the eldest of the Loney brothers, owned the small farm where her family lived. He had seldom a good word for anyone, least of all

12

herself, and he complained endlessly. If it wasn't the rain, it was the lack of it. If it wasn't the poorness of the income from the farm, it was the weakness of the government. If it wasn't one of his nephews or nieces not doing what he told them, it was his sciatica or his chest.

She had never seen Uncle Joe smile. She sometimes wondered if he had forgotten how to or whether the muscles of his small, wrinkled face had set so firmly in its habitual scowl he could no longer manipulate it, even if some unusual circumstance were to provoke him to make the attempt.

'He and Bobby are turning the hay in the low meadow,' she said lightly, knowing she must say something.

'Ah shure it's great weather for hay,' said Henry, his tone implying an intimate knowledge of the maturing process of hay. 'With this heat there'll be grand drying. The quality will be exceptional this year.'

Rosie nodded and smiled dutifully as Henry reached over the counter for her empty shopping bags.

There were few subjects on which Henry was not an expert. The fact that he lived over the shop, had never married, seldom left the village and read only the newspapers which he ordered with the goods for his trade, presented him with not the slightest difficulty in pronouncing on any matter that might arise.

'And what about yer da? Does he like his new job?'

Henry paused in the process of packing her

bags and Rosie eyed the remaining pile of groceries. Were another customer to come into the shop Henry could pack the remainder in a matter of seconds and she would be out into the sunlight in the time it took for him to say 'Cheerio, Rosie, tell your mother I was askin' for her'.

But today, no other customer came to her aid. Henry would pack the items one at a time with concentrated attention until he had satisfied himself there was nothing of any significance left to be found out.

'Yes, he does,' she agreed, nodding. 'It's further to cycle every day, but he says it'll keep him fit.'

After many years working as an engineer at the local jam factory, her father had been offered a job with the company where he'd had his first job away from home, many years earlier, in the days when he still drove a traction engine. He'd told her about getting it one day when she was sitting in the barn watching him measure up a piece of metal sheeting for a boiler he was about to mend.

He'd come over from Banbridge on the train and walked up from the station on a lovely sunny morning, passing their own house, never thinking he might one day live there. He'd been offered the job right away and went home as pleased as Punch to tell her granny and granda. It had been a bad time for him and they'd been worried about him, because he'd had an accident at the haulage company where he'd been working since he left school. He'd broken his leg and

14

been given his cards. It had nearly knocked the heart out of him, he'd said, his face darkening at the memory, but didn't we all have bad times and get over them, he'd gone on, nodding to her, encouraging her, for he'd guessed she'd had another dressing down from her mother that day and had come out to the barn to get away from her.

'It's a grand firm to work for,' Henry continued confidently. 'I have it on good authority that they're one of the best motor companies in the North of Ireland. Maybe your da'll buy a motor himself,' he said, looking at her sideways.

'That would be nice,' she said promptly. 'Then he could bring Ma up for the groceries.'

The moment she spoke and saw the smile broaden on his face she regretted it. She'd meant to say only that it would be nice, a harmless remark he could make nothing of. She couldn't think what had possessed her to say more. Maybe it was because her back was aching with standing still while he took his time over packing her bag, or maybe she was just tired of having to watch every word she said.

'Aye, she could act the lady then like yer granny does. Mrs Hamilton from Rathdrum House,' he said with a little bow. 'Have ye been over t' see *her* at all, or is it only yer da goes ivery week?'

Rosie felt her face flush with anger and could not be sure if it showed in the dimness of the shop. Henry was leaning towards her across the counter, her shopping bags enclosed in his arms so that she couldn't pick them up without

15

moving closer to his smiling face.

'Granny is very well, thank you,' she said coolly. 'I'm hoping to see her next week when school finishes.'

She stepped over to the door and propped it open with the brick that lay beside it. Then, without looking up at him again, she reached for the shopping bags, pulling them away from his restraining arms.

'Ma'll be wondering what's keeping me,' she said crisply turning her back on him. 'I'll tell her you were asking for her.'

'Aye, an' tell her I put in a good word fer ye up at the castle. She told me ye'd no plans for when ye left Miss Wilson's wee school. But I think they'll have ye. The Richardsons know I can spot a good worker when I see one.'

He came round the counter and followed her into the street. She walked away quickly, the heavy bags dragging at her arms, her chest tight with fury. Even though she knew he couldn't leave the shop to follow her, she moved as fast as she could. Once clear of the village, she was so breathless she had to prop the bags against a gatepost, lean against the bars and wipe tears from her eyes with the back of her hand.

'So that's what she's been planning,' she whispered to herself. 'Her and Henry, behind my back.'

The thought appalled her. Only once had she been inside the handsome seventeenth-century house that stood behind its wrought-iron gates at the top of the hill. Lizzie Mackay's aunt was the housekeeper there and she'd smuggled them in

16

one day when the family were away visiting one of the other landed families in the county, the Stronges at Caledon or the Achesons at Markethill.

She'd taken them on tiptoe round the family rooms showing them portraits and silver and well-polished furniture. She'd even shown them the shaped timbers that held up the roof, each one numbered centuries ago by the builder, and pointed out a great stone eagle that sat poised on one of the tall chimneys.

There was a strange smell about the place. Dust and old carpets and metal polish. But it was the back kitchens that had oppressed her most. Dark and gloomy, they had a list of rules and regulations pinned to the wall that Aunt Maisie insisted on reading out to them. Lizzie hadn't much liked the place either, but it was Rosie who caught her breath and longed to be out in the open air again, away from the dark panelling and the cold stone floors.

'What am I going to do?' she exclaimed. 'What am I going to do?'

She picked up her bags, straightened her shoulders and moved on. If she delayed any longer she was sure to be told off for dilly-dallying. If she couldn't think of anything different in the next week, she might end up having to go up to the Richardsons after all. She couldn't stay at home for long, she knew that. Things were bad enough as they were, her mother constantly finding fault with everything she did, but if she had to spend every day at her beck and call she'd never be able to keep her temper.

For the last year, since she'd left the National School, she'd been going to Miss Wilson's small school on the outskirts of the village. Miss Wilson was white-haired, wore a monocle and was very strict, but she was also kind. She'd suggested that Rosie might train as a teacher or become a nurse, but Rosie knew her mother would never stand for it. There'd been trouble enough over her going to Miss Wilson's for a year, even though her grandmother had paid the modest fees.

All her mother wanted was for her to get a job, in the office of the jam factory like Emily, or be apprenticed to the dressmaker, like young Dolly wanted to be just as soon as she could leave school. Who did she think she was that she couldn't do what her sisters did?

'It's all very well for yer grandmother, she can well afford it,' her mother had protested, when Rosie had told her of her grandmother's offer. 'An' while your sittin' readin' books, I suppose she expects me to feed an' clothe ye fer the year,' she went on furiously.

'I think we can manage that, Martha,' her father said coldly. 'There are five of our family addin' to your purse forby what I give you. Ye can let me know if ye run short.'

The year was almost finished now, but she was no further on. Another week and there would be no Miss Wilson, no books, no French lessons, no painting or poetry. She would even miss the deportment and embroidery which she'd never enjoyed.

For a long time now she'd been anxious about

leaving school but her father had tried to reassure her.

'Give yourself a bit o' time, Rosie. Sure there's no great hurry to make up your mind. There's plenty to do here over the summer now Emily's out at work and Margaret spends all her time helping her aunt up at Sandymount. You can give your mother a hand with the house and keep an eye on Dolly and Jack. Things might be clearer in a month or two. Maybe ye need a bit of a rest from school work.'

She crossed over the main road, the sun high in the sky, a short misshapen shadow at her feet, and began the long, slow descent to the valley bottom. She could rely on her father trying to help her, but it was always at a price. If her mother saw her coming out of the barn where he had his workshop and where he and her brothers slept, she'd be accused off slipping out to avoid doing her work, leaving it all for someone else. Once started on the theme of Rosie's idleness, and particularly her sitting around reading books when she could be doing something useful, there was no stopping her. Only the appearance of one of her brothers, or a visiting neighbour, would stem the flow and create an immediate change of tone.

'Ach hello, Mrs Hutchinson. Come in and sit down. Rosie was just goin' to make us a cup of tea.'

Although she'd walked as quickly as she could, going up to the village and on the return journey, Rose was only too aware that time was moving on. Henry had been slower than usual and although there was no clock in the shop, she knew the sun was higher and the shadows much shorter than when she'd set out. It was a bad sign too that there was no one about. Not a soul on the lane itself, and no one in the gardens or farm-yards she passed. When she picked up the odour of boiled potatoes and fresh-baked bread, she knew it was certainly past one o'clock.

The smell of frying onions drifting over the wooden gate that led to the open door of their nearest neighbours reminded Rosie she was hungry as well as tired, but her thoughts were not on food. Part of her was already anxious about her mother's reception. Another part was think-ing longingly of a large mug of water from the enamel bucket in the wooden press.

The gate into the farmyard was open as it often was during the day. Only when the four cows were brought up for milking did Uncle Joe send Bobby running to close it. She tramped through gratefully, her eyes watering in the bright light, her neck and back aching from the weight of the bags dragging on her narrow shoulders, her gaze on the open door ahead and the thought of the cool dimness beyond.

'Hello, Rosie. Ma thought you'd got lost.'

A small voice greeted her brightly as she cross-ed the threshold into the stone-floored kitchen.

'Hello, Dolly,' she replied wearily, managing a small smile for the little girl who sat by the stove rubbing a brass candlestick with a piece of black-ened rag.

She lifted up her bags, lowered them gratefully on to the kitchen table, propped them up against each other and began to unpack them quickly.

'Mrs Hutchinson was here,' Dolly went on, as she poured Brasso on the matching candlestick with more vigour than skill, her fingers as black as the rag she was using. 'Ma's just walking down the road with her. She said she thought you'd got lost.'

Rosie sighed and said nothing. The remark about getting lost was another way of saying she was late. Like many of her mother's remarks, made to a neighbour, with a little laugh, it sounded like a joke, but it only *sounded* like a joke. Unless Mrs Hutchinson was still here and her mother had to behave as if it really was, then its true meaning would emerge. Unless some piece of news, or gossip, had put her mother in a good mood, that remark about getting lost was simply advance warning that she could expect a telling off.

Halfway through the second bag and before she had dared pause for a drink of water, Rosie heard her mother's step in the yard. Moments later the light from the door was blocked by her small, square figure.

'Ach, so ye did come home after all. We thought you'd lost your way,' she began, as she came to the table, an unpleasant smile on her face.

Rosie was not at all surprised when she turned away towards Dolly.

'Aren't those just lovely, pet,' she enthused, as she picked up the candle sticks and placed them back on either side of the mantelpiece. 'Haven't you done a great job. Good girl yerself. Now

21

away over to the barn and clean up your hands in the wash house. And then go and have a wee look and see if you can find where the white hen's nest is. She's laying away again. Have a good look an' I'll call you to yer dinner when it's ready.'

Rosie saw the smile on her mother's face disappear like snow off a ditch the moment her young sister was out of the house. She went on unpacking from the bottom of the second bag, a tight knot of apprehension gathering in her stomach.

'What kep ye?' Martha began, her lips snapping shut after her utterance.

'There was a lot to get today. Uncle Henry said I'd a brave list,' Rosie replied mildly.

'Ye cou'd ha' bought the whole shop in the time ye've been away,' her mother replied, tossing her head.

Although her mother had grown increasingly stouter over the years, for some reason Rosie could not fathom her face had not changed. It was still as she remembered it from her childhood, sharp and almost unwrinkled, the eyes small and bright, the nose pointed, her sparse hair drawn back into a meagre bun, pinned at the nape of her neck.

'Maybe ye were seein' yer man,' Martha said with a sneer.

Rosie folded up the empty bags and stared at her, a look of amazement on her face.

'Don't you try to fool me, Miss Rosie,' her mother said sharply, her tone heavy with sarcasm. 'Aggie Hutchinson saw you the other night. And right embarrassed she was to hafta tell me what any chile of mine was up to. Ye should be ashamed of yerself,' she went on, poking her chin forward and flushing red with the fury of her words.

'What are you talking about, Ma. What night?'

'Last Wednesday night, as you very well know,' she replied, nodding her head for extra emphasis on every word. 'Choir practise was what you tole me. A pack o' lies. That wee huzzey, Lizzie Mackay, an' you, comin' down the lane with a couple of boys. Kissin' and huggin'. Lettin' yourselves down a bagful. Paddy Doyle, indeed. Not even one of yer own sort,' she spat out viciously.

Rosie felt the blood drain from her face as she recalled what had actually happened in the lane. A group of boys had rushed out from behind a hedge, mostly the young Doyles who had recently come to live nearby, shouting and egging each other on. Paddy had grabbed her, managed to kiss her awkwardly on the cheek and run away laughing. Lizzie didn't even know the name of the red-headed lad who was more successful and kissed her on the lips before disappearing with his friends.

'It was nothing, Ma. Just a couple of boys catching hold of us for a dare.'

'Well, that's not the way I heard of it,' her mother snapped back. 'Are you tryin' to tell me that Mrs Hutchinson is stupid? That she hasn't eyes in her head?'

Rosie looked away, the anger on her mother's face too much to bear. Mrs Hutchinson might or might not be stupid, but she was well-known as a gossip. The more unpleasant the gossip, the better she enjoyed it.

She knew she couldn't say that, but before she had considered carefully enough what she could say, she heard herself reply.

'Perhaps, Ma, if Mrs Hutchinson had watched a bit longer, she'd have seen the boys running away into Mackay's field.'

Martha came round the table, where Rosie had abandoned her efforts to sort out the groceries, and advanced upon her.

'How dare you! How dare you! You're as bad a wee huzzey as Lizzie Mackay. I'll not hear you say a word against your elders and betters.'

Rosie saw her draw back her hand to hit her, moved backwards to avoid the blow to her face and tripped on the uneven worn stone of the floor. As she felt herself falling, she grabbed wildly at the back of a chair standing against the wall that gave on to the farmyard, but she couldn't stop herself. She hit the upper part of the open door, her head banging against its solid shape, her cheek scraping past the latch of the half door below as she crumpled on the doorstep.

Dazed and confused, she lay where she had fallen, her eyes closed against the blinding light.

'Get up outa that.'

She felt the shadow of her mother come between her and the light and waited for her to go on. The fall had jerked tears to her eyes and she put up a hand to wipe them away. She felt blood on her cheek, warm and sticky.

'What's happened to Rosie?'

From a little way away, she heard her father's voice, calm and steady as it always was. A moment later, she picked up the smell of lubricating oil as he put his arm around her and drew her to her feet, her face buried in his working dungarees.

'Did you lift your hand to her?'

'Not at all. She tripped over herself on that bad bit of floor,' replied Martha quickly. 'Sure she's never lookin' where she's goin' her head's that full o' books and stories.'

'We'll see about that later,' he said shortly. 'Send Dolly over with some tea and plenty of sugar in it.'

He picked Rosie up in his arms as if she were a child and carried her over to the barn.

Two

Sam Hamilton placed his empty plate quietly on the table beside him and looked down again at the slight figure of his daughter. She lay asleep on one of the four single beds placed in each of the corners of the large, low-roofed room that ran the full width of the barn above his workshop and the washroom he'd fitted out for his family when they'd first come to live at the farm with Uncle Joe, his wife's eldest brother.

The high sun of early afternoon made two bright patches on the bare boards by the tiny windows overlooking the yard, but the rest of the sparsely-furnished space was cool, quiet and shadowy. Neither the random bellowing of cattle distressed by the heat, nor the whistle and hiss of the engines that steamed past on the railway line nearby, penetrated the thick walls. As he sat watching the sleeping girl, his broad shoulders angled towards her, his large, square face immobile, the only noise he could hear was the regular click of the alarm clock that sat beside his empty plate.

Her dark hair had fallen across her face, but he could already see the outline of the bruise on her forehead. The scrape from the door latch wasn't deep but it had bled a lot. He'd sat her down in the wash house, cleaned it and dabbed it with iodine from his First-Aid kit. Painful, but reliable. He'd used it himself many a time and never suffered infection in a cut or a wound. She'd not said a word of complaint as he painted it on, though he knew well how much it stung.

The bruise would come and go, the cut would heal. She'd be none the worse. He sighed and looked around the room as if it would answer the questions shaping in his mind.

She'll be all right, he said to himself, as he saw a hint of colour come back to her pale face.

Although she'd been confused for a while after he'd brought her over to the barn, he could see she'd taken no great harm. He thanked God it wasn't as bad as he'd feared when he cycled into the yard and heard her cry and the bang of her head on the door.

The tea had helped. She'd drunk the whole mug his youngest daughter had brought over in the short time it took the child to pass on her mother's messages. *There'd be no dinner till evening when Billy was home. Did he want his bread and cheese on a plate where he was?*

He had a fair idea of what had happened, but as soon as she'd drained every last drop of the tea, he'd tried to get her to tell him herself.

'Tell the truth and shame the Devil,' he said encouragingly.

It was always so difficult with children. One moment you were trying to teach them not to carry tales and the next you needed to know exactly what had happened so you could do something to protect them. It was not the first

27

time Martha had struck Rosie, though he had spoken to her sternly about it.

He shook his head sadly. But why was it always Rosie? She was such a willing girl, a hard worker who never complained when her mother gave her the jobs she didn't want to do herself. Martha had never laid a finger on any of the boys. She might have smacked Emily or Margaret when they were very small and being naughty, but she certainly never raised a hand to them once they were older. As for Dolly, the youngest, the child born after he'd left Martha's bed for good, she spoilt her outrageously, petting her and favouring her in a way she'd never done with any of the others.

There was no making sense of it. But then, he'd known for a long time there was no making sense of Martha. He'd accepted years ago that she didn't love him. As the years passed, he'd finally come to the conclusion that she never had loved him, even when she was happy to have him in her bed. Martha was a law unto her self. The best he could do was to avoid angering her, to make sure she had enough money to care for the children properly, and to take pleasure in seeing them grow and thrive.

Nine children, five boys and four girls. A fine, long family, as they would say around Banbridge where he'd spent most of his own childhood in a well-built farmhouse that looked out over the rich Bann Valley to the Mourne Mountains beyond. He wasn't sure if they had the same expression here in County Armagh, but then, apart from the men he worked with at Pearson's

Haulage Company and the other Quakers he saw on a Sunday at the Friends' Meeting House in Richhill, he didn't have much time or opportunity for conversation.

There was certainly no conversation with Martha. Mostly she ignored him, or sent him messages via the two youngest, Dolly and Jack. When he went over to the house, she set his food in front of him without a word. If something in the day had happened to please her, she'd talk excitedly while he was having his meal without once looking at him. Then she'd stop suddenly and before he'd had time to make any comment, she'd complain that he never listened to a word she said, that he was interested in no one but himself and his work.

Rosie stirred restlessly, her sleep troubled. He leaned towards her, saw beads of perspiration break on her forehead and noted the darkening skin of the rising bruise.

What Martha said wasn't true. He loved all his children and was happy to see them in his workshop. He could speak freely there and listen to their stories for Martha never came over to the workshop where he spent most of his time repairing tools and machinery when he was not doing his everyday job at Pearson's. Maybe she so seldom saw him talking to the children, it did seem to her as if he wasn't interested, but then he remembered how angry she was when Rosie used to come and sit hour after hour in the barn watching whatever he was doing. He sighed. Nothing he'd ever done was right for Martha and it wasn't likely to change now.

29

He got slowly to his feet and moved cautiously across the bare wooden floor, avoiding a couple of boards that always squeaked. Downstairs in the workshop, he collected a piece of clean, spoilt cloth, folded it into a pad and stepped into the washroom. The cold water gushing from the tank on the roof splashed his blue dungarees as he soaked the fabric and pressed the pad between his large hands.

Suddenly and unexpectedly, he thought of his own mother, Rose, standing over the sink in the small, chilly dairy of their house at Ballydown, her hands red and chapped as she struggled with his and his father's work clothes. Often stained with oil or grease, or the plaster from a wall where his father had squeezed into some awkward corner to repair a loom or a weaving frame, she would work away with a beetle or a washboard, a drip at the end of her nose, the steam from the hot water condensing on her cold face, singing.

When he was small she would sing nursery rhymes to him and his little sister, Sarah, as they played in the big kitchen, the door open so she could keep an eye on them. When they were older, at school, or at work, they would come in upon her unexpectedly and find her still singing, but those songs were different, quiet and sad, and she sang as if no one was meant to hear.

Years later, Sarah had explained why he could never make out what the songs were about.

'It was Irish, Sam. That's why you couldn't understand it. Did you think it was your ears?' she asked, laughing at him, teasing him as she always did, till he'd smiled and admitted that indeed the harder he listened the less he could make of it.

Rosie had turned on her right side while he'd been gone, making it easier to lay the pad gently on the bruise. As the cool fabric touched her damp skin, he was surprised to see her smile.

'That's nice,' she said, her eyes flicking open. 'I think I heard you going down, but I was busy dreaming,' she went on, her smile broadening. 'But it's gone. Can't remember a thing about it.'

'That's the way with dreams,' he said soberly. 'The bad ones wake you up and the nice ones run away. That's what your Aunt Sarah always used to say. She was a great one for dreams,' he added, encouraged by the steady tone of her voice. 'She used to keep us all sitting at the breakfast table while she told us every wee detail of some dream or other she'd had. We'd all 'ave been late for school if your granny hadn't put in a word or two.'

Rosie sat up, caught the damp pad as it slipped, turned it over and pressed it back over the bruise.

'Didn't she *ever* scold you?' she asked, a frown wrinkling her brow.

'Ach, I'm sure she did,' he replied, a small smile touching his lips. 'Shure we were naughty too. But I never mind going to bed without a hug and a kiss. She always taught us never to hold a grudge or be upset with each other, even for a day.'

'"Life is too short for hurting one another. If you can't love someone, then at least let them be",' Rosie repeated quietly.

'Aye, that was another of her sayings.'

He looked at her closely, wondering what else she'd picked up from his mother.

Each summer, two at a time, from the beginning of the school holidays, she had invited all the children to the farmhouse, halfway up Rathdrum Hill, his old home in Ballydown. Billy and Charlie had slept in the bedroom where he and his brother James once slept, followed a week later by Sammy and Bobby.

He paused. Dear James, the older brother he'd followed around so devotedly throughout his childhood. Clever James, so ambitious he'd rejected his parents and himself for being foolish and backward, unaware of political and economic realities, indifferent to all the things James himself thought so important. James had spoken so bitterly to the parents that loved him, said untrue and unkind things to Hannah and Sarah, then turned his back on all of them, walked out of their home at Ballydown and out of their lives.

Sam shut his eyes momentarily and repeated to himself the blessing he always said for James: *God protect you, James, if you are still with us, and keep your soul if you are not.*

What had happened to his brother was a mystery. Were he still in Ireland, someone surely would have come across him, or at least read his name in the paper, but there'd been no word of him for long years now. Perhaps he had simply shaken the dust off his feet, like his own uncles who'd left the family home in Annacramp, gone to America, hadn't written and never returned.

He began to smile again when he thought of

Emily and Rosie and how much they loved going to stay with their granny. Being younger, only a few of their visits were to the farmhouse. For them, visiting Granny and Granda meant going on up to the top of the hill to the lovely old house where they had a garden to play in, books and photograph albums to explore, and a bathroom. He could still remember the excitement when the two girls came home after their first visit and told him how they floated in the long, deep bath, something they'd never met before.

Only the two youngest girls, Margaret and Dolly and his young son Jack had never visited their grandmother. Though they had all been invited as warmly as Emily and Rosie, Margaret always refused to go, insisting that her aunt couldn't manage without her. From the time she'd been old enough to visit away from home, she'd taken herself off to her Aunt Maggie's house just up the road at Sandymount. Now she lived there permanently and her aunt, who had no children, always backed up her refusal.

Dolly never wanted to leave her mother and for some reason, best known to herself, Martha absolutely refused to let young Jack go to Rathdrum House either with one of his sisters or on his own. There had been arguments about it, but when he saw how distressed the little boy had become, he'd dropped the subject, knowing his mother would understand.

There was colour in Rosie's cheeks now. She'd thrown her dark hair back from her face and was wiping face and hands briskly with the pad he'd brought for her bruise.

'Did yer mother lift her hand to you?' he said calmly, without looking at her.

Rosie's smile vanished, she dropped her eyes and twisted the damp cloth in her hands.

'Did she?' he persisted.

She moved her head in an almost imperceptible nod.

'I'll give it thought,' he said quietly. 'It will never happen again.'

Although Rosie protested and said her mother would need her help with preparations for the special dinner she always made when Billy came home, Sam insisted she stay where she was and have another wee sleep. This Saturday, Emily had the half day from her job at Fruitfield Jam Factory. She could do whatever was needed, he said, as he got to his feet and went back down to his workshop.

There, he stood undecided, his eye running over the jobs lined up on the workbench, his mind still resting on his daughter, the image of her small, pale face as she lay on his bed, the lightness of her slim body in his arms as he carried her over from the house.

Rosie fell asleep almost immediately and woke surprised to find it was so late in the afternoon. She sat up hurriedly, ready to swing her legs out of bed, push her feet into her shoes and go back over to the house, but the moment she moved her head throbbed with pain and set up an oscillating beat like the one a motor makes when the engine is ticking over. She lowered herself cautiously on to the bed again and was grateful to feel the throbbing slowly die down. A little later, she discovered the pain went away as well so long as she kept quite still.

High above her head in the pitched roof the motes danced in a broad beam of sunlight that fell through the one small skylight window. She followed its slanting path to the floor where it lit up a rag rug, its colours still bright, though she and Emily had made it from the carefully folded pieces from dresses and skirts out of Granny's box, some of them years old, a few even going all the way back to the days when Auntie Hannah and Auntie Sarah were still at home.

On one of the few wet days in their visit the previous summer, their grandmother had sat in the conservatory at Rathdrum and showed them how to stitch the hemmed pieces on to the hessian backing. They knew already that visit would be their last holiday together for Emily was about to start work at the jam factory and Rosie begin her year at Miss Taylor's small school in Richhill.

She closed her eyes and walked round her grandmother's garden. The details of the paths and flowerbeds were so clear in her mind, for a moment, she imagined she could smell the perfume of the old roses after the rain, but the moment passed even more quickly than a pleasant dream when she caught the tone of a sharp little voice down in the workshop below.

'Ma says, is our Rosie going to lie aroun' all afternoon an' leave us to do all the work?'

Her father's voice was soft but firm.

'Rosie hurt herself, Dolly. She's not feeling

well. Do you not remember when you fell and cut both your knees? You sat by the fire for a long time. Is Emily not home yet?'

'Aye, she came a while ago, but Ma sent her a message to Loneys.'

'Well, tell your mother that if Emily is delayed at Loneys and she needs help, I'll come over myself as soon as I've finished fitting this blade.'

Rosie smiled in spite of herself. Now ten years old, Dolly had grown so like her mother she'd picked up her mannerisms and her sharp way of speaking. Her father's offer would have brought a sour look to her face for she knew it was not the answer her mother wanted.

When he made an offer to help in the house, she could never be quite sure whether or not he did it deliberately, for he knew as well as she did the last thing her mother ever wanted was to have him in her kitchen.

She eased herself up in the bed and leaned back against the headboard. The throbbing didn't start up immediately, but suddenly she felt so weary all she wanted to do was go to sleep. She smiled wryly and admitted to herself how much she was dreading stepping in to the kitchen and facing the comments which would inevitably come her way. At this moment, she had not the remotest idea how she could bring herself to go, but she knew it would have to be done.

As she bent over gingerly to lace up her shoes, she heard a different voice below, a hasty word to her father and a flurry of skirts on the wooden stair.

'Ach, Rosie dear, what happened at all? You

look ghastly.'

Her sister Emily dropped down on the edge of the bed beside her so awkwardly that the springs protested and she nearly knocked Rosie sideways.

'Thanks very much,' Rosie replied, managing a smile.

Over a year older, tall and skinny, with the same pointed features as her mother, Emily resembled her in no other way. She put her arm round Rosie and hugged her, then pushed her sister's hair back and scrutinized the bruise and the cut outlined with iodine. She screwed up her face in concentration.

'Ma said you fell against the door,' she said, her voice heavy with disbelief. 'Well, if you did, you hit it the queer dunt. That wou'd be more like somethin' I'd do. It's not like you at all.'

To her great surprise, Rosie found tears had begun to trickle down her face. She didn't know why she was crying, but the more she tried to stop the faster the tears flowed.

'Ach, dear a dear. Is it very sore?' Emily asked, her face screwed up with anxiety.

Rosie shook her head and poked about in her pockets for a handkerchief.

'Here y'ar, here's mine,' said Emily quickly, pulling out a crumpled square and putting it in her hand. 'Now, c'mon on. Tell me what happened for I don't believe a word of what I've bin told.'

It was only then Rosie realized it was Emily herself had brought the tears, the big sister who had always stood up for her, who'd listened to her even when she knew she hadn't much idea what she was talking about. Emily and Sammy, her older brother, were her best friends. They had been her playmates, her companions on the walk to Richhill school, the two people she could rely on day by day. While she had them she felt safe, even when her mother was in one of her rages, but now Sammy was working in Armagh and only came home on Sundays and Emily was putting away every penny not demanded by their mother. As soon as she had enough money saved she would buy her ticket to America.

Rosie cried in Emily's arms until the tears finally stopped. Then she told her what had happened.

'Ach dear, what are we goin' to do?' Emily said with a great sigh. 'It's not fair that you get the worst of it. She's never as bad with me. But then she knows I'm goin' as soon as I can,' she added, wiping Rosie's damp face with the sleeve of her second-best blouse. 'Did you see anything in the paper last night?'

Rosie nodded.

'Six jobs for "smart boys",' she said briskly. 'Two in Armagh, two in Richhill, one in Portadown and one in Loughgall.'

'No smart girls?'

Rosie laughed.

It was the earnest look on Emily's face that cheered her. It was so characteristic of her. Emily's greatest gift was figures. From the day she'd been asked to count wooden beads she'd changed her mind about not liking school. Numbers made her happy. She recited the multiplication table for pleasure. Counted the money in her mother's purse. Measured and recorded the milk given by each of the four cows. Laid out the nails and screws from the workshop in multiples. Words were a different matter. Emily often had no idea what to say.

When Rosie laughed, Emily beamed with relief. She couldn't bear to see her sister all upset and worried. There were so few jobs around and that made it all the harder. Billy had had to work on the farm until he was old enough to join the police and she'd been at home for over a year before one of the clerks at Fruitfield left to get married. There were so many in for that job she probably wouldn't have had much chance if her father hadn't worked there for years and all the bosses knew him.

Poor old Bobby was just the same. He'd left school the previous year and couldn't find a job of any sort. He wanted to be a mechanic, but he was still having to put up with Uncle Joe on the farm for a few shillings a week. Rosie was smart, far cleverer than any of them, but that wasn't much help if all the jobs going were for boys.

'Rosie,' Emily said suddenly. 'I've thought of something.'

'What, Emily? What have you thought of?'

'Something I read in *The People's Friend*. There was this story about this girl who goes to America and marries a rich man and the first thing she does is send a ticket to her sister,' she said quickly.

'I could do that. Not find the rich man. Not with my face,' she said, laughing. 'But I could save up again and send you a ticket. And it wouдn't take near so long as it's taken me this time. It'll take me sixty-five weeks at two shillings a week here and I've lost over three weeks with expenses at work I hadn't reckoned on, but wages are higher there and I could save maybe a dollar a week for thirty weeks or two dollars for fifteen weeks or even three dollars for ten...'

She broke off.

'Isn't that an idea?' she asked quickly, not sure what to make of the look on Rosie's face.

'That's a *great* idea, Emily,' Rosie replied, giving her a hug. 'That's awfully good of you.'

Rosie hadn't the heart to tell her sister that if she went and she herself had to stay at home, waiting to find work, then she would feel so lonely and vulnerable that even a week would seem more than she could bear.

Three

'Shure the Govermint is far too soft on them 'ems. They oughta be put out. Why aren't they sent down to their own Free State, as they call it? Shure what do we want with them up here, a lot o' Fenians and troublemakers.'

Rosie's heart sank and she felt her hands go moist as they always did when she was anxious. She didn't even need to glance across the kitchen to where Uncle Joe sat in his usual place to the right of the stove to see the twist of his lined and wrinkled face and the bright, malicious flicker in his eyes as he stared up at Billy, the eldest and tallest of her five brothers, who stood with one arm casually stretched along the mantelpiece, a small smile on his face as he looked down at the old man.

The meal had hardly been finished when Uncle Joe got launched. The sound of his voice was often enough to make Rosie feel queasy but she'd managed perfectly well so long as he held forth about the farm, the hard work he and Bobby had put in on the low meadow in the desperate heat with not a soul lifting a hand to help them. She'd even smiled to herself at one point as her uncle went on to complain that the new-cut grass was lying moist on the ground with not the ha'pence worth of a breeze to dry it. So much for Uncle Henry and his confidence about what a good year it would be for the hay.

How the conversation had moved from the hay to the subject of their few Roman Catholic neighbours and Joe's uncompromising attitude towards them she had no idea.

It might simply be the way Billy was standing in front of the stove, his large frame dominating the still-seated figures of his family. It didn't take much to irritate Uncle Joe and that might have been enough to do it.

'Well now, I think you're too hard on the Government,' said Billy, whose tone had grown more assured since he'd been away from home. 'If you wou'd read the provisions of the Special Powers Act, I think you'd take heart.

'An' I can tell you, in confidence, of course,' he went on, lowering his voice significantly, 'that there's more to come. But we in the police are not supposed to talk about it,' he added pompously.

Outside, the long June evening was fading to a warm, pale dusk, the smell of cut grass on the evening air, but indoors, even with the door propped open, it was so dim Emily had just been instructed to light the lamp. In its glow, Rosie watched the faces of her brothers and sisters. Moist with sweat, they gleamed in its light. Though she was sitting at the end of the table furthest from the lamp, she could feel the heat vibrating above the hot mantle. The faces at the other end of the table began to waver in and out of focus. The smell of the rising fumes from the paraffin was beginning to make her feel sick again.

When the meal was served up, the very sight of food had almost been too much. The plate set in front of her was piled high with mashed potato well-moistened with thick, brown gravy. While her mother's back was still turned to the stove, she moved the roast meat from underneath on to Sammy's plate. Later, when her mother's entire attention was devoted to Billy's second helping she managed to pass over the vegetables she'd only been pretending to eat.

Sammy asked no questions. He always had a good appetite and it wasn't the first time he'd helped her avoid her mother's sharp comments when she wasn't feeling well, but she noticed he and Emily kept looking at her whenever they could do it without their mother catching them at it. It occurred to her that she probably still looked ghastly. Even Billy had given her the odd sideways look when he arrived home.

When Emily got up to light the lamp she'd bent down and whispered that maybe she should go and lie down, but although it would get her out of the kitchen, it wasn't going to help very much with Billy and Charlie now hard at it with Uncle Joe. You could probably hear the three of them down at Richhill Station, never mind in the wee room she shared with Emily on the other side of the fireplace wall.

As the kitchen became hotter Rosie wondered if she could possibly manage to go outside. Sandwiched in between Sammy and Emily, it would be difficult to get out without attracting attention. Her mother had ignored her all afternoon, but now, from time to time when she wasn't looking up at Billy and smiling, she cast her a sour look. The other problem was standing up. She was soon going to have to go to the privy at the far end of the yard. The thought of being outside and in the cool air was very appealing but she felt so shaky she wasn't entirely sure she could make it.

Billy was talking now about the provision for whipping in the 1922 Act, and Charlie, who had recently joined the B Specials, the new part-time police force, was paying close attention.

'An' ye mean that male offenders can be whipped in private as well as whatever punishment the courts give them,' he asked thoughtfully.

'That's a fact. The police'll not be as soft as some here might think,' Billy replied sharply, glancing down at Uncle Joe who was filling his pipe. 'An' you'll find, Charlie, that when the new act goes through next year, you can be sure the provisions will extend to *all* the forces of the law. B Specials included. It's only a matter of time.'

The stove had been allowed to burn out after the meal was served, but the low-ceilinged room continued to grow warmer. Not a breath of air moved between the open door and the single small window set in the thickness of the back wall of the house. Dolly had been sent to bed and her father had left quietly when Joe began to hold forth about the hay, but the room was still uncomfortably crowded, bedroom chairs having been brought in to the kitchen to provide enough seating round the big table.

'Sure maybe, Charlie, you'll go for the police yerself when you're the age, like Billy here,' Martha began. 'Hasn't he had a great time to himself down in Enniskillen? Good pay. An' the uniform looks powerful well on him. It wou'd suit you too.'

Rosie heard her mother's voice echo as if it was reaching her from a long way away. She glanced towards her where she sat opposite Uncle Joe. He was puffing crossly at his pipe and poking the stem of it with the end of a spent match.

As the blue tobacco smoke drifted towards her, she caught the familiar acrid smell, saw her mother's face crease in a warm smile as she turned her gaze upon Charlie and felt her own eyes close as she fell sideways into Sammy's lap.

When Rosie opened her eyes she had no idea where she was. Looking down at herself, she saw she was wearing her best skirt and blouse and she was lying comfortably on top of the bed-clothes in a room she didn't at first recognize. The ceiling above her was neither the white-washed square with the damp mark in one corner of the room she shared with Emily, nor was it the high-pitched roof of the barn.

She couldn't remember what day it was either. Suddenly, the light fragrance of lavender from her pillow brought it all back. It was Sunday. She was at Rathdrum, in the room she and Emily had often shared, the room Granny always kept ready in case family or friends would suddenly find the opportunity to come and visit.

She took a deep breath and sighed. This must be what Heaven was like. To lie on soft covers, with blue sky and birds singing in the trees outside, the pretty flowered curtains moving silently in the light breeze, in a room full of well-loved, familiar things, a big, comfortable chair you could curl up in, a small bookcase with some books you still hadn't read and a table by the window where you could sit to write or paint.

She twisted her head back and forth to view the framed watercolours hanging on the pale walls. Most of them, including her favourite, a magnolia bud just beginning to open, had been painted by her cousin Helen when she was still at school in Lisburn, but there were one or two of an old house in Kerry done by a strange lady who used to live in Dublin, someone whom everyone called Aunt Lily, though she didn't appear to be a relative.

She sighed and made an attempt to push away the less pleasant memories that now poured back into her mind. The very word 'relative' conjured up a whole train of thoughts and images jostling for her attention, her mother and Uncle Joe especially.

'Go away,' she whispered to herself.

It was one of the things Miss Wilson often spoke about when she gathered her girls together for morning prayer. Life, she said, was full of difficulties and discouragements. Whether you were a member of the aristocracy or a servant girl, it didn't matter. Everyone had their burdens and sadnesses. What was important was to treasure the good things, the precious moments of rest, or pleasure, or joy. Only if you concentrated on them when they came to you would you have something to help you in the bad times.

She agreed with Miss Wilson and could see what a wise person she was, but she found it surprisingly hard to put her good advice into practise. Here she was, where she was always so welcome, so comfortable and easy on this little bed, in this room she loved, yet she couldn't get out of her mind the noise and the smell of the kitchen back at the farm and the look on Uncle Joe's face. And all that talk between Billy and Charlie about whipping.

Surely what they'd said couldn't be right. She'd thought whipping was something that belonged to the last century. She'd read about it in *Uncle Tom's Cabin* and in many of Dickens' novels. That was so long ago, yet here were Billy and Charlie talking enthusiastically about whipping suspects, men who had not been charged with any crime, men who might not have done anything wrong in the first place.

She rolled on to her side and began to run her finger round the shapes of flowered cotton that made up the quilt. She concentrated on the tiny individual flowers in each of the small pieces. Granny had promised to teach them how to quilt the next time they came.

Quilts were like stories or photograph albums, she said, you could put your whole life history into one if you really wanted to, provided you could find pieces that reminded you of the people and the places important to you. You couldn't expect just to have them all in your bag

47

or box. Some of them you'd have to go looking for, like the way one had to recall memories.

Perhaps she hadn't got enough pretty, bright pieces in her box to make a very nice story, but that might change. Someday, if she worked very hard, she might have a room like this. After all, Granny had been poor and had lost her home in Donegal when she was only eight. Her whole family had been thrown out of their cottage by a landlord who wanted rid of them so he could put sheep on the land in their place. Then Granny had worked for years as a ladies' maid until she met Granda. Away down in Kerry where *her* mother had taken her when she found a job as a housekeeper after her husband had died.

Ah, God be with you Kerry
Where in childhood I was merry...

She could remember the lilting tune her father sometimes sang when there was no one about, but the rest of the words had gone.

Her father had been there when she'd opened her eyes in the wash house. He'd been holding up a lamp from the workshop so that Emily could see to bathe her face while Sammy supported her in his arms.

'What happened, Sammy?' he asked anxiously.

'I think it was the heat, Da. She just passed out, but she fell into m' lap, so she diden hurt herself.'

'Thank God for that.'

Sammy's shirt smelt of glueing compound, the kind he used to mend punctures in the bicycle shop where he worked. She recognized the smell

48

immediately. She could hear them talking, Sammy and Emily and her father, but the lamp dazzled on the whitewashed walls and she couldn't keep her eyes open. The cold water was nice on her hot face, but the voices kept coming and going and were sometimes a long way off.

'She'd be cooler if she slept in the loft.'

'Should we send for the doctor?'

'Couldn't Charlie and Billy sleep over in the house and you and Sammy and I can keep an eye on her.'

'Would the doctor come now or will we have to wait till the morning?'

She found out later that it was Sammy who suggested driving her over to Granny the next day. He'd arrived home in his boss's motor so that he and her father could weld together a metal fitment Harry Mitchell had designed and drawn for them. When they attached it to the back of his motor he would be able to pull a trailer and transport his precious motorbike to race at Clady and on the new Dundrod Circuit in County Antrim. He'd been planning it for years.

Early on Sunday morning, while her father checked over the job they'd done the previous evening, Sammy walked the two miles to the nearest Post Office, spoke to the postmaster's wife, who was feeding her hens, and explained why he needed to use the telephone. He'd arrived back smiling. Yes, so long as he was back early on Sunday evening when Harry Mitchell needed the car himself, he was welcome to drive his sister over to Banbridge. Harry hoped the wee lassie would feel better soon.

Rosie smiled to herself. She didn't see very much of Sammy these days, but, like Emily, he was always glad to see her when he came home. At least *he* wasn't planning to go to America. What Sammy most wanted was to own a motorbike and race it, like Harry Mitchell, but he wanted to go beyond the circuits in Northern Ireland and take part in the Isle of Man T.T.

'What's T.T. Sammy?' she'd asked, the first time he told her about it.

'Tourist Trophy. It means anyone can enter, so they get some of the big names.'

'And would you like to be a big name?'

'Well, it's not so much that,' he said thoughtfully. 'You see, if you race with the big people you learn a lot. You learn about racing technique, and about the bikes themselves. Racing is a kind of test. You find out weaknesses in the bike you wouldn't have known about.'

'And about yourself?'

'Aye, I suppose you do. I never thought of that,' he said laughing. 'That's you all over, Rosie. You're always looking to see a bit more, aren't you?'

She couldn't see anything very much at the moment. She certainly couldn't see where she could go or how she could go about finding a job. Except when she visited Granny and Granda, she'd never been away from home. While she and Emily had been with them, Granda had taken them into Banbridge to help Granny shop and to Newcastle and Kilkeel for outings, but beyond that the only places she'd ever visited were Armagh and Portadown.

50

Miss Wilson had hired a charabanc and taken them to visit the two cathedrals and the museum in Armagh. They'd climbed up the tower of the old cathedral and looked out over the whole city, then walked down the hill, through the Shambles and climbed all the dozens of steps up to the new cathedral to marvel at its exotic decorated interior, full of the strange, unfamiliar smell of incense. Afterwards, they'd been so glad to go and sit under the trees on the Mall, eat their sandwiches and watch the nursemaids with their large perambulators and the groundsman cutting the grass in front of the little cricket pavilion.

It was last February she'd gone to Portadown. Her friend Lizzie was one of the guides in the Guard of Honour that lined up outside the station when the Duke and Duchess of York had arrived on their visit to the province. Mr Mackay had cleaned up his timber lorry and she'd gone with Lizzie and her mother and some of their neighbours to see the Royal couple.

It had been a very different sort of day. No great buildings or old stone houses, but crowds of people, bands and parades. The Duke and Duchess smiled and waved, the Duchess wearing the longest gloves she'd ever seen and one of the new cloche hats. She and the Duke had seemed so happy together. The crowd had roared and clapped and waved their handkerchiefs and scarves, but she hadn't. She'd fallen silent and felt her eyes fill with tears, but she'd never worked out why she should have felt like that.

'Come in,' she said quickly, as she heard a foot on the landing and a knock at her door.

'Ach, yer awake. Are ye feelin' better?'

'Yes, I am, Granda. I don't know why I keep falling asleep. I'm sorry I'm being such a nuisance.'

'Not a bit of it. Sure that was a nasty accident you had,' John Hamilton said, shaking his head. 'We'll have Dr Stewart over tomorrow to have a look at you. Granny was wondering if you'd be able to come down for a wee while. Sammy says its time he and yer da were going back, so he can return the motor.'

'Yes, I'm fine. I'll just put my shoes on.'

'Don't hurry yourself now. I'll away down an' tell them yer comin'.

Just in time, Rosie remembered not to bend over quickly. The last time, she'd nearly passed out again. She pushed her toes into her shoes, stood up, then tied them carefully one after the other by putting her foot up on the edge of the low windowsill and holding her head as high as she could.

She stepped out on to the landing, saw the afternoon sunlight streaming into the house through all the open doors and heard the sound of voices from the sitting room.

'Oh, Rosie dear, you *are* looking better,' her grandmother said, as she slipped into the room and stood smiling at them.

Sam Hamilton stood up, his glance casual as he watched her come back into the room. Only his mother noticed the change in his face as he saw his daughter smile.

'Granny says you can stay here for the week,' he said, giving her a kiss. 'We'll see how you are

52

then.'

'But what about Miss Wilson?'

'I'll walk up tonight an' have a word with her,' he said reassuringly. 'Sure you could go an' see her yourself when you come home, couldn't you?'

'Yes. Yes, of course I could.'

She turned towards her grandmother and grandfather.

'She's been so good to me,' she added, 'I could not possibly leave without thanking her.'

Rosie didn't see the glance her grandparents exchanged as Sammy moved forward to give her a quick hug.

'I'll see them off,' said John firmly, as Rose was about to get up.

'Your granny has a bad back, Rosie. See if *you* can keep her sittin' down,' he added, giving her a wry smile over his shoulder.

He followed his son and grandson into the hall and turned towards the back door and the former stable yard where Harry Mitchell's motor stood waiting.

Four

'I'm sorry about your back, Granny. Were you gardening?'

Rose laughed as her granddaughter sat down in the armchair opposite and pushed her dark hair back from her face.

'No, not guilty this time.'

She straightened herself awkwardly in her chair.

'It just takes a notion to itself from time to time. It'll go away if I behave myself. But what's good for us isn't usually to our liking, is it?'

'I know you're not much good at watching the weeds grow,' Rosie replied, grinning at her.

Even as she spoke, Rosie was aware what a relief it was to talk to someone who didn't criticize, someone who listened to what she said and actually asked questions when she didn't understand or wanted to know more. It was nearly a year since her last visit to Rathdrum and she had almost forgotten that her grandmother loved her and cared about her whatever her faults and failings. The awareness was such a shock, she forgot completely what she was going to say.

'Have you still got the headache, Rosie,' the older woman asked quietly.

'Yes, it's still there, but I hardly notice it at all

54

if I keep still.'

Even before her grandmother spoke, the silence had filled up with unwelcome thoughts. She could hear her mother's nagging voice, the high-pitched tone that warned her there was trouble ahead, that she'd best stay silent and unobserved if possible. If she had to work under her eye then the tone warned her she'd be well advised to work faster and yet more vigorously, even if it exhausted her.

If she was scrubbing the kitchen table, or washing the stone floor, her mother would be sure to say, 'Don't hurt yourself now'. It was the sarcastic, cutting edge in her mother's voice that gave the meaning to the words. No matter how hard she'd worked or how clean the result might be, she could be sure of a hurtful comment. If she paused, even for a moment, to work out what it was best to do next she'd be told off for 'standin' there daydreamin'.'

'I'm sorry I've been such a nuisance,' she said, when she realized she'd fallen silent again.

'You mustn't say that, Rosie,' her grandmother replied, looking quite shocked. 'You've had a very nasty accident and you need to rest until you feel better. We'll get Dr Stewart to come over and see you tomorrow.'

Rosie opened her mouth to protest, but her grandmother was ready and waiting.

'He's very nice,' she said reassuringly. 'Rather good-looking too,' she continued, raising an eyebrow and hoping to get a smile. 'Besides, he's my godson and I don't see him as often as I'd like.'

'I thought Dr Stewart was quite old.'

'Yes, he is. We are *all* old now. Richard and Elizabeth, your granda and me. Richard has almost retired. *My* Dr Stewart is his son. He's Richard as well. James Richard Pearson Stewart,' she added. 'Elizabeth has always called him Richard, or Richard P. when his father is there as well, but I remember thinking it was such a big name for such a tiny baby. Then, of course, two month's after he was born your Auntie Hannah and Uncle Teddy had their first child and they called him Frances John Molyneux Harrington, which is even longer.'

'Why do you think parents give babies long names like that?' Rosie asked suddenly.

'When you and I got just plain Rose?' her grandmother retorted, her eyes twinkling.

Rosie laughed and sat back more comfortably in her chair.

'It's partly a matter of social class, I suppose. Certainly the Molyneux family all had long names made up of important ancestors. I remember when I first met your granda down in Kerry, he was working for Sir Capel Molyneux from Armagh and I was working for Sir Capel Molyneux in Kerry. Capel was a family name so they both had it. It was very confusing at times. I suppose little Frances was lucky he didn't have Capel as well.'

'And why didn't he?'

'Do you know, I don't know. Or maybe I did know and have forgotten!' she said, laughing again. 'Oh dear, Rosie, I do keep forgetting things these days. I hope I'm not going to grow into a silly old woman.'

'No, of course you're not,' Rosie protested vigorously. 'I don't see how one can possibly remember everything. There wouldn't be space in your head if you remembered absolutely everything, would there?'

'Well, I certainly hadn't thought of that,' Rose said levering herself cautiously to her feet, 'but it's a much nicer idea than thinking I might end up being silly.'

'Can I help? Can I fetch anything for you?'

'No, my love. I need to stand up from time to time. Besides, I'm supposed to be looking after you, and *you* are very pale and have big dark circles under your eyes. Do you want to lie down again and let Granda bring you up some supper on a tray?'

Rosie shook her head.

'What I'd really like is to go out into the garden and sit on your seat,' she replied, as she got to her feet and stood looking down at the small, compact figure who regarded her so closely.

'You've grown, Rosie. I can't look you straight in the eye anymore. I won't be able to scold you,' she declared, her tone light and teasing.

'But you never *have* scolded me, Granny. Never ever.'

To the surprise of both of them, Rosie dropped back down into the armchair, burst into tears and wept as if her heart would break.

'Is she reading?' Rose asked, looking up from her knitting as John came back into the sitting room.

He bent down and put another log on the small wood fire he'd lit when the long summer evening began to grow chilly under a pale, yellowing sky with not a trace of cloud.

'I think that was the intention all right,' he said, nodding as he sat down gratefully in his comfortable armchair. 'But by the time I'd got her the towel and the wee cake of soap you asked for, she was asleep. I had to take the book out of her hand. But she looked very comfortable. Apart from that big bruise.'

'What do *you* think happened?' Rose asked, catching his eye.

'Oh, I think it *was* an accident. Our Sam wouldn't tell us a lie. He's very particular about that sort of thing. But, as you would say, I don't think he told us the half of it.'

'So you think it *was* Martha?'

'That wumman's capable of anythin'.'

Even if she hadn't glanced up at him, Rose could tell he was badly upset. Over his many years as a director of Bann Valley Mills, dealing with people of all sorts, fellow directors, customers, foreign buyers, machine builders, bankers and insurance assessors, John had lost much of his Armagh country accent. The one time it really came back was when he was seriously upset.

'Sure she's fit for anythin',' he went on hastily, 'an' you know she picks on Rosie. Sure Emily as good as told us that the las' time the pair of them were here.'

'But why Rosie?' she asked, bewildered. 'I know Martha's a law unto herself, but Rosie's the most willing, good-hearted girl. She'd do anything to help anyone. From what I can see she just about runs that house now Emily is out at work. Martha's never there. When have we ever called to see them and Martha's been there?'

'That's only because she knew *you* were comin',' John replied promptly. 'Any time I've had to go to Armagh and dropped in to deliver something or other she's been there all right. Usually with some neighbour clocked by the fire,' he added, surprised that Rose hadn't read Martha's absences for herself.

'Me?'

'Aye, you. Don't tell me you haven't noticed she's afraid of you?'

'What?'

Rose dropped her knitting on her knee and stared at her husband not sure what to make of the small smile on his lined and weather-beaten face and the firm set of his shoulders.

'She's afraid of you, because you might just tell her what she doesn't want to hear. She's a greedy, selfish wumman and the likes of her can't stand those that aren't the same way as herself.'

'Yes, you're right,' she said quickly. 'When I think of the neighbours she's so thick with, they're just like her. Money and gossip. And yet I think she's always looking over her shoulder to see what they're saying about her. She's not a happy woman, John.'

'An' you're right there. She doesn't spread much happiness around her family either,' he said bitterly. 'Which brings us back to the wee lassie upstairs. God bless her.'

'Yes, it does,' Rose replied as she picked up her knitting again. 'But you haven't answered my question. I asked you why you think Martha picks on Rosie?'

'Ye mean to say ye don't know?'

'No, John, I don't. That's why I'm asking,' she said shortly.

'It's because she's like you. Sure she's looked like you since she was barely able to walk. And she just gets more like you all the time. Except maybe for the odd bit of crabbitness that they say comes with age,' he added, with a sly smile.

Rose laughed aloud. She hadn't heard the word 'crabbit' for years, a word John's mother had used, long ago now, when her arthritis was bad and she felt herself being sharp with her grand-children.

It was typical of John that he'd make her laugh when she'd been sharp with him. It had been like that through all their long years together. She'd never been able to be really cross with him, or if she had, she'd not been able to keep it up for very long.

The room had grown dim and shadowy, the corners dark except where the lively flames re-flected in the well-polished furniture or the small diamond panes of the china cupboard. Beyond the tall windows, the trees stood motionless against the pale sky, heavy now with the dark-ness of full leaf. The hush of evening had descended on the farms and fields. No sound at all flowed into the quiet room. Apart from the flicker of the fire and the small whisper of ash settling from a glowing log, the silence was complete.

Rose put down the matinee coat she was knitting for her young neighbour's expected baby, the light now too poor to see. She was about to ask John to light the gas lamps when suddenly, as clearly as if she were a girl of sixteen again, she remembered what it was like to be a servant. To be at the beck and call of senior servants, themselves answerable for the order of the house. It had been a hard life. Long hours and heavy work. But then she had always had her mother to help and comfort her. Whenever she was tired, or anxious or upset, she knew there would be reassurance, a kind word, a cup of tea.

With a clarity she thought had disappeared with advancing years, she saw just how right John was. Martha had always disliked her, avoided her, disparaged her behind her back. Now she was treating Rosie like her servant. *Mistreating* her, in fact. When what she should be doing was helping her to grow into womanhood, a hard enough task for any girl.

'John, what are we going to do?'

Even as she spoke, Rose was suddenly aware the question she'd asked was the one he'd so often asked her whenever there was some crisis. Now it was the other way round. But why not? Why shouldn't that change like everything else?

If there was one thing she had come to accept in these last years, so full of the distress and anxieties of the long years of the war and all the heartache that had come after for their own land, it was the way things could change, at any

61

moment, for good or ill. Nor could you tell to begin with which way it was going to go.

'I don't know, Rose. I leave these things to you,' he said steadily. 'But you tell me what you think's best an' I'll go along with it. It's a long time since I saw our Sam so anxious. He'd break his heart if anything hurt that wee lassie.'

'Well, we'll not let that happen,' she said softly, knowing that there was someone other than their son who had lost his heart to a slip of a girl called Rosie.

'Here y'ar, miss. A nice boiled egg and toast. Yer granny says to eat it all up an' she'll be up to see you after the doctor comes. She said she could do the stairs once in a morning but not twice. Though she's better, mind you. I see an improvement since Friday...'

Rosie had been awake for some time, but she'd felt so easy and been so comfortable she'd gone on lying with her eyes closed just listening to the familiar sounds of the house and the rapturous song of a blackbird in the garden.

She sat up in bed and watched Mrs Love, the housekeeper, fuss around the room, putting down her breakfast tray, drawing back the curtains, straightening the cushion on the big armchair by the window.

Mrs Love talked all the time and once she got going she was very hard to stop. She always reminded Rosie of the Ancient Mariner in Coleridge's poem. But Mrs Love was such a kind-hearted soul that even when Rosie longed for quiet, like this morning, she did her best to pay attention.

'Yer granda went out early and drove over to Dromore so ye'll maybe have young Dr Stewart here before too long. Would you like another pot of tea?' she demanded, as Rosie poured a second cup and drank thirstily.

Rosie reassured her that she never had more than two cups at breakfast. What she didn't say was that she'd be lucky to get a second cup if one of the boys emptied the pot before she got to it.

'I suppose yer sister's working away. She must be nearly saved up by now.'

Rosie nodded, her mouth full of toast.

She was intrigued by Mrs Love. She talked all the time and appeared never to hear anything you said in reply, yet weeks or months after you mentioned something it would come up in conversation as if you'd been talking about it only the previous day. It was almost a year since Emily had said she planned to go to America as soon as she had the money for her fare and enough in her pocket to satisfy the immigration authorities.

'Maybe you'll go too now yer finished the wee school?'

Mrs Love always referred to Miss Wilson's school in Richhill as if it were not quite proper. Having learnt to read and write and do sums, which she was willing to admit came in handy for getting a job when you were young, she could see no point in reading novels, reciting poetry or speaking French.

'But I have no money saved up, Mrs Love.'

'Sure if you went to America you'd have your

grandmother's people to go to,' Mrs Love replied. 'Her brother Sam's family. God rest him. The McGinleys. I know they're Catholic, but I'm sure any relative of your granny would be a decent sort and good to you. There's good and bad in all sorts as my dear husband used to say. He had a great friend was a Theosophist. I wouldn't know one of those from a horse and cart on a dark night, but he was so kind to me when Billy passed on. Ye have to keep an open mind about these things,' she added, as Rosie despatched the last of the toast and emptied her teacup.

Richard Stewart arrived shortly before noon, parked his motor outside John's workshop and came in by the back door.

'Richard, how lovely to see you,' exclaimed Rose. 'How are my dear friends at Dromore?'

'Both well and they both send their love. It's you we're all concerned about. When is it you and Uncle John are planning to go off?'

'Some time this week or early the one after. As soon as he can organize a particular Lagonda he's set his heart on. Don't ask me for its model and number, I'm just so relieved that you and your father managed to persuade him to hire in Kerry. He really was quite prepared to drive all the way there and back.'

Richard smiled and followed her through the kitchen, down the hall and into the sitting room.

'And what about *your* back, Auntie Rose? Do you think the journey will do it any good?'

'It's getting better, Richard. I *have* done what you told me, really I have. Mrs Love said I was walking much better this morning than I was when she went off to see her sister on Friday.'

He shook his head.

'I know how much it means to you both, but you really must take it gently. It is a long way.'

'It's another world, my dear. But I've wanted to go back all my married life and we've never managed it. This might be our last chance,' she said quietly, looking up at the long, sensitive face and the grey eyes.

He was just so like his mother, in manner as well as looks. Cool, calm, competent on the surface but underneath full of restless energy. There was nothing that passed before his sharp gaze that he did not observe, question and try to understand. It had been no surprise to her when he'd won the gold medal for the best student of the year on the results of his Finals in Edinburgh.

'And what about your wee granddaughter, Auntie Rose? Is there anything you want to tell me about her?'

'No, Richard dear. It's the other way round. I need *you* to tell me all you can about her and this accident she's had,' she explained, looking up at him. 'I'm not coming up with you. You know your way.'

She followed him as he moved towards the sitting-room door.

'She's not usually shy or awkward,' she added thoughtfully. 'If she's uneasy, it'll tell *me* something.'

'I'll see what I can do. Uncle John seemed more concerned about her mother than about the bang on the head.'

Rose laughed as she left him at the foot of the stairs.

'Like your dear father, Richard, you don't just look at a set of symptoms. I confess freely that I think my daughter-in-law Martha is probably a greater danger to my granddaughter's health than any bang on the head.'

Rosie looked up from her book as she heard a light tap on her door. In answer to her soft 'come in' a tall, trim, young man with thoughtful grey eyes slipped quietly into the room and crossed to her bedside.

'Good morning, Rosie. You look very comfortable.'

'Yes, I am. It was worth a bang on the head just to be here,' she responded cheerfully, as he picked up the battered leather-bound volume she had just put down.

'*Pride and Prejudice*,' he commented, as he ran his eye over the bruise that stood out so sharply from the creamy skin.

'Granny and Aunt Sarah's favourite book. I always read it when I come here,' she said, answering his unspoken question and beaming at him, as he drew a chair across to her bedside.

'And what do you read at home?'

In the two years since qualifying as a doctor he had become adept at asking innocent questions, but even with two years' experience he was shocked at the effect of his words upon this young girl.

The whole set of her face had changed. The bright sparkle in the dark eyes disappeared. Even her shoulders, draped in a light bedjacket, took on a rounded shape quite out of keeping with her years.

'I don't have much time to read,' she said awkwardly

'You live on a farm, don't you?'

'Yes.'

'I expect it's very busy at times.'

She nodded, her face closed, the bright smile so completely erased he began to wonder if he had imagined it.

Deciding that only a professional approach would now serve, he asked her what exactly had happened.

'I tripped and hit my head against the door,' she said quickly.

To his ear, there was something about the way she said it that wasn't right at all. It sounded too pat, too practised.

'May I have a closer look?'

He took his time examining the bruise, touching it gently and asking her where it hurt most. He took her pulse and looked at her tongue, though he knew they'd tell him nothing he didn't know already.

'Rosie, when someone suffers a bad fall there are a number of possible causes,' he began, grateful to see how intently she was listening. 'Some of them are quite simple and obvious, like tripping over the cat. But some are more complicated. With older people there's often a momentary blackout. That's unlikely in your case, but one has to be very cautious with head injuries. It would help me if you could remember exactly what happened?'

Rosie looked him in the face and was surprised to find he didn't turn away. Very few people ever looked straight back at you. Apart from her father and Granny and Granda, in fact, she couldn't think of anyone. Then she remembered Miss Wilson and Lizzie Mackay, but that still wasn't very many.

She glanced down at the cover of her book, aware he was still looking at her, waiting patiently for her reply.

She sighed and took a deep breath.

'I can remember exactly what happened, so it wasn't a blackout.'

'Good. That's splendid. You should be as right as rain in a day or two and Uncle John will be able to take you home.'

He stood up and walked across to the open window, looked up at the blue sky and down into the cobbled yard where his motor was parked near the little gate that led to the garden. He said what a lovely day it was, how well the garden was looking and that she could go outside now if she wanted to. He turned round just in time to see her hastily wipe a tear from the corner of her eye.

He crossed the room and sat down again by her bed.

'Perhaps Rosie, just to be on the safe side, you should tell me every detail of what you remember. Then I could be quite sure I was prescribing the right treatment for you.'

Five

Less than a week after her arrival at Rathdrum, her bruised face healing rapidly and her good spirits completely recovered, Rosie found herself sitting beside her grandmother in the back seat of her grandfather's motor.

'Are you right there, ladies?'

'Yes, we're fine,' they chorused.

Uncle Alex, friend and neighbour of Rose and John, touched the accelerator gently and moved out of the yard and under the heavy shade of the limes.

'Kerry, here we come,' he called out vigorously, as they turned left down the hill, past his own home at Ballydown, as excited about the journey as if he himself were setting off to drive the whole way there.

The July day was hot but not oppressive. Although the brilliant light reflected from the lush grass by the roadside was dazzling, great white clouds had built up on the horizon and there was a pleasant breeze as they drove to Portadown Station to catch the Dublin train.

Even when they followed the porter through the booking hall and she saw her father standing on the platform watching for her, a small suitcase in his hand, she couldn't believe she wasn't going home with him on the local train.

'Ach yer lookin' well,' he said, as he bent towards her, put an arm round her and kissed her. 'Aren't you the lucky girl?'

He moved forward to greet his mother and shake his father's hand.

'It's very good of you,' he said, looking from one to the other.

'Not a bit of it,' John responded vigorously. 'Sure isn't she the one will have to do all the work looking after the pair of us?'

Sam laughed, relieved and pleased. Rosie would certainly make herself useful and she'd be good company.

The bang of carriage doors from the further platform, where the huge engine of the Dublin train gleamed in the sunlight, hissed slightly and sent sudden clouds of steam swirling up into the metal rafters of the train shed high above her head, told them it was time to go.

'See you're a good girl now,' Sam said, hugging his daughter.

Rosie smiled up at her father. He still said the things he'd said to her when she was a child, but whether she was sixteen or twenty-six, she'd never mind, for the gentleness in his tone was the one sure comfort she had always had.

He was watching for them as they walked down from the footbridge to the further platform.

'See ye enjoy yerselves,' he called across as they paused outside their reserved carriage where an elderly porter was loading their hand luggage on to the racks.

'Givus yer wee case, Miss Hamilton,' the man

said, touching his cap as he climbed down on to the platform.

She handed him the case without a word, gave a last wave to her father, standing quite alone on the far platform, and got in quickly beside her grandparents, her eyes suddenly misted with tears.

She had never been further from home than Banbridge, nor left him for more than a week. She had never before been called 'Miss Hamilton' except when her mother was being especially sarcastic.

Suddenly, the carriage jerked and slowly began to move. She leaned out of the carriage window as far as she dared and went on waving to him till he was long out of sight.

'You sit here by the window, Rosie, and I'll sit beside your granny,' John said suddenly, as she turned away, grateful the clouds of steam could be blamed for the tears streaming down her face.

'I'm all right, John. Really I'm all right,' her grandmother replied, as she straightened herself up in her seat.

Rosie looked from one to the other. No, her grandmother was not quite her usual steady self and there was a note in her grandfather's voice she'd not heard before. Perhaps they were as anxious as she was, going so very far away. It was easy to think you might never come back. Something might happen to them, or to her father. They might never see each other again.

'Ye needn't be one bit afeard,' he said softly. 'Sure this engine could pull two trains and sure there's hardly anyone on it.'

71

Rose shook her head and smiled across at Rosie.

'It's years since I've been on a train,' she explained rather brightly. 'It was 1916 after your Uncle Sam was killed in Dublin. We went down to see his grave and stay a night or two with a woman friend of his. That's eight years ago now. Time goes so quickly when you get older,' she added, her smile fading as she noticed how closely Rosie was watching her.

'She's not telling you the half of it, Rosie,' said John quietly. 'But we'll not say another word about it.'

'That would be best, John. For now,' she said, as she turned away to gaze unseeing across the passing countryside.

They all fell silent. John unfolded his newspaper. Rose leaned back in her seat and closed her eyes. Rosie looked out of the window, absorbed and fascinated by houses and fields and hedgerows she had never laid eyes on before. She saw strong farms with well-tended stables and barns. Poor houses with grass grown thatch. Paths and lanes and cart tracks. Golden fields of cut hay, the after-grass sprouting bright green in the stubble. Wheat and oats not yet ready to cut, shimmering like a green-gold inland sea, rippled by the breeze. In the dense shade of a mature chestnut, horses swished their tails. Cows gathered in the short noonday shadow of a hawthorn hedge.

I'm going to Kerry, she said silently to herself. I'm going to the furthest corner of Ireland to stay in a hotel and we're going to drive round and see the sights and go and look at the big house where Granny used to work and where she and Granda met.

She'd been through it a hundred times since the morning Rose had suggested it, coming up with her breakfast tray herself to show her how much her back had improved and to tell her what she and John had decided the previous evening.

Even when all the arrangements had been made, when Emily had been phoned at work and asked to pack her case, a single room requested from the hotel in Kerry, the hire firm contacted about a larger motor than the Lagonda John had already booked, she could still not believe it. But here was the proof. The green fields of Ulster, its villages and towns, streaming past her eyes, names she knew only from Miss Wilson's battered atlas. Poyntzpass. An unknown place as exotic as Paris or Prague.

Down there in that narrow main street people lived and worked and bought their groceries just as she did in Richhill. But these people were separate and as completely unknown as Poyntzpass itself. She wondered if they went for Sunday walks to the strange, broken earthwork called the Black Pig's Dyke. Looking down from the high embankment, she saw its random shape breaking across the smooth landscape of small fields. She'd read that the dyke was thrown up as a defence against raiders from the south. There were those who declared is was made by a huge, angry monster furiously gouging the earth. But surely that would leave a trench, not a ridge.

She was still thinking about stories and legends

and where they came from when she became aware that the countryside had changed. Now the fields were full of rushes, the cabins scattered and poor. On the horizon mountains rose, peak behind peak in shades of grey, their heads in cloud. The Mournes. Granny's mountains. The ones you could see on a clear day from the bottom of her garden or from the lane running down the hill from Rathdrum to her old home at Ballydown. Sombre now seen from this distance. Their outline unfamiliar from this different angle.

She glanced across the carriage. Her grandfather was absorbed in the *Banbridge Chronicle*. Her grandmother had fallen asleep, her head to one side and her mouth slightly open. With a chilling shock, for the first time Rosie realized her grandmother was old. Without her quick smile and the twinkle in her eye, the wrinkles of her seventy odd years spelt out the length of her life rather than the quality of her living.

She looked from her grandmother's face to the face she saw above the rim of the newspaper. White-haired now, but still broad-shouldered and fit, her grandfather was a year or two older than her grandmother. He was still absorbed in his newspaper, reading methodically from front to back. He liked to know what was going on in the district and still kept in touch with the mills, though he'd retired from his directorship when he was seventy. She knew how much he enjoyed being called upon when there was a particularly difficult problem with the machinery.

She wondered what it would be like to be old.

It must be strange to have most of your life behind you, seeing your youth from far away, instead of looking forward to having all your real life in front of you. Perhaps it was like seeing the mountains from a completely different angle. They were the same rugged peaks, but you were standing somewhere different.

As the train slowed down on the outskirts of Newry, a cloud passed over the sun. As if a giant hand had covered the globe of a lamp, the sunlight was shut off. The fields lost their glow. The mountains retreated further from view. With a sudden gasp, as if her heart had stopped, she realized that being old, her grandparents would die. Unless there was some awful accident, they'd not die together, so one of them would be left alone, desolate, after a whole lifetime of loving.

The thought appalled her and she had to look yet more vigorously out of the window in case either of them should notice how upset she was. She was grateful when the train whistled and slowed to a halt alongside a more crowded platform. The carriage door opened and a man and woman got in, apologizing politely for having to step over their feet in the narrow space between the seats.

Rose woke up and collected herself as the newcomers settled by the window at the far side of the carriage.

'Goodness, Rosie, I must have fallen asleep. How rude of me. Were you bored?'

'No, not a bit. It's all so new and so interesting. I wish I had Miss Wilson's atlas so I could follow where we were.'

'Remind me when we get to Dublin, Rosie, and I'll buy you a map of Ireland,' John said, folding up his paper. 'It might come in handy for your granny as well,' he added with a smile. 'She's been up and down to Dublin a few times now, as well as the first time we did the journey together, but she's not been back to Kerry since she came up to Dublin in a coach. I was out with the driver that time, but I'm not sure how much chance she got to see where she was going. She had a lady-ship for company.'

To Rosie's delight, her grandmother laughed and caught a hand to her mouth in sudden recollection. Her own dark thoughts disappeared as rapidly as the shadows off the land when the sun broke through again. Her grandmother began to tell her about the longest journey she had ever made, by coach and train from Currane Lodge in Kerry, to John's mother's house at Annacramp, a few miles outside Armagh.

'In a coach, Granny? But weren't there any trains?'

'Oh yes, there were trains, but the old families went on using their coaches. If they hadn't had coaches, your grandfather and I would never have met. You don't need a groom with you when you travel by train.'

'But were you a groom, Granda? And how *did* you meet him then?' she asked excitedly, turning from one to the other.

'Well, ye see, it was like this,' John began, angling himself in his seat so he could look across at his granddaughter more comfortably.

Rose smiled and said nothing. John was happy to tell the story yet once more. Whatever reservations she might have about the details which had been added over the years, she'd certainly not spoil his pleasure in the telling nor his enjoyment of his granddaughter's response by pointing them out.

Rosie too sat back in her seat, the broken hill country of southern Armagh forgotten for the moment. Just sometimes she had managed to get her father to tell her stories about the past, but it was always difficult. He would never talk about his experiences if her mother were there, so it was only if she could go over to the barn that there was any hope at all. Getting him started depended on the job. It was no good if the job was complicated or noisy, it had to be something simple and routine. But when he did begin, he'd use exactly the same words as her grandfather had just used: 'Well, ye see, it was like this.'

Her mother never had any time for stories and got very angry if she found her husband telling the children about what happened long ago. She'd say he lived in the past. That he needed to move with the times. Shake himself up a bit.

It wasn't just telling stories that made her angry. There was something in the way her father did things, perfectly ordinary things like cutting a loaf of bread, or cleaning his boots, that her mother couldn't tolerate any better than his talking about the past. He was so calm and steady, so methodical, in everything he did, his very calmness, his steadiness, seemed to exasperate her.

She'd often seen her mother look across at him

from her seat by the fire, her face taut with displeasure, then jump up and busy herself with jobs she hated and normally left for Rosie herself to do. She'd work quickly, sweeping the floor so vigorously she knocked the brush against the table or dresser. She'd clean the windows and rub so hard they rattled, or blacken the stove fiercely, or polish its silver edges so rapidly the emery paper tore.

Hastily, she put her mother out of mind and concentrated on what Granda was saying. He'd got to the point where Sir Capel Molyneux asked him to go to Kerry as a groom, because the groom's old mother was ill and a coach can't manage without someone to help the driver.

She listened hard, already aware she could easily persuade him to tell her many more stories, now he had time and leisure for a whole fortnight. And Granny too. She was sure Granny had stories to tell, but when she and Emily visited, there'd never been the opportunity, for Emily always wanted to do things and go places. She hated listening to anyone, even Granny. She said it reminded her of school.

The July sunshine sparkled on the Irish Sea and turned the empty beaches to pale gold as they steamed south towards Dublin. It continued to shine through their brief stay in the city and was still unbroken on the long day's travel from Dublin southwards to Cork. Then onwards from Cork, ever westwards, till they finally reached the small station at Kenmare and drove the last miles of their journey to Waterville, the little town that had grown up on a narrow neck of land between the shimmering waters of Ballinskelligs Bay and Lough Currane itself.

By the time they reached their hotel, Rosie understood exactly why, whenever she'd asked Granda what Kerry was like, he kept saying the same thing: 'Sky and water. Sky and water everywhere you look. Not just the sea, the lake as well and the mountains beyond. Just magnificent.'

She barely noticed the heavy furniture and wide staircase of the reception area as they went upstairs to see the luggage deposited. All she could think of was the sea such a very short distance away. Looking out of the windows in her grandparent's room, she could hardly believe it was so close, closer than the bottom of Granny's garden.

All she wanted to do was stand on the sandy shore and look around her. However splendid the views from the train, it was not the same thing as having your feet on the ground, looking up at the small feathery clouds in the clear blue sky, feeling the soft air on her face and smelling its unfamiliar, salty tang.

'I think I might just have a little rest before dinner, Rosie. But you and Granda must go and have a walk if you want to. I'm sure he needs to stretch his legs.'

'Granda, is Granny all right?' Rosie asked anxiously, as they went down the wide, carpeted staircase together.

'Aye, she's fine. Just tired,' he said reassuringly.

They went out by the main door, crossed the road, and followed the short grass path down to the beach in companionable silence.

'You're right enough though, she's not quite herself,' he said suddenly. 'Maybe a wee bit sad for the moment. Sure she has a lot of memories of this place,' he continued. 'She's wanted all her life to come back. I was only here a couple of weeks and I was driving here and there with the lords and ladies who were visiting. Taking them to see the sights, like I was telling you. I only saw your granny in the evening when we walked out down by the lake. But this place was her life from wee girl to full womanhood. I don't know just how long,' he pondered, twisting his face in an effort of memory. 'Certainly from the time her father died and her mother brought her here from Donegal. That would have been 1861 or '62.'

'Donegal?'

'Aye, that's where she was born. Did she never tell you about the family being evicted? Thrown out on the street one bitter April. A whole valley full of people...'

He broke off as they came to the soft sand at the highest point of the beach and paused to look around. There were only a few people about, walking down by the water's edge, their shadows reflected in the damp sand. The sea was smooth as beaten metal. Where the minute waves broke on the shore, they made only the tiniest splash before they ran back silently over the gleaming sand pulling small seashells in their wake.

'But Granda, *how* did that happen?'

John looked down at her sharply, registered the

80

sudden anxious concern in her dark eyes, the tensing of her narrow shoulders. She was so like the young woman he had first met on a hillside not all that many miles away. A little taller now, but the same fine eyes and dark hair, the slim waist and womanly shape. What was different about this one was her mind. Unlike her grandmother, who could rest quiet if the chance came to her, this one never rested, always wanting to know more, whether ordinary things like the difference between a male and a female blackbird, or complicated matters like why this poor island had been divided into two parts.

So often now, she reminded him of his youngest daughter, Sarah. She would always ask and ask till she understood. A trial at times he had to admit, when she was very young and sometimes hard to stop, but it stood to her now, the wife of a diplomat, surrounded by the high affairs of the day.

The sand near the water's edge was firm and rippled, the tiny indentations full of small shells and broken fragments. She stooped to pick up a handful, choosing from the most perfect ones those with faint colour, pink or mauve or purple. She held them out to him arranged in a circle on her palm.

He bent forward to look at them and found her eyes firmly fixed upon him, still waiting for an answer to her question.

He laughed shortly.

'Greed, Rosie, greed. A man that had money enough to do all he might want, but he wanted more. He put those people out so he could fence

81

the land and make a deer park for his friends to come and shoot for pleasure,' he went on, his tone hard and his face grim. 'But if it hadn't been for his wickedness, then your granny would never have come to Kerry and we'd never have met each other. And I don't know where I'd be without her.'

He looked away quickly towards the low cliffs that bounded the far end of the long beach and strode off again. Rosie followed after, but she had not missed the words or what they were saying.

Six

'According to Miss Wilson, it's because the moist air from the sea rises up the sides of the mountains, cools and condenses and then falls as rain,' said Rosie solemnly, as she buttered a piece of toast.

'Yes, that's all very well,' said John, eyeing her, 'but it doesn't explain why it rains at night.'

'But it would be cooler up the mountain at night, wouldn't it?'

Rose laughed, her weariness departed, her good spirits restored by the days just past. She'd had time to rest. To delight in the changing play of light on the mountains, the reflections from sea and lake, the remembered loveliness she had never stopped longing for in one small part of herself.

'Well, all I can say is, *aren't we lucky*? This wonderful freshness every morning and not ·a drop of rain all day.'

'Was it like this when you were here, Granny?'

'I can't remember. I think I noticed if it rained on my afternoon off, but apart from that, work had to go on, rain or shine. It didn't make much difference. At least I don't think it did.'

'Bad weather would have meant more work, wouldn't it?' asked John, looking across the breakfast table at her. 'Dirty feet on the carpets and suchlike. But then, that wasn't your job.'

'No,' she agreed, nodding. 'But it was my mother's job to oversee the whole house.

'Yes, you're quite right,' she went on, as she refilled their cups. 'I can remember now her saying how worn out she was when we got days of wet weather, or when it was colder than usual. She had to watch everyone to make sure the extra work was done, not just their routine jobs. They weren't lazy,' she added, 'they just didn't think.'

To Rosie's surprise, John laughed heartily.

'Sure most of my life's work has been clearing up after people who didn't think,' he said, still smiling. 'I remember my father telling me that the old blacksmith he was apprenticed with once told him it was a good thing people were so careless, because he made a living straightening out what other people bent.'

They were still laughing when a pale, uneasy girl, neatly dressed in black, with a spotless white apron and cap, came to enquire if there was anything they'd like. She asked if she could bring more toast, or a fresh pot of tea, or if they'd like her to get reception to telephone through to another hotel to book their lunch should they be going for a drive.

'Ah, well now, we haven't discussed that yet, Bridget,' responded John. 'Would you like to come back in a wee while and ask us again?'

Rosie watched Bridget's face soften into a shy smile. A girl about her own age, daughter of one of the cooks, she'd been sent to unpack Rosie's

84

suitcase as soon as they'd arrived, but Rosie had so few clothes, she'd emptied the case herself before she appeared, so there was nothing for Bridget to do.

She'd stood by the door so awkwardly not knowing what to do and Rosie felt instant sympathy for her. She asked her about the hotel, about her job, and if she'd mind telling her whether she ought to wear a dress for dinner. She knew perfectly well from what her grandmother had told her, in hotels as grand as this, that people dressed for dinner, but she knew asking Bridget would make her feel easier.

'Well now,' said John, breaking across her thoughts, as Bridget bobbed a curtsy and departed for the kitchens. 'And what would my ladies like to do today? Now that I have my very elegant motor, you can go anywhere you want. The further the better. Valentia Island to see the cable station? Very historical,' he suggested. 'Or the Dingle Peninsula? Or Daniel O'Connell's birthplace?'

He listed the well-known viewpoints on the Ring of Kerry route, quoting the guide book which he'd read in detail after finding little to interest him in either *The Kerryman* or the *Tralee Clarion*.

Rosie waited to see what her grandmother might say. All week she'd been so excited with everything there was to see and do she never minded what was decided, but she'd begun to wonder why they'd not taken the lakeside road to visit Currane Lodge and the little church a short distance away where her grandparents had been

85

married and where her great-grandmother, Hannah McGinley, lay buried.

'Well,' Rose began, 'seeing my back is behaving itself so beautifully, I thought it would be a good morning for some shopping. There is a birthday present to be bought.'

John suppressed a sigh as he caught his wife's fleeting glance towards Rosie. Shopping in Cahirciveen or anywhere else for that matter, was not at all what he'd choose, but he knew she'd Rosie's birthday in mind. She'd mentioned several times already that her only dress, a green and white check gingham she'd had to have for Miss Wilson's, had never suited her and now no longer even fitted her properly.

'An hour or two is as much as I could manage, I think,' Rose continued, 'so I thought after lunch we might go to Currane Lodge and take a picnic tea. The hotel does a very nice one, I'm told. And you and I could sit in the sun and let Rosie explore all she wants. They say the road is much improved,' she added, as she saw him brighten.

'Well, it would need to be better with all the visitors these days driving their motors along the lake for the scenery or going there to fish. Sure wasn't it the roughness of that road that made Pegasus lose his shoe in the first place?'

'Not a word, not a word,' Rose said quickly, putting her finger to her lips as Rosie opened her mouth to speak. 'We've a busy morning and it's time we were moving. You can ask Granda all the questions you like when we get to Currane Lodge.'

'Well, that's fine by me,' John said agreeably.

'I found a book in the visitors' sitting room about this man Lindberg and his flying machines. I'll just park outside the shop and read it like the way your old friend the coachman used to sit reading his paper waiting for the ladies. What was his name?'

'Thomas,' she said promptly. 'Isn't it funny how some things come back without you even having to think and others have you puzzling for days?'

The little grey church stood back from the road, a rusted iron gate leading into the churchyard, most of it overgrown, the paths barely visible, the lush vegetation smothering all but the taller gravestones.

Rosie led the way while Rose and John followed more slowly.

In the shadow of the boundary hedge tall spires of foxglove reached up through the tangled grass and bloomed in a profusion of colours. Their first faded blooms had been wafted away to fall among the bright faces of buttercups growing in the sunlight beyond its shadow. The hedge itself was thickly entwined with wild clematis, the fluffy seeds rising like a swarm of exotic insects whenever there was a more vigorous movement of air in the soft breeze from the lake.

Close to the church itself there were new graves, the turned earth still bare, planted with posies of bright flowers in jam pots. Rosie saw her grandmother pause, heard her repeat a name that seemed familiar, but she herself pressed on. Stepping carefully along the overgrown path, drawn by a group of white marble stones, still visible above the sea of ripening grass and wild-flowers.

As she had guessed, the slabs were engraved with names she knew. Servants from Currane Lodge from her grandmother's time lay among neighbours who'd lived in the scattered habitations further along the lakeside. Somewhere, further into the long grass, would be the graves of Lady Caroline's sons, the longed-for boys who never lived for more than a few months.

She stood reading the dedications, totally absorbed in the lives of these unknown people who had once been an everyday part of her grandmother's world here at the opposite end of Ireland. Behind her, she heard the low, sad tones of her grandparents. Among the new graves, they'd found a young man whose father and grandfather they had known. He'd been killed the previous year, a victim of the Civil War.

She moved further away, drawn by the older stones where the lichens grew more profusely, spreading their delicate colours so deeply into the cut stone that she could no longer trace the words even with her fingers. She found the grave of Thomas the coachman and his wife, another handsome white marble slab. The dates and places still perfectly legible. Low down on the stone, she read: *Well done thou good and faithful servant. This stone was erected by Sir Capel Molyneux in grateful thanks.*

A short distance away the upper part of a similar memorial was just visible above a huge mound of briar rose that almost completely obscured its white marble face with its prolific stems and masses of tight pink flowers.

She made her way across the humps of vegetation cautiously, for the strong stems were spiked with jagged thorns. She picked out a stem close to the marble. Taking hold of it by a mass of bloom, she pulled some of the vigorous growth away from the stone. At last, she had found what she was looking for. Protected by the rose, the words on the still-white marble were free from lichen and perfectly legible.

Hannah McGinley, nee Mackay
Born 1815, Drumcraig, Galloway
Died 1886, Currane Lodge

The intertwined stems and dense blooms obscured the rest of the inscription. Should she be able to clear away all of the growth, she was sure she would find Sir Capel had had the same words inscribed, for Hannah too had been 'a good and faithful servant'.

She stood staring down at the words the dense growth masked. 'Thou good and faithful servant'. Was that what her own life was to be? Her schooldays were over. She'd stayed on into the senior class at Richhill Public Elementary and then she'd had gone to Miss Wilson's for a year. But that was over now.

Not a day had passed since Dr Stewart sat by her bedside encouraging her to talk about her family and her plans for the future that she had not thought what was to become of her. When she'd owned up to her anxiety, her grandmother had been reassuring. Told her to forget all about it till she was quite recovered from her fall. She herself had thought it might be easier to forget about the future when she came to Kerry. Every day she promised herself she'd push the question out of mind and then she'd see Bridget in her black dress and white apron and back it would come.

What was there for her beyond the work of the farm? She wasn't old enough to be a governess like those in the novels she'd read, even if there were any families that needed one these days. So far, the only prospect of a job had been the one in Richhill castle. She'd refused to go to work there and had been roundly abused by her mother for upsetting her Uncle Henry, who had 'put in a word for her'.

But what else was there? An assistant in a shop in Portadown or Armagh? A worker in one of the mills or the fruit packing factory? The question of whether the jobs appealed to her or not simply didn't arise, for there was so little possibility of her getting one. Jobs were so scarce, mostly they were filled without any need to advertise in the local papers. Emily got hers because her father worked at Fruitfield and heard about the vacancy in the office from the girl who was leaving to get married.

Her brothers had found out how hard a time it was for everyone, but it was even harder for girls. It was as if no one really expected girls to be fit for any job other than domestic service or shop assistant. If you went into service, you had to accept the regime of the big house, as her grandmother had had to fifty years before, or find one near enough so you could go on living at home, for jobs paid so little there was no possibility of setting up on your own.

She sighed and looked down at the mass of tiny pink roses. Was it a floribunda? It might be. She ought to know its name for she'd seen it before in the garden at Rathdrum, but there her grandmother had trained it to climb a wooden trellis and she pruned it vigorously each autumn so the blooms were bigger and the thorns not quite so fierce.

Currane Lodge was less than a mile from the churchyard. Set back further from the road, it had once had a driveway curving through well-kept shrubberies beyond handsome wrought-iron gates. It was no surprise that the gates were gone, that even the pillars supporting them were crumbling, their capstones removed, a generous growth of grass and foliage well-established in the decaying mortar.

After his wife died, Sir Capel had moved to Dublin with his unmarried daughter, Lily. The house continued to stand empty for many years after his death, for none of the English relatives to whom it was entailed had any wish to bury themselves in this remote corner of Ireland.

Only for some years at the turn of the century had the house been wakened from its long sleep. A returned emigrant, his fortune made in the motor industry in Detroit, bought the place, repaired the roof and outbuildings. He then invited his remaining relatives to come and live with him only to discover none of them wanted to leave the homes in which they'd spent their lives any more than they'd wanted to seek a new life in America.

Rosie wondered if her grandfather would risk his handsome motor on the grass-grown surface of the driveway, but he turned between the massive pillars quite confident it would take no harm. The chassis was high off the ground, he told them, and the springs far superior to his own vehicle at home. But he still drove very slowly.

None of them were prepared for the sight that greeted them as they emerged from the shady tunnel made by the over-arching trees and un-pruned shrubs. Currane Lodge had been burnt. Only part of the front façade still stood, the windows dark staring eyes, blackened with soot. Most of the roof had gone, except for one fragment, its surviving timbers dividing the startling blue sky into tiny rectangles, its jagged beams in silhouette.

'Oh my goodness,' gasped Rose. 'No one told us there'd been a fire.'

'Sure who would there be to tell us now?' John said softly, as he stopped the car on the charred and littered space in front of the stone steps. 'We never thought to ask at the hotel. They might not have known anyway.'

'No, why should they?' she agreed. 'It's well out of the way and no one lived here. I wonder what happened.'

'I expect some of the volunteers thought it was time it was gone,' he replied crisply. 'Anything they thought was British would be fair game. Or maybe someone was storing arms there. Black and Tans or Pro-Treaty or Anti-Treaty. You've plenty to chose from in the last few years. It could even have been an accident.'

Rosie was puzzled by the strange look on her grandmother's face. She'd been so shocked when she first saw the burnt ruin, but now, a small smile played around her lips as she stepped down from the motor and walked closer to the ruined house. She ran her eye over the wide stone steps that led up to the empty space where once the front door had been.

'Lady Anne used to ride her horse up those steps,' she said suddenly, turning towards her.

Rosie stared back at her in amazement.

'His name was Conor and he was huge,' she went on. 'Goodness knows how many hands high. But she was a wonderful horsewoman, was Lady Anne, and Conor would do anything for her. Do you remember him, John?'

'Indeed you'd never forget a horse like that. There'd be few enough men would have the way of him, never mind a young girl.'

Rosie saw her grandmother's eyes blink and move away from the steps.

'Is Lady Anne dead?'

She nodded sadly.

'Eight years ago now, though it seems much longer. Her husband, Harrington, died in May 1916 and she had a fall from her horse about a month later. She broke a hip and never really recovered. I don't think she wanted to recover. She as much as told me so when I went over to see her,' she added, with a small, wry smile.

'The worst thing about growing old, Rosie, is that you lose your friends, even ones that are younger than you are. Like Anne and my baby brother, Sam. And Lily, a year later.

'Lily Molyneux,' she went on to explain, 'Anne's younger sister, the one who painted those watercolours you always admire at Rathdrum. She lived here too, the prettiest of them all.'

'But she never married?'

'No, she never did.'

Rosie said nothing. The look that passed across her grandmother's face was so unlike her she was sure there was a sad story to be told. Too sad for such a lovely summer day standing looking at the ruins of a once handsome house and thinking about dear people now lying under the tangled growth of a neglected churchyard.

Rosie left her grandparents sitting in the motor and walked up the wide stone steps. The lower ones still bore the shallow indentations made by long years of use, but the upper ones were shattered at the edges by the heat of the fire. Grass was sprouting from the cracks.

She moved cautiously. In the soot-blackened gap, she stopped and gazed at the ruins beyond. The upper storey had collapsed, pieces of wall had bent and fallen on top of each other, like a book dropped on its open side, the pages splayed, the binding poking up in the air. The burnt timbers gleamed and shone in the sun. Here and there, small patches of weed and wildflower, fresh and green, waved in the breeze, thriving in the rich ash.

'Not long ago,' she said aloud to herself.

She had seen enough abandoned cottages near her own home to know how quickly tree seedlings could spring up, but even here, where growth was so prolific, there was nothing older than this present season. The undamaged trees in the nearby garden and driveway had not yet colonized the tangled ruin.

She stared at the waving fronds, imagining what they would become. In ten years. In twenty years. Left to the wind and rain, the soft breezes from both sea and lake and the luxurious vegetation all around, the desolate space would close over, settle and heal. Like with the churchyard, you would soon have to know the story to be able to find the fragments that remained.

'Well, what next?' asked John as she arrived back at the motor, but made no move to get in.

'I'd like to see the stable yard and the rooms where you lived, Granny.'

'Well, I'm not sure what we'll find there,' her grandfather replied. 'The back drive is over there. It looks no worse than the front though. The stable yard is over yonder, beyond those chestnuts,' he went on, pointing to a gap in the trees. 'What do you think, Rose?'

'Why not? We may as well do the job properly and let Rosie have the whole story.'

They proceeded even more slowly than before, but it was not many minutes before the grass grown track stopped at a handsome pair of stone built pillars. The gate had been removed but ahead of them the cobbles of the stable yard were still there.

'My goodness, that's a surprise,' exclaimed John, coming to a halt outside a two-storey building with stone steps running up to the living quarters on the upper floor.

All around them the single-storey buildings, workshop, barns and storehouses, stood open to the sky, their roof timbers green with growth, their slates gone, yet the living quarters Rose and her mother shared and the main stables opposite where John himself had been quartered for the length of his stay, still had their roofs intact.

'Well, what do you make of that?' he asked in amazement.

Rosie looked up at the tiny windows above the pale, flaking whitewash. The room behind them must be much smaller than the room over the workshop at home.

'But didn't the man from Detroit put new roofs on?'

'Ach yes,' said John laughing. 'I forgot. I thought they'd lasted a bit too well since our time here. But that's it. Do you want to go up and have a look?' he said turning to Rose. 'It'll be safe enough inside if the roof's sound.'

'No, John. I think I'd rather walk a little way down the path and sit by the lake, but I think I know who will want to go and have a look.'

Rosie nodded vigorously and then had a sudden thought.

'Wouldn't it be locked up, Granda?'

'Not very likely,' he replied, shaking his head. 'The only thing worth stealing is the slates. They mustn't have had a ladder long enough.'

Rosie climbed down from the motor, ran across

to the foot of the steps, then paused halfway up the steps to watch her grandparents setting off down the back drive. Her grandmother was limping slightly, but she seemed not to notice. As they moved away from the motor, to her great delight, she saw them look at each other and laugh.

Smiling herself, she ran up the remaining steps to the rooms where Hannah McGinley had made a home for her daughter and her youngest son, Sam. She turned the handle on the door at the top and stepped into a room with two small windows and a black metal fireplace. Beyond the windows she could see the clock on the stable block, its face still painted blue, its hands long gone. Below stood the parked motor, its elegant shape in sharp contrast to the mellowed stonework of the old stone building.

She turned back into the room. The floor was dusty, but not as dirty as she had expected. The new planks still showed where it had been mended, much paler than the original ones which were darkened with age and tramping feet. The black metal fireplace was still intact.

Opposite the door by which she had entered stood another, presumably leading to the bedrooms. Suddenly, she noticed something lying on the floor by the bedroom door. She stepped across, picked it up and stood staring at it in amazement. A page torn from a notebook, perfectly fresh and clean with the number six written clearly at the top.

She carried it back to the window where the light was better and began to read what had been

97

written. She studied the unfamiliar hand and the even more unfamiliar words for some minutes before it struck her that her problem was not so much understanding what it said, but how this piece of paper came to have a smudge of ink on it as fresh as if it had only just been written.

As she ran her eye along the unfamiliar words once more, her body bent towards the light, she heard the creak of the bedroom door opening behind her. Startled, she whirled round and looked up as a young man with red hair stepped into the room.

'Good afternoon,' he said formally. 'I don't think I've had the pleasure of meeting you before.'

Seven

'What on earth are you doing here?' asked Rosie, looking the young man up and down.

He shut the door behind him, leant nonchalantly against the doorpost and regarded her with a slight smile. Red-headed, with a creamy skin and the freckles that usually go with such colouring, he was dressed in an open-necked shirt and a pair of grey flannels, the shirt crumpled and none too clean, the trousers marked with black streaks below the knee.

'I could ask you the same,' he said quickly, a hint of pique in his tone, 'and with more cause.'

'But I asked you first,' she replied, holding her ground.

She was sure he was older than she was, perhaps as much as twenty, but that didn't give him the right to be sharp with her. But then boys were often like that. They behaved as if they knew everything, had the right to say the first thing that came into their head and then stand over it whether it made any sense or not.

She lowered herself carefully on to the low, narrow windowsill. She was perfectly aware that she was blocking its light and making the room even dimmer, but if she was going to have to wait for him to explain himself she might as well try to be more comfortable.

He returned her gaze, studying her thoughtfully.

'I'm sorry my sitting room is so ill provided,' he said sarcastically, 'but I can't possibly invite you into my bedroom.'

'Is it better provided?'

'Yes. It has a chair and a small barrel. I moved them in there when the motor stopped. Along with my desk and bookcase.'

'And why did you do that?'

'Precaution. I don't get many visitors here. In fact, visitors are not welcome.'

'Are you hiding then?' she asked abruptly, looking him straight in the eye.

Without giving her an answer, he turned his back on her, went into the room he'd described as his bedroom and fetched a roughly-mended chair which he placed to one side of the empty fireplace. Through the open door, Rosie caught a momentary glimpse of a blanket thrown over a heap of wilted bracken and a packing case on which sat a small pile of books, a bottle of ink and a notebook.

He rolled the barrel across the floor, upended it on the other side of the fireplace and sat down, glancing into the empty grate as if to ensure the fire did not need another log or a shovel full of coal.

Rosie sat silent, puzzled by his reticence, but unwilling to give way to his attempts to deflect all her questions.

He gazed around the completely empty room as if it were full of interesting objects, then settled his eyes upon her with a small smile.

'You might be a spy,' he said coolly.

Rosie burst out laughing and shook her head, almost prepared to forgive him for his unco-operativeness.

'Though you are a bit young, I must admit,' he added, looking her up and down. 'You can't be more than fourteen or fifteen.'

'I'm sixteen,' she retorted, without even bothering about the small modification of the truth.

What did a few more days matter? Except, of course, that it did. People made judgements based on age that were quite false. Miss Wilson had explained that to her girls most carefully.

'My dears, I have to keep my age a secret,' she'd said firmly, one afternoon when the subject of age came up in discussing the novel they were reading. 'There are some people who would assume I was too old to run a school if they knew how old I was. They would say I was too out of touch to know what went on in the world, or too feeble to do the things a teacher needs to do. Keeping my age secret is nothing to do with vanity.'

Rosie remembered how she had gone on to caution them about the dangers of making such ill-founded judgements about people, either old or young. Now here was the very proof of what she'd said. This young man assumed she could not guess what was going on just because he judged she was younger than he was.

In fact, as Rosie sat watching him fidget on his hard wooden barrel she began to wish she'd said seventeen while she was about it. Wearing one of the two new dresses her grandmother had bought for her birthday, with its trimly fitted waist and soft, full skirt, she felt sure she could have got away with it.

'I'm here for the good of my health,' he said abruptly. 'There are two IRA men searching for me. If they find me, they'll kill me. They'll probably torture me first, or tie me to a landmine, or some such variation to provide entertainment,' he added, as if shocking her would keep her in her place. 'There are quite a lot of options from recent events,' he said, his pale face flushing angrily.

'But why would they want to kill you? What have you done?' she demanded.

'Nothing that I know of personally, but I have red hair and I'm a Walsh. That'll be enough for the same pair who are after me.'

She was sure he was telling the truth, but could she be sure that he was not frightening himself. Many people were fearful without good cause, but as many did indeed go in fear of their lives. Terrible things had been done in the last years in every part of Ireland with family set against family, brother against brother.

'But the Civil War ended last year,' she began as calmly as she could manage. 'There was a treaty last summer, wasn't there?'

'And do you really think that would have the slightest effect on two men who have made up their minds that I, or my brother, betrayed them?'

Rosie dropped her eyes and stared at the prettily patterned fabric of her new dress. If that was the way of it, then he had good cause. After the

Black and Tans had left there'd been deaths enough at home in County Armagh which everyone knew were the settling of old scores. Feuds and fallings out that had grown to hatred were being taken up under the shadow of the political troubles. She'd listened to the stories of stolen guns and night raids her brothers brought home. There were plenty of guns to be had and plenty of opportunities. Hundreds had died, both Catholic and Protestant.

Suddenly, she saw again the newly turned earth in the churchyard, the jam pot of flowers, her grandparents standing close, their heads together. Walsh. That was the name freshly cut on the small white stone.

'Was your grandfather Thomas Walsh, the coachman here at Currane about fifty years ago?'

He stared at her in amazement.

'What if he was?' he said, with a visible effort to collect himself.

'And your elder brother Thomas was killed last year, in May, in an ambush of Free State soldiers,' she went on very quietly, 'in the hills above Waterville.'

To her absolute amazement, he dropped his head into his hands and burst into tears.

'I'm sorry. I'm so sorry about your brother.'

Quickly she crossed to him, then hesitated, looking down at him, his shoulders crumpled, his face in his hands, tears trickling silently down his fingers. Then she knelt down beside him and put her arm round his shoulders.

'Now, please tell me what's going on. There must be something we can do to help.'

103

'We?' he said quickly, his unease springing up again as he wiped his tears crossly with the back of his hand. 'Who's "we"?'

'My grandparents and myself,' she said, taking his hand and drawing him over to the window. 'Look, you can see them down there, near the motor. They've been to the lake together because that's where they used to walk when they first met. My grandmother used to live here. In this room. She knew Thomas and your father. Apparently your father and her brother, Sam, were good friends.'

'Sam McGinley?'

'Yes.'

'And you are...?'

'Rose Hamilton,' she said easily, 'but everyone calls me Rosie.'

'They soon won't,' he said, as he wiped his eyes firmly with the sleeve of his shirt. 'You'll be a Rose when you've grown up just a little bit more.'

Before she had time to decide whether this was meant as a compliment or another edgy comment, he clasped her hand more firmly, drew her to him and kissed her warmly on the mouth.

'Rosie Hamilton, you're an angel in disguise,' he declared, releasing her. 'I haven't spoken to a soul for three weeks and unless it rains a bit harder tonight I won't even have enough water for a bowl of porridge tomorrow.'

A few minutes later Rosie made her way back down the steep stone steps and into the stable yard, aware that Patrick Walsh was watching anxiously to see what would happen. Uneasy herself, she wasn't quite sure what she was going to say to the two figures who sat in the motor and turned towards her, smiling, as she approached.

'Well, did you have a good look?' asked Rose, as she came and stood by the driver's side. 'There can't have been very much to see.'

Rosie decided there was no simple way. She'd have to be direct.

'I found a young man hiding, Grandma...'

'What?' gasped John, horrified, before she could continue. 'And we let you got up there by yourself. Sure we should have known better, the times we've been through. Are you all right?'

'Yes, Granda, I'm perfectly all right But he's not. He's Thomas Walsh's grandson and there are two IRA men after him. He's been living on porridge for a week. He thinks it's got too dangerous for his young brother to bring him food. He was leaving it in a hiding place down by the lake for Patrick to pick up at night, but there's been nothing now for a week.'

'Oh the poor lad,' said Rose. 'How long has he been here?'

'I didn't ask him that, but he said he hasn't spoken to a soul for three weeks.'

'And living on porridge ?' said John, shaking his head. 'Where is he now?'

'Watching us, I expect,' said Rosie with a smile, turning and waving up at the small window, which showed no sign of an observer. 'I couldn't persuade him to come down till I'd made sure there was no one around but yourselves.'

'Ach, not a soul the whole afternoon,' said

John quickly. 'Even on the shore where you might sometimes see the odd fisherman.'

Rosie could tell from the look on her grand-mother's face she'd already made up her mind what they had to do and she suspected it was as clear to her grandfather. She breathed a sigh of relief when she caught the look that passed between them.

'There's one sure way of getting him down,' said Rose confidently. 'Go up and tell him there's nobody at all around and we've got Ther-moses of tea and a big hamper full of sandwiches and cake.'

All three of them were silent that evening as they sat in the hotel dining room, the sunlight still sparkling on the silver and glass, while the young girls cleared away their empty plates and the young men brought the next course.

Rosie could think only of Patrick. Darkness would fall much more quickly in the small room where he might still be trying to read in the pale evening light. He'd be forced to go to bed as darkness fell. Unless, of course, he went down to the lake, to check again the hiding place his younger brother had used whenever he'd felt it safe to make the journey from Waterville.

A hard enough journey. Patrick told them how fifteen-year-old Kevin used his bicycle over the lakeside road for the first five miles or so. But then, to avoid being seen or followed, he hid the bicycle in the waterside bushes and took a cir-cuitous route inland, up one deep valley between the hills, across the watershed and down the next, to come out on the lakeshore unobserved.

At least tonight Patrick would have some supper. Her grandmother had gathered up everything the hotel had provided for their picnic tea, wrapped it in the sports pages from John's newspaper and insisted he take it back upstairs with him.

Poor Patrick. She'd watched him out of a corner of her eye as she poured tea from the Thermoses into Bakelite mugs. She'd seen the look in his eyes when her grandmother brought out the first packages of food from the hamper. He'd said 'thank you' so politely when she'd offered him a sandwich, sank his teeth into it ravenously and then struggled with himself not to gobble it up.

Her grandfather had been watching him too.

'Eat up, Patrick,' he said encouragingly. 'We'll just drink a cup of tea to keep you company. There'll be a dinner tonight would do half a dozen people. But careful now, don't eat your fill all at once, or you'll pay for it.'

'Here, have these now and a piece of cake or two after them,' he went on, picking up a generous handful of sandwiches and putting them on a plate. 'But the rest you should take with you and eat later.'

They'd sat together in the motor drinking tea while Patrick ate devotedly. Rosie wondered if someone passing by might think they were just a family party on an outing, but she was grateful it wasn't put to the test when she looked at him, his hair dishevelled, his trousers marked, his shirt-sleeves rolled up.

'Did young Patrick tell you whereabouts in Waterville he lives?' John asked, when they began their main course.

'No, he didn't. He wasn't going to say anything at all when he first appeared. It took me ages to get him to tell me what he was doing there, though I guessed he was hiding from someone.'

'That's hardly surprising, I suppose,' he said, nodding. 'Sometimes you could hardly believe the badness of people.'

'You said he had some books, Rosie. Did you get a look at them?' her grandmother asked.

'I would have tried but I didn't manage it.'

Her grandfather looked at her surprised and puzzled.

'Granny and I think you can tell a lot about someone by the books they read,' she said to him. 'He'd been making notes on something when I arrived. That's how he gave himself away. There was a fresh page lying on the floor. But I couldn't read it. It was in Irish.'

'Did your friend Thomas speak Irish?' John asked abruptly.

'No, he didn't,' Rose replied, shaking her head. 'I'm quite sure of that. But his son might well have learnt it in Land League days. There was a big revival then. Teachers going round the country giving classes in schools and halls. My Sam taught now and again when he was very short of money. Did Patrick mention his father?' she asked suddenly.

Rosie shook her head and they fell silent again as a young man came to offer them further thick

slices of roast beef and yet more roast potatoes.

'I can think of someone who could do damage
to that salver of beef,' John commented grimly,
as they declined second helpings and saw the
loaded serving dish being carried away.

'It's not for long, John,' Rose said to comfort
him. 'We'll take him some toast and marmalade when we collect him in the morning and
see he gets a good lunch before we put him on
the train. He's young enough not to take any
harm. It would be different if the weather was
cold.'

'Aye, I'm sure you're right. And I'm sure the
uncle in Dublin will know what's best for him. I
can't keep up with the comings and goings but it
would be different if you lived there.'

'Yes, John, but it doesn't really matter what's
happening at the political level. These two men
who want Patrick are Waterville men. Now
they're out of jail, they'll have to find work or
emigrate. They're not likely to go searching
round Dublin for a student. And if they leave
Waterville, everyone will know. Its no different
from Banbridge, everyone knows everyone
else's business. If they head for Dublin, his
mother or brother will know and can send him
word. His uncle can pack him off to London, or
America. I'm sure he's got relatives there. And if
he hasn't, then the McGinleys would be only too
glad to help him.'

John nodded, looked relieved and said a polite
no to apple pie with cream, or custard, or both.

A little later, as coffee was being served, he

excused himself. He'd just go out and have a look at the motor's handbook. It might be a good idea to put up the top on the motor for tomorrow's job, even if it didn't look much like rain.

Eight

Rosie did not sleep well after her visit to Currane Lodge. For a long time she lay awake intensely aware of the low voices of her grandparents in the bedroom next door. It was no more than the faintest murmur, but she knew they were working out what to do about Patrick and just thinking about his situation made her anxious. They'd promised to go back to Currane Lodge in the morning and take him to somewhere he'd be safe, but it would be no simple matter to decide what was best.

The two O'Connors, newly-released from internment, who held him responsible for tipping off Free State troops about their movements a year earlier, were members of one of the nine Kerry IRA Brigades. When her grandfather had questioned him, Patrick had explained they recruited young men from every part of the county, though rather more from the north than the south. The Waterville men were well-known to his family, but there were any number of others who might also be on the look out for him.

Rosie tossed and turned and so wished she could hear what they were saying, wished there was some simple solution she herself could come up with, wished he was safely on his way to

111

Dublin, or London, or America. Then, to her intense surprise, she found herself wishing nothing of the sort, because she'd only just met him and very much wanted to see him again.

For one thing, she knew so little about him, and would like to know much more, even though she'd not even liked him very much to start with, especially when he'd treated her as if she were only fourteen or fifteen. When he'd cried over his brother's death, though, she'd changed her mind. Then he'd kissed her, so quickly she hadn't had time to think how she felt.

Sweet sixteen and never been kissed.

People were always saying that. She'd no idea where it came from, but she kept on hearing it all the time these days. Song or not, it happened to be true in her own case. The nearest anyone had come to kissing her had been Paddy Doyle, one of the new neighbours on the lane back at home, but he'd only done it for a dare, so it didn't mean anything. She knew Patrick's kiss was very different, but what it was saying, she had no idea.

It could just be he was so relieved to have someone to talk to after all those lonely weeks, but then again, he'd said she was an angel in disguise. The trouble was she had no way of telling whether or not he really liked her or whether that was just the sort of thing he would say to any girl who took his fancy.

She fell asleep without coming to any conclusion and was pursued by ugly dreams all through the night.

Uncle Joe was there in most of them, unwashed and unshaven, poring over his newspaper, reading out accounts of gun battles and ambushes. At one point, he appeared standing on a low hill cheering as two groups of men shot at each other.

'That's it. Go on ye boys,' he shouted, above the crack of pistols. 'Kill each other off. The only good Fenian is a dead Fenian.'

'All Fenians have red hair. Kill the bastard!'

Suddenly, there was Patrick too, his red hair matted with blood, little rivulets flowing down his ash-white face.

She cried out and woke up, her body bathed in sweat.

She lay there shaking until her heart began to beat more quietly then she slid out of bed and drew back the heavy curtains. It was only six o'clock but already it was a fine, sunny morning. Although her room faced west, long fingers of light crept round the hotel and lay across the gardens. Beyond the lawns and flowerbeds, the tiny waves ran silently up the beach and the low sun set them sparkling. The wet sand was dazzling as they slipped silently back into the calm waters of the bay.

Comforted and reassured by the familiar sight from her window, she spoke severely to herself and went to the wardrobe. In it there now hung three dresses and the skirt and blouse that had been her Sunday best. The green and white gingham check had been obligatory wear at Miss Wilson's and she'd never liked it, but that still left two dresses and her blouse and skirt to chose from. For the first time in her life, she had the problem of what she would wear for this second

113

visit to Currane Lodge.

Her grandfather was more silent than usual at breakfast. Even while eating his bacon and egg, he kept glancing towards the handbook for his hired Bentley and a new roadmap he'd parked beside his plate.

Rosie noticed that her grandmother had brought a large handbag to breakfast. When it was opened she saw it was quite empty, except for a large sheet of tissue paper with which it had been carefully lined. In the course of breakfast, they filled it with well-buttered toast thickly spread with marmalade made into sandwiches.

'Is there anything I can get you this morning, ma'am?' enquired Bridget, approaching the table a great deal more confidently than she had the previous week.

Rosie wasn't surprised that she was easy with them. Unlike the way she'd seen other guests behave, they all treated her as no different from themselves, a girl doing her job for their benefit.

She smiled at them as John nodded to her, unfolded his map and disappeared behind it.

'Yes, thank you, Bridget. We're going to visit some old friends today, over in Dingle, so we'd like a picnic lunch.'

'Certainly ma'am.'

She listed the available sandwich fillings, several kinds of cake, apple tart and fruit and noted down what Rose chose in a small pad she took from her apron pocket.

'Actually, Bridget, they are rather *elderly* friends,' her grandmother added. 'Do you think you could make lunch for five? We haven't told them we're coming and we don't want to put them to any trouble.'

Bridget beamed.

'Certainly, Mrs Hamilton,' she said, bobbing her little curtsey. 'I'll bring the hamper out to the motor in about twenty minutes. Will that be all right?'

'That will be splendid,' Rose replied, smiling. She slid a few coins from her pocket unobtrusively under her saucer, picked up the handbag and got to her feet.

'Have a nice drive, miss,' Bridget added, as Rosie followed her grandmother out of the dining room.

Just as Rose had had second thoughts about taking Patrick into a hotel for a good lunch, John had changed his mind about putting up the top on the motor. It promised to be yet one more beautiful day, the barometer high, the weather set fair. The hood might indeed conceal his passenger, but it would be more likely to attract unwelcome attention on such a fine summer's morning.

They set off, taking the same road as the previous day, in the same warm sunshine. But nothing else was the same. A young man's life was at risk. If his young brother tried to contact him he might simply reveal his hiding place. He had no means of transport but his own two feet, and negotiating unfamiliar territory where his presence would immediately be noticed was far too dangerous.

They drove in silence. The sun-drenched landscape, the prolific blossoming of hedges and wayside flowers and the bright splashes of colour in cottage gardens were ignored. They had eyes only for anything strange in their immediate surroundings or any other traffic on the road.

Apart from a couple of fishermen, one or two carts heading in the direction of Waterville and a man driving cows to new pasture, they met no one coming towards them. Only two motors caught up with them. John slowed down and observed their occupants closely as they passed. They were all relieved when one vehicle contained well-dressed ladies, the other an elderly priest.

There was no one anywhere in sight as John swung the motor into the overgrown drive at Currane Lodge and proceeded as quickly as he could to get the motor out of sight of the road. They bumped a bit as they met the cobbles of the stable yard, but moments later they came silently to a halt outside the stable block.

Rosie looked up at the window where she'd sat the previous day, expecting to see a face, or a hand waving in greeting, but everything remained silent and still. She felt the tight grip of anxiety as the minutes passed and there was no sign of him.

'Maybe he didn't hear us stop,' said John quietly.

'Or perhaps he's being very cautious in case anyone followed us,' said Rose, looking behind her, back down the drive.

'He could be in the other room, Granny. If he's writing. That's where he had his things,' Rosie suggested.

'I think you could go up and fetch him, Rosie. Here, give him this and tell him to wear the cap. If it's too big, we can pad it with some clean handkerchiefs.'

Rosie took the parcel her grandmother handed her and got down from the motor quickly before John had time to protest. She ran across the yard and up the stone steps. As she arrived at the top, he pulled the door wide open and stood staring at her.

'I thought you mightn't come,' he said, shaking his head and drawing her into the room. 'I only let myself look out the window every ten minutes. But I was awake from six.'

'So was I.'

She handed him the parcel, acutely aware of how closely he was observing her.

'What's this?'

He looked so confused and anxious she wondered if he had slept any better than she had. Certainly, there was something different about him today and for a few moments she couldn't work out what it was. Then she saw that he'd washed his hair. It was soft and shiny and even redder than she'd remembered. His shirt looked cleaner too but it was even more crumpled than before. She glanced cautiously at his trousers. They no longer had black marks below the knee, but in their place, large, dark smudges all over them.

'It might be trousers,' she said tentatively. 'I know there's a cap.'

'Cap? But it's not raining.'

'No, but you have very red hair.'

He pulled open the brown paper and found a pair of corduroys and a motoring cap.

'Where did you get these?' he asked in amazement.

'I didn't. They look like Granda's to me. But I know Granny asked Bridget for some sewing things last night. You'd better go and put them on.'

He hesitated for a moment and then disappeared into the other room, pulling the door very firmly shut behind him.

She smiled to herself and sat down on the windowsill to wait, amazed at how confident she now felt that everything would be all right.

'Well, what do you think?'

He reappeared looking remarkably respectable. He was wearing a comfortable tweed jacket that just might have been bought to go with the trousers her grandmother had shortened the previous evening. Only a small part of his shirt showed under the jacket and not a single shred of red hair escaped her grandfather's spare motoring cap.

'Goodness, I wouldn't recognize you,' she said, delighted.

'But I recognize an angel when I see one.' He hesitated and smiled shyly. 'I have a present for you.'

He put his hand into the jacket pocket and took out a slim, leather-bound volume.

'With love, and kisses,' he said, as he handed it to her, took a step towards her and drew her into his arms.

It took only a few moments for him to collect

118

his books and writing materials and put them in a knapsack he'd hung on a hook on the back of the bedroom door. He'd already thrown away the bracken that he'd used to take the edge off the hardness of the floor. He picked up the folded rug and handed it to her and then stood looking round the almost empty room. A chipped enamel bucket stood in one corner. Nearby, a tin plate and mug sat on the floor. Beside them, the smoothed out paper from yesterday's sandwiches and his discarded trousers.

She saw him glance at them undecided.

'Those were Thomas's. Army issue,' he said awkwardly.

'The trousers, you mean?' she asked, following his gaze.

'No, the plate and mug. It's the first thing they give you when you join up.'

'Then you'll want to keep them,' she prompted.

'Will I?' He came back at her, his tone full of bitterness. 'If he hadn't joined up, he might be here now.'

'But he's not here. And being bitter won't help.'

'Why not?' he asked, glaring at her.

'Because bitterness disables. It stops you from doing the best you can and from taking the comfort there might be for whatever you've lost.'

She heard herself speak the words and stopped in amazement wondering wherever they'd come from. He was still staring at her angrily when she remembered. Out of a story her grandmother told

119

about the time her family was evicted from their home in Donegal.

Sitting in the garden of the hotel the previous week, she'd spoken of the day their cottage had been battered to the ground. It ended with a gathering of some of those evicted that day in the house of an old man who knew his home would itself be knocked down the very next morning. It was his words that had come to her, warning all those who'd suffered and were about to suffer that it was bitterness damaged people most, not hardship, because those who were bitter could take no comfort for their loss.

Rosie saw his belligerent scowl soften as he knelt down on the bare boards. He tore the paper in two, wrapped the metal plate in one piece and the tin mug in the other.

'Here, hold this,' he said, thrusting the knapsack into her hands so abruptly she had to let go of the rug she'd been carrying.

While she held it open, he wedged the plate in easily enough, but he could see nowhere to put the mug. He stood clutching it in his hand, looking down in dismay at the well-packed books.

'If you take the ink bottle out, the mug might fit in the space.'

The mug slipped neatly into place. She then pointed out that the ink bottle would fit inside the mug. He shook his head and smiled a strange, rueful little smile, did up the straps and hitched the knapsack over one shoulder.

'What *am* I going to do without you?'

He glanced back at the floor. His blackened trousers lay where he'd dropped them.

120

'What about those?'

'They could do with cleaning.'

She picked them up and wrapped them inside the rug she'd retrieved from the floor.

'I did try. I went down to the lake and swam and washed my shirt. But I couldn't get the marks out.'

'How *did* they get there in the first place?' she asked, trying not to smile.

'Cooking my porridge. I lit fires in the ruins, in among the fallen timber. That way the smoke could have been accidental. There were plenty of bits of broken glass around to get one going. It was hard work climbing in there and the burnt timbers rubbed off on me. I'm not going back for my saucepan and spoon,' he declared, as he slipped an arm around her and led her towards the door.

Rosie noticed how uneasy her grandfather looked as they came across the cobbles to the motor, but he greeted Patrick warmly and nodded enthusiastically when he saw the transformation in his appearance.

Her grandmother opened her handbag and laughed when she saw his eyes light up.

'There's not time to make tea,' she said, 'but you can eat as we go. We've worked out a plan to put to you, but you must decide if it's any good.'

Patrick nodded, his mouth full of marmalade sandwich.

'The obvious way to go to Dublin from Waterville is by train from Kenmare,' John began. 'There's two things against it. One, that your men might be about the place. Two, that that's what they'll be expecting you to do.'

Patrick nodded again.

'So we thought we'd take you to Tralee and put you on a train for Galway. Then from Galway, where no one knows you, you should be safe enough getting across to Dublin tonight or tomorrow morning.'

Rosie saw the flicker of unease in his eyes, but so had her grandmother.

'I'm sure you haven't any money left by now, Patrick,' she said, 'but John here always carries more than we ever need. You can pay him back one day if you want to. Treat it as a long, long loan.'

'That's very generous of you, sir,' he said, looking up at John. 'To be honest, I didn't have any money in the first place, Mrs Hamilton,' he added, smiling at her. 'When my father died, his pension was so small my mother had to give up the Dublin house and come and live with her sister down here. That's why Thomas joined up in Waterville. I was only able to stay on at college because I got a job evening and week-ends in a pub and my uncle and aunt let me stay with them for free. I was looking for work when I came home, but then the O'Connor's got let out and I had to run for it.'

'So how about Tralee?' John asked, aware that time was moving on. 'What do you think?'

'You're quite right, Mr Hamilton. However many IRA men are back home in Tralee, they don't actually know me to see. And they may have their minds fixed on other things like trying

122

to find work. There's not much about. I thought it was bad in Dublin but its much worse here.'

'Right, Patrick. That's agreed then. Come and sit in front with me and let the ladies sit behind,' said John briskly, helping Rose down from her seat. 'That's the way all these visitors drive around. Two by two. If we have to stop for any reason, pretend you're Rosie's brother.'

Rosie looked around as he turned the motor in the cobbled yard. This was the place where it all began, she thought. Over there was where her grandfather once sat with the other grooms, waiting for her grandmother to come back from work. Then they walked out together along the lakeshore.

Up there, where Granny had lived with her mother, she had met Patrick. They had not walked out, but they had talked and he had kissed her. Twice. As the motor moved slowly past the ruins of Currane Lodge, she fingered the pocket of her skirt where she'd thrust the small, leather-covered volume he'd given her. She longed to see what it was and if he'd written anything in it for her.

They slowed right down at the end of the drive. Cautiously, the motor edged forward on to the road. Her grandfather looked both ways to see if there was anyone in sight, but there was no one. Apart from the song of a skylark and the soft murmur of a light breeze from the lake, not a single sound broke the empty silence of the road.

'That's good news, Patrick,' she heard her grandfather say.

Once safely on the road, to her great surprise,

he put his foot down and drove faster than she'd ever seen him drive during all their time in Kerry. Despite the roughness of the road, the motor he had longed to drive, responded beautifully. In a very short time Lough Currane was left far behind.

Nine

Driving back to Waterville by the coast road, alone in the back seat of the motor, as Patrick's train carried him away in the opposite direction, Rosie could not make up her mind whether she was happy or sad.

It had been such an extraordinary day so far, so full of confusing and contrary feelings. There'd been real anxiety when they'd set off from Currane Lodge, but once they left the lakeside road and climbed steadily higher on the long pass between the mountains, it felt as if good fortune were smiling on their journey as brightly as the July sun.

As they headed north and east through green, empty country, not only did nothing overtake them, but they met hardly anything at all, not even a turf cart. Miles passed and wide vistas of valley and mountain unfolded before them, rich and luxurious as the sun rose higher. Still nothing came up behind them and the anxiety of the morning quietly faded away.

After the first hour her grandfather was happy enough to stop, convinced by now that there could be no pursuit from the direction of Waterville. They paused often. Each time they drew in to view the newest prospect or let the engine cool on the steepest gradients, Patrick was there at her side.

His jacket now discarded in the bright sunshine, she could feel the warmth of his body through his thin shirt as he stood close beside her, sharing the road map, pointing out to her places he'd heard of from his grandfather for whom these mountains, the Magillycuddy's Reeks, had been home, until he'd got his first job as a groom in Waterville a few years before Sir Capel took him on at Currane Lodge.

In a small curved area where road stone had been quarried from a convenient outcrop, they'd drawn off the road and spread their picnic on a broad, flat rock. Surrounded by wildflowers and shadowed from the heat of the noonday sun by the bare cliff behind them, they'd eaten together, talking and laughing.

After the meal, while her grandparents read and rested in the comfortable back seats of the motor, she and Patrick explored the nearby rock faces and the sheltered crevices, home to a whole variety of small plants. Neither of them knew the names of the flowers they found, but he'd helped her to find the freshest of the blooms and together they'd arranged them carefully and pressed them between the clean pages at the back of her sketch pad.

Only when they arrived in Tralee and made their way through the unfamiliar streets to the railway station did some of the old tension return, but even that soon disappeared. The station was crowded, full of visitors. Some of them were English, some American tourists, easily distinguishable by their clothes and accents, but most were family parties from Cork, or Galway, or Dublin. No one gave them a second glance as they threaded their way on to the platform together, one more family going to welcome friends or setting off to visit relations at the height of the summer season.

Quite without planning it, they'd arrived only moments before the scheduled departure of a train that would take Patrick well away from Kerry. He bought his ticket and began to say thank you to her grandparents as the train itself steamed in.

There were only minutes left as he shook hands vigorously with her grandfather and said something to him she didn't catch. Then her grandmother moved forward, hugged him and wished him well.

Encircled by a family party already pushing past them from the open carriage doors, he turned towards her. Their eyes had met and she found herself overcome with shyness.

He'd hesitated for a moment only and then, taking her by the shoulders, he'd kissed her vigorously on both cheeks.

'Take great care of yourself, sister dear, till I see you again,' he said with a broad grin.

They had laughed as he climbed in, stepping carefully around a small boy who refused to move away from his vantage point at the window.

He waved and disappeared into the crowded carriage as the train began to move out of the station. They watched it disappear in a cloud of steam and smoke knowing he could not look back at them or wave. All she could think of was whether he felt it safe enough now to remove his headgear and reveal his capping of shining red hair.

Now the sun was going down in an orange glow in the shimmering waters of Dingle Bay and the shadows were lengthening across the road ahead. She wondered where the same evening sun would find Patrick and what different prospect he might be viewing from the windows of a train steaming east across the map of Ireland. She was painfully aware the miles between them increased as each minute passed. Not only had no one ever left her before, but she had no idea if she would ever see Patrick again.

Saddened by the thought of their hasty and confused parting, another thought as sad came in on top of it. She caught her breath and stared indifferently at the lively activity filling the large central square in Cahirciveen.

In three more days their holiday would be over. There would be no more drives. No more magnificent prospects of mountain and sea. No more walks on the beach or long talks with her grandmother in the hotel garden. She would be going home. Home to Ulster. To the Six Counties, as people here in the south now called it. First to Banbridge to spend a night at Rathdrum, then home to the farm by Richhill Station.

Tears sprang to her eyes. She fumbled in the pocket of her skirt for a handkerchief. It was only when she'd wiped her eyes and was putting her handkerchief back in her pocket that she touched the slim, leather-bound book Patrick had given her only that morning.

With a great sigh of relief, she took out the book and held it firmly in her hand. Here was a token, some tangible evidence of what had been between them, however brief the time and whatever it might mean. Even after so few hours, it seemed as if Currane Lodge and her meeting with Patrick was slipping away from her as fast as the miles between Tralee and Waterville.

She examined the small volume closely, a well-thumbed copy of Shakespeare's sonnets, the pages brown and brittle and spotted with age. On the title page, the name of some former owner had faded from black to misty grey. Inside the back cover, a very modest price had been scribbled in pencil. A single leaf from a notebook, folded double and identical to the one she had found on the floor of Patrick's hiding place, served as a book mark.

'Shall I compare thee to a summer's day...'

She read the familiar sonnet and smiled, then read it again. She leaned her head back against her seat. Had he simply left the folded sheet to mark the place where he'd been reading, or was it placed there deliberately, to send her a message? She'd so like it to be meant for her, something that reached across the growing miles. Something to cherish. But she couldn't be sure. Like Patrick's kisses, she was sure they were sincerely meant at the time, but something told her that Patrick's gestures might come and go very easily.

She opened the book again. Inside the front

cover, was a freshly written message, slightly smudged, with a generous scrawled signature at the end. She was sure it began 'To Rose', but that was as far as she could go for Patrick had written his message in Irish.

Next morning over breakfast, they began to discuss what they might do in the precious few days that remained. Although he seemed tired after the long drive to Tralee, her grandfather was in the best of spirits. He said what he wanted was to make the best of the greatest motor he had ever driven.

Her grandmother smiled to herself, not at all surprised that all he wanted to do was drive. She confessed what she wanted was to see the mountains, from any angle, even from a seat in the hotel garden. She'd lived with the remembrance of these mountains, she said, for almost half a century, and she wanted to make sure they'd be with her for the rest of her life.

When they turned to Rosie and asked her what she'd most like to do, she made them laugh, because she suggested they just opened John's guide book at random because there was nowhere she'd been so far she hadn't loved.

In the end, they did two drives. They went west to Valentia Island, took the ferry to the island itself and saw the place from which the very first telegraph message had been sent across the Atlantic. The next day they went east to see the lakes at Killarney, for her grandmother said that no one could come to Kerry and not go to see them.

The time passed even more quickly than Rosie had expected. Sitting at breakfast on the very last morning she felt unspeakably sad. It needed a real effort to eat the tasty breakfast which Bridget had just served.

Looking down at her plate, she knew there'd be no bacon and eggs for breakfast when she got home. Nor smoked salmon kedgeree. Probably not even a second cup of tea, unless she was quick enough. She couldn't imagine that ever again anyone would ask if there was there anything she'd like, or anything they could do for her.

The previous evening, after dinner, Bridget had knocked on her bedroom door.

'I've come to do your packing, miss,' she said politely.

'Oh Bridget, come in. I've done it. It only took me a minute, but I'm so glad to see you. Come and sit down.'

'I'm awful sorry yer goin' miss,' Bridget said bluntly, as she followed her to the window seat that looked out over the garden.

'And I'm awfully sorry to be going,' she replied honestly, as they sat down facing each other.

'Maybe ye'll come again next year, miss. Yer granda and granny enjoyed themselves, diden they?'

'Oh yes, they did. We *all* did. But it was a special holiday for them. They've wanted to come for a long, long time, but something always came to stop them. For a very long time they couldn't even afford the train fare. Then, when they could, there was family and work. They had it all planned in 1914 when the war broke out and then there were all the troubles that came after. Some people thought they shouldn't even have come this year with all the bad feeling there's been over the Boundary Commission but Granny said they weren't getting any younger. So they came. But I don't think they would come again.'

'But *you* could come, miss.'

'Bridget dear, you mustn't call me *miss*. There's no one to hear you now and I'm not a guest any more. I'm just a girl like you, though I've turned sixteen now and you're probably younger.'

'I'm fifteen an' this is m' first job since I left school. An' I only started last week the day you's came, miss.'

She paused as Rosie smiled and shook her head.

'Rosie,' Bridget corrected herself, with a shy smile. 'It's a nice name, it suits you, miss. I mean, Rosie.'

She laughed at herself and then looked at Rosie cautiously.

'What'll ye do Rosie, when ye go home? D'ye live with Granny and Granda?'

'No, I wish I did,' she admitted. 'I live on a farm about fifteen miles away and I don't see them very often. I've eight brothers and sisters and I've been trying to find a job. No luck so far.'

'I'm saving to go to America,' said Bridget suddenly. 'And your granda was very good to me. He gave me a wee envelope with money. Paper money,' she added, her eyes wide. 'If there were a few more like him I could go next year.'

She paused and hesitated. Then it all came out with a rush.

'Maybe we'll meet in America,' she said brightening, her dark eyes flashing into life. 'Irish people always meet each other over there. There's so many clubs and societies, ye'd never be afraid of being lonely. That's what my sister says. She went last year.'

'My sister Emily is hoping to go too.'

'Sure, you could come as well. Sure what's to keep you here if you haven't a job and don't live with your nice granny and granda?' She paused and added shyly, 'Though I know you wou'den want to leave them.'

'That's true. I'm so lucky to have them.'

'Aye, an' they're lucky to have you,' Bridget replied, as she stood up. 'Sure don't old people need young people to keep the life in them and to stop them thinkin' long.'

Rosie looked up at her and smiled, watched as she straightened her apron and her cap with a practised twitch, a skinny, vulnerable figure.

'If I don't go now, someone 'ill be lookin me,' she said quickly, though she still made no move to go.

'Yes, I suppose you must. A pity we couldn't go out for a walk on my last evening.'

Bridget hesitated, as if she had something more to say, but felt to shy to say it.

'Rosie, would you write to me?' she managed at last, blurting out the words as she put her hand

133

on the well-polished door knob.

'Yes, of course I will, if you want me to.'

She got up and followed her to the door. 'Maybe not very often if I'm living at home, but I *will* write.'

'That would be great, really great,' Bridget replied, holding out her hand and giving Rosie a great beaming smile. 'And then we can plan where to meet if we're both goin' to America.'

'Two messages for you, Mr Hamilton,' said Bridget, approaching their table quickly as they finished breakfast. 'The young man from Tralee is here.'

For one startling, heart-stopping moment all Rosie could think of was Patrick. But that was silly. Patrick had *left* from Tralee. The last thing he would be doing was coming back to Waterville.

'Ah, thank you, Bridget,' John said, folding his *Irish Times* and looking at his watch. 'He's a good bit early, but the cases are all ready and I settled up last night. Would you tell him we'll be with him shortly.'

'He's in no hurry, Mr Hamilton,' she replied, giving him a big grin. 'The housekeeper is his mother's cousin. She has him sat down with bacon and egg.'

Leaving them all laughing, she had just hurried away when she stopped, put her hand to her mouth and came back again.

'I'm sorry, sir, there's another message,' she apologized, putting her hand to her apron pocket and taking out a badly crumpled piece of paper.

'It came last night late and there was only the night porter on reception. It's not very clear and Jimmy's a desperit bad han' with a pen.'

'It says,' she began, peering at it crossly, 'Mr Hamilton's cat safe. Dublin ... something ... something ... will send to North.'

Rosie smiled and said nothing, a great wave of relief sweeping over her.

'I wonder,' said her grandmother slowly, 'could it be that cap you left behind in Dublin, John.'

'Aye, cap, not cat,' said John, his face lighting up.

'I left my other driving cap behind in Dublin, Bridget,' he explained. 'Maybe the hotel thought it best to send it to our home address.'

'Ach yes, they would. It's what we do here as well. You wouden believe what people leave behind that has to be packed up and sent. England and America inta the bargain.'

'Well, we'll try not to do that, Bridget,' said Rose, getting slowly to her feet. 'Will you come out to see us off?'

'Indeed, I will, ma'am. As soon as I see ye's gettin' inta the motor, or yer man finishin' up his tea, I'll take a wee run out. I've sent the porter up for yer cases.'

Rosie went back up to her room knowing she had nothing left to do but look out at the garden, at the pattern of shrubs and flowers that had been her companion for nearly two weeks now and at the sea beyond. She stood by the window not knowing whether she wanted to treasure these last precious moments in this world, or wishing she was back and settled in the very different world that awaited her.

Now that the cases had gone, the small one her father had brought from Richhill and the larger one her grandfather had bought her for her birthday, all that was left of her presence in this bright, pretty room was a woven bag from a gift shop in Killarney. In it she had put a book for the journey, the maps her grandfather said he no longer needed, her half-filled sketch book with its treasure of small pressed flowers secured by rubber bands and the slim volume of Shakespeare's sonnets.

She took it out and leafed through it yet again, her mind moving back and forth over her meetings with Patrick. He had seldom been out of her thoughts since they'd sent him off on the train from Tralee. Now they knew he was safe. From somewhere in Dublin he'd phoned his coded message to let them know he'd arrived.

It was almost time to go down to the courtyard. The motor would be waiting, the young man from the hire company ready to drive them to the station at Kenmare before returning with the Bentley to Tralee. She was about to close the book and put it back in her bag when she caught a slight noise outside her door. There was the briefest of knocks as her grandmother came into the room.

'Goodbyes are so sad,' she said, taking one look at Rosie's face.

'Yes,' she agreed, making an effort to smile. 'Is it time to go?'

'Yes, it is. He's finished his tea, and Bridget is

waiting.'

To Rosie's own surprise, she held out the book to her grandmother.

'Granny, could you tell me what this means?'

'Well, yes. I'm a bit rusty,' said Rose, slightly taken aback. 'But this is quite easy. It says: To Rosie, who will always be my angel and my rose. Patrick.'

'Thank you,' she said, as she took the book and put it away. 'I meant to ask you sooner...' she added awkwardly.

'He's a very charming young man. I'm sure you'll meet again some day.'

She slipped an arm round her waist and drew her out of the room and along the landing to where the broad, carpeted stairs led them down to the courtyard from which they would begin their long journey home.

Ten

There were wisps of cloud on the far horizon as they drove briskly along the southern stretch of the Ring of Kerry to the station at Kenmare, but by the time they reached the little town heavy grey swags had covered the sun. As they unloaded the luggage, tiny stabs of warm rain fell. Sitting by the window, as the train steamed steadily eastwards, smoke billowing around the carriages in the strengthening breeze, Rosie watched the heavier rain catch up with them, driven by the strengthening westerly wind from the Atlantic, and spatter noisily against the window beside her.

The rain continued to chase them eastwards throughout the day. She watched the green countryside slip past beyond the streaming carriage windows, its rich colours even more intense under the laden grey skies than in the brilliant sunshine of their journey down.

They arrived in Dublin in a downpour, heard thunder in the night and set off again next morning as the first gleams of light broke through the massed clouds. As they stood outside the hotel waiting for the luggage to be loaded, she watched the wet pavements begin to dry, the pale centre of each flagstone expanding outwards in the fresh breeze, moment by moment.

Halfway to Drogheda, the clouds parted and the sun finally broke through. Rosie, focused on the ruffled white caps fretting the navy-blue of the sea, stared in amazement as the broad expanse of dark water was transformed to a deep turquoise. She would never have believed that any stretch of Irish coast could look like the cover illustration on *Coral Island*, a tropical sea bathed in sunshine and rimmed with golden sand. Only the palm trees were missing.

She wondered if she would ever see this gleaming expanse of sea again, or stand by the shore on the west coast gazing out over the Atlantic with nothing but ocean between her and America. Her grandmother had waited a lifetime to revisit her beloved mountains of Kerry. She wondered where her own life would take her and whether she'd have the chance to return to somewhere she'd been so happy.

As so often since they'd left him at the station in Tralee, she found herself thinking of Patrick. Somewhere in the city rapidly being left further and further behind them, he was going about his everyday life. Doing whatever job he'd been able to find to earn enough money to stay at college. Meeting friends. Reading History, his chosen subject, or poetry, clearly his passion, or any of the hundreds of books he would have access to, as a student in a very literate city.

She wondered if she wasn't more than a little envious of him. It was surely hard enough for him to exist on very little money and keep up his studies, but at least he had the choice. Being a woman, it would be impossible for her. She simply didn't have that choice. In fact, she saw so clearly now, once she got home she hadn't very much choice about anything.

She glanced across at her grandmother and saw she'd closed her eyes. Over the last weeks, she'd worked out that she was seldom asleep even when her eyes were closed. Rose herself had admitted she was usually thinking. So many memories had been awakened by this very special journey, she could hardly take them all in.

Suddenly, she remembered a story her grandmother had told her when they were sitting together in the garden of the hotel in Waterville. She'd been struggling to catch the tones of the mountains with some new watercolours they'd bought that morning and Rose was encouraging her. Then, quite suddenly she began to talk about the mountains of Donegal where she'd been born.

Often before she'd talked about her childhood home, but this time she spoke quite slowly and in detail about the terrible morning when her parents and her brothers and sister were evicted from their home.

What so surprised Rosie was the cool, steady tone of her voice, so at odds with the heartache of the story she was telling. She could hear it even now.

'I remember my mother going round the house, looking at everything, touching things, gathering them up. I didn't understand at the time, but later I realized what she was doing. She was gathering all the thoughts and memories together so that she would have the home she'd made for us all safe inside her head when the house itself was only a heap of rubble.'

A cloud moved across the face of the sun, the tropical sea resumed its dark, ruffled aspect. Rosie stared at it as she went over her grandmother's words in her mind, yet once more. Perhaps that's what she herself had been doing all these miles from Kenmare. Gathering up the memories of this wonderful journey, so that when life was reduced to the farmyard, the lane up the hill to Uncle Henry's shop, she could be sure there *was* another world out there, a world she might one day be able to reach out for.

'Porty-down, Porty-down. All change for Richhill, Armagh, Monaghan, Cavan...'

Rosie almost laughed aloud as the train slowed to a halt. If there was one thing that made Miss Wilson really cross, it was when one of her pupils failed to pronounce the name of their nearest town in the proper manner.

'Port-a-down,' she would repeat. 'Port-a-down.' Then she'd add a little homily on the importance of correct pronunciation. It was a matter of courtesy, she insisted, to get the names of people and places exactly right.

'Home James,' said John Hamilton, folding his newspapers into a neat bundle and peering out at the stationmaster as he tramped past the carriage window, reeling off his long list of stations. 'I hope our reception committee has got here all right,' he said, more than a hint of anxiety

141

coming into his voice as he glanced up at the well-filled luggage racks and thought of all the heavy items in the guard's van.

'Yes, we did expand a bit, didn't we?' said Rose to reassure him, 'But you've a lovely tweed jacket to show for it.'

'And I have *two* dresses *and* a suitcase,' Rosie added quickly.

'Ach, sure there's Alex,' he broke in, the relief in his voice only too obvious. 'An' someone else with him,' he added. 'I can't make out at all who it is with that pillar in the way.'

'Oh, how nice,' said Rose, as she looked out herself and began to laugh at his puzzlement. 'It's your godson. Saturday must be his day off.'

'I hope all's well over at Dromore,' John replied, his eyes screwed up against the light as he tried to catch sight of the young man for himself.

'Aunty Rose, Uncle John, welcome home,' said the tall figure, bending down to kiss Rose as soon as he'd helped her safely to the ground. 'Alex here thought you were a bit squashed on the way over, so he's let me come to help take you home,' he added, as John stepped down to the platform and clapped him on the shoulder.

There were kisses and handshakes all around.

'My goodness, you're looking well,' Alex declared, turning and lifting Rosie down lightly from the carriage.

'Indeed, Alex is right. You *are* looking very well. Much better than the last time I saw you.'

It was only when she heard his voice that Rosie registered the tall young man in an open-necked

142

shirt, so warmly greeted by her grandparents, was the same young man as the dark-suited doctor who sat by her bed a mere three weeks ago encouraging her gently and with great kindness to tell him about her family and her plans for the future.

She looked up at him, saw the sparkle in his grey eyes as he held out his hand and bowed over hers in a slight theatrical gesture. To her own amazement and distress, she blushed.

'My goodness, it was as well I brought Richard,' said Alex cheerfully, as he surveyed the luggage a porter had brought from the guard's van to join what a second one had fetched out from the empty carriage. 'Sure I thought you were going for the scenery.'

'And to get driving a Bentley,' added Richard, as they followed after the porters and their trolleys.

Alex sized up the luggage now piled high on the pavement of the station forecourt. Deftly, he and Richard began to load the two waiting motors.

'It looks as if there were shops as well as scenery,' he commented, beaming down at Rose.

'You never know what might be in those cases, Alex,' she came back at him. 'We don't forget our good friends or their family just because we go on holiday.'

He handed her into John's well-polished Austen saloon.

'I'm sorry we can't run to a Bentley, but as they say in these parts, now you're home you'll have to sit on an egg less.'

John laughed heartily as he levered himself into the driving seat. Alex swung the starting handle and, as she fired first time, he jumped in beside him, waving at Richard and Rosie as they set off.

A few minutes later, Richard's Morris followed after with Rosie in the front seat beside him. How she came to be there she wasn't entirely sure. Alex had loaded two heavy cases into the back seats, but who it was suggested it would balance the weight if she drove with Richard she really couldn't remember, there had been so much talk and laughter over her grandmother's determined defence that she'd only bought presents on this holiday to make up for all the ones they'd never had.

'So, did you have as good a holiday as it seems, Rosie?' Richard asked, glancing towards her with a smile as they came clear of the station traffic.

'Yes, I did. It was all quite wonderful. I can't imagine I shall ever have such a lovely holiday again.'

'Oh surely not,' he said gently. 'Think of all the marvellous places you can go when you're older. Not just Ireland. Scotland, England, the Continent, even America. Would you like to travel?'

She glanced sideways. His eyes were fixed on a horse-drawn dray loaded with some heavy piece of machinery, proceeding towards them at a snail's pace and taking up most of the road. His face was rather long and not handsome at all when she came to think of it. Certainly not by the standards of the film magazines Lizzie Mackay was so devoted to. On the other hand, he had large grey eyes that looked directly at you. Kind eyes that seemed to see the best in you. They smiled easily too as if he was always ready to find something to be pleased about.

'What do you think that is?' he said, frowning, as the dray edged slowly past their stationery vehicle.

'It might be a transverse engine,' she replied thoughtfully, 'judging by the size. What I can't understand is why they're using horses and not a road engine for such a heavy load.'

'Actually I meant that slight hiccough coming from our engine. Though I do agree it seems strange to see a team of horses these days working on something so heavy.'

The dray moved past, its projecting load so wide there were only inches to spare. He put the Morris into gear and drove off cautiously. The hiccough grew less frequent, but was still there.

'It's pinking,' she told him, as soon as the road was clear.

'Is that dangerous?'

'No, just a bad sign. A symptom of an unhappy engine,' she added laughing. 'It could be one of about three things: plugs, distributor or magneto.'

He looked at her in surprise.

'With any luck, we'll make Rathdrum and you'll get the best repair service for miles around. Granda and Uncle Alex will just love taking your engine to pieces.'

'You think they can fix it?'

'Oh yes. It's finding the problem that's diffi-

145

cult. It's relatively simple once you've worked it out. I suppose it's the same with diagnosis. You can't really prescribe for a patient until you know what's wrong, can you?'

She didn't know what to make of the brief look he gave her as they turned on to the familiar road to Banbridge. He said nothing more and seemed to be concentrating on his driving, so she turned away and cast her eye round the still saturated countryside, lit up by a sun now high in a clear blue sky.

The low-lying meadows between the small, humpy hills were still flooded in places. The cattle who'd come to drink were reflected in the pools of water along with the taller clumps of grass and the branched stems of buttercup. Wherever a track ran to a barn or a field entrance the light struck back from the flooded wheel ruts and made parallel silver lines through the rich green of meadow or the sodden yellow of stubble.

'Have you thought any more about what you're going to do next?' he asked as the silence extended.

'Yes,' she said wryly. 'I've thought lots, but I've not made much progress. Granny has been very good. We've talked about all sorts of possibilities, but she knows she can't do anything to help me unless my father agrees.'

'And wouldn't he want to do anything that would help you?'

'Oh yes, he would if he could. But my father is very fair. Granny and I know he thinks it would be wrong to give me something he couldn't give to all my brothers and sisters. There are nine of us, you see. My older brothers and sister have all gone out to work straight from school while I've had a extra year at Miss Wilson's. I still don't know how Granny managed that, but I doubt if she could persuade him to let me do training of any kind. My mother wants me to go into service in some of the big houses. My Uncle Henry had it all lined up for me at Richhill Castle...'

'You mean as a servant?'

Rosie looked at him quickly, taken aback by the shocked tone of his voice.

'It's that or being a shop assistant in Portadown or Armagh,' she said matter-of-factly.

She studied his profile as he negotiated a cluster of vehicles in the narrow main street of Gilford. When he was concentrating, his face did seem long and rather thin, but when he talked or laughed it looked quite different. It reminded her of Uncle Alex, who actually looked cross, his face set in sombre lines, until he laughed.

'What would you do if your fairy godmother waved her wand and said you could do whatever you liked?' he said suddenly as the road opened ahead of them without another vehicle in sight.

He threw out one hand to wave an imaginary wand over her.

She laughed, closed her eyes tight and then looked up at the bright sky.

'I'd like to be a lady,' she said, grinning. 'Lady Rose, if you please. I'd have lots and lots of money and people who were clever and could do things to help me and I'd do important things like Aunt Sarah. I'd see what people needed and

147

I'd be able to do something about it. I could set up nurseries for poor children, and workshops, and dispensaries, just like she did. There's nothing like that where I live. There are poor people who haven't enough to eat, and old people who can't even keep clean unless they've got family to help them, and not everyone has family. And anyway not all families get on with each other...'

She broke off, aware that her light-hearted tone was no longer light-hearted. She hadn't meant to go on at such length.

'Hmm,' he said. 'So the first thing you need is a very wealthy milord. The richest ones are usually old and fat. Would you mind?'

'Oh yes, I would. If I ever marry, it'll have to be someone I like as well as love and they'll probably be just as poor as I am. Like Granny and Granda. They had nothing much to start with and they were very poor when Granda was working in Drumcairn mill and they had four children to feed, but they really cared about each other. That's what I'd want.'

'And have you found anyone yet who might fit the part?' he asked lightly.

She paused, considering, aware he was looking at her, the motor slowed right down as he prepared to swing into the steep left turn to take them up through Ballydown to Rathdrum House.

'I might have,' she confessed at last. 'There was a young man in Kerry. He was hiding in Currane Lodge and we took him to Tralee to escape the people who were threatening to kill him. I liked him, but I might never see him again.

He's at college in Dublin and he's poor. But he gave me a book of Shakespeare's sonnets,' she added, as if it explained something important she was now quite willing to share with someone as kind and friendly as Richard Stewart.

Halfway up Rathdrum hill the pinking grew rapidly worse, the engine coughed repeatedly, spluttered and died. Only Richard's quick action on the handbrake prevented them from rolling backwards down the steep slope.

'We'd better get out one at a time and chock the wheels,' declared Rosie, moving cautiously so as not to destabilize the vehicle.

He followed her with equal caution and together they looked around for the nearest dry-stone wall. They found only flourishing hawthorn hedges, their blossom long gone, the new growth shooting out in all directions, berries already formed in pale green clumps.

'Not a stone in sight,' said Richard ruefully.

'We *could* use the suitcases,' suggested Rosie. 'They'd be much better than stones, but getting them out might shake the motor.'

They stood staring at the Morris which now rested precariously on the steepest part of the hill, several hundred yards short of Alex and Emily's house and a good half mile more from Rathdrum.

'If you leaned against it to steady it, I could get the suitcases out,' she offered.

He looked at her in amazement.

'You can't possibly lift those suitcases,' he protested. 'It took Alex and me all our time getting them in.'

'Of course I won't lift them. I couldn't manage that. But I often have to move heavy things. There's a knack in it. It's all in the way you manoeuvre them. But it takes time ... and cunning. You'd have the harder job keeping the motor steady.'

'Right then, boss. Tell me what to do,' he replied, pulling his forelock.

She giggled and opened the back doors of the Morris and squeezed slowly and gently into the tiny space between the suitcases and the front seats. The new leather cases were shiny. She was able to edge the top one towards the door, just as she'd thought. When it was ready to pivot on its mid-point, about to tip over and fall, she lay across it and called Richard to spread a car rug on the road before she let it slide to the ground. Once the case was safely landed, she helped him drag the rug with its burden into place behind the back wheels.

Manoeuvring the second suitcase was easier, the vehicle now more stable and less liable to run backwards with one heavy obstacle already in place.

'You are an extremely practical young lady, if I may say so,' Richard declared, as they paused to rest, perspiring in the hot sun and breathless from their efforts.

'Thank you, kind sir,' she replied laughing, as she wiped her forehead on her bare arm and smoothed down her crumpled skirt. 'I daresay Emily will give us a glass of spring water if we can make it that far.'

'Should I take the starting handle?' he asked

thoughtfully, as he considered the stationery vehicle.

'Not much point I'd say. Only neighbours come up here on a Saturday and they're not going to be able to start it anyway!'

'What about the suitcases with all the presents?' he asked, looking rather sheepish.

She laughed aloud and shook her head.

'The only person who could pinch those cases would be a professional weightlifter who wasn't afraid of being run over as he picked them up.'

Richard grinned and fell into step beside her. The thought of a large glass of spring water was suddenly very appealing.

They paused only briefly in Emily's cool, shady kitchen for Mrs Love had a special lunch prepared at Rathdrum and everyone would be waiting for them to appear, especially as Emily thought it was at least half an hour since John drove past and tooted his horn.

'He'll be getting worried about you if you don't arrive soon,' she said as she walked out to the gate with them. 'Give them both my love. I'll be going up to see them tomorrow when Alex is here to mind the girls.'

'Does Uncle John worry a lot these days?' Richard asked casually, as they slowed down on the steepest part of the road, the far horizons blocked for the moment by the hawthorn hedges, the inserts of young oak trees casting welcome shade as the day grew even hotter.

Rosie looked at him quickly, but there was nothing in his face to give her a clue as to what

151

he really wanted to know. But something was troubling her, a niggle at the back of her mind. In these last weeks she'd often seen her grandfather upset, anxious about the time, or the right running of the Bentley, or whether they'd be able to find petrol when they needed it.

She'd noticed too, how often her grandmother reassured him, as she'd done this morning when he worried about their reception committee.

'Why do you ask?'

'Oh, I just wondered,' he said, his tone lightly dismissive.

They paused to catch their breath, walked across and leaned on a five-barred gate. Sloping away from them lay a meadow where cattle stood, twitching their tails, in the shade of one of the young oaks. Below and beyond stretched the green lowlands of the Bann valley, the river itself glinting wherever it was not hidden among the trees. On the horizon lay the mountains, their outline sharp against the sky though the heat haze increasing by the hour made them seem insubstantial.

'Granny's mountains,' she said, half to herself.

'I can see why neither of them wants to move from Rathdrum. Imagine looking out on mountains from the end of your own garden. I don't think I could be prised away if it had been *my* home.'

'Is anxiety a symptom of something?'

'Yes,' he said, his eyes still firmly fixed on the far horizon.

She looked sideways at him and waited.

'Like pinking. It can mean different things.

Plugs, magneto and...'

'Distributor.'

'But unlike a car you can't lift a man's bonnet up and see which it might be,' he ended, as they stepped back on to the road and continued up the hill. 'In many cases you just have to wait and see.'

'I'd find that very difficult if I were a doctor. In fact, I find it difficult even though I'm not a doctor. I sometimes hate not knowing what's going to happen next.'

'Don't worry, *that's* not a symptom. It's just something we poor mortals have to live with. I'm probably no better than you when it comes to thinking about the future, but things usually work out all right in the end.'

They arrived at the top of the hill and tramped into the welcome shade of the big sycamore overspreading the entrance gates which had been left open for them.

To her great surprise, he reached out and took her hand as they passed between them.

'Come on, Rosie, let's put an inch to our step. Just think of Mrs Love's nice lunch.'

Eleven

Rosie woke early next morning and drew back her curtains to find a dark and threatening sky so overcast she felt oppressed by its weight. Not only had the previous day's bright sunshine disappeared, but also the freshness that followed Friday's heavy rain. There was not a breath of wind to stir the foliage of the trees, dense and darkened with the maturity of late July.

Sunday morning was always quiet at Rathdrum. No distant murmur came up from the beetling hammers at Ballievy, or crash of sudden rock falls in the quarry at Lisnaree, or the rumble of vehicles moving on the Katesbridge road across the fields on the other side of Corbet Lough. No activity in the yard below until the motor came out to take them to church. The Sunday quiet was familiar from other visits. But this morning even the birds were silent.

There were a few large spots of rain as they came out of church and Rose and John stopped to greet friends and neighbours, but the threatened downpour didn't materialize. The overcast skies were enough however to make John anxious that it would rain during the afternoon when they were to take her home.

It was not a comfortable drive. Roomy as it

was, the Austen felt dark and confining, a strange rubbery smell emanating from the seldom used hood her grandfather had felt obliged to put up. Sharing the back seat with the smaller of her two suitcases, she could only glimpse the passing countryside through the transparent panels in its heavy waterproof fabric and register only the most obvious of the familiar landmarks. Her stomach rumbled uncomfortably as the miles passed as if her lunch hadn't agreed with her. She knew it was because she was anxious, dreading the coolness of her mother's reception and the barbed remarks sure to follow once her grandparents were out of sight.

She felt the vibration as the motor turned off the Portadown road and moved more slowly on the rutted surface and steep slopes of the narrow lane running down to the level crossing. Just before the station itself, they swung left through the open gate, turned round neatly in the empty farmyard and stopped outside the barn, exactly opposite the front door of the house.

She took a deep breath and pushed wide the rear door. As she climbed out she heard her father's voice. He was already kissing his mother and clasping his father warmly by the hand.

'Ach it's great to see you,' he exclaimed, beaming at the two of them.

'Hello Da,' she said, coming towards him and holding up her face to be kissed.

'Dear a dear! Who's this young lady you've brought me back?' Sam demanded. 'My goodness, she's looking well,' he added, his eye moving surreptitiously to her left temple where the scratch and bruise were nowhere to be seen.

'That dress suits you powerful well. I suppose that was your doing,' he continued, turning towards his mother.

'A birthday present, Sam. One wee dress from me and one from your da. Now you wouldn't deny us that, would you?'

'Ach no, I couldn't say a word and you so good to *all* of them. Come on away in an' we'll see about a cup o' tea. I think maybe Martha had to go down to see Cissie Loney. One of her we'ans has took bad, but she'll be back any minute.'

Rosie followed them into the kitchen. To her amazement, there was no one there at all. Neither Uncle Joe reading his Sunday paper, nor young Dolly absorbed in her *Girls Own* comic, nor any of her brothers or sisters, not even young Jack who always used the table for his models whenever he could lay hands on it. She watched her father draw forward the kettle on the stove and pull back the rings to stir the fire. The sudden flicker brought the only brightness in the oppressive gloom of the empty room.

'Ach, Granny, Granda, hello. It's great to see ye.'

Without the slightest warning, Emily burst into the kitchen like a gale of wind, her hair and clothes tossed and untidy, her face wreathed in smiles.

'I heard the motor all right but I couldn't let go what they had me holdin'. I had to give Uncle Joe and Bobby a hand mendin' the fence,' she explained hastily, as she put her arms round Rosie and hugged her.

'The wee brown heifer is the very divil for breaking out into Hughie Lamb's field and aul Hughie doesn't be one bit pleased,' she gasped, finally running out of breath.

'Did ye's have a good time?' she demanded, releasing Rosie, but keeping an arm round her waist. 'Granny, I'll swear she's grown since she left. Don't you think so? If she goes on like this she'll grow out of this nice, new dress.'

'Oh, don't say that, Emily,' Rosie begged. 'I like this dress so much I want it to last forever.'

The words came out so fervently that even her father laughed his slow, gentle laugh.

Emily took over making the tea, while Rosie fetched cups and plates from the dresser. There was no cake in the tin, but she found an un-opened packet of biscuits, which would be better than nothing. Emily was just pouring the first cup of tea for Rosie to hand to her grandmother when they heard the scrape of boots in the yard.

Bobby came in, did a shy and awkward shuffle towards the stove, but greeted his grandparents warmly. Uncle Joe didn't so much as glance at the assembled company. He pulled open the door by the fireplace and tramped through to his bedroom without a word to anyone, banging it closed behind him. His studded boots echoed back from the bare boards.

'Is Uncle Joe not feeling too good?' asked Rose.

'No, he's not right,' Bobby admitted, shaking his head. 'It's his stomach, he says. But then,' he added, lowering his voice, 'Uncle Joe always has something wrong with him, as you very

157

well know.'

'We've been tryin' to get him to go to the doctor,' Sam explained, as he took his cup of tea from Rosie and pulled a kitchen chair over to the stove. 'He's got an awful bad colour and he's eatin' next to nothin'. But sure whatever I say wouden be right,' he added, shaking his head and smiling ruefully. 'Joe'll do his own do, as the saying is.'

'And how's Bobby?' asked Rose, turning away from Sam to smile up at the sturdy young man who was doing his best with a cup and saucer when what he'd really have liked was his usual half pint mug.

'I'm rightly, Granny,' he said, grinning at her, 'but I'm still lookin' a job with motors if I could find one.'

'Jobs are very hard to come by these days,' said John very slowly. 'I was talking to a man from Belfast the night we stayed over in Dublin and he told me, "There's green grass growing in the ship yards". If it's that bad in Belfast, it affects everybody...'

He broke off, suddenly short of breath. Teapot poised to pour second cups, Rosie paused and looked towards him. She caught her own breath and looked quickly away. It wasn't the first time she'd seen him go pale, his speech slow, his manner withdrawn, or anxious, but that was before Richard Stewart had asked his casual question as they walked up the hill to Rathdrum. Now she saw her grandfather with different eyes and was so distressed by what she saw she had to busy herself with the teacups to hide her feelings.

She was sure her grandmother had noticed. Before she had even finished her tea, she bent over and began to produce presents from a large shopping bag. There were presents for all the grandchildren. Rosie watched Emily's face light up when she unwrapped a pretty blouse she herself had helped to choose. There was a biplane model for Jack. Books and board games for Margaret and Dolly.

Bobby watched his grandmother take the last boxes out of the shopping bag. He could be sure he was not forgotten, any more than Sammy, who couldn't get home this weekend, but he was puzzled as the bag emptied and still no gift had emerged.

'I'm afraid you and Sammy will have to wait just a little while for your present,' Rose began, smiling at the young man 'I don't think you'll mind sharing it,' she went on, looking across at John, who stirred himself and managed a small smile.

He raised his hands to his face, placed his thumbs against his cheeks and wiggled all his fingers at once.

Bobby's face lit up.

'Cat's whiskers?' he demanded, hardly able to avoid tripping over the words.

'Aye,' said John. 'We saw the advertisement for a kit in a magazine in the hotel. It might take a wee while to come, but it's all there. All the parts you need. Next time I come I'll be wanting to hear all the news.'

'Wireless,' Rosie whispered softly to Emily, totally perplexed by John's grotesque gestures

159

and Bobby's beaming smiles.

'Well now,' said Sam, 'that's very generous of you, Da. There won't be many round here that has all the latest news straight from London.'

'Aye, and beyond,' insisted Bobby, unable to contain his excitement. 'Once Sammy an' I get an aerial up on top o' the barn we'll be able to get stations abroad forby. We've got all the frequencies from outa the magazines, its just a matter o' tunin'...'

Rosie and Emily were sitting side by side at the kitchen table, the empty teacups still scattered across its worn surface. The door had stood open since Sam had brought them across from the barn. Now, some change in the light, some small sound of footsteps or rustle of clothing, caused Rosie to look round.

Martha stood in the doorway, her face expressionless, her pale, bright eyes moving quickly over the small gathering.

Rosie opened her mouth to speak, but Martha ignored her.

'I see I've missed the tea,' she said, a small smile playing round her lips. 'It's a pity that, for it's not often I get a cup made for me,' she went on, her tone thin and cutting as Bobby stopped speaking and John and Sam got to their feet.

'Ach, sit yer ground. Sure, don't ye need all the rest ye can get with the busy lives ye both lead, driving to the far ends of Ireland or lying down on the railway banks chattin' with your friends?'

John sat down gratefully, glanced across at Rose and said nothing, but Sam remained standing, a look on his face that Rosie could not read.

Aware of the tense situation, Rose did her best. 'How are you, Martha?' she began.

Martha looked at her as if she were about to reply, then turned on her heel and addressed Bobby.

'Mrs Loney has her hans full with that girl of hers. I told her you and Emily would go down an' see to the milkin' to help her out. I diden think your sister wou'd be much help, even if she did arrive back. Rosie has never been one for work on the farm,' she added, to no one in particular.

'Perhaps, Martha, that's because you find so much work for her in the house,' said Sam, who had kept silent as long as possible, observing the small, tense figure of his wife, and now felt compelled to speak.

'An what do you know about keepin' house?' she fired back at him. 'An' what are you two waitin' for? Do I have to tell you everyhin' twice?' she went on, swinging round to glare at Bobby and Emily.

John got to his feet, excused himself, and walked out of the house. At the same moment, Emily got up and followed Bobby across the yard and into the lane.

Rosie saw her grandfather set off in the direction of the privy behind the barn, but she was sure he would not come back into the kitchen. He would go into the barn or sit in the motor and leave it to Rose to extract them from a situation he found unbearable.

'Sam dear,' said Rose, getting to her feet, 'there's a conversation you and I must have

161

before we go back to Rathdrum. Shall we go over to the barn and get out of Martha's way? There's nothing worse than visitors who don't know when to go, is there?' she continued sweetly, turning to Martha. 'Especially when you've been so busy helping your neighbour.'

'Oh, suit yourself, Rose,' Martha retorted. 'You and your pet granddaughter are very good at that. I have the hen's feed to make.'

She pulled out a bucket of scraps from the low shelf under the dresser with a noisy rattle that would drown any response and then stamped out into the yard and across to the potato house where the Layer's Mash was stored.

Left alone in the empty kitchen, Rosie put her head in her hands and let the waves of despair flow over her. She'd been dreading coming back and apart from Emily's big hug and her father's shy smile, her welcome, or lack of it, had been pretty much as she'd expected. The presence of her father and grandparents had somewhat modified her mother's customary hostility, but no doubt that would come soon enough. In all the ordinary working days and weeks that lay ahead she was only too aware neither her father, nor Emily, nor her grandparents would be there to deflect her mother's anger and frustration.

She studied the deep grain of the much scrubbed table, cast her eyes to the floor below and considered the accumulation of dust and crumbs. The floor certainly hadn't been swept for some time and there were no signs it had been scrubbed either. The windows were dirty and marked with the squashed bodies of blue-bottles swatted with a rolled newspaper, a favourite pastime of Uncle Joe. The stove hadn't been blackened, nor the fender polished.

In the heavy atmosphere of the late afternoon, the lingering smell of boiled potatoes and cabbage lay on the warm air mixed with the faint aroma of paraffin oil and greasing compound almost certainly emanating from two pairs of very dirty blue dungarees hanging on a hook beside the front door. From the small bedroom beyond her own, she heard Uncle Joe hawk and spit. Moments later, she heard the sound of running water as he peed in the large chamber pot which *he* was never required to empty.

There was nothing for it, she decided, as she got to her feet. Sitting here would only leave her more vulnerable should her mother return and find her doing nothing. She picked up the suitcases she'd parked by the door and moved as quietly as she could along the echoing boards to the bedroom. She shut the door firmly behind her, took off her dress with its pattern of tiny dark blue and light blue squares and opened the wardrobe door. The stink of mothballs was overwhelming, but there was nowhere else to put it.

She took out her black working skirt, pulled it on, and then, reluctant to give in completely to the situation she now faced, she searched in her suitcase for an old red blouse, faded and mended but still wearable. She unpinned her hair, brushed out the dark mass and caught it back with one of the neatly trimmed pieces of ribbon she and her fellow pupils at Miss Wilson's gave to each other as birthday gifts or marks of friendship.

She looked at herself in the long mirror on the open wardrobe door. Despite the dim light and the starred and broken reflection where the silvered backing had peeled with age, what she saw surprised her. Even without her grown-up dress, with her hair down and wearing her old skirt, she looked different. What made her so, she couldn't work out yet, but the change was one she found strangely comforting.

When Sam and Rose emerged from the barn, John was already sitting behind the wheel, anxious to drive off before the threatened rain finally arrived. Rosie heard the sound of voices and ran out to join them, leaving the washing-up bowl and the clean cups and saucers behind her.

'Your da will tell you everything later,' her grandmother said, as Sam took up the starting handle and stood waiting.

'He's promised to consult his conscience about what should be done for you, so you know he'll do his best. I've asked him to bring you over one Sunday towards the end of August,' she went on, as she put her arms round Rosie and hugged her. 'It's only a month and the children are at home,' she whispered softly in her ear before she released her.

They walked hand in hand round to the passenger seat.

'Write me the odd wee note if you can. I'm going to miss you after all the long talks we've had,' she added, as she stepped into the motor and settled herself for the drive.

Sam swung the handle vigorously. The engine

fired first time. Father and son looked at each other with satisfied smiles.

'She's in good order, Da,' commented Sam, as he placed the starting handle back in the motor.

'Aye. She's a good motor, even if she's not a Bentley,' John replied. 'We'll see you soon. Take care of yourselves,' he called to them as he let in the clutch and moved slowly forward.

Rosie and her father stood watching as they crossed the yard. John took his time, for he was always on the lookout for a stray hen or the elderly, half-blind sheepdog. As the vehicle turned right up the hill, they saw two arms shoot up in the air and wave.

They waved back, even though they knew the elderflower bush to the right of the gate had grown so big it now blocked the view from the yard to the lane.

'Accordin' to your granny, you were great company on their holiday,' said Sam, as the last vibrations of the motor faded from the still air. 'She said you were a great help to her, an' that you could turn your hand to most things. She's not keen at all to see you goin' into service or gettin' a job in a shop.'

Glancing round him, Sam caught sight of Martha, bucket in hand, appearing at the gate into the orchard. Without another word, he moved them briskly over to the barn and closed the door firmly behind them.

He sat down on an unopened barrel of lubricating oil and left Rosie the ancient armchair. Long evicted from the house, he'd mended its broken leg with angle iron and padded its sagging seat with cotton waste and an old blanket. Rosie had sat in this chair so often, over so many years, she'd come to love its oily smell and the happy memories it brought of so many hours spent watching her father work.

'Granny says she and Granda would like to see you go for trainin' to Belfast,' he went on without further ado. 'He says you've a real eye for paintin' wee flowers an' there's good jobs in the mills for people like that. Better paid even than the weavers, he says. Forby, some of the mills has scholarships to encourage young people to do courses. Would that be something you'd really like, Rosie? I knew you did a wee bit of paintin' and suchlike at Miss Wilson's but you'd never said much about it.'

'That's because I didn't think I was any good, Da,' she explained. 'Miss Wilson said I drew very well, but what I liked was watercolour and my landscapes never came out right. But down in Kerry, I started to paint flowers. Granny said my first attempts were very good, so she made me try all sorts of things, garden flowers and wildflowers and even leaves and berries and bits of grass. The funny thing was, it was so *easy*, and everybody said I was so clever. But I wasn't. It just seemed to come out right.'

'An' you enjoyed it?

'Oh yes, I loved it. I have three sketchbooks full home with me.'

'Ah well then, that's all I need to know. That's a gift, an' you know that we should all use whatever gifts we have. But there is a problem over the trainin', an' you're old enough to understand.

Granny an' Granda have a bit of money and they could afford to pay your lodgings in Belfast. But I couldn't do that myself with what I've put by. An' if I could, then there's Bobby who'd like to be apprenticed, an' Jack who's not long more at school, and young Dolly. The question is, Rosie, should I favour one of my children at the expense of the others?' he said, a sad and troubled look crossing his face.

Rosie sat silent. She *could* say that he wasn't favouring her, that it was Granny and Granda who were offering to pay for her. Yet she knew it wouldn't help him to have it pointed out. Her older brothers and sister had had to make the best of whatever they could find. Billy had only had money since he joined the police. Without apprenticeship, it would be years before Charlie or Sammy would be paid other than as helpers, however skilful they'd become. Emily had been lucky, but even she could only put a few shillings in the Coronation tea caddy on a Friday night till it was worth the journey to the Post Office.

'Granda says the courses don't start till September,' she said quietly, when the silence began to lengthen.

'Aye, an' I'm glad to have time to take counsel. It helps to have someone outside the family to put the case to. I have to think what's best for the whole family. It would maybe be easy to say *yes* without due thought and then find there was bad feeling or bitterness that one could have avoided.'

Rosie wondered what he could be thinking about. She couldn't imagine any of her brothers or sisters being bitter about her going away for a year to train as a textile artist. But then Granny and Granda hadn't offered to pay for training for them.

She sighed. It all seemed much more complicated than she'd imagined and it really didn't look very hopeful. But then Granny had warned that her father would need time.

'I maybe should tell you that your Ma is very keen on you goin' into service. There's a place going at Castledillon in September,' he said slowly. 'Ladies' maid, I hear.'

He paused, took in the look on her face, and said, 'Ah well, we never know the way doors open for us. Don't forget that's how yer Granny started her life. An' look what she made of herself.'

It was true, quite true, but the thought appalled her so much she couldn't think of anything whatever to say.

Twelve

As Uncle Joe sat himself down at the breakfast table next morning and gestured at Rosie to hurry up and pour his tea, he commented on the recent activities of Sinn Fein, the Shinners, as he always called them, the failure of the government to throw them out of what was now a Protestant state, and the disloyalty of people like her and her grandparents, who ran off for their holidays to the enemy's country which was just the very thing to encourage them.

Clearly, he was feeling better.

To her own surprise Rosie found she was quite indifferent to the old man's tirade. She'd heard versions of the same complaint so often, over many years, and it had always distressed her before, yet this morning she saw him mouthing the familiar words as if she were watching a performance in a play.

Sitting in an out-of-the-way corner of the workshop while some neighbour occupied the one and only armchair, she'd heard tales of disaffection often enough. While other men complained of their job, their boss, the unprofitability of their farm, the demands of their family, or even the unreliability of the weather, only Uncle Joe had selected the political state of Ireland. Out of it he had woven a grim and hopeless garment that covered his entire dissatisfaction with the world.

At last, she understood why he never listened to any reply, nor indeed required any answer, to the irritable questions he threw out so freely. She decided she could safely ignore his morning devotions and get on with her work and not allow anything he said to trouble her further.

Her small satisfaction at coming to terms with Uncle Joe's behaviour and the relief from his nagging tone as he drank thirstily and noisily from the tin mug which he insisted on using, disappeared promptly when she glanced across at her mother. Standing at the far end of the table, wisps of stray hair bobbing up and down with the vigour of her activity, she was cutting slices of baker's loaf and buttering them for both Uncle Joe and Dolly and Jack. Unlike Uncle Joe, she couldn't be ignored and left to rant. Her mother needed something much more immediate and tangible as a vehicle for her anger.

Thinking about it now, she could see her father had always been her mother's chief target, but she'd observed over recent years he'd developed a cool, distancing manner which made it more difficult for her mother to goad him into comment. Looking back, she realized with a shock, how seldom he'd been available in the months before her visit to Kerry.

In the evening when he came home from work, there were farm implements and machinery awaiting his attention, lined up inside and outside the barn. She wondered if it was his absence

170

from the house that had finally directed all the force of her mother's anger towards herself. At the thought of the awful day of the accident, she felt herself shiver with apprehension. Should her mother treat her again as she had that day, she'd no idea how she would cope.

As to what she might expect or what her mother's state of mind might be, the previous evening gave her little to go on. Martha had continued to ignore her while her father and some of her brothers and sisters were present. That was usual enough. The real test would come after breakfast when her father and Emily had gone to work and Jack and Dolly disappeared.

'I'm sorry the place is so dirty, Rosie,' Emily said in a whisper, as they got ready for bed the previous night. 'I'd have done a bit more in the evenin's after work, but she wouden have it. An' ye know there's no arguin' with her.'

'Never worry, Emily,' she responded, as she pulled on her nightdress, 'I honestly don't mind the work. It just makes me angry the way she's always looking for something to complain about. I'm afraid I'll lose my temper one of these days.'

'Now don't go doin' that, Rosie,' Emily replied hurriedly. 'It'll only make her worse. Sure what does it matter for a few weeks if yer gettin' away to Belfast to do this course ye told me about in yer letter?'

Rosie sighed and dropped down on the side of the bed.

'Emily, I'm not sure Da will let me go.'

'What!' Emily exclaimed, so horrified she forgot to whisper. 'Sure he wouden keep you here scrubbin' and cleanin' an' runnin' her messages when you coud be doin' somethin' better,' she went on, whispering now, as Rosie put her finger to her lips and shushed her.

'He's worried that it isn't fair,' Rosie whispered back. 'I know he has money saved, but it wasn't enough to let the boys be apprenticed. You know he wouldn't do one without the other.'

'You're all right, you clever girl,' she went on, smiling at her sister, who had stopped applying curlers to her uncompromisingly straight hair and was staring at her open-mouthed, 'but there's Bobby and Jack and Dolly as well as me to think about.'

Emily shook her head and went back to struggling with the unyielding metal as Rosie told her quietly about their conversation in the barn.

'Our da's a good man,' her sister said after a moment's deep thought, 'but sometimes he thinks *too* much about things. He shou'd jump at the chance of gettin' you away to somethin' you want to do.'

'He did say he'd take counsel and consult his conscience,' replied Rosie reassuringly, as Emily got into bed.

'Aye well, I hope he hurries up about it. Mind you, I'm that fed up with baker's bread and Ma's cookin', I'll be glad to have you home for a wee while for some decent grub, if ye can put up with it.'

Rosie smiled, as she blew out the candle and climbed into bed beside her.

'Well that's something. At least someone will appreciate what I do.'

To Rosie's surprise, her mother made no comment at all as she set about her normal morning routine, clearing the breakfast dishes, sweeping the floor and putting water to heat on the stove so she could make a start on scrubbing it. Martha herself disappeared to feed the calves and collect the eggs and still had not returned late in the morning when the first of her day's visitors arrived, knocking at the open door, just as Rosie finished blacking the stove and cleaning the fender.

'Hello, Rosie. Are ye back?' a loud, high-pitched voice hailed her from the open door. 'Sure, your ma'll be glad to see you an' her has so much to do. Is she still out workin' with Uncle Joe?'

Before Rosie had even risen from her knees, the emery paper in her hand, the fender now restored to its silver-like finish, Martha appeared at the door, a warm smile of greeting for the heavily-built, grey-haired woman who was already standing by the stove, her bottom poised over the further of the two armchairs.

'Sit down, sit down, Mrs Allen,' Martha cried. 'I'm sure you could do with a rest an' you like m'self up from all hours.'

Rosie began to put away her cleaning materials in the bottom of the dresser, her ear already anticipating the familiar line, Rosie was just going to make us a cup of tea. When it didn't come, she was completely taken aback.

'I'll make us a cup of tea in a wee minute,' Martha began apologetically, 'but Rosie here has messages up to her uncle's. We're right out of

173

flour and bacon. Is there anything she can fetch for you while she's about it?' she continued, as she produced her purse, a piece of paper and a shopping bag.

'Maybe Rosie, before you go, you might pay a wee visit to the wash house,' Martha went on, smiling indulgently as she glanced at her hands, streaked and smudged with black lead. She cast a knowing glance towards Mrs Allen, now settled comfortably by the stove.

'Aye Rosie, ye niver know who ye might meet 'tween here an' the village,' the older woman said, winking at Martha.

Martha nodded and smiled. The look that passed between the two women was simply to reinforce their often expressed view that all these young girls ever thought about was boys and if you weren't watching them every minute of the day, you'd never get them to lift a hand to do bit of work about the house.

'Hallo, Rosie. Fancy seein' you twice in one week. What's got inta her?'

Lizzie Mackay put down the egg from which she'd just removed a speck of chicken manure and a small curling feather and placed it in one of the cardboard trays belonging to the wooden crate the egg man collected every week. She stared at her friend in amazement.

'I'm not asking,' said Rosie, laughing as she saw the look on Lizzie's face. "Why don't you take a wee run up and see Lizzie?" she said, when I started to get out the baking board, so I did what I was told. I've run, before she could

174

change her mind. Though I did meet Mrs Hutchinson on her way down the lane and I'm not asking you to guess where she was going.'

'She keeps wantin' to get ye outa the house,' said Lizzie shrewdly. 'She's always sending you messages or out to look for hens laying away. But that's just great, for I'm fed up with these. Why can't hens do what they have to do outside and not get it on the eggs for me to have to rub off?

'Hold on a minit till I tell Ma I'll be back in a while,' she went on. 'She must be havin' a lie down for I haven't seen her since lunch time. Sit yerself down a minit an' wait for me an' we'll go for a walk.'

'Isn't it a lovely afternoon,' Rosie began, as she and Lizzie fell into step on the short drive in front of the Mackay's house. 'Where shall we go?'

'What about going over to Sandymount to see if they're still pickin' strawberries. Ma gave me money for sweets, but if there's any still left, I'll buy her some. She loves strawberries.'

'How is she today, Lizzie?'

'There's no change,' she said flatly. 'The doctor says she'll never be strong. I don't think they ever knew what was wrong with her when she took so bad, but at least she's better than she was. Da thought she was a gonner an' he was near off his head. She said to tell you she was askin' for you.'

'That's nice of her, Lizzie,' Rosie replied, touched by the sick woman's thoughts. 'I'll come and see her when she feels more like it.'

They walked quickly down the lane and passed the Hamilton farm without even glancing towards the open door. Across the railway line they moved more slowly, following the steep lane up as far as Harry McGaw's smithy.

They turned left along the gable of the low, whitewashed building with its high-pitched roof. The much gentler slope along the hillside gave them back breath for talk.

'So have ye heard anythin' yet from yer man?' Lizzie asked.

'I had a letter this morning. It was five pages.'

'Five!' she exclaimed, her eyes wide with amazement. 'What did he say?'

Rosie had considered bringing Patrick's letter to show to Lizzie. They were, after all, very good friends who shared all their secrets. Unlike many of the other girls at Miss Wilson's, Lizzie never gossiped or talked behind one's back and she was far too good-natured ever to be jealous if Rosie had a boyfriend and she hadn't. But Patrick's letter didn't exactly seem the kind you shared with a girlfriend the way she'd seen the other girls do, reading out the 'good bits', going into peals of excited laughter, teasing and making sly comments.

Most of Patrick's letter was about books, telling her at length what he was reading and what he hoped to read. He went into great detail about W.B. Yeats and some argument he was having with the Abbey Theatre and what his friend Sean thought about the matter. About the Abbey, all she knew of it was its reputation for putting on controversial plays. She had no idea at all who

Sean was.

To be honest she hadn't known what to make of the letter. On her first hasty reading, as page followed page, she'd begun to wonder if he would even mention their meeting, the time they had shared, or the events in Kerry that had brought them so suddenly together. She was halfway down the last page, her heart sinking as she realized the letter was almost at an end, when he began a new paragraph quite unrelated to what had gone before and wrote in his flourishing script: 'I think of you often my lovely Rose and hope you flourish in your far country until we can meet again.'

There followed a fragment of Irish. She recognized some of the words he'd written in her book of sonnets. Then his scrawled signature, Padraig.

'It's a pity he's away in Dublin,' Lizzie said, puzzled as to what one did when the object of one's affection didn't live down the road, over in the next townland, or at least within cycling distance.

The narrow lane was dusty and made narrower still by the untrimmed hedgerows, shaggy with the growth of a hot summer, laden now with ripening berries and threaded with honeysuckle. The hedgebanks themselves were spiked with rosebay willow herb, its drying fragments floating in the warm air like fibres gyrating on a spinning floor. Dark brown stalks topped by fine rayed spikes, the remains of cow parsley, already stood out amidst the long, seeding grass, stiff skeletons bearing little relation to the soft fronds of green and cream that in springtime had waved in every breeze like the surging of a stormy sea.

Lizzie looked at her friend curiously

'Will ye write back? What'll ye say?'

The idea of writing to anyone, never mind the longed for *someone* had never entered her thoughts. But then, Rosie was different from all the rest of the girls at Miss Wilson's. She was cleverer for a start. She even read books because she liked reading books.

Reading books didn't appeal to Lizzie at all. What she enjoyed most was being out and about. Going into Portadown on her father's lorry. Buying things in shops for her mother. Making clothes. Looking at the film magazines. Reading about the Hollywood stars and their frequent marriages and divorces. But, when she thought of her friend, she always remembered what her mother said, 'Lizzie, people are different. You have to accept them the way they are, otherwise you'll get very disappointed.'

'You've gone very quiet, Lizzie. Have I upset you?' Rosie asked anxiously.

It was so unlike Lizzie to be quiet that Rosie wondered if this talk of Patrick had reminded her that *she* hadn't got a boyfriend. With her dark curls and large, bright eyes, Lizzie was prettier than most, but Rosie had noticed how often she would laugh and be happy to be the centre of attention when there was a crowd of young people, yet grow shy and awkward should any particular boy speak to her.

'An' how wou'd you upset me for goodness sake?' Lizzie demanded. 'Sure we never fell out in the whole year we were up at Miss Wilson's, did we?'

'No, we didn't,' agreed Rosie, taking her hand. 'But I so hate upsets and arguments and I wouldn't for the world upset you of all people. Oh how I wish we could just all say what we wanted and agree to differ if we couldn't agree in the first place,' she went on, releasing Lizzie's hand to sweep stray hair back from her cheeks.

'Sure there's people thrive on argument,' Lizzie came back sharply. 'It's just you're not one of them. It's one reason I like you.'

She looked away and studied the lane ahead.

There was nothing out of the ordinary anywhere on the lane ahead, but Lizzie was sure she'd seen tears as Rosie brushed back her hair, tears that had come unbidden, prompted by the very thought of 'argument'.

They could see the gate to the strawberry field stood wide open as they came round a bend in the lane and gazed across to the sloping fields where the pickers had been at work day after day. The freshly gathered fruit was sent down by the cartload to a special halt on the railway line used only during the short strawberry season, or direct to the factory at Fruitfield.

'C'mon, Rosie. I think they're still pickin',' Lizzie cried, surging ahead enthusiastically.

Rosie had just spotted a flourishing clump of blue scabious in the hedgerow and was lost in thought, wondering if she should take some home to paint. It was some moments before she collected herself, hurried after her friend and almost collided as she shot out of the field, red-faced and flustered.

Lizzie pulled her away from the gate and back into the lane.

'Whatever's wrong, Lizzie?'

'There's someone there. A boy. But I don't think he saw me,' she went on. 'He was lookin' up at the sky.'

'But what was he doing?'

Lizzie blushed yet more deeply.

'You know,' she said, nodding her head, as if her meaning was perfectly plain. 'In the hedge.'

'You mean he was having a pee?'

Lizzie was so upset, all she could do was nod again.

Rosie slipped an arm round her waist and gave her a little hug.

'It's all right, Lizzie. Boys go behind hedges all the time. If you had brothers, you wouldn't pay any attention. Mine used to have contests to see who could pee the farthest or go on the longest, or hit a tin can or knock the clock of a dandelion. Why were you upset?'

'He might have seen me,' she said breathlessly.

'And why does that matter?'

'Well, he might have been annoyed if I'd seen him.'

Her voice faltered and her face crumpled as she bit her lip.

'Lizzie dear, he might not have been bothered at all. He'd probably have pretended you hadn't seen him. But even if he knew you had, what does it matter?'

'I don't know, Rosie. I don't know,' she replied, near to tears.

'Now, come on Lizzie. We can go back home

or we can go and see if there's any strawberries. He's only a boy and he can't hurt you if I'm with you. Did something frighten you?'

'No,' she admitted, collecting herself quickly. 'Let's away an' see if there's any left.'

When they went into the field, Rosie recognized the boy at once, one of the Loneys of Tullygarden. He was stacking wooden boxes inside the gate and looked up as he caught sight of them. A tall, ginger-headed lad with blue eyes, creamy skin and freckles.

He nodded in a friendly way to Rosie, whom he knew by sight from bringing tools to her father's workshop and turned shyly towards Lizzie who'd recovered her usual liveliness.

'Are ye's lookin' strawberries?' he greeted them easily. 'The field's finished,' he explained, 'not worth the pickers comin' again, but there's plenty o' wee ones if ye know where to look. I'll give ye's a hand,' he went on, addressing himself to Lizzie.

'So you're still open to sell?' asked Rosie.

'Ach no,' he said, shaking his head and looking puzzled. 'I asked Mr Lamb what to do if people came and he started to tell me this story about a woman in the Bible called Ruth. She was a cleaner, he said. But then he got called away, so I didn't hear the end of it. But as he was goin' out the gate, he called back that if anyone wanted fruit for their own use they were welcome.'

Rosie tried not to smile, but Lizzie burst out laughing.

'Have you never been to Sunday School?' she demanded.

181

'Not unless I could help it,' he replied, beaming at her cheerfully.

'Well that would explain it. Ruth was a gleaner, not a cleaner.'

'An' what's that, when it's at home?'

'It's someone who gathers up what's left after the pickers have been.'

'Like we're goin' to do now?'

She nodded her head and waved her hand at him, waiting for him to lead the way to whichever part of the field he judged most promising.

Rosie hitched up her skirt and got down on her knees in the dry, sandy soil. Other people might bend over to pick, but she found it made her back ache. Besides, she liked the feel of dry soil, even if it got into her shoes and she loved searching for the small, bright berries hidden under the ribbed leaves.

To her surprise, she found late flowers and green berries on the plants as well as the sweet-tasting strawberries. As she dropped the shiny, red berries into the punnet Hugh Loney had provided, she thought of placing dark, pointed leaves behind the fragile white flowers with their yellow stamens and then adding in some long, curling tendrils with their hint of pink.

She'd always loved flowers. Even as a very little girl, she'd picked twigs and leaves and whatever blooms or berries the season offered to put in a jam pot in the workshop or a vase in the kitchen window. She'd taken flowers to her teacher at Richhill Public Elementary and at Miss Wilson's she'd won little prizes for the best arrangements of flowers from the large, rambling garden behind her house. But she'd never thought of painting flowers.

During those first days in Kerry she'd taken out the paint box her grandparents had bought her. She'd worked on both landscapes and sea-scape. But, although she loved the idea of painting, and thought longingly of her cousin's watercolours at Rathdrum, she admitted she couldn't get the feel of either. It was then her grandmother suggested she try her hand at painting flowers in the hotel garden. Once she began, it came so easily, and now, everywhere she looked, she saw shapes and colours she longed to paint.

From a little distance away she heard the sound of laughter. She glanced up, but immediately dropped her eyes again. Sitting on either side of a row of plants, their hands reaching across the small distance between them, mouths and fingers stained with juice, Lizzie and Hugh were divid-ing strawberries with their teeth and passing them across to each other in some private attempt to find the sweetest fruit.

Rosie felt her spirits rise so much she felt hap-pier than she could ever remember. Completely overwhelmed by a sudden and unexpected joy, she got up and moved further away from Lizzie and Hugh, so bound up in themselves they didn't even notice her going. She settled herself again on the warm earth, her eyes moving over the receding lines of plants as they followed the curve of the hillside and led her eye down to the valley below.

The shadows were lengthening as the afternoon moved on, but the sun was warm on her hands and face, the far hillside patched with pale gold where the stubble left from the hay harvest had not yet sprouted new growth. Further away, beyond orchards and stretches of woodland, a finger of stone stood on the flattened summit of a green hill, its sharp outline gleaming in the sunlight as it pointed up at the clear blue sky.

'Rarely, rarely comest thou, Spirit of delight,' she whispered to herself, laughing at the picture she must present, a girl sitting in the middle of a strawberry field, her head thrown back, her eyes closed, the warmth of the sun on her face. Even as she whispered the familiar line, the dark shadows which had clung to her through these two long weeks back at the farm dissolved into warmth and laughter.

Thirteen

Reluctantly, as the sun dropped lower in the sky, Rosie collected her thoughts, picked up her punnet and waved to Lizzie and Hugh. It would be a pity to anger her mother by not being home in time to prepare the vegetables for the evening meal.

Lizzie caught her eye, waved back and came running towards her, followed more slowly by Hugh. He was carrying in both hands her punnet, now full to overflowing with gleaming, ripe fruit.

'I could stay here all day,' said Rosie, smiling at them, as she stood waiting on the grassy margin near the open gate, 'but there might be no dinner if I did.'

'An' Ma would wonder where I'd got to,' added Lizzie.

Hugh let them go through the gate before he swung it closed behind him and tied it with a piece of rope.

'What's the rope for?' Rosie asked, puzzled as to what possible use it might serve, tied in a loose knot that wouldn't keep anyone out.

'Ach it's just to say to certain people that they've no business to be pickin' to sell. Sure any like yerselves knows just to climb over.'

They moved along briskly. By the time they reached the forge and turned down the hill, Rosie noticed Hugh had managed to take Lizzie's hand. Moments later, the winding lane leading off to Tullygarden, his quickest way home, was passed without his giving it so much as a sideways glance.

'Goodness, is that the time?' Lizzie asked, as they approached the level crossing at the foot of the hill.

The gates were closed, the signal down and from far away they heard the long drawn out whistle of the approaching train.

'Aye, that'll be the five twenty from Portadown, due Armagh five forty,' declared Hugh confidently. 'It takes a brave while to pick strawberries,' he went on, his eyes on Lizzie, before the roar of the on-coming train drowned out his words as it rattled through the station without stopping.

The smoke and steam cleared. The long white gates swung slowly back and dropped into place with a loud clack as Rosie said goodbye to them both.

'I might see ye again tomorrow, Rosie.'

They paused by the open gate to her own farmyard.

'Maybe,' she replied. 'Shopping in the morning. And I haven't baked today, but I'll probably get up some time on Sunday if Billy comes home...'

She broke off as she caught sight of a figure moving out of the wash house halfway down the yard. It was her father in his braces, with a towel

186

over his arm.

'See ye then,' said Lizzie. She and Hugh continued up the hill, Hugh's arm now firmly round her waist.

Neither Lizzie nor Hugh had registered the look of anxiety that passed across Rosie's face, for she'd turned away too quickly, her eyes fixed on her father, who had stopped at the door of the barn the moment he'd caught sight of her.

Something was wrong. She was *quite* sure of it. Normally her father wasn't home till after six. He'd freewheel down the last of the hill, turn into the farmyard and park his bicycle against the wall of the barn. But it was nowhere near six and there was no bicycle to be seen.

As she ran to meet him, he walked towards her, moving slowly, as if he was overcome by fatigue.

'Da, what's wrong?' she demanded, as she came up to him.

He glanced at the punnet of strawberries. For a moment, she was sure he was not going to answer. Then he reached out and put his arm round her.

'Yer granda's had a bad turn, Rosie. He might not do,' he said coolly. 'I'm catching the next train over.'

For a moment, all Rosie could think off was the sand in her shoes, the working clothes she was wearing and what she was going to do with the strawberries. She looked up at him. Of course he'd have to shave before he went as he normally shaved at bedtime. She guessed too, that his boss had brought him home, which was why there was no bicycle against the wall of the barn. His boss was a Quaker, and Quakers helped each other. Working out the answer to these puzzles gave her time enough to resolve her own problem.

'I'll need to come with you,' she said matter-of-factly.

He looked at her, his features immobile, giving nothing away. She watched his large grey eyes flicker round the farmyard, pause at the open door of the house and move back again to meet her anxious gaze. He glanced down at her dusty clothes and the pink stains of strawberry juice on her hands.

'Aye. I think ye might maybe help yer granny more than me,' he said, nodding. 'The train's in fifteen minutes.' He paused and then went on. 'She might well want you to stay. Take a few things with you. Pack a wee case while I go an' get changed m'self.

In the last few days of July the kitchen of the south-facing house had become dim and shadowy at this hour. Dolly sat by the stove reading *Girl's Own*, Jack was hunched over the end of the table nearest to the door studying the assembly instructions for a model biplane, the pieces laid out in a row in front of him.

'Oh goody, strawberries,' exclaimed Dolly, eyeing the basket of fruit greedily.

Jack looked up, said hello and returned to his instructions.

'Where's Ma?' Rosie asked quickly.

'Out,' Dolly replied.

'Don't know,' said Jack, at exactly the same

time.

Rosie walked over to the dresser, placed two saucers on the table and put a generous handful of strawberries in each.

'Here you are,' she said, handing them a saucer each. 'And *no* more. The rest are for Ma. She may want to make jam. Jack, will you see to it, please.'

'All right,' he said promptly, popping a berry into his mouth and watching her as she dipped the edge of a dish cloth into the rainwater bucket and rubbed at the stains on her hands.

Moments later, she shut the bedroom door behind her and drew out from under the bed the smart leather suitcase her grandfather had bought her.

She touched its shiny surface, surprised it hadn't yet acquired a patina of dust. But then, she reminded herself, as she peeled off her old red blouse and her everyday black skirt, it was only two weeks since she'd packed that same case to come home.

She took her nightdress from under the pillow, borrowed some of Emily's knickers, because her own were hanging on the clothesline in the orchard and dressed in her old Sunday best. She brushed her hair hastily, tied it back and found the ribbon pulling so tight she had to loosen it and tie it all over again.

He may not do.

Her father's stark words rang in her mind. She tried to silence them, but they wouldn't go away. Granda was not just ill, he was so ill he might die. If he died there would be a funeral. What would she do then?

Unbidden, a thought came to her. If she took her very best dress, the one he had bought for her, she wouldn't need to wear it, because he wouldn't die. She took the dress from the wardrobe, shook it vigorously to disperse the smell of mothballs, folded it gently and placed it in the half-empty case. At the same time, she remembered her new shoes which she'd put away wrapped in the tissue from the shoe shop in Cahirciveen. She added them, her hairbrush, some clean hankies and the tiny bottle of scent Emily had given her for her birthday. She took a deep breath and snapped closed the catches.

As she came back out into the kitchen, she caught sight of her father crossing from the barn. He was wearing a clean shirt and his Sunday suit. She hurried outside to meet him before Dolly started asking questions. If she stopped to answer them they might miss the train.

'Ma and Uncle Joe have started the milkin', but I've had a word,' Sam said, as he took the suitcase from her hand. 'Yer ma'll tell the children later where we've gone and I'll speak to them tomorrow,' he continued, striding out so fast she had to run to keep up with him as they heard the whistle of the approaching train.

They said little to each other on the way to Portadown. It appeared her father knew nothing beyond the brief message from Alex his employer had given him when he'd arrived back from a delivery earlier than usual to carry out the regular Friday afternoon maintenance.

Rosie glanced across at him as he sat looking out of the carriage window, his eyes fixed on the sunlit landscape. She was sure he was seeing no detail of the familiar fields and hedgerows now bathed in golden light. From the set of his body and his even more pronounced stillness, she decided he was praying. He wouldn't be asking God to spare his father, but rather, asking to know His will and for the strength to do what was required of him.

She thought of the way Emily had declared two weeks ago that their father was a good man. Yes, he was. But she knew he was not a happy man. How could he be, when he slept in the loft over the barn rather than with the woman who had borne his children?

That made her sad enough, but she felt all the sadder when she compared his solitary life with the close companionship of her grandparents, Rose and John. She could quite easily imagine them as a young couple, like Lizzie and Hugh, walking hand in hand along the lane from Currane Lodge to the lakeside. Yes, they were Granny and Granda, old in years. But she had been with them and she knew they still loved each other.

She'd seen them sit talking often enough, heard them discuss what to do next, tease each other. Laugh at the mention of some shared memory or old contention she herself couldn't possibly understand. Day by day, they shared their life, the good times and the bad, each of them appreciating whatever the other one did to make their time together as good as it could be.

To love and to cherish, indeed. Just as it said in the prayer book her mother never used.

She turned and looked over her shoulder as they entered a cutting. A road bridge over the line cast a sudden deep shadow. She used the moment to wipe away her tears, so as not to attract her father's attention.

But he was a long way away. His prayer complete, he had put his trust in the Lord. Feeling free now to think about his father his mind had moved backwards in time. The image of his mother came to him, singing to him as she washed his face before he set off for school. He saw himself trundling an egg on a windy, sunlit hillside, his father and mother watching, cheering him on. There was bag of sweets as a prize, but he couldn't remember who won, for the sweets had been shared among them. James and Sam. Hannah and Sarah. His brother and sisters.

The long drawn out whistle of the train as they approached Portadown Station caught him unexpectedly. For the time it took for the train to slow down and come to a halt by the platform, he was back in another train on a summer morning, the Methodist excursion to Warrenpoint.

It was James who saved them. Leaning out of the window he'd seen the men divide the train, putting stones under the wheels to stop the separated carriages from running backwards. He hadn't understood himself what James was saying about the vacuum brake being off, but then he'd said the carriages would run back into the on-coming passenger train and he'd seen the look on his face. His mother had understood immediately. She'd made them jump out and take shelter from the sun under a hawthorn bush.

He remembered how she'd gone back along the line to look for her friend, but her friend was dead. But he and James, and Hannah and Sarah, had walked all the way home to the house opposite Robert Scott's forge at Salter's Grange. They had been spared, when all around them friends and neighbours had been killed and injured. He sighed deeply. The will of God was hard to understand. *God protect you, James, if you are still with us, and keep your soul if you are not.*

They changed trains at Portadown and continued to Banbridge, silence still heavy upon them.

Rosie wondered if dying was easier if you were old. Not the actual process of dying, but getting used to the fact that it was bound to happen. Was it something you could get used to, like not being able to read without spectacles, or having difficulty bending down, or your teeth falling out.

She knew of many people who had died. Neighbours whom she had sometimes seen in the workshop, but more often people who were just names she'd heard. So and so from Kilmore or Kilmacanty, Cloghan or Cornascreeb. Familiar names of local townlands, even if she'd no very clear idea exactly where they were. News would come and then, on Sunday, after Meeting, still wearing his suit, her father would walk to some neighbouring church for a service at two thirty or three o'clock and come home looking sad and solemn.

But it being John Hamilton of Rathdrum was very different. Not an unknown person in an unknown place, but her own dear grandfather.

Banbridge Station itself was busy and Rosie found herself jostled and struggling as she tried to keep alongside her father against the press of people trying to board the train even before they'd had time to get off.

'There's your granda's motor,' Sam said, as he stood outside the station scanning the busy street.

For one single moment, she thought everything was all right. There'd been some mistake and Granda was here in his motor to meet them, after all.

She felt a sudden light touch on her arm.

'Uncle Alex,' she said, turning to the familiar figure who'd been waiting for them on the platform and missed them in the crowd.

She was completely taken aback by the look on his pale, drawn face. No, there was no mistake.

'I thought you might be on this one,' he said flatly, as he turned to Sam, caught his hand and pressed it in both of his. 'He's still with us,' he added, in the same lifeless tone. 'Or he was an hour ago. I met the last train as well, just in case.'

They said no more as they drove off, for the Friday evening crowd paid no attention to the odd motor and wandered at will, back and forth across the main road.

Once out of the town Alex put his foot down and sped along the now empty road. He swung up the hill at Ballydown with practised ease. Suddenly, they were passing between the open gates and under the dense shade of the limes. Rosie could hardly believe they'd arrived so soon as they drew up beside the two other vehicles parked facing the hedge of sweetpea that divided the yard from the garden beyond.

'Ach, there ye's are, God bless ye.'

Before she'd set foot on the ground, a distraught figure ran from the back door, her skirt and apron flying with the speed of her movement, like a great bird about to rise into the air.

Alex and Sam paused, their faces immobile as Mrs Love clutched at Rosie and enveloped her in a fierce embrace.

'Ach, you poor chile,' she said, overcome with emotion. 'Yer granny said ye might come. Sure Granda was talkin' about ye this mornin' before he was took bad.'

She released Rosie, looked at Alex and Sam with red-rimmed eyes and made some small effort to collect herself.

'How is he?' Alex asked, the words coming out one by one without the slightest trace of his Canadian accent, which had survived unmodified all these years since his return.

Tears poured down her long, wrinkled face.

'He can't speak right, but the pain's gone. It was somethin' desperate,' she went on, wringing her hands together. 'The doctors is with him now. Maybe they'll tell us somethin' better when they come down.'

Rosie had never before seen Mrs Love so utterly distraught. She was one to get upset over even tiny domestic disasters but she'd never been like this before. The poor woman was beside herself.

'Have ye's had yer tea?'

The question took them all by surprise. Food was the last thing any of them were thinking about.

The two men shook their heads and Rosie observed the sudden change in the anxious figure.

'Sure, you'll need a bite to eat,' she insisted, as she led the way back into the kitchen.

'I'll give you a hand, Mrs Love,' said Rosie. It would keep her occupied till the doctors had gone. Then she might see her granda. Granny would be with him, for she knew she wouldn't leave him.

Making sandwiches for anyone who might be able to eat them, Mrs Love became a different person. She talked all the time, as she always did, but this time Rosie paid close attention.

John Hamilton had been to one of the mills in the morning, she began. Although officially retired for some two years now, he'd been pleased when the directors asked him to give them the benefit of his long experience. Since he'd had some trouble with chest pain before his retirement, he no longer did any of the work himself, but after all the years he and Alex had worked together that didn't present any problems.

'An' he had his lunch, just as usual, he an' your granny, in the conservatory. Though, mind you, I had to pull a couple of the blinds for it was gettin' that hot. An' then, after he reads his paper, he goes out to the motor an' starts up the engine.'

Rosie felt herself grow tense. Standing here in the kitchen, imagining him outside, bending over the engine as she'd seen him do so often, made it

196

so immediate.

'An' the engine runs an' it runs. An' I wonder to myself what he's doin' to need it runnin' for so long. An' after a wee while I look out an' I can't see him. An' I know he wouldn't go away an' leave an engine runnin'. So I take a wee walk out to see where he is, an' he's lyin' up against the back wheel behind the motor with his eyes shut an' his han' up to his chest.'

Rosie had to stop buttering, because her hand was shaking so much she was afraid she'd drop the knife, but Mrs Love continued quite matter-of-factly.

'To tell you the truth, Miss Rosie, I thought he was dead. But he opened his eyes when yer granny came an' she sent me down to Missus Emily Hamilton to get help, for she cou'den lift him.'

'But Aunt Emily couldn't come, could she?'

'Ach no, not the way she is. Sure she's over her time already. But as good luck would have it, the breadman was there an' the minute he heard, he came up an' helped us get yer granda to bed. An' then he went down to Ballievy an' got the office to phone for the doctor and get your Uncle Alex back from Lenaderg. Sure, they couden do enough to help when he tole them what had happened. An' he's a new breadman too, only a young chap with ginger hair, and looks as if he couldn't lift a pan loaf. But he was tougher than he looked, good luck to him,' she added, firmly, as she started slicing the ham, 'we cou'den a done wi'out him.'

The sandwiches were made and wrapped in a

clean, damp cloth. Rosie began washing up the knives and plates they'd used making them and Mrs Love stopped talking for long enough to step into the hallway and listen to see if she could find out what was going on.

'Yer da and Uncle Alex are sat in the sittin' room. There's not a word outa them. An' there's no sound at all from upstairs,' she reported, striding noisily across to the kitchen window and staring out at the three motors parked by the sweetpea, her face twisted into an anxious grimace.

One look at her and Rosie decided something would have to be done.

'Do you think we should make some tea, Mrs Love, to go with the sandwiches?'

After the way in which time had speeded up on their journey from Banbridge station, Rosie was now having difficulty with the way it had slowed down again. Despite the audible click the large hand on the kitchen clock made when it moved, it seemed as if it had stopped. It reminded her of her days at primary school and the last half hour of the afternoon. Sometimes it seemed as if three thirty would never come. She had to keep reminding herself that in the end it had. Sooner or later, they'd hear footsteps on the stairs.

But the first thing they heard were voices in the hall.

'Rosie!'

Placing cups of tea carefully on a tray, she was startled by the soft voice, familiar, yet quite unexpected. She glanced up and found Richard Stewart standing in the doorway gazing at her in surprise.

'Auntie Rose said she thought you might come,' he said, moving out of the way when Mrs Love picked up the tray and headed for the sitting room. 'She'll be so pleased to see you,' he added, coming round the kitchen table to stand close to her.

'I'm so sorry, Rosie,' he said softly, taking her hand.

She looked up at him, surprised and almost amused to see he was wearing a dark, herring bone tweed suit, the accepted uniform of a country doctor. Despite its heavy formality, he actually looked younger than he had in the shirt and flannels he'd worn coming to meet them at the station just two weeks earlier.

'Is there no hope, Richard?' she asked quietly, amazed the way the words seemed to speak themselves.

She saw him press his lips together, pause, then run a finger round under his stiff collar. His face was damp with perspiration.

'Could we just step outside, Rosie? I'm boiling over in this jacket.'

She nodded, opened the door and led the way across the yard and into the garden itself. A slight evening breeze had begun to stir the tall perennials. She stopped by a seat, hesitated, then sat down.

'Would you mind?' he asked, catching his lapels.

'Of course not,' she replied. 'Even in a blouse I was too hot,' she added as he took his jacket off. 'Or maybe I'm so hot because I keep forgetting to breathe.'

'You were very brave to come.'

'No, I wasn't,' she protested, shaking her head. 'I just couldn't bear not to be here. I may not be much use...'

She looked at him closely and wondered why taking off his jacket made him look so much more vulnerable,

'You haven't answered my question,' she reminded him.

'I was trying to think of the best way of putting it. No, there isn't much hope. Sometimes Father and I disagree, but not this time. We both knew Uncle John had angina and it was getting worse. That's why we persuaded him not to attempt the long drive down to Kerry.'

'But he drove a lot in Kerry while we were there,' she said quickly. 'He so loved driving. One morning when we were deciding what to do, he said he didn't mind what we did as long as it was a long drive away.'

'We must both remember that then, mustn't we?' he said firmly. 'They so wanted to go to Kerry and they managed it, and enjoyed every moment of it.'

'But he's going to die, isn't he?' she insisted, trying to say the words without letting tears come into her eyes.

'Yes, I think so.'

'What will happen? Will it be like what happened this afternoon?'

'How do you know about that?' he asked, suddenly alarmed.

'Mrs Love. She gave me a detailed picture.'

He looked away hastily, studied a rose bush which had shed a pile of pale petals on the well-trimmed grass path, and then turned back to her.

'If we're lucky it shouldn't be as painful. The heart is already weak. It won't be able to take much more if there's another one. Or rather, *when* there's another one.' He paused. 'Are you *really* going to stay?'

'Yes. Unless Granny needs my bed for someone else. Auntie Sarah or Auntie Hannah, if they can come.'

He nodded briskly and reached for his jacket.

'I'm staying here tonight. After that, Father and I will take it in turns. Mother will come tomorrow. I'm glad you'll be here ... for your granny's sake.'

He stood up, took her hand and led her back into the house.

Fourteen

On the day of John's collapse, July's oppressive warmth and heavy cloud had been left behind and August begun, a month which Rosie had always liked for its maturing colours and more varied weather. For once in her life, she didn't even notice the change. It was true no one turned over the page on the kitchen calendar to reveal a new Irish landscape, but everyone's concern for John's well-being, along with the disappearance of the regular activities that usually marked the passing days, was more than enough to account for it.

On Saturday, Alex took Rosie to do Friday's shopping. On Sunday, no one went to church. Mrs Love thought it not proper to do the weekly wash on Monday and Elizabeth Stewart's regular Tuesday visit was postponed, because Elizabeth herself had sat with Rose and John through most of Sunday and Monday and needed a day at home in Dromore.

At first, Rosie found the days at Rathdrum strangely extended. Sitting with her grandmother on Saturday evening, while John slept peacefully, she felt she'd been there by his bedside for so long, the bustle and noise of shopping in Banbridge that morning was so far away it felt like something she'd done on an earlier visit. But as a second, and then a third day passed, with no visible change in John's condition, time seemed to speed up again.

The news of John's illness had spread quickly. Even before the minister of Holy Trinity and the local priest had both said prayers for his recovery on Sunday morning, visitors had called to make enquiries or leave gifts. On Monday, the manager of Ballievy arrived seeking the latest news even before Rosie had begun her breakfast. He told her the other mills had asked him to keep them closely informed, so he would send messengers up at regular intervals to see if there was any improvement, or if there was anything the household might need. He himself would see to the dispatch of any telephone messages or telegrams they needed to send.

After that, visitors arrived throughout the day and into the early evening. Some came in by the back door, like Alex and her father, or Elizabeth and her doctor husband and son, greeted her and went straight upstairs. Others knocked at the front door, people of all kinds and conditions, from directors to delivery men, and had to be brought into the sitting room while she ran upstairs to ask what her grandmother would like her to do.

There were so many who wanted no more than to shake hands with Rose at the bedroom door. They would look at the sleeping figure, call blessings upon him or cross themselves. Of their wishes for his speedy recovery there could be no doubt at all.

Almost always, Rose said that the various callers might come up to see him and for each one she had a smile and a gentle word.

'Yes, he'd had a peaceful night. No, he was no better. Yes, we must hope for the best.'

Rosie heard the words so often, she almost began to believe that there was indeed a best to hope for. That if they all went on living this strange life of quiet vigil upstairs and continuous activity downstairs, then some miracle would bring John back from the faraway place where he slept so devotedly.

On Tuesday evening, as Rosie was preparing a supper tray for her grandmother, she heard a motor stop over by the sweet-pea hedge. Last night it had been Dr Richard Stewart himself. Tonight it was Dr Richard P as his mother called him. He came through the kitchen door, looked around warily for Mrs Love and dropped into a chair when he saw and heard no sign of her.

'How's Uncle John?'

'No different from when you left on Monday morning,' she said, observing him closely, to see if his expression would tell her anything.

But he gave no sign apart from a small smile when he looked up at her.

'Is that good or bad, Richard?' she asked.

'Neither. We can only guess what's going on. The heart can't repair itself,' he said sadly. 'Too well we know that, but in a state of rest, the deterioration might be slow. We'll be able to tell better when he recovers consciousness.' He paused and looked down at the floor. 'That is, if he *does* recover consciousness.'

204

'You mean he might not?'

''Fraid so.'

'And you still don't think he *might* recover?'

'What do you want me to say, Rosie?'

She stared at him, puzzled by his question, then glanced down at the tray she'd just completed.

'I must take this up before the pot of tea gets cold. I'll make some more for you when I come down.'

'Is Auntie Rose on her own?'

'No. Da and Emily came over after work. They're with her now,' she explained, as he stood up and held open the kitchen door for her.

All was quiet as she brought the tray into the big bedroom where her grandparents slept. Rose sat on one side of the bed, her hand gently resting on John's, which lay inert on the bedspread. Her father and Emily sat on the other side, Emily's face taut with distress, her father outwardly as calm as ever.

Her grandmother looked up as she heard her come into the room.

'Did I hear Richard P arrive?' Rose asked easily.

'Yes, just now. I was going to make him some tea, unless you want him to come straight up.'

'No, no need. If we want him, he's close by and I have two good messengers here.'

Rosie arranged her grandmother's supper on a small table, poured cups of tea for her father and Emily and hurried back to the kitchen.

Richard was waiting for the kettle to boil on the gas, pot and tea caddy at the ready.

'When did you last look in the mirror?' he

asked, before she had time to speak.

'Why?' she replied, laughing. 'Have I got a dirty mark on my face?'

'No, you look entirely respectable. Neat, trim and businesslike, a credit to the household. *'But,'* he went on, 'you are at least three shades paler than when I left you yesterday morning. When did you last see the light of day?'

'Saturday, I think,' she said honestly.

He laughed, poured water into the teapot and set up another tray with cups and saucers and a jug of milk, as if it was something he did every day.

'Have *you* had any supper?'

'No,' she admitted. 'I didn't feel like any. But I did have a proper lunch. Casserole and vegetables followed by prunes and custard. Mrs Love insisted.'

'Where *is* the formidable lady?' he asked, as he cast his eye over the cake and biscuits tins, picking them up one by one and shaking them gently to see if there was anything in them.

'Granny sent her down to help Emily. She's started and her friend Nellie hasn't arrived yet to look after the little ones.'

'Poor old Alex. His best friend dying and his wife in childbirth. Sometimes life is very hard. Has he been up today?'

'Yes, twice. Emily is very upset she can't come herself. She's always been fond of Granda and Granny and the two little girls adore him. Even the baby can say "John", though she can't manage "Granda". She calls him Ganda,' she added, an undisciplined tear threatening to cloud her vision.

'Come on young lady, outside,' he said abruptly. 'There'll be sun on the far end of the garden. Open the door and lead the way. I'll carry the tray.'

To Rosie's surprise, it was warmer outdoors than in. The kitchen had been in shadow and she'd spent a long time working there, clearing up and making tea for the familiar stream of visitors. Her back ached from standing and her hands had gone icy cold. She felt suddenly so grateful for the sunlight, filtering through the trees and shrubs, soft and golden as the sun dipped in a cloudless sky, and for the gentle movement of air stirring the herbaceous borders and archways of roses, releasing their mixed perfumes.

They walked right to the end of the mown grass path and sat on her grandmother's favourite garden seat from which there was an uninterrupted view of the mountains outlined in the paling evening sky. Richard had poured her tea and passed her a piece of cake before she'd managed to draw her eyes away from the distant prospect, never mind collect her thoughts.

'You're doing my job,' she said lightly, as he poured his own tea.

'And I could say you've been doing mine. Providing for the needs of an anxious family is part of good doctoring. At least I think it is.'

She thought about what he'd said, began to consider a reply, but found she couldn't concentrate. What kept coming back into her mind was the question he'd asked her before she went upstairs: 'What do you want me to say?'

Suddenly finding the effort of explaining too much for her she simply repeated his words and then went on.

'But what can you say about him, except to tell me the truth? You haven't got a choice of things to say, have you?'

To her great surprise he laughed and shook his head.

'Oh Rosie, Rosie, if only you knew how little people want to hear the truth,' he said quickly. 'Not just about dying. About living, about making a life, about creating a world fit for us all to live in. Truth is very unfashionable these days. But some people appreciate it. They're the ones who'll be most sadly deprived by Uncle John's loss, though they probably won't know exactly what they've lost.'

She thought of the stream of callers, the bulletins posted up in the mills, the letters and cards and gifts.

'Is that why Granda is so loved?'

'I think so,' he said soberly. 'In fact, I'm sure that's why. You see he's always been himself. There's never been any pretension about him. He's never tried to impress or be something he wasn't. One of my patients mentioned him to me this morning. When he found out I knew him, he told me a couple of little stories. He ended up saying, "Even when he got on in life and had to wear a suit to the boardroom, John Hamilton would still get down on his knees to fix your motor if he came on you stuck on his way home", and that just about sums up your grandfather.'

Rosie smiled. It wasn't just the words them-selves, it was the broad country accent Richard had used. Sometimes he seemed so sober and solemn, but then, she thought, being a doctor can't be easy. People would expect him to be sober and solemn, but his dark eyes twinkled when he made her laugh and that she loved.

'Do you think you could persuade Granny to come out for a breath of air? She only leaves that room to go to the lavatory or to wash.'

'No, I wouldn't even try, Rosie,' he said, shaking his head. 'Not many men are loved as John has been loved. I wouldn't deprive them of a moment of their being together. Would you?'

Rosie just shook her head. If Richard said John would die then he would. What she could not yet come to terms with was the fact that his death would separate her dear grandmother from the love of her life.

Richard left on Wednesday morning soon after his mother and father arrived and the two men had spent some minutes with John. His pulse was stronger, they agreed, but there were still no signs of him opening his eyes.

'Be a good girl,' said Richard lightly, as he tramped through the kitchen where Rosie was already at work. 'Up and down the garden as often as you can and a nice sit in the sun when Mrs Love comes back.'

He paused and looked at her with mock severity.

She returned his look and sensed how tired he

was. This was the third night he'd spent dozing in a chair beside John's bed and now he was driving back to Dromore to take his surgery before going out on his calls.

'You haven't had breakfast,' she said accusingly.

'No, but I *do* intend to when I get home. I *always* have breakfast, I promise you, but that's because I don't always get lunch,' he confessed with a wry glance. 'I'll see you tomorrow.'

She smiled and nodded and felt strangely sad as she watched him stride across the yard and drop his leather bag into the back of his motor. Minutes later he was gone. Before the sound of the engine had faded from the fresh morning air, she heard the doorbell. The day had begun and it was not yet eight o'clock.

Slowly and quietly the hours passed. They were surprised when Mrs Love did not return, but Elizabeth did arrive and insisted on cooking lunch and Rosie went and sat with her grandmother until it was ready. They ate it together at a small table at the foot of John's bed.

Rosie had never met Elizabeth before, though Rose had spoken of her dear friend so often. A tall, stately woman, her hair iron-grey, her face still soft and given to smiles. When she laughed, her large, grey eyes lit up and Rosie was startled to discover how beautiful she still was.

There were fewer visitors today though the messenger from Ballievy arrived at regular intervals. It was he who told them Emily was now well advanced in labour, that her friend had not yet arrived from Belfast and that Mrs Love

210

was fully occupied with the three lively little girls, the youngest just starting to crawl.

Rosie did as Richard had asked and walked out into the garden whenever she had a free moment. It gave her the chance to pick sweet pea and put it in vases in the sitting room. There were creamy pink roses just opening which she arranged with spikes of lavender and the shiny leaves of magnolia for the hall table. She took a single, short-stemmed rose in a small bud vase up to the bedroom where Elizabeth and Rose sat in companionable silence. It was still tightly rolled with only a small tip that told her what colour it would be, but it was beautifully shaped, plump and perfect. In the warmth of the sunlit room, it should open very soon.

She examined the rosebud carefully next morning as she sat by John's bed while Rose washed quickly and changed her clothes and Dr Stewart drank a cup of tea in the kitchen before he went home. Though she could smell its rich perfume already, to her surprise it had still not opened.

As she sat watching her grandfather's face, she heard voices in the kitchen and a step on the stair. It was not Dr Stewart, for she'd heard his motor on the driveway and it was certainly not the young man from Ballievy who always came to the front door.

She had just stood up, wondering if she'd be needed, when Rose appeared from the bathroom at the same moment that Alex reached the top of the stairs.

'How is he, Rose?' Alex asked, as they came

211

into the room together.

'Another peaceful night,' Rose replied, smiling briefly at him, as she took up her place by the bed.

'Hallo, Rosie.'

Alex ran his eye over the sleeping figure and then looked from Rosie to Rose and back again to John. 'I've news for you all.'

He paused and Rosie held her breath.

'There's another wee Hamilton arrived at Ballydown. A bit hard on Emily this one, harder than any of the others, but she's all right now.'

He paused yet again and Rosie felt a surge of joy, sure she knew what he was going to say next.

'It's a wee boy.'

Much as Alex loved his three little girls, he'd admitted freely how much he wanted a boy. Having no parents that he knew of, only the name, once pinned on the collar of his coat on an emigrant ship carrying orphans to Canada, the family he had made with Emily was even more precious to him than to most men.

Rose beamed at him, stood up, put her arms round him and kissed him.

'That is wonderful, Alex, quite wonderful.'

'John Alexander Hamilton, he said softly, looking from her to the sleeping figure. 'But he'll be called John.'

Whether it was pure chance or the sound of his own name, no one would ever know, but at that moment John opened his eyes and looked around him, a slight hint of surprise on his face at finding Alex and Rosie as well as Rose by his

212

bedside.

He turned his face towards Rose, clearly expecting an explanation.

'Good news, John,' she said, quite steadily, as if she had been expecting him to open his eyes any minute now. 'Alex has got a wee son and Emily is fine.'

John tried to speak, coughed, cleared his throat, and jutted out his hand to Alex.

'Ach, congratulations man. Sure that is great, just great. Tell Emily I was asking for her.'

Alex nodded and shook John's hand vigorously. Only Rosie saw that his eyes were so full of tears he dare not risk speaking.

When the young man from Ballievy arrived to make his usual morning enquiry, Rose said he must come upstairs and see for himself the great improvement the night had brought. Within the hour, many friends and colleagues, hearing the news via the four mills, set out to wish John well. Visitors arrived throughout the day, as delighted to see John sitting up in bed as he was to see them.

John himself wanted to get out of bed, but accepted Rose's decision that he'd better wait until Richard P arrived later in the day. Meantime, Alex gave him a hand to shave, Rosie made toast for his breakfast and a little later, when Alex had gone back down the hill to his wife and family, Mrs Love returned in a flurry of skirts unable to contain her excitement about the new arrival at Ballydown.

Rosie was puzzled that John did not seem to be

213

at all curious as to why he was in bed or to be aware that time had passed. Only then did she herself go to the calendar in the kitchen, turn over the page and strike off the large squares under the picture of Ben Bulben. Today was Thursday, the seventh of August. It would be a full week tomorrow.

As the afternoon passed and the usual hour of the evening meal drew near, the doorbell rang less frequently. John dozed in the late afternoon sunshine, opening his eyes when Rosie came into the room carrying a tray.

'Were ye paintin' flowers?' he asked, as she put the tray down on the table at the foot of the bed.

'No,' she said, smiling at him, 'but I've put sweet pea in the sitting room and roses in the hall.'

'That's good,' he said, nodding as if it were a matter of great importance. 'I'll come and look at them when young Richard let's me out of bed. Your granny say's he's coming to see you this evening.'

Rosie looked at her grandmother and wondered if she'd picked up John's mistake. If she had, it was clear she didn't intend to point it out. She simply gave him his tea in a china mug which he grasped firmly in his large brown hand. When some of the tea dribbled down his chin, she wiped it up without him even noticing.

With Mrs Love back in the kitchen and the doorbell now less demanding, Rosie took the opportunity to go and wash her hair. Coming out of the bathroom, a towel round her shoulders, on her way to her own room, she caught the sound of voices. Rose and John were talking to each other. Through the open door, she saw her grandmother was no longer sitting in her usual chair, but had moved to sit on the edge of the bed, her back to the door, her face close to her husband.

She tiptoed past and went out into the garden to dry her hair in the sun.

'So he's awake?' Richard said, as she met him by the sweet-pea hedge.

'Yes. It happened quite suddenly when Alex came this morning,' she replied as they walked towards the kitchen door.

'So I heard. Your man at Ballievy rang me before I left for my calls. And Alex has his son,' he continued, grinning at her.

She nodded happily.

'Have you had a lot of visitors?'

'Yes. Particularly this morning. But its been quiet since about five. Granny said we'd wait and have a bite of supper when you came. Granda is expecting you to let him out of bed. At least, that's what he said earlier.'

'So he's in good spirits then?'

There was something in his tone that made Rosie pause. She looked up at him.

'Is that a Richard question or a doctor question?' she asked, a hint of anxiety in her tone.

'Both,' he responded quickly. 'Whose with him now?'

'Just Granny. I was there when we all had a cup of tea, but she said I might like some fresh air. I think she wanted to be by herself with him. She sent Mrs Love back to Emily, because she kept

215

popping in and out. But I expect the children will keep her busy and she'll leave Emily in peace.'

'I think perhaps I'll go straight up,' he said, a grave note in his voice.

'All right. Is there anything you'd like?

'Yes. I'd like you to come with me.'

Rose had heard their voices on the stairs and was sitting in her usual chair, one hand outstretched to where John's lay on the bedspread.

'Ach Richard, how are ye? How's your mother and father? Are they well?'

Rosie listened as they had the sort of conversation she'd heard a thousand times. John seemed unaware of his illness, yet was perfectly clear about the arrival of Alex's son. Richard made all the predictable replies, his tone warm and relaxed, but she saw that he made no move to take John's pulse or even open the leather bag he'd dropped casually by the foot of the bed.

There was a pause. John appeared to be about to say something. They waited. It was more than a minute before he opened his mouth again to speak.

'This is the wee girl that paints the flowers, Richard,' he said, jerking his head towards her. 'I was telling you about her yesterday when you came to see us. She's great company for her granny when I'm busy in the workshop...'

Rosie felt a sudden sense of tension. Something wasn't right. John had turned to look at Rose and lifted his hand as if he wanted to touch her hair. He seemed confused, as if suddenly he could no longer see quite clearly. He glanced at Richard, a look of puzzlement on his face, then

216

turned back to Rose, to whom he always turned for explanation. His hand, suspended for a moment in mid-air, fell suddenly, jarring the bedside cabinet where the single rose in a bud glass had now opened its dark red petals. The glass fell over and it dropped to the floor, followed by a trickle of water.

Rose got to her feet and caught him in her arms as his body slowly fell forward.

Richard reached for Rosie's hand and led her from the room.

Fifteen

Despite the warmth of the August afternoon and the mass of dark-clothed bodies packed into every corner of the spacious parish church of Holy Trinity, Rosie felt cold. When she'd taken her place at the end of the long pew where her sister and her brothers were already seated her hands were so numb she'd dropped the printed service sheet left ready in her place

Now she was grateful for the soft, black wool shawl Rose had lent her. She'd wanted to wear 'Granda's dress' and had been anxious, because it was a deep, autumn red, the colour of ripe hawthorn berries, not perhaps what some people would think appropriate for a funeral.

'Now don't worry,' Rose had said. 'Granda would be pleased you wore his dress. Besides, I'm certainly not wearing all black. He hated me in black. Skirt and coat, yes, but I'll wear a blouse or a scarf he liked and so will Sarah and Helen. Remember Aunt Elizabeth is a Quaker and they don't wear black for funerals.'

Rosie found it hard to believe how calm Rose had been. Even shortly after John died, Rose had come down to the kitchen to find her weeping in Richard's arms and not shed a tear herself. Instead, it was she who'd comforted them both.

'There'll be a time for tears, Rosie dear, but it's not now,' she'd said to them both, smiling. 'Now we must give thanks. John and I had an extra day. A whole, happy day, when we might have had nothing at all. He was safe and comfortable and not anxious and there was no pain, just the puzzlement my good friends had warned me about,' she added, taking Richard by the arm and squeezing it gently.

To Rosie's amazement, she'd sent them both down to Ballievy. The night watchman had instructions to open the office at any hour if someone from Rathdrum needed the telephone.

'I'm quite happy to be on my own,' she'd said firmly, when Rosie suggested she should stay and keep her company. 'This is the last time for many days when John and I can be quiet together.'

It was quite true. From the arrival of Richard's parents less than an hour later, closely followed by the undertaker, the house had not been empty or quiet since except in the deep night hours. The once calm haven of her grandparent's bedroom became a public place, where John lay still and pale beneath a creamy linen cover, at whose centre, carefully remounted in recent years was set a wreath of rosebuds embroidered long ago entwining the initials J and R.

'Are you all right, Rosie?'

Rosie nodded and grasped Emily's hand. Her sister had long bony fingers like her mother, but unlike her mother, Emily's awkward touch always brought comfort. Now she clutched the warm hand as if it would prevent her own from turning to ice.

Throughout the great vaulted church, there was a murmur, an ebb and flow of echoing sound that was also a kind of silence. Dark figures made their way to the remaining spaces in the front pews reserved for the family and close friends. Behind them, every pew was full and men lined up against the walls leaving their wives to take the folding chairs being carried from the church hall to give extra seating in the outer aisles.

'Who's that lovely-looking girl with the long, dark hair?' Emily whispered.

'That's Helen Sinton, Aunt Sarah's daughter. She's the one that goes to the art school in London. She's very nice.'

'Is Auntie Sarah here?' Emily mouthed, looking puzzled. 'I thought she was away somewhere foreign.'

'Yes, she was. In Berlin. But she started out when Granda took ill, so she was already in London with Auntie Hannah when he died. They came together yesterday morning with Helen and Auntie Hannah's son, Frances.'

'Is she the one that's a countess or somethin'?'

'Yes. But she never mentions it. Granny just says "my daughter Hannah", but I did see "Lady Harrington" printed on her suitcase. That's Frances sitting beyond Helen with Hugh, Aunt Sarah's son.'

Emily studied the faces of the two young men she could never remember meeting. Frances lived in an English mansion called Ashleigh Park but Hugh lived in Belfast. He had something to do with flying, she thought, but didn't know quite what.

'How is Granny?'

'Amazing. I really can't understand why she doesn't cry all the time. I would if it was me.'

Emily fidgeted awkwardly in her seat.

'Maybe when yer old it's not the same,' she said abruptly.

'What d' you mean?'

'Maybe things don't matter as much. They sort of wear out.'

'Do you mean things like feelings?'

Emily nodded.

'Well, if you mean love, then it doesn't. They loved each other more than couples I know saving up to get married.'

The organ stopped playing. The congregation stood up, the silence now complete but for the rustle of clothes and the ripple of movement. As the 'Funeral March' began Rosie took a deep breath and wondered how she would ever get through the service without bursting into tears.

The coffin was carried down the central aisle and laid on trestles so close to her she could almost have reached out and touched it. Immediately behind it, her grandmother walked steadily, a small composed figure, her hand on her father's arm, her eyes never moving from the sheaf of red roses, the only flowers to lie on the coffin itself out of the multitude of wreaths that had arrived.

They moved into the pew in front her, so that Rosie found herself suddenly looking at a delicate silk scarf John had bought for her grandmother in Kerry and the immaculate black and white of her father's coat and stiff collar.

Hannah, her blonde hair now streaked with grey, and Sarah, her face pale, dark circles under her eyes, weary from days of travelling and the saddest of homecomings, walked together behind them, then turned aside to the places awaiting them beside their own sons and daughter.

As the first hymn began, the vigorous uplifting of so many voices was so utterly unexpected it left Rosie stunned. Even more unexpected was what followed. A tall, thin man of military bearing, whose name on the printed sheet was followed by rows of letters, honours and decorations, few of which made sense to her, walked briskly from his seat to the great brass eagle of the reading desk. He laid a small piece of paper on the open Bible and then, without making the slightest reference to it, launched into his address.

'They say we must speak no ill of the dead,' he began, his tone commanding attention, yet light, easy, almost conversational. 'It is my feeling that it would be a task of considerable magnitude to find any ill we could speak of in considering our friend John Hamilton.'

From the congregation came a sound, soft like a sigh, not as positive as laughter, but yet somewhere on the edge of pleasure, a movement of agreement, a relaxation of tension. They listened devotedly as he continued.

'John Hamilton was born in Annacramp, near Armagh, in 1851, the youngest son of a blacksmith. He left school at twelve, as so many did in those days, and went into the forge with his father, leaving to find work with a local land-owner Sir Capel Molyneux when his father died some three years later...'

Rosie listened fascinated. There were so many things about her grandfather that were new to her. She knew the story of his meeting with Rose in Kerry and the coat that was too small for him, of course, a story which Sir Lindsey retold with obvious pleasure, but she'd not known about her grandfather's inventions, nor about his part in improving working conditions in the mills.

'It was typical of the man,' Sir Lindsey went on to say, 'that he listened both to the urgings of his daughter, Sarah, and the advice of his close friends Dr Richard Stewart and his wife Elizabeth.

'It was one of John Hamilton's gifts,' he continued, 'that what he knew he shared, and what he didn't know he was willing to learn. I would hazard a guess there is not a man or woman here today who has not spoken to John Hamilton knowing he would listen to whatever they had to say.'

Even when this unknown man, a fellow director of Bann Valley Mills, went on to speak of the long and happy marriage that had blessed John's life, Rosie managed to remained dry-eyed and attentive. She glanced cautiously at her father and saw him smile at some of the stories that were brought back to him. Rose herself looked pleased. Out of the names of those who had said they would be honoured to pay tribute to John, Sir Lindsey had been her own choice.

He stepped down from the reading desk at last

and walked briskly back to his place, leaving a lightness in the air. But for Rosie, the sense of uplift that followed his generous and accurate tribute was swept away as the organ began the opening bars of the tune Crimmond and they stood to sing 'The Lord's my Shepherd'.

Suddenly, she could hear her grandfather's voice: 'Ach, it's a lovely psalm that, whatever the tune they put it to, but I like Crimmond the best.'

Tears streamed down her face and simply would not stop.

Both her own handkerchief and one of Emily's were sodden before they stood for the Benediction, but by then her tears were spent. Sitting at the aisle end of the second row of pews, she gathered herself to follow Hannah and Sarah. If she didn't move at exactly the right moment, she and her brothers, Alex, the Stewarts and three women she didn't know, would not be behind Rose as the coffin left the church.

She walked as steadily as she could, aware of Richard and Elizabeth and Richard P following her, then Sammy and Bobby, Billy and Charlie. In front of her, on both sides of the aisle, the solid mass of dark clothes and pale faces. She had never seen so many people in one place ever in her life before.

The organ was playing something triumphant which she found oppressive, but suddenly they were out in the sunshine. For a few moments there were hugs and handshakes as close family greeted Rose, Sam, Hannah and Sarah. Then, as

Sam responded to a signal from the undertaker and moved away, the three women took up their position and waited to receive the greetings and condolences of the entire congregation.

Rosie looked around her, beyond the known figures who waited at some distance from her grandmother and her two aunts. On all the space between the short driveway and the enclosing trees of the small churchyard the flowers had been laid out in the sunshine. Now, as the warmth played on the carpet of chrysanthemums and roses, lilies and dahlias, large formal tributes and bunches of homely garden flowers, it drew out a heady perfume that floated on the still air.

Absorbed by the colour and perfume, it was some minutes before she noticed that the coffin had not been put back in the hearse which had brought it from Rathdrum. Her father and Alex, Hugh Sinton and Richard P stood ready to take it from the shoulders of the undertaker's men. She watched as her four brothers fell into step behind them and they moved slowly towards the gates. Then, four by four, in some pre-arranged pattern, after speaking to Rose and her daughters, the men from the congregation lined up behind her brothers.

It dawned on her then that so many men had wanted to pay their respects by carrying John's coffin for a short distance they were going to shoulder it the whole way to Seapatrick, well over a mile from the church.

Rosie watched her father and Uncle Alex settle the weight of the coffin on their broad shoulders, their arms clasped beneath the casket. As a little girl she had always thought Uncle Alex was her father's younger brother. It was only when she was older she'd learnt that Alex was an orphan, sent with a ship-load of children out of Liverpool to an orphanage in Canada that provided cheap labour for the farms.

He couldn't have been more than five, a little boy with a label on the collar of his coat. As he'd said to her himself more than once, all he possessed was his name, Alexander Hamilton, written on that label, until a chance meeting with Granny's brother, Sam, had awakened a lost memory and sent him searching for his family.

Sam had spoken of Annacramp, where generations of Hamiltons had lived. Granda had been born there. He'd brought Granny from Kerry to her first home there. James and Sam, Hannah and Sarah had all been born there.

Alex had come to Ireland in search of his family and had found Granda and Granny in Ballydown. Whether or not these particular Hamiltons were his actual family, Rosie was sure there was no one in this vast concourse of people, their eyes upon the steady movement of her grandfather's coffin, who could imagine Alex as anyone other than John Hamilton's son.

Slowly, the head of the procession made its way through the gates of the churchyard and out into the empty, silent streets, the shops closed because it was Sunday, the blinds on private houses drawn down because of John's death. Behind it, yet more men took their place. Group after group, they moved like a dark, flowing river that would never end.

'What do we do now?' Emily whispered, as quietly as if they were still in church.

'I'm not sure. Granny told me it's only the men that go to the graveyard. There's tea at Rathdrum. I do know that because Mrs Love and I made loaves and loaves of sandwiches last night.'

She looked around again and saw clusters of women walking away from the church in twos and threes. The undertaker's men were loading the wreaths into the empty hearse. Yet there were still men shaking hands with Rose, older men, bent with age, who did not hurry to join the groups of four who would carry the coffin all the way up the long hill. She could still hear the murmur of their voices, repeating and repeating the same simple phrase.

'I'm sorry for your trouble. I'm sorry for your trouble.'

Richard P was so right. He'd asked her yesterday if she'd ever been to a funeral and she'd shaken her head, so he'd described what it would be like. He'd explained everyone would say 'I'm sorry for your trouble' to her grandmother as she stood at the church door. Though it looked a bit like a formula, it wasn't. It was, as he put it, a hallowed phrase, only ever used when sincerely meant.

She felt so grateful to him now for telling her as much as he had about the customs and traditions and the rituals of mourning, but nothing he'd said had prepared her for the sheer numbers of people nor for the atmosphere created in the parish church.

'Hallo Rosie. That's the worst over.'

Helen Sinton had come up quietly behind them and slipped an arm round them both. 'You must be my cousin, Emily,' she went on smiling. 'I think the last time we saw each other, I fell out of a tree in your orchard.'

'Ach dear, fancy you rememberin' that,' responded Emily, her face lighting up. 'Your poor ma looks tired out.'

'She had rather a bad journey from Berlin to The Hook,' Helen replied, pressing her lips together. 'She just caught the first possible train with no booking, so she'd no sleeper. I think she actually stood part of the way, but she's not letting on about that. Have you ever seen so many people at a funeral before?'

'I've never been at a funeral before,' Rosie confessed.

'So Richard P told me. He seems very concerned about you,' she said with a small smile.

'He's been very kind,' Rosie replied honestly. 'He tried to warn me what it would be like. I was so afraid of doing something wrong.'

Helen took them both by the arm.

'There are some taxis waiting over at the hotel. They're going to ferry us all up to Rathdrum and then collect the men as they make their way back from the churchyard. I've to go now and summon them,' she added, 'unless you'd like to come with me.'

Rosie glanced across at Emily, knowing how shy she could be with people she didn't know well, but she was looking pleased and relieved. However different from them this elegant young woman might seem to be, with her smart London costume and beautifully manicured hands, she was warm and friendly, just like her mother.

They set off together, slipping out by the small side gate behind the church, but there they had to wait for some time before they could cross the road. They stood silently on the pavement until the last of the solemn figures had past by, then took one last look at the long, dark line winding its way over the bridge, past the Crozier Memorial and through the town, on the journey John had made at least once a week through every week of his working life.

Rosie, Emily and Helen were the first to arrive back at Rathdrum. The front door stood open, the sitting room and hall were full of flowers, but all was silent as they made their way through to the kitchen. To their surprise, they found there not only Mrs Love, who had insisted on staying behind, but two young girls in black dresses and white aprons laying out cups and saucers and a smart young man polishing wine glasses.

'This is Mary and this is Bridget,' said Mrs Love quickly, introducing the two girls. 'Auntie Hannah said that you and I had done enough,' she went on, addressing Rosie. 'We're not to spend the afternoon in the kitchen, so she borrowed these two from the hotel.'

Rosie wondered why she hadn't introduced the young man who was polishing away quite devotedly, but before she'd remembered Mrs Love was a vigorous teetotaller, Helen had stepped forward towards him.

'I'm Helen,' she said sticking out her hand. 'And these are my cousins Rosie and Emily. Who are you?'

He looked up from his tray of sparkling glasses, stared at her in amazement, blushed as red as the stripe on his Irish linen tea towel, and finally shook her hand.

'I'm Willy Auld. Pleased to meet ye.'

'Does your father by any chance work in the Post Office?'

'Aye, he does. He's the postmaster,' he replied, looking startled.

'You must talk to my mother when she gets here. She and your father are old friends. I've often heard her mention him. Now let's take these through to the sitting room. Where have you set up the booze?'

Rosie had no idea what she was going to do about the look on Mrs Love's face as she saw Helen and Willy disappear together. To make it worse, Emily said excuse me and headed for the lavatory and Mary and Bridget picked up their trays and moved out into the hall to follow Helen and Willy.

'Yer granda wasn't a great man for drink,' she said accusingly.

'No, I don't think he ever got drunk,' Rosie replied, choosing her words with care, 'but he always enjoyed a wee whiskey. And he liked wine,' she added emphatically, remembering the bottle of sparkling white wine he'd ordered for her birthday supper.

Mrs Love pressed her lips together and jerked her head in righteous disapproval.

230

'Ye haven't see the boxes that came with that young man from the hotel. And it the Sabbath day,' she said, tight with ill-concealed anger.

'Where did he put them?' Rosie asked, looking round her, there being no visible sign of drink of any kind in the kitchen.

'Out in the workshop. There wouldn't have been room in here. They'd a' filled the place.'

'I'll go and look,' Rosie offered, desperate to get away from her black looks.

There were indeed a dozen or more cardboard cartons neatly lined up along her grandfather's workbench, their lids turned back ready for use. She examined them carefully. Whiskey, port, sherry, as she had expected. But alongside the familiar names like Bushmills and Powers was a whole range of soft drinks.

She sighed with relief. She could go and tell Mrs Love that only some of the boxes contained the demon drink. But as she moved out into the sunlight again it occurred to her that Mrs Love and 'drink' was the equivalent of Uncle Joe and the Fenians. It wouldn't matter what facts you gave her, she'd made up her mind and nothing would change it.

She paused as a second vehicle from the hotel drove slowly into the yard and stopped short of the motors already parked by the sweet pea. To her great relief, she saw Elizabeth Stewart coming towards her accompanied by two grey-haired women and an uneasy-looking younger woman.

'Hello Rosie, come and meet two old friends of Granny. This is Selina Scott from Salter's Grange and Peggy Wylie from Annacramp and

231

this is Ellen Scott, Selina's daughter-in-law. Ellen and Robert are at the forge house now, beside the one where your father lived as a little boy,' she added helpfully, as Rosie shook hands. 'Do you think we could slip in by the back door to save walking round to the front? Not proper at all to bring visitors in by the back but we're all so tired with standing.'

For a moment Rosie thought of asking Elizabeth to speak to Mrs Love, but when she saw how wearily Selina Scott was leaning on her stick, she made up her mind.

'Of course you can. It might be a bit of a squash with the two girls making tea, but it's much shorter.'

She led the way and found the kitchen was now empty, another group of women were coming down the hall from the front door, the sitting room was beginning to fill up and Mrs Love nowhere in sight.

Sometimes things did come to help you, she thought, as she breathed a sigh of relief.

What surprised Rosie most about the afternoon was the laughter. Richard P had not mentioned that. Nor had he told her how those who have suffered loss renew their ties with those who have also suffered, not by grieving, but by telling stories, weaving between them a web of memories that comfort and sustain.

Now in her eighties, Selina told Rosie about how John Hamilton had worked with her husband, Thomas, in the forge at Salter's Grange. How they'd stuck to their principles when the two of them were threatened and intimidated by

Orangemen protesting over Home Rule, making no difference between their Catholic and Protestant customers, and how they'd suffered for it financially.

'But you know, Rosie dear, the amazing thing was, if your grandfather hadn't been forced out of the forge and into the mill to keep bread on the table for his four wee ones, he might not have ended up a director of Bann Valley Mills. He'd have been a good country blacksmith like my Thomas, with enough to bring up a family and leave a little by, but he'd not have made such a go of it as your granda did. Though having said that I'm not sure if Granda could have done so well if it hadn't been for Granny there behind him,' she added, looking across the room to where Rose sat, listening to Alex and Sam, among the first to arrive back from the graveyard at Seapatrick.

Selina fell silent and Rosie was just about to ask her if she would like another cup of tea, when she turned towards her, her pale eyes bright, a sober look on her face.

'Rose once told me that her mother used to say that some good may come from even the most heartbreaking events,' she began. 'But that's only if you have the courage to accept what has happened. I think Hannah McGinley was right, and your grandmother has always done the same. You have to face things, Rosie, not pretend they haven't happened. Life is never all bad, or all good. You'll miss your Granda, but other things will come and you'll always have the memories.'

Rosie nodded, though she was not sure she

fully understood.

'But what about Granny, Mrs Scott? I know I have all sorts of experiences ahead of me, good and bad, like you said, but don't you think she'll be terribly lonely by herself?'

Selina smiled and wondered what to say to a girl so thoughtful, yet so inexperienced.

'I talked to my Thomas for years after he went,' she began. 'I knew him so well I could guess what he'd say. There were times I could just imagine him laughing at me for getting in a state about something. And there were other things came to help me too. People I'd lost touch with. My friend Peggy and her family, for instance.'

'Rose has her son and daughters and all you grandchildren,' she continued reassuringly. 'No, its not the same, but it *is* something. That's what helped me when the house seemed so empty. That and a kitten a neighbour gave me,' she added, beginning to laugh. 'You might not believe me, but that wee scrap of divilment was the first thing that made me laugh again.'

She paused, looked across the room at Rose, then back at Rosie.

'Now away dear, and talk to some of your young cousins,' she said smiling and patting Rosie's shoulder. 'You're good company, but I'm happy here to sit and watch the comings and goings till I get a word with your grandmother before I go.'

Rosie moved out into the hall, simply because a space opened in that direction. As she came through the sitting-room door her cousin, Hugh

Sinton, arrived with Billy and Charlie and Richard P. Moments later another motor stopped. This time it was Frances Harrington, Sammy and Bobby and Dr Stewart. Together the eight men filled up the narrow space, some greeting her warmly, others squeezing their way into the kitchen where Willy stood, with a tray of glasses at the ready.

As soon as there was movement, she reached the stairs and ran up quickly, hardly able to believe the house could accommodate so many people. But then, everyone gathered below wanted to support her grandmother. They'd make light of any difficulties and be as helpful as they could in whatever way was needed.

Talk and laughter rose in waves from the downstairs rooms. From her window she could see some people had moved out into the yard, others were now walking in the garden. For a moment, she felt totally alone.

How could one be alone when there were more known people downstairs than she'd ever experienced before all gathered together in one place? Not only Granny and her own family, but her aunts and cousins whom she'd never met till now, like Frances, or met so long ago that they might as well be a different person.

Beyond her open door, she heard a footstep on the landing. She paid no attention, but went on staring out of the window wondering when she'd stand here again. She caught her breath. Till that moment, she'd never thought losing Granda might mean losing Rathdrum.

The knock on her door was gentle but firm

enough to reach her over the waves of sound echoing from downstairs.

She turned round and saw Richard P entering the room.

'Have you had some tea?'

It was the only thing she could think of to say.

'Not yet,' he replied, coming to stand beside her at the window. 'You looked very thoughtful,' he went on. 'Sad?'

'Yes,' she said honestly, 'but not like I was in church. I was wondering when, or if, I would ever stand here again.'

'That's a very philosophical question.'

'Is it?'

'Well, you know the saying that you can't step in the same river twice...'

She shook her head, wondering what was in his mind.

'You can't step in the *same* river twice, because it has moved on. Whatever happens, some things will have changed. You in particular.'

'And what about you?'

'Oh yes, me too.'

He paused as if he wanted to be sure of his words for what he had to say next.

'Perhaps what I mean is that I've changed a great deal since I was sixteen. Going to medical school. Coming back and going into practice with Father. I might not change as much in the next few years as *you* will.'

'But not everything changes, does it?' she asked, puzzled by his train of thought and an expression she couldn't read. 'You'll still be Richard P and I'll be Rosie. There are some things I can't ever imagine changing.'

'Yes, I think you have a point. We'll have to compare notes...'

He broke off as he saw two figures moving purposively across the yard below.

'Actually I came up to say "Cheerio". Auntie Rose has persuaded Helen to go back tonight. She was in the middle of producing scenery for a play that has its first night next week. It seems she just put down her paint pot and came. I said I'd take her to the boat.'

'And you won't come back later?'

'No, I'll go straight home from Belfast. Mother and Father will want to stay this evening, so I need to be on call.'

For a single moment she felt overcome with disappointment. She'd just assumed she'd see him one more evening before she herself went home.

'It's going to be a lovely evening for the drive,' she said quickly.

She watched as Aunt Sarah and Helen put a small suitcase and a couple of parcels in Richard's motor. Helen threw her arms round her mother, hugged her, and climbed into the front seat, her dark hair caught back with a bright red scarf.

Richard followed her gaze down into to the yard below.

'Take care, Rosie. I'm sure I'll get all your news from Auntie.'

For a moment, she saw him hesitate. Then he took her hand, kissed her cheek and strode off without a backward glance.

She stayed by the window, watched him as he emerged from the house, crossed to his motor, climbed up into the driving seat and reversed away from the sweet pea hedge. As they manoeuvred Helen turned to him and said something which made them both laugh. The motor set off down the drive and disappeared.

Rosie thought her cousin Helen was quite the loveliest and liveliest person she'd ever met. She was sure Richard thought so too.

Sixteen

When Rosie went to say goodbye to her grand-mother next morning she found her weary and not quite her usual self though Rose hugged her warmly and said she was to come and see her as soon as she could manage it. Aunt Hannah was still trying to persuade her to go back to England with them, if only for a short rest. In direct contrast, when she went to the kitchen, she found Mrs Love completely restored to her normal good spirits, tackling two weeks' washing on a morning with exactly the kind of fresh breeze she liked to give her the best of drying.

Rosie left Rathdrum in her grandfather's motor with Aunt Sarah at the wheel. On her way to Armagh to visit her former brother-in-law, James Sinton, who'd been too ill to come to the funeral, Sarah said how glad she was to have her company. As they set off down the hill they agreed how grateful they were, to be driving briskly under a wide, cloud-strewn sky after the confine-ment of the last days, the first pink and gold leaves of the chestnut trees suggesting a touch of autumn even this early in August.

'So what now, Rosie?' Sarah asked as they headed for Banbridge. 'We've not had much chance to talk, but Ma told me in a letter you were keen to do a year's training for textile design.'

'Yes, I was. It was something we talked about in Kerry, but I don't think it'll happen now.'

'Why not?'

Rosie sighed, not sure where to begin. The more she thought about it the more complicated it all seemed.

'Well, to begin with, Da can't afford the fees himself. Or rather, even if he could, he'd not be happy about it, because he wasn't able to help the boys to do apprenticeships. He thinks it might not be fair if he were to say yes and let Granny and Granda help me.'

'That sounds so like my dear brother Sam,' she said sharply. 'Did he *ask* the boys if they wanted to be apprenticed?'

'I don't know. I'm not sure any of them did. Except perhaps Sammy. But he's doing so well now I don't think it matters any more. He likes his boss and he's had two pay rises so far, so he's earning far more than an apprentice. He's saving up for a motorbike,' she added smiling.

'And he's planning to ride in the T.T. races in the Isle of Man whenever he's got enough experience, isn't he? I had a few minutes with him yesterday and I heard all about it,' Sarah replied. 'I like your Sammy,' she went on thoughtfully. 'How do you feel about staying at home?'

'I don't really know. I was dreading it when I came back from Kerry, but it wasn't as bad as I expected. Ma had been very down on me before...'

'You had your accident with the door that jumped up and hit you. Ma told me all about that as well.'

Rosie took a quick look at Sarah, her eyes focused on the road ahead, her motoring hat pulled down firmly over her ears.

'When I came back she was different,' she explained. 'Mostly, she ignores me, but quite often she sends me out. Messages and so on. She even suggests I go and visit people. Lizzie or Miss Wilson, or some of the other girls I went to school with. I can't think why she's suddenly changed, but it does make things easier. Especially if I can't go to Belfast.'

'What do you think might have made the change?'

'I really wish I knew. Lizzie said she thought Da said something to her while I was away. He was very upset when—'

'Shrewd guess of Lizzie, I'd say,' Sarah interrupted, glancing at her briefly. 'The thing about your da is that he seems to do nothing, and do nothing, and then, quite suddenly, he acts. I used to get so cross with him when I was your age, the way he put up with things I'd never have stood for five minutes. I suppose now I've achieved the incredible age of forty either I've learnt patience or I've finally accepted that other people work differently from the way I do,' she said, laughing. 'Sam bides his time. And I must say, though I never became a Quaker, even when I was married to one, I *do* respect their principles. Not *always*, but mostly. Your dear father *always* tries to be fair, even if he gives himself a

241

bad time in the process. Had you noticed?'

'Emily says Da is a good man, but he thinks too much,' Rosie replied, laughing herself.

'Yes, that's perfectly true,' Sarah agreed. 'But rather that than these people who never think at all. What *is* the state of play on your going to train? Don't the courses start in September?'

Rosie nodded.

'Yes, I think they do. I might be too late already to sign up. When we came back from Kerry three weeks ago Granny spoke to Da. He told her, he didn't think he could give to one of his children what he hadn't been able to give to all of them. But he did promise her he'd take counsel and consult his conscience.'

'But wasn't it Granny and Granda who were going to put up the money?' said Sarah frowning.

'Oh yes, it was their offer, but only if Da said yes.'

Sarah nodded and concentrated on overtaking a long trailer carrying a huge metal object like a giant flowerpot being pulled at a snail's pace by a road engine.

'Perhaps Granny will be short of money now Granda has died,' said Rosie anxiously, the thought having just occurred to her.

'No, don't worry, she'll be fine,' Sarah reassured her. 'But there are always tedious things about money when anyone dies. Probate, for example. She may not be able to get at what is actually hers until the solicitors produce the papers. More to the point, Rosie, is that even when she's got access to her money, your father may not be able to let you go.'

'What do you mean, Auntie Sarah?'

'Much as I love Sam, I have to admit he's not exactly made a happy marriage. He works hard, he does his best for his family, but there's not a lot of joy in his life. If you go, he's got even less. He could never admit that you're probably the best thing in his life. But that's why he may not be able to let you go, especially just now when we've lost Da.'

Suddenly and unexpectedly, Rosie saw her father standing on the empty platform at Portadown when they'd waved from the Dublin train. He'd looked so solitary, so alone, she'd been overcome by a dreadful feeling she might never see him again.

'So you think I should stay at home?'

'No, by no means. You must do what is right for you. When I remarried, I had to leave Ma and Pa after being close by for ten years. I knew it would be hard on them, loosing me and Helen and Hugh as well, but they'd have been even more distressed if I hadn't gone. Ma always said a woman *must* move on. She must leave her father or mother when the time comes, otherwise she never grows up to become the person she has it in her to be.'

Rosie took a deep breath. Sometimes things suddenly became clear. Aunt Sarah had known him all her life and what she said about him waiting, and waiting, and then acting, made perfect sense. She was sure now he had indeed spoken to her mother and found a way of ensuring she no longer treated her so badly.

But as for leaving him, that was a different

matter. She felt so confused. Her aunt had said he might not be able to let her go, yet she'd also said a woman must leave her father or mother when the time comes otherwise she never grows up properly. How did you reconcile the two?

She wondered if going to Belfast was still a possibility or if her grandfather's death had in fact taken it away for the moment.

'You're looking very thoughtful, Rosie,' Sarah said, as she drove slowly through Richhill. 'I hope I haven't said anything to upset you. I still have the Quaker habit of speaking when the spirit moves me. Or perhaps I just use them as an excuse,' she added, her eyes sparkling as she laughed at herself.

'No, you haven't upset me,' Rosie said, shaking her head. 'You've helped, just like Granny does. I wish I had someone to tell me the things I need to know. Miss Wilson was very good. I miss her.'

'Couldn't you go and visit her? She might miss you too.'

'I never thought of that,' she admitted. 'She told Da she'd like to see me when he went to explain about my not being able to come for the last week at school, but I haven't managed it yet.'

'Then you must. I know things haven't been easy for you. I'm sure there are good things ahead but you mustn't be shy about going after them.'

She slowed down, swung left into the farmyard and did a neat manoeuvre to leave the car pointing outwards.

'You won't mind if I don't come in, Rosie, will you? I never was a favourite with either your mother or your dear Uncle Joe,' she explained, leaning over and kissing her cheek. 'Write to me when you can spare the time. I'm back in Sloane Square for the foreseeable future. Berlin was just one of Simon's assignments and he'll be back himself in another two weeks.'

Rosie picked up her case from the back seat.

'Good luck and give my love to your dear da.'

Rosie had not been expecting a welcome when she returned home and so she wasn't disappointed. Apart from a kettle boiling its head off on the stove, there was no sign of life as she walked through the open door. The kitchen was empty, dim and muggy with the warmth of the day and the steam from the kettle. She put her suitcase down and moved the kettle back from the heat.

She looked around, noted the general untidiness and the accumulated layer of dust and crumbs under the table. A couple of large blue-bottles buzzed in the bucket where scraps for the hens were kept, the lid having fallen off and not been replaced. She guessed there might well be two weeks' washing awaiting her out in the wash house. There was nothing to be done except change her clothes and pick up where she had left off.

Some time later, going down to the orchard to hang out the first instalment of working shirts and dungarees, she met her mother coming towards her carrying a bucket of eggs in each hand.

'That brown hen is laying away again,' she said

shortly, barely pausing in her step as Rosie lowered her heavy basket of wet washing to the ground. 'I'll hafta get Dolly to look for her nest when she comes back from Loneys. She's a great han' at finding nests,' she added, continuing on her way, speaking to herself as much as to Rosie.

She pegged out the first of her brothers' shirts and looked up at the bright sky, the white clouds streaming out of the west, the sun warm on her damp hands. The breeze was brisk. She thought of Mrs Love and the garden at Rathdrum and smiled to herself. Her washing might well be dry by now.

'Hallo, Rosie. Are ye back?'

Rosie turned hastily to see a tall, ungainly figure standing behind her, looking her up and down.

Their closest neighbour on the uphill side of the farm, Maisie Jackson, was one of the few people in the immediate vicinity Rosie actively disliked. The rolled up magazine Maisie held in her hand indicated she was on her way to visit her mother, the disorder of her lank, straggling hair a sign she'd now taken to using the hole in the hedge the children had made as a shortcut between the orchard and the Jackson's over-grown back garden.

'Shure ye've had a time of it this last while. I'm sure yer granny was glad to have you and her so fond of you, but what'll she do now, the poor woman?'

Maisie's daily bread was gossip. She stood now, her face a study in sympathy, her large, cowlike eyes wide with concern, her mouth

246

twisted in distress. Now thirty-five, the eldest of her large family at work, the younger ones left to amuse themselves, Maisie had recently become one of her mother's closest cronies.

'I really don't know,' said Rosie, shaking her head.

'I'm sure ye've had a time of it, Rosie dear, and you with your own future to think of. D'ye think you'll like it at Castledillon?'

For a moment, Rosie couldn't think what she could possibly mean. Then she remembered her father had warned her about her mother's plan for getting her out of the house by sending her into service.

'I haven't heard any more about it,' she replied warily, trying to stick as near to the truth as possible.

'Maybe you should have a rest before ye look for a wee job, Rosie. What does that nice lookin' woman who brought you home in her motor think? Is she the one that's a ladyship or is it the other one?'

'They both are,' said Rosie, not seeing how to avoid the question. 'Auntie Hannah is a countess and Auntie Sarah is now Lady Hadleigh.'

'Oh, isn't that just lovely, Rosie?' said Maisie, pressing her hands together in an exaggerated gesture of felicity. 'I'm sure you must be thrilled to be able to speak to people like that. Maybe one of them will give you a job and you could marry some sir or lord yourself. 'An you could sit all day doin' nothing, like they do.'

The thought of either of her aunts sitting all day doing nothing was so ludicrous she couldn't think what to say, so she bent quickly to the ground, picked up her father's dungarees and stretched up to pin them on the line.

'Ach, here dear, let me do that,' Maisie said quickly, laying down her magazine on the grass. 'Sure I'm taller than you an' better able for it. I'm sure you'd far rather be readin' one of them books of yours than doing the washin',' she went on with the sort of laugh that she used to encourage confidence.

'Miss Wilson says you're a very clever girl, so I'm told,' Maisie went on, twisting her head to see how this piece of information would be received.

'There are lots of people much cleverer than I am who can't get a job these days, Mrs Jackson. Emily was one, for example. All my brothers and sisters are clever,' she said, trying her best to keep her irritation to herself.

'Yes, indeed they are. I often say that to your mother. What a clever family she has and what a credit they are to her. But not all of them as clever as you, Rosie,' she said coyly. 'No wonder your granny looks after you and buys you nice dresses. Though maybe she won't be able to do that anymore. Wouldn't that be terrible sad after the good time you've had?'

Rosie handed her a clothes peg, then another. After the dungarees, there were only a couple of pairs of underpants left at the bottom of the basket.

'Bereavement is such a terrible thing,' Rosie said suddenly, turning to Maisie as she handed her the next garment. 'You really have no idea what is happening or what people are going to do. Haven't you noticed that yourself, Mrs Jackson, with all the people you've gone to help at times like that? They just don't know what is happening,' she said sadly.

'Ach, indeed yer right. You never spoke a truer word,' Maisie agreed, as she pinned up the last garment and prepared to hoist the whole load on the clothes pole.

Rosie made up her mind she'd been patient long enough and given Maisie no obvious cause for complaint.

'I must get on, Mrs Jackson,' she said with a smile she certainly didn't feel. 'This is only the first lot, there's quite a bit more steeping in the wash house and I'm sure Ma's expecting you.'

'Aye indeed she is, for she's not just herself at the moment. She's very concerned about your Uncle Joe, him not being well and your Da inta the bargain, with this business at his work and all the responsibility fallin' on him. I'm sure he's told you all about it,' she added, as they walked back through the orchard and into the farmyard.

Rosie nodded and said nothing, though a stab of anxiety came upon her at the mention of her father. Whatever was going on at work and whether it was good news or bad, he would tell her in his own good time. The last person she wanted to hear such news from was Maisie Jackson.

She turned aside at the wash-house door with a cheery goodbye she certainly didn't mean and stepped over to the window to watch Maisie walk on across the yard.

'Thon Maisie has a desperit roving eye,' Emily had said, one day when they'd been at home and she'd arrived to visit.

At the time, she'd protested, saying she couldn't imagine anyone more unlikely to have any success with a roving eye, Maisie's unfortunate looks being exceeded only by her unfortunate manner. What Emily had really meant, however, was perfectly demonstrated as Maisie crossed the yard.

Backwards and forwards her eyes moved as she looked everything up and down. She studied the surface of the yard, the paintwork round the windows, the floor brush left outside to dry, the summer flowers in half barrels on either side of the door. Nothing escaped her eagle eye.

With a sudden pang of anxiety Rosie wondered if Maisie had seen something in her own looks she might not be aware of herself, something she'd much rather not have reported to her mother in Maisie's terms. Her clothes could hardly attract attention as they were only her ordinary everyday working things. Her hair was no different from usual, simply pulled back and tied, not even with a new piece of ribbon that could be noticed and commented upon.

Still, she knew well enough we can't always see ourselves. Sometimes in the months before her accident, she'd replied to her mother as coolly and as reasonably as she could and yet her mother had flown into a rage, shouted at her and roundly abused her for 'being sarcastic'.

She wondered if her mother used phrases she'd heard without knowing exactly what they meant, so 'sarcastic' appeared to mean no more than that she was being rude, or cheeky, or guilty of 'answering back'.

It was hard to tell what her mother could possibly have seen that created this anger. The words themselves, the tone and the manner of their using, were the only clue she had, but no dictionary would help her towards understanding what she really meant.

She pounded the saturated dungarees vigorously and rubbed the bits stained with grease or motor oil or grass with slivers of Sunlight soap. Hot water would help, but she was reluctant to go over to the house to boil kettles with Maisie in residence by the stove. She rinsed and mangled three more pairs, one each for Charlie, Sammy and Bobby. They made the clothes basket so heavy to lift, she decided to go back down to the line with them before she added anything more.

The sun was high and dazzled her eyes as she lowered the clothes pole. The wet dungarees blew against her face and caught at her hair as she reached up with the first pair and held them one-handed to put in the first pegs. She stepped aside and wiped her cheek with the back of her wrist and reached up again with the next pair. From somewhere nearby a blackbird sang, indifferent to the flap of the long line of clothes or the rattle of a passing train.

She hung up the third pair, lifted the clothesline on the pole, saw the breeze catch them and inflate them so that they looked like three headless figures. As she lowered the clothespole back into its socket, they showered her with drops of water. She moved back quickly, laughing at herself for not jumping back quickly enough. She wiped her face again on her arm, a handful of pegs still in her hand, her eyes half-closed against the bright light.

'It could be worse,' she whispered to herself. 'It could be worse.'

This was not how she wanted to spend her life, but here and now, at this time, it was a beginning. She thought of her grandfather and the story he liked to tell about 'the fortieth horseshoe'. Day after day in the forge, doing the same things, you had to look for the good things, the wee things, the happy things to set against the boredom of the endless repetition. He said you could always find something, but you had to look.

She thought of two girls, both called Bridget, one in Kerry and one in Banbridge, each in a skimpy black dress with a little white apron. She had a lot more to make her happy than either of them. Running the house, cooking and cleaning and keeping an eye on the two youngest was hard work, but if her mother continued to ignore her, left her the freedom to get on with her work in her own way, she could cope.

Suddenly she remembered the afternoon in the strawberry field the day the news came of her grandfather's sudden collapse, those happy hours when she'd picked fruit and sat on the dry earth looking at leaves and flowers and the view out over the valley beyond. She'd been so content. So unwilling to move or even to speak. There could be times like that in the long days ahead, hours when she could sit in the orchard after the work was done, walk up the lane to see Lizzie, or slip into the barn with a book or her paintbox.

It was up to her to make the best of what she had out of the freedom she could create inside her head, the small pleasures she could contrive, reading and writing letters, or enjoying the company of Emily and Sammy and her father.

Beyond the orchard and the farmyard, beyond the lane that led up to the village and the shops in Richhill, there was a larger world. Twice she had stepped into that world, once in joy when she went to Kerry and once in sadness when she'd shared the loss of her dear Granda. But having once ventured into the world, she now knew there were possibilities out there she might never have been able to imagine had she not done so.

She picked up her basket and made her way slowly back along the path to the gate into the farmyard. For the moment, this was where she had to be, but it would not always be so. She had no idea what might lie ahead of her, but whenever things got really difficult she would have to remind herself that there *was* a different world out there. That some day her life might change as sharply as it had changed twice in the last two months. And when the moment came, as Aunt Sarah had said, she had to seize it and move on.

Seventeen

Autumn lingered that year of 1924. Even in late October, when frost dusted the long grass in the early morning, the afternoons were still often warm and sunny. Rosie made good use of them, taking her sketchbook out into the orchard or up the lane. Sometimes she walked as far as Cannon Hill and climbed the steep slope to the obelisk, a point from which she could look out over the familiar countryside to the mountains beyond Lough Neagh and the pale, misty shadows even further away which were sometimes cloud and sometimes the mountains of Donegal.

She had set herself the task of sketching or painting all the familiar hedgerow plants and flowers she could find and she was amazed at how many there were she'd never noticed before. One of her favourite places for sketching was the old Quaker graveyard at Money, a name which had nothing to do with shillings and florins. It was simply a corruption of the Irish name, Muney, according to Miss Wilson, which meant a bog. True enough, only a little distance from the graveyard, where many of her mother's relatives lay buried, there was indeed a stretch of sodden ground with plants she had never seen before and had not yet been able to identify.

She had no difficulty whatever about going out every afternoon. Sometimes she'd barely finished clearing away the midday meal before some of her mother's cronies arrived. Had she not already announced she was going out, her mother would immediately come up with a good excuse to ensure her absence. Having observed her mother's strategies for a few days, Rosie quickly found ways to make it easy for her.

She and Lizzie went for long walks and shared the story of her growing love for Hugh, a young man whom Rosie could not help but like despite his marked lack of competence in everything he tried to do. Of her own relationship with Patrick Walsh she said little, partly because Lizzie's delight in her own affair appeared to take up almost all their conversation, but also because Rosie herself found it difficult to decide what would be of the slightest interest to Lizzie or indeed exactly what part Patrick *was* playing in her life.

Nevertheless, it was a great comfort to have his letters. True, they were somewhat erratic in their frequency but they were always lengthy when they did come. Together with those from her grandmother, her Aunt Sarah and Bridget O'Shea in Kerry, they gave her something to look forward to.

Rising now in darkness as the November days grew ever shorter, the water on the washstand yet more icy, the lino beyond the bedside rug like marble under bare feet, she encouraged herself each morning by the thought of what the post might bring, rather than on the endlessly

255

repeating chores, the floor which had to be washed more often once the yard became wet and the orchard and fields muddy, the extra bowls of eggs to clean now that the year's chickens were mature enough to lay, and the rips and tears in working clothes as hedges were cut down and ditches cleared before the winter.

She'd tried hard to remember the wisdom of 'the fortieth horseshoe' and do all those things Aunt Sarah had encouraged her to do when life grows oppressively dull, or difficult. For all her efforts, however, in those first months at home, nothing seemed to give her the pleasure she might have expected from it.

On a lovely afternoon, she would find some new plant, or have an unexpected success with a sketch or watercolour, yet find it brought no joy. Bound up in her own happiness though she was, even Lizzie commented on how flat she seemed, how often she missed jokes, or didn't laugh at her lively account of Hugh's latest misfortune.

Standing by the stove waiting for the kettle to boil one morning early in December, the breakfast dishes stacked beside the tin basin on the kitchen table, she looked up at the calendar and smiled to herself. Today was Thursday, her favourite day of the week, the day of her regular visit to her former teacher, now her friend. Even though the days were short and there was less and less daylight for walking or sketching she realized how much better she now felt. She was sure it was thanks to Miss Wilson.

Aunt Sarah had been quite right about going to see her, but she'd delayed for rather a long time, although she'd always liked the older woman. It was October before she finally got round to it and when the time came she'd actually been rather nervous.

She'd dressed very carefully in 'granny's dress', the one made of soft, blue fabric with its pattern of tiny dark and light blue squares. She'd brushed her hair thoroughly, polished her shoes and made sure she had a clean handkerchief tucked up her sleeve.

The moment Miss Wilson opened the door, she knew she'd been silly to be anxious, for her greeting was so warm and direct.

'My dear Rose, how delightful to see you. I did appreciate your note. I'm afraid not all my former pupils deploy the courtesies which they embraced while they were under my tutelage. Please, do come in. Mother is with me in the sitting room but I fear she can take little part in conversation. Nevertheless, she must not be excluded. I'm sure you understand.'

She led the way past the large front rooms that served as schoolrooms and opened the door to a dim and crowded sitting room lit only by one small window overlooking the garden.

Rosie had never seen old Mrs Wilson before. The sight of the small, squat figure filling the armchair by the window distressed her. Like an illustration from an old book, or a painting symbolizing age, she was dressed entirely in black except for a startlingly white mob cap. From the way her eyes moved it was clear she was almost blind. From the nature of Miss Wilson's introduction, it appeared she was also very deaf.

'Now do sit down, my dear. I want to hear what's been happening to you. I was so very sad you couldn't be here for our *conversazione* and our leaving celebrations. I'm sure Elizabeth will have told you all about them.'

Rosie nodded and smiled, grateful she'd remembered in time there was actually one person in the world who called Lizzie by her baptismal name.

'Now, how is your grandmother, Rose? Have you been to visit her since her bereavement?'

Rosie shook her head.

'I'm afraid Granny has been quite ill. Auntie Hannah thinks it's shock and exhaustion after all those nights she sat up with Granda, but Auntie Sarah says it might just be bad luck. She was perfectly well when she went to London to stay with her, but by the time she'd moved on to Auntie Hannah in Gloucestershire she'd developed some sort of chest infection. She was really very poorly for several weeks. But she's much better now,' she added quickly, seeing the look of concern on Miss Wilson's face.

'Loss breeds loss, Rose. It is a sad thing to say, but true. When we lose someone we love, we often lose other things as well. Our courage, our hope, our health. I'm afraid I've known too many individuals who have become ill after a major loss. How have you been feeling yourself?'

Rose hesitated. She'd not been at all ill herself but she remembered Lizzie had asked her more than once if she was all right.

'I'm not sure how to answer your question,'

258

she began, aware of the clear blue eyes that focused closely upon her.

'I thought I would feel very sad, but I didn't. I could see that Granda's going was not nearly as bad as what might have happened. One of his doctors told me what it could have been like. But since I've come home, I've felt very dull and flat, even when I'm doing things I like to do, sketching, or painting, or writing letters. I can't quite explain the feeling...'

Miss Wilson was sitting upright in her chair just as she'd taught her girls to sit, back straight, feet placed neatly together, hands folded, her attention alert but relaxed. Poor Lizzie had never managed to sit in the approved manner for more than five minutes. She herself had done better, finding that practice did help. The thought that Lizzie might practice sitting still made her smile to herself, but she didn't let it distract her from what she was trying to say.

Miss Wilson waited patiently to see if Rosie had anything to add, but in the end, Rosie admitted to herself that she found it impossible to say more about how she felt.

She looked hopefully towards the familiar figure in her rather faded, brown, everyday dress. She'd worn the same dress all through the year Rosie had been her pupil, but then, as now, she'd decorated it each week with a freshly-laundered collar embroidered with small, pale flowers and pinned with a little brooch.

'I had a dear friend once,' the older woman began when Rosie remained silent, 'who lost her father when she was in her thirties. He'd been so

259

ill, it *was* a merciful relief when he died, but for months and months afterwards she felt all the joy had gone out of her life. She was older than I was and fortunately she had a wise friend who said something to her which I have never forgotten. She said, "Grief is not sharp and pointed, it's grey and flat, like a fog, and because you can't see it, you don't know why life seems so dreary" '.

Rosie nodded enthusiastically.

'That is *so* exactly right,' she declared, taking a deep breath. 'Because I wasn't crying, or feeling desperate, I thought I was somehow my normal self, though Elizabeth did keep asking me if I felt all right. But what you've just said is so true. I couldn't see anything was wrong, so I didn't think anything was.'

Rosie had once found Miss Wilson rather formidable, but now, sitting in the small, over-crowded sitting room, the old woman asleep in her chair, she saw a different person, a rather sad, but very kind person who would certainly answer her questions and give her the advice she was sure to need, just like Aunt Sarah had suggested.

She had no idea why Miss Wilson had never married, but she suddenly realized that she couldn't have had a very easy life, working to support herself and her mother and caring for her as she herself reached her seventies. Remembering things she'd said in the last year, little stories she'd told to illustrate points she was making in class, it seemed that friends she'd once had were no more. Either dead or now removed far beyond regular contact.

'I was wondering, Rose, whether you might do me a small service.'

'I most certainly will if I can,' Rosie replied promptly.

'I've been finding it very difficult to go and collect my library books. It's only a short distance to my kind neighbour's house, but she has some difficulty with walking and I feel I cannot leave Mother unattended. Were you to come and visit me one afternoon a week, you could collect the books Mrs Rountree's daughter brings from the library in Armagh while you were here and we might, if you wish, share our literary explorations together.'

Reflecting on her first visit to Miss Wilson, Rosie was still putting plates back on the dresser when she remembered she'd be collecting a new *Flora of Ireland* for them, this week. It had been on request for some time now. Finally, it had become available. With its help, they hoped to identify not only the plants she'd found in Money bog, but also the pressed flowers she'd brought back from Kerry, now mounted on sheets of drawing paper.

Turning away from the dresser, Rosie caught sight of her mother hurrying towards the house.

'Ye may come an' give me a han',' she said abruptly, as she arrived breathless at the door. 'Bobby's away t' Portadown an' Joe's slipped on the squit the cows left. Not lookin' where he was goin' as usual. He's filthy an' he says his leg's broke.'

Rosie followed her quickly as she turned back

261

towards the byre. Obviously in pain and equally obviously in a temper, Uncle Joe sat on the splattered surface of the yard.

'It's broke. Ah know it's broke. Ye may get the doctor.'

It was not the smell of fresh cow dung that made Rosie feel ill as she put her arm round him, it was the stale odour of tobacco and sour sweat from his unwashed body. The stubble on his chin scraped against her cheek as they lifted him to his feet.

'Sure ye know I can't walk,' he said, glaring from one to the other, while he stood on one leg, their arms still supporting him.

Rosie had been concerned they might have difficulty lifting him, for her mother had never had much strength in her arms and always complained she couldn't carry buckets of water if they were full, but Uncle Joe had been far lighter than she'd expected. Even so, they couldn't possibly carry him all the way up the yard and over to the house.

'If we support you, Uncle Joe, you could hop on your good leg,' Rosie suggested.

He twisted his face towards her and scowled, his tobacco-stained teeth only inches from her face.

'Or we can set you down again and bring you a chair till the doctor comes,' she added, glancing up at the sky.

'Aw, that's a great idea, isn't it? What d'ye think of that, Martha? Leave me out here an' the rain about to pour down.'

'Well, it would wash the shit off ye,' her

mother threw back, so promptly that Rosie had the greatest difficulty in keeping her face straight.

When he finally agreed to hop, he'd leaned on them so heavily they'd ended up half carrying him.

'Ye may go up to Woodview an' phone for the doctor,' Martha said, as they deposited him thankfully in his chair by the stove.

'I could go up to Lizzie's. It would be quicker.'

'Have Mackay's got the phone?'

Rosie wondered yet again how her mother could express such a wealth of meaning in one brief phrase. She managed to make acquiring a telephone sound as if it were a deliberately disloyal challenge to the normal and proper way of conducting life.

'It's for Mr Mackay's business,' she explained.

'Take my purse and pay for it then. We don't want to be under an obligation to the Mackays. We're just as good as they are, phone or no phone.'

Uncle Joe was quite right about his leg. It *was* broken.

The doctor was a man in his fifties. His hair had receded creating a long, gleaming forehead that looked as if he might have polished it each morning at the same time as he shone up his spectacles and his gold watch. Rosie heard him mutter to himself about a 'greenstick fracture', but she judged he was not the kind of doctor who would welcome questions or be very forthcoming with his explanations.

'I'm afraid we'll need X-rays, Mrs Hamilton. That means Armagh Infirmary. Do you have transport?'

'What kind of transport?'

'A motor car would be ideal,' he replied, with an unpleasant smile, clearly indicating that he felt he was dealing with one of the less able-minded of his patients.

Martha shook her head.

'Then I'm afraid it's a matter of waiting for the ambulance. I'll telephone the hospital when I get back to my surgery this afternoon. They might be able to come today. If not, sometime tomorrow.'

Rosie didn't have to look at her mother or Uncle Joe to know how they'd react to this. It was still only mid-morning and Joe was clearly in considerable pain. Richard P would be horrified. In this situation he'd take Uncle Joe to hospital himself, cow shit or no cow shit.

She took a deep breath, picked up the old jotter in which she made lists of things needed in the house and smiled at him sweetly.

'Perhaps I could make the telephone call and save you the trouble, doctor. We don't have a motor, but we do have a kind neighbour with a telephone. If you would just tell me who to ask for at the hospital, I can find the number myself in the telephone book. I expect they will need your authorization,' she added, her pencil poised. 'Just tell me what I'm to say.'

He did as he was asked without further ado, collected his fee and disappeared while Rosie ran up the hill and made the call. The ambulance arrived less than an hour later driven by a large man with an even larger young lad as his helper. They picked up Uncle Joe as if he were an overgrown child.

'Ye spoke up rightly to yer man,' Joe said, eyeing Rosie as she and Martha went out to the ambulance with him. 'Maybe a bit of education comes in handy after all. I'm beholden to you, as the sayin' is.'

They banged shut the heavy doors of the ambulance and drove off. Rosie thought how out of place it looked, still painted camouflage green, for it was one of those paid for by the people of Armagh in 1914 and given to their local regiment.

Two weeks later, Joe died in Armagh Infirmary. Not from the leg injury which had taken him to hospital, but from a cancer, probably long established, they said, which became suddenly active, turning his face to a sickly yellow and dropping off what little flesh remained on his gaunt frame.

On a damp and misty December afternoon, Rosie saw him carried up the hill on the shoulders of her father and brothers to the quiet Quaker graveyard, where, years earlier, some more devout member of his family had ensured burial rights, even for those, like Joe, who had not set foot in a Meeting House since his boyhood and who had never to the best of her knowledge managed to say a good word for the Quakers who now provided his resting place.

Joe's departure inevitably meant there would have to be changes in the routine of the household, but at this low point of the year, with the cattle stalled for the winter months, there was little obvious change to the farm routine for Martha and Bobby. Recently, Joe had avoided the milking and he'd left all the heavy work to Bobby.

Rosie did sometimes feel there was an easier atmosphere in the house. For a start, her father came over from the barn in the late evening more often to sit by the fireside in the chair Uncle Joe had habitually occupied. She herself was glad enough not to have to wash his smelly underclothes, when he could be persuaded to change them, and even happier to escape having to clean his room. While he would not spit in the kitchen under Martha's eye, he had observed no such limitation in *his* room.

No, she could not be sorry he was gone and yet she found herself puzzling over his life, fitting together the few fragments she'd picked up about his adventures as a young man prospecting in Alaska and working on the Canadian railways with his brothers.

Why he had come home no one knew. Some said there was a woman in it, as so often in these stories. Others said he was homesick. But nothing anyone said about Joe suggested he'd ever made any contribution to the happiness of another human being.

If the details of Uncle Joe's life puzzled Rosie, her mother's reaction to his death puzzled her even more.

From the moment the news of his death arrived, she'd been in the best of good spirits. Naturally, she'd gone through the appropriate rituals with her neighbours. Poor Joe was lamented as a man who hadn't made much of his life. God Bless the crater. Thus the pieties were observed, but with moderation. Martha did not try to soften the picture of a waspish and egocentric man. Rather, she took the line that we all have it in us to make a poor job of life and, but for the grace of God, we any of us might end our days like Joe.

More relevant to Rosie than merely the lift in spirits which Joe's death had produced in her mother, however, was the change in her behaviour towards herself. It came as a shock the first time Martha was polite to her. Where once she'd replied to any enquiry about a meal or a job with a sharp, 'Suit yerself', she would now say, 'Whatever suits you best'.

She was baffled and for once Lizzie could think of no possible reason, even though she did manage to forget about Hugh for long enough to give the matter her full attention.

The respite was invaluable to Rosie. There was no objection now to her spending a weekend with her grandmother when she finally arrived home just after Christmas, to escape the predictable January storms.

Back at the farm again, much encouraged by her grandmother's obvious pleasure in her return to Rathdrum and her modest plans for occupying herself during the worst winter months, she was able to redecorate Uncle Joe's bedroom. She suggested to Bobby and Jack that they share the room. There would then be space in the barn for a long workbench where Charlie and Sammy

267

would have a much better place for their new wireless receiving set. Already, the previous September, they'd managed to pick up the first Northern Ireland broadcast.

After a little good-natured teasing Charlie and Sammy, delighted by this plan, agreed that a small area of the new work bench, just under one of the two small, north-facing windows would be kept free of wires, aerials, soldering irons and valves, so that Rosie had a space were she could work.

Even with the paraffin heater lit and a rug round her knees, it was very hard to keep warm in January, but having a place of her own with a piece of bench where she could paint, or write letters, was such a pleasure that she used it every afternoon until the point at which her hands got too cold to hold either brush or pen. A hundred times better than writing by candlelight sitting up in bed with a coat round her shoulders, she thought, every time she started out on another letter to Patrick.

Writing to Patrick was not as easy as she'd imagined it would be. At first, she thought it was because the shadow of her grandfather's death had come so soon after the happiness of her time in Kerry. As time passed, however, and Patrick's letters grew less frequent, she realized how anxious she was as she took them up.

Always they were lengthy, as much as a dozen small, closely written sheets, but each time, as she read, she felt a strange disappointment creep over her.

It wasn't that what he wrote wasn't interesting

in itself and quite new to her. Yeats and Joyce and Synge he'd studied closely. He had so much to say about them, but they were simply names to her and when she asked questions so that she might understand better, he never answered them. He just went on about the literary scene in Dublin and his own observations on it, as if she knew the people he mentioned and was as involved in their disagreements as he seemed to be.

She wondered why he never took up any of the things she said about her own life, never asked what she was doing, or even what she was reading. More than once, it came into her mind that it was so different from the way Richard P. related to her. But then, she told herself, she had to accept her talk with Richard had always been face to face. Letters couldn't be expected to have that kind of immediacy.

Then there were passages where Patrick rode off, as she put it to herself, saying such extravagant things about Ireland and its past, or about love and its transforming power. Scattered with phrases in Irish, she wondered if she should find such passages romantic, but sadly, she had to admit to herself, they just made her feel uneasy, even a little cross as she'd said she couldn't read Irish. Sometimes it felt as if he were addressing someone she simply didn't recognize.

She encouraged herself by considering that he might have problems with being direct, just like Emily. Meantime, she did her best. Writing letters was one of her pleasures and she continued to write in the hope that she might begin to understand better someone who was so different from anyone she had ever met.

It was a bitterly cold morning in February when the happy state of affairs that had existed since Uncle Joe's death came to an end. Walking cautiously back from the ash pit, her eyes scanning the yard for any telltale gleam of ice, Rosie saw the postman leave his bicycle by the gate.

'Hallo, Rosie. You're outa luck today,' the young man greeted her.

He'd asked her to go out with him so often that she'd finally let it drop she had a boyfriend in Dublin in the hope it might discourage him. Clearly a mistake, she decided, as she came up to him. All he'd done was to identify Patrick's letters, measure the gap between them, and wait hopefully for them to stop. His face was always downcast when there was a fat envelope with a Dublin postmark and Patrick's unmistakable scrawl.

'One for yer ma ... ah hello, Mrs Hamilton,' he said quickly as Martha suddenly appeared from her bedroom and almost snatched a long, stiff envelope from his hand.

'What about the dance in the Orange Hall, Rosie?'

'On Saturday?'

His face lit up.

'Sorry, I'm going to see my granny in Banbridge.'

'Ah well, maybe the next one then,' he said, grinning hopefully.

Going back into the kitchen, she found her

mother searching for her spectacles. She found them for her in the spare sugar bowl on the dresser, a place she used regularly when a neighbour surprised her and she didn't want to be seen wearing them.

'The oul bugger. The ould bugger,' Martha screeched. 'Damn his soul for a liar. May he rot in Hell,' she shouted, as she threw the heavy sheets of paper on the floor and rushed out of the house.

Crossing to the door, Rosie saw her stride up the yard and turn out of the gate, heading down the lane towards the station. It looked as if Aggie Hutchinson, her nearest neighbour and cousin, was the most likely destination.

For a moment she hesitated. Then she picked up the sheets of paper. A single glance told her it was from the solicitor in Portadown with whom Uncle Joe had always done business. The main letter was quite short, the second page was a typed copy of an earlier document. She scanned them both quickly.

'My goodness,' she said to herself, as she read the letter through again and began to make sense of the information revealed by the formal language.

Her mother's anger was at least understandable. For years Uncle Joe had said he was leaving the farm to her. Family and neighbours had heard him say so many, many times. She herself was quite used to hearing her mother say, 'one day when I own this place'. In fact, the phrase was something of a warning. Her mother used it whenever she was in a really bad mood, particularly if she wanted to annoy their father.

The letter revealed that the farm was not Uncle Joe's to leave to anyone. It had been left to him for his lifetime and was then to pass to his surviving brothers in America, or to their male offspring in the event of their prior decease. The second sheet of paper was a transcript from the original will made by Joe's father.

She put the sheets down on the table and picked up the envelope as if it might have something more to tell her, and indeed it had. The letter was addressed to *both* her parents. Probably her mother had never even noticed. The size, shape and weight of the envelope told her where it had come from and she'd simply ripped it open, expecting to read she was now the new owner of the farm, left to her by the will of her late uncle, Mr Joe Loney, deceased.

She had not for one moment expected to find that the solicitors were already engaged in tracing the new owners in Pennsylvania and hoped shortly to be in direct contact with them. Nor would she have appreciated the courteously worded warning that in the circumstances it would be provident to assume the new owners might prefer to sell the property rather than to receive a weekly rent.

Rosie took a deep breath, folded the letter in its original creases, replaced it in its envelope and put it behind the clock where her father would be sure to see it when he came in from work.

The news completely changed the situation. It was possible they would have to give up the farm and find somewhere else to live. That would mean her father having no workshop, her mother having no animals to care for and poor Bobby having no work at all.

However much she thought about the family and the effects a move might have on each of them, what was clear to her was much more personal. The improved atmosphere since Uncle Joe's death had come to a sudden, dramatic end. The person most likely to suffer from Martha's bitterness and disappointment would be herself.

Eighteen

After a wild and blustery March, with Martha's violent outbursts as turbulent as the gale force winds and her comments as sharp as the continuing frosts, April brought no change in her bitter mood. In complete contrast, a sudden settling of the weather blessed them with blue skies and sunshine and the first real warmth of the year.

The coming of spring had always been marked for Rosie, not by the budding of trees, nor even the visible growth of new grass, but by the flowering of a particular patch of lesser celandine on the steep bank of the lane exactly opposite the drive leading up to Lizzie's house.

'Hallo,' she said out loud to herself, smiling broadly. 'Good to see you again.'

She stopped to stare into the hundreds of small bright faces which had not been there even the previous day when she'd walked past on her Thursday visit to Miss Wilson.

As she stood looking down, the sun warm on her shoulders, the ecstatic song of small birds all around her, she wondered what else the sun might have coaxed into leaf or flower. Glancing across the lane, she caught her breath in pure delight. A south-facing branch of Mackay's ancient magnolia was outlined against the pure blue of the sky, its exotic pink and white buds unfolding almost as she watched.

'I shall have to take one of you home with me,' she announced in the deserted lane, as she collected her thoughts, for once almost reluctant to move on, to pass beneath it and make her way up the drive and round to the back kitchen where Lizzie would be waiting for her.

Lizzie and her mother were there together, wiping the day's eggs, a large bowl on the table between them.

'Hallo, Rosie, any news?'

To her surprise, it was Mrs Mackay who addressed her. Standing in a patch of sunshine that fell through the kitchen window and lit up the table where they worked, she was smiling broadly. Grey and drawn even on one of her infrequent 'good days', her face now looked quite different, softer and with a hint of colour. What really surprised Rosie were her eyes. She'd never before noticed that they were so vivid a green.

She shook her head.

'Maybe, Rosie, these American relations will turn out to be *sooo* rich they won't be interested in a wee place in Ireland,' she went on.

'Well, that would be one solution.'

The suggestion had been put with such light-heartedness, Mrs Mackay's way of referring to 'a wee place in Ireland' had so distinct an ironic edge to it, that she could not help but laugh.

'Now away on the pair of you and enjoy your walk,' she said briskly, beaming at them both.

'Sure it's beautiful out. I'll finish the eggs, Lizzie. And then I'm going to sit in the garden and *do* nothing,' she announced with a wink and a vigorous nod of her head.

'Lizzie, what's happened to your ma? I can't believe it,' Rosie demanded, the moment they were out of earshot.

'You'll not believe me if I tell you,' said Lizzie, staring at her wide-eyed.

'Of course, I'll believe you.'

Lizzie viewed this comment with scepticism, but nevertheless she pressed her lips together, stared up at the sky and launched forth.

'She has this friend she used to go to school with that comes and visits her. She's quite nice really, but a bit religious, always quoting the Bible and saying she'll pray for me,' Lizzie began, shrugging her shoulders impatiently. 'Anyway, this friend had this idea about Ma going to some kind of a healer over Loughgall way. Ma wasn't keen. She's been to so many doctors and specialists she says they only make her worse, because she gets depressed, as well as feeling awful when they've finished with her. Anyway, a couple of weeks ago, she must have given in to Faith, or Mercy, I can never remember which, an' gone to see yer man. She never told me, but I noticed she was gettin' up more and eatin' better. An' Da and I couldn't believe it when she started to laugh and pull our legs again. Do you remember, she always used to laugh an' pull our legs when we were at Richhill School?'

Rosie nodded and waited for her to go on.

'This man, it seems, waved his hands around a

276

bit over her, told her something she wasn't to repeat to anyone and gave her a list of things she's not to eat. Eggs and milk and butter, I think it was. And she's near back to normal. But it might wear off, Rosie,' Lizzie ended, suddenly bursting into tears.

'Oh there, love, don't cry. Don't cry. It's wonderful news.'

She put her arms round her and found them a place to sit on a grassy bank nearby.

'Do you not think it will?' Lizzie sniffed. 'Sure, we're always hearin' about miracles from these Tent Missions, but sure they never last.'

'But this wasn't a Tent Mission, Lizzie. This was different,' she said firmly. 'There was something about your mother today that isn't going to go away. I don't understand it any more than you, but I think she's back to stay. And I'm so happy for you,' she added, hugging her again, her own eyes filling with tears.

Rosie thought of Richard P as she stroked Lizzie's hair and heard the sniffs grow less frequent. In these last months, she had to admit to herself it wasn't just things with a medical connection that made her think of him. She'd come to accept how much she wished she could talk to him the way they'd talked in the kitchen or the garden at Rathdrum during that long, long week of her grandfather's dying.

Often enough, she'd asked herself how such a sad time could have brought her such moments of happiness. Gaiety even. When she thought of Richard himself, of the hours she'd spent with Aunt Sarah and with Helen she wished so much she could see them all again.

Even Frances Harrington and Hugh Sinton, her cousins, very mature young men now down from university, she'd been able to be easy with, though at first she'd not been sure what to make of their formal manners and their English accents. Once she'd got over the unfamiliarity, she'd discovered just how friendly and approachable they both were. She'd only to say there was a job needing an extra pair of hands, or a trip into Banbridge to be made, and they were there, ready and willing to do whatever she asked.

Lizzie had wiped her eyes and was now looking much more like herself.

'I've got some news for you, Rosie.'

Although Lizzie was smiling now, a wave of anxiety swept over her. News, these days, always seemed to make life yet more difficult.

'Hugh and I are going to get married.'

'What!'

Rosie was completely taken aback. Apart from the fact that Lizzie was a month younger than she was and wouldn't be seventeen until August, she'd made no secret of the fact that Hugh had been trying to get a better job and had been completely unsuccessful. She couldn't possibly think they might live on the pittance he earned from doing odd jobs and running messages for Mr Lamb of Fruitfield.

'Ach, keep yer hair on Rosie, I don't mean now this minit,' Lizzie replied sharply. 'It'll be a year or two yet, but we've made up our minds. We're engaged. But it's a secret, except for you.'

'Oh Lizzie, that's lovely. I'm so pleased for you both and I'm very honoured. I won't tell a soul. I promise.'

'We've worked out a plan. Do you want to hear?'

'Of course I do.'

'Well, it does depend on Ma staying the way she is. I couldn't leave her if she was poorly, but if she stays well, I'm goin' to Belfast to do a course in typing and bookkeeping. Hugh's never going to get anywhere where he is, but if I had the money to start a shop or a wee business, he'd be fine. He's grand talkin' to people an' helpin' them, so long as I was there to keep an eye on him and do the paperwork.'

Rosie nodded and listened. There was no doubt Lizzie had got the measure of her Hugh. She was quite unperturbed by the fact that his only apparent capacity was a very appealing good-naturedness. Apart from that, she knew that he'd always be willing to try and he would listen to her and do what she asked.

'But where would you get the money to start a shop, Lizzie? Would your father be able to help you?'

'He might, but I'd rather get started first, so he sees what a good job we can make of it. I've had a bit of a surprise,' she went on, her face lighting up, her tears totally forgotten. 'We worked out what we were going to do an' it was all fine, but for the money. Guess what?' she demanded. 'Ma had this letter from Toronto,' she went on without waiting for a reply. 'I've a godmother I've never met. She was Ma's bridesmaid and she went to Canada. She's just died an' left me a hundred pounds. We only heard yesterday.'

'Oh Lizzie, that's just great,' Rosie said, clutching her hand. 'What did Hugh say when you told him?'

'He said, would you believe it, that whatever we did we'd always be all right. That we'd never want for money.'

She raised her eyes heavenwards and shook her dark curls.

'If I didn't love him, I'd think he wasn't quite right in the head.'

'But you *do* love him. I think loving someone makes everything different.'

'How d'you mean?'

Rosie frowned and pressed her lips together.

'I know Hugh's right, but I can't explain why. Not properly. I think it has something to do with having someone to help, having a friend, a partner, someone who'll tell you things you don't know for yourself and listening when you do the same for them...'

She stopped in mid-sentence, a familiar voice saying to her, 'Two heads are better than one, Rosie.'

It was her grandfather's voice and the phrase was one of his favourites. Whether it was a problem at the mills or difficulties with the people who worked the machines, he always assumed there was something he might not have thought of, something crucial that someone else would see immediately.

Time and time again, and especially when they were all together in Kerry, she'd heard him ask

Granny what she thought. Yes, they sometimes disagreed, but they always talked things over and they always listened to each other. Yet she felt it was something more than talking and listening. It was what was between them. Maybe it was love itself. She really didn't know, but it wouldn't surprise her at all if Hugh and Lizzie ended up making a most successful team, just like Granny and Granda.

'When had you thought of starting the course, Lizzie?' she asked, aware she'd fallen silent. 'Would you travel by train every day or go into digs and come home at the weekends?'

'I'd go into digs. I've an auntie who takes people. Then, you see, I could do my studyin' in the evenings and not have anythin' to do but see Hugh when I came home at weekends.'

Rosie laughed. She never thought she'd see the day when Lizzie would make plans to study. But here she was setting aside four evenings a week and looking happy about it.

With so many new ideas to explore, they walked and talked all afternoon. When they parted finally on the lane beside the lesser celandines, Rosie was so full of thoughts of her own she forgot all about the spray of magnolia blossom she'd wanted to take home and paint.

Days passed and still there was no news from the solicitors. Martha came hurrying up the yard every time she saw the postman, or sat down and wrote to them herself every few days. On one occasion, she took the train to Portadown only to find the person she needed to speak to was out all day at the Petty Sessions in Armagh. She continued to bite everyone's head off until the middle of April when at last the expected letter arrived.

The Loney relatives had been traced. Clearly they had not made a fortune in Pennsylvania, as Lizzie's mother had hoped. They were delighted to have acquired a farm in Ireland and assumed it was worth a great deal of money, despite having been given a description of the house and the acreage of the land. They wanted it sold as quickly as possible.

As her mother stumped off to regale her neighbour with this latest piece of news, Rosie knew there was nothing she could do but accept there'd be another furious row the moment her father came home. At least the stew she'd just made for the evening meal could sit waiting on the back of the stove without spoiling until the worst was over.

'An' what are you goin' to do about that, may I ask?' Martha demanded, as she thrust the letter into his hand the moment he came through the door.

Before her father even had time to scan the contents she was at him.

'Are we goin' to be put out on the street before you lift a finger?'

He made no response, re-read the short letter a second time and placed it gently on the table.

'What would you like me to do, Martha?'

'Well, you could do somethin' an' not leave it all to me,' she spat out, quite indifferent to the presence of Dolly and Jack who now disappear-

282

ed as quickly as they could.

'And what purpose have your letters served? Or your visit? There was nothing to be done till we had more information,' he went on in the same even tone.

Rosie saw that he was very tired. He had a way of sitting in his chair and rubbing his forehead when the day had been heavier or more demanding than usual.

'Ye can't just let them sell this place over our heads.'

'Have I proposed that they should?'

'You've *proposed* nothin',' she came back at him, her voice heavy with sarcasm. 'You've done nothin'. You've just sat there and let me worry about what's to happen to us all.'

'Well, if that is what you think, Martha, then you'll be pleased at the news I have for you tonight,' he began, speaking even more slowly. 'I'll not be here to annoy you for the next couple of months. We've got the contract for the transverse engine job and I've accepted the charge of getting it to the mill. I'll be home for a few hours from time to time and possibly an occasional Sunday, but meantime you can send me the solicitor's letters with Bobby or Rosie. Now there is something that might be done, I shall give them my full attention.'

Not waiting for a reply, he stood up stiffly and made his way out of the house and across to the barn.

Undeterred, her mother's voice continued to hurl abuse after him, her parting shots quite predictable and equally unreasonable.

Rosie watched him go. Hungry and tired after a day's work this was what he had to come home to. Night after night, she greeted him with hostile silence or an ill-tempered nag. The thought of what he'd suffered through all the years she'd been old enough to observe and understand came near to overwhelming her. At that moment, all she could think off was escaping herself to some safe place where her mother's anger could not reach her, but she knew she had nowhere to go.

Suddenly she remembered what Auntie Sarah had said as they drove back from Rathdrum after Granda's funeral. That her father had put up with things she herself would never have tolerated for five minutes. That he waited and waited, but in the end he acted.

She remembered how he'd spoken to her mother after her own 'accident'. What he'd said she could not even imagine, but he had succeeded in altering her behaviour out of all recognition. In this latest crisis, she had to hope he would find as successful an answer.

Moving out of the corner by the dresser, where she'd been filling a jug with spring water for the supper table when her father arrived, she crossed to the stove, took a warm plate from the oven, served a generous portion of stew, covered it with another plate and carried it carefully over to the barn.

Her mother called after her, but she pretended she hadn't heard.

'Here you are, Da,' she said, taking a knife and fork out of her apron pocket. 'Don't let it spoil your appetite.'

He managed a smile as she took the top plate away and the smell of well-cooked food rose into the air. He made no reply but began to eat slowly as if he had barely the energy to lift the fork to his mouth.

Rosie sat down in the old armchair and waited. If she didn't go back to the house, her mother might well hand out generous second helpings to Dolly and Jack and leave no more than the scrapings of the pot for Emily and Charlie when they arrived home. It was a risk she would have to take.

Neither her father nor herself had ever had a problem sitting silently together in the barn, for they had never felt any need to talk for the sake of talking. If they did have to leave the farm, it would be the barn she'd miss far more than the house. Here in his workshop surrounded by the strange smells of oil and lubricant, acetylene and petrol, she felt at ease in a way she never felt in the house, even when her mother was out in the byre or in the fields and she had the place to herself.

'That was very nice, dear,' he said, clearing his plate. 'You're a real good cook. I'll have to cook my own dinner for a while now, or let one of the boys do it. I'm not sure which of us would be the worst at it,' he added with a little laugh.

'How long, Da?'

'Two months, maybe three. Depends on the weather.'

'To Milford?'

He smiled his slow smile and there was a hint of laughter about his eyes.

'Sure I know you could do it in an hour on a bicycle,' he declared, leaning back against the workbench behind him. 'The load is half the size of this barn. If we do half a mile in a day, it'll be good goin'. An' we may have to move at night. Forby, there's a couple of bridges on the way, we may have to by-pass or re-build. There'll be a road engineer to advise us and the police are involved as well. There'll be a few headaches, I'm tellin' you.'

'Won't you be able to leave it at night, or on Sundays? I can't see anyone pinching it, can you?'

'No, there's no fear of that,' he agreed. 'But there'll be two, maybe three, road engines and all their gear. There's plenty of worthwhile stuff to tempt thieves. Besides that we'll have to show lights at all times. There's a caravan where we'll cook and sleep. Two on every night and I'm responsible for the whole show.'

'When do you start?'

'Monday.'

'So soon?'

'Ach it should have been last autumn, but there was a delay at the foundry. Then the weather was bad. Now they've finished arguin', it's urgent. The mills are not in a good way since the war. If they don't keep up to date they'll lose what orders there are. It's hard times for everybody, Rosie, and you and Bobby have your share to put up with,' he added with a sigh.

He stood up, opened a drawer in the work-bench, poked around among packets of differently sized nails and produced two battered

286

envelopes.

'When Joe died, I decided you and Bobby should have some payment for all the work you do, even if the sum is very small. But with this business over the farm, I felt it wise not to mention it,' he explained, handing her an envelope. 'Now that I won't be here very often for some months, I'm givin' you your half year's pay now. It'll mean you can go and visit your granny whenever you want. Or maybe there's somethin' you're savin' up for, like Emily,' he continued, a flicker of anxiety passing over his face. 'I'll see Bobby before I go.'

Rosie put the envelope in her apron pocket, kissed his cheek and picked up his empty plate.

'I'll borrow a bicycle and come and see you. You won't be far away for quite a while, will you? And I can bring you something to heat up in your caravan.'

'Can ye ride mine?'

'Yes, of course, but won't you need it?'

He laughed silently, his face breaking into the broad grin which so delighted her.

'I won't be goin' anywhere on a bicycle after Monday mornin' goin to work. I'll ask the boss to drop it back when he's passin' and you an' Bobby can use it. Don't let Jack out on it,' he warned. 'It's too big for him.'

He turned away, glanced over his workbench to see which of the urgent jobs sitting there he might finish before he went, then turned back towards her.

'I doubt if I'll even get away for a few hours to go and see your Granny,' he said sadly. 'I'll drop her a line. But it would do her more good to see you. Will you go as often as you can? Don't let your ma stand in your way. The family'll not starve for a weekend.'

She assured him she would and gathered herself for whatever she'd find when she went back over to the house.

Rosie couldn't quite believe it when she opened the envelope and took out a carefully folded five-pound note. Unlike the envelope which was grubby and covered with oily fingerprints, the large parchment note with its silver stripe and beautiful flowing script was perfectly clean. Only rarely had she seen a five-pound note before and she'd certainly never possessed one.

She thought of Bridget O'Shea when she'd come to say goodbye the night before they'd left the hotel in Waterville. She'd told her that her granda had been very good to her. Paper money, she'd said. If there were a few more like him she'd soon have her ticket and her travel money saved.

As she refolded the large note and put it back in the envelope Rosie's first thought was that she could now pay her debts. She'd come home from Kerry with the money her grandparents had given her for her holiday, money she'd never been able to spend because every time she went to buy something, her grandfather had bought it for her. But that money was long gone. Stamps and watercolour paper had used it up by Christmas. A few sixpences from her mother when she'd been in a good mood after Uncle Joe died had bought some new tubes of paint, but since then it was Emily who'd paid for her stamps and her drawing paper.

'Well, I've some good news for you, Emily,' she announced, as they walked up the lane together on Saturday afternoon to do the weekly shop.

'That would make a nice change,' Emily replied sharply.

Rosie looked at her, surprised by the tone. One of Emily's gifts was the ability not to let their mother upset her. She could sit in the kitchen looking at the newspaper and appear not to notice what was going on around her, whoever might be getting the sharp edge of their mother's tongue. It was seldom Emily herself, for she had a knack of not hearing what was said, or looking completely baffled at hostile comments should they come her way.

'Oh Emily, what's wrong? Have you had some bad news I don't know about?'

'Ach no, it's just the usual. I wish Sammy got home oftener. An' now Da's goin' away...'

Her voice trailed away and Rosie recognized the familiar weakness. Emily could seldom tell you right out what was upsetting her, but it did sound as if she was feeling the sort of loneliness that's not just an absence of people you love, but a more personal kind of desolation. By the look on her face, Rosie judged there was little she could say to comfort her.

'Emily, I have a problem,' she began quietly. 'I need change of five pounds.'

'Ye don't!'

289

'I do.'

The effect was immediate and encouraging. Emily wanted to know every minute detail of this extraordinary occurrence and by the time they'd reached the top of the lane, her low spirits had completely disappeared.

'But how do I get change, Emily?' she persisted. 'I can't take my five-pound note to Uncle Henry's or he'll tell all of Richhill. And if I can't get change, I can't pay you the ten shillings I owe you.'

'You don't owe me anything,' Emily retorted. 'Look at all the nice dinners you cook for me, forby washin' my knickers and smoothin' my clean blouse every week.'

'Oh yes, I do,' Rosie came back at her. 'Da's just paid me for all I do in the house. So that's not fair. I owe you at least ten shillings.'

'No, you don't. I only lent you nine and sixpence.'

Rosie laughed and shook her head.

'Well, you're the one that can do sums, I won't argue. But I can't pay you till I get change of this note.'

'That's easy. I have four pounds ten and sixpence put away at home. If you really want to pay me, then I'll have the five pounds for my ticket.'

Rosie stopped dead and looked at her.

'And what about the fifty dollars you have to have before you go?'

'I saved that first. It's in the Post Office.

'So you could go anytime now?'

Emily nodded and said nothing, but the look on

her face told Rosie all she needed. She was longing to escape. Now she had the money she could go. Only a weeks' notice was required by Fruitfield. From the beginning of May there would be dozens of advertisements in the newspapers. With the ice melting in the St Lawrence, she'd have a choice of both Canadian and American destinations.

There was no doubt in Rosie's mind. Emily would be gone before the apple blossom came and she would be left to face the future without her support and comfort.

Nineteen

Nothing would have given Rosie greater pleasure than spending all her weekends at Rathdrum, but she knew perfectly well her life would be made unbearable if she did. However, bearing in mind what she'd promised her father, she made it plain to her mother she was going to visit every second weekend. She would do the shopping on Friday instead of Saturday, prepare a casserole to heat up for Saturday's meal and leave immediately after supper on Friday evening.

The thought of her weekends brought her great comfort as April turned to May and her father's steadying presence was no longer there. Even when he was at work or busy in the barn, she'd been aware of him, but now, night after night, when there was no footstep to listen for, she missed him sadly. Sometimes she found herself wondering if this was how Granny felt now that Granda was gone. The thought that one day her father might really be lost to her and not simply tied to a job a handful of miles away, upset her so much she had to push it out of her mind.

'Hallo, Rosie, you look tired. Come in and have some lemonade.'

She put her small suitcase down thankfully,

perched on the garden wall and turned to greet Emily Hamilton, standing with her young son held in her arms.

'Yes, I am a bit slow tonight, but if I stop I might not get going again. My goodness, isn't he growing fast?'

She stood up to return the gaze of the bright blue eyes that followed her every movement.

'Hallo, John,' she said softly.

John gurgled, stuck out a small arm and reached for her hair.

'This child has slept the entire day and now wishes to be entertained,' his mother declared. 'Just when I was hoping to sit down and have a conversation with my dear husband. I don't know when we last exchanged words. The other three are asleep long ago,' she said, shaking her head and laughing.

'How is Uncle Alex?'

'He's fine. Working a bit too hard, but that's to be expected for a while. He misses your granda. Did Granny Rose tell you the company had bought his motor and given it to Alex for the job?'

Rosie shook her head.

'They'd been planning to let Alex have a motor for some time, then one of the directors had the idea of buying your granda's. Alex is very pleased. He loves that motor.'

'So he's got something of Granda's he can use everyday,' Rosie said smiling. 'And how is Granny Rose?' she asked, taking up the name Emily's little girls always used.

'I don't really know, Rosie,' Emily said

thoughtfully. 'You could say she's well enough. Maybe a bit stronger in body since you were over a couple of weeks ago, but she's not herself. She'll be glad to see you though, she always looks forward to you coming. She told me your Emily had gone. She was very concerned about you. You'll miss your sister, won't you?'

Rosie nodded and said nothing. Thinking about those last days getting her ready to go, then standing on the station platform with her and waving till the train disappeared round the first bend still made her cry.

'I really must go, Emily. I told Granny which train I'd be getting, so she'll be expecting me.'

'Well, in another month or two you'll be able to phone me and tell me which train you're coming on and Alex will meet you. Did you not notice the telegraph poles?'

'No, I didn't. There was a huge pile of wood in Lavery's yard as I was passing, but I thought they were building a new hayshed. I never thought of the phone,' she said in amazement.

'Apparently your grandfather said no when the company offered to put in the telephone a couple of years ago. The cost was tremendous at the time because of the hill and there being only two houses on it, but now they say Alex *must* have it. I think maybe the cost has come down as well,' she added, as she rocked the baby gently in her arms. 'Anyway John's fellow-directors have insisted the lines go up to Rathdrum. You'll be able to phone Granny as well, though that will take a few months longer.'

'Look, he's gone to sleep. Just like that,' said

Rosie quickly.

'Thank God for small mercies.'

She picked up her case and stepped back on to the road.

'Give Uncle Alex my love. You might get a few words together if no one wakes up.'

'Sorry I'm late, Granny. I hope you weren't worried,' she said, as she came round to the back door and found her grandmother standing on the doorstep. 'I stopped for a bit with Emily.'

'No, I wasn't worried, but I heard your step on the drive. Oh, you do look tired, Rosie. Has it been a bad week?'

'No worse than usual,' she laughed, as she dropped her suitcase and hugged her grandmother. 'There was a lot of shopping. Sometimes it gives me backache.'

They exchanged knowing looks and headed for the sitting room, arms round each other's waists.

Rosie eyed a loaded tray on a low table by the fire.

'I know you've had supper, but that was hours ago. I've made us some sandwiches. I was going to make a pot of tea, but looking at you, my dear, I'm going to give us a glass of sherry.'

She sat back in her armchair and sipped the golden liquid tentatively.

'Oh, this *is* nice, Granny.'

'You like the sherry?'

'Oh yes, that's lovely, but I meant being here, the smell of the logs and this room and all your special things. And the quiet...'

She broke off.

'I know what you're thinking, my love. That it might just be *too* quiet.'

Rosie nodded, but it eased her mind to see her grandmother was smiling.

'The quiet doesn't trouble me at all. What was almost unbearable when I was too ill to come home was all the noise and bustle and everyone being so kind. Keeping me company, so that I wouldn't miss John. They did mean it so kindly, Rosie, but I should never have gone to England.'

'Why not, Granny?'

'Oh, nothing to do with Sarah or Hannah. Bless them. All they wanted was to try to help me. But sometimes no one can help you. I needed to be here. I needed to face the empty house while I could still hear John walking about. Hear the sound of his voice. Hear the motor in the yard or on the hill. It was never going to be easy, but I've realized in the last week or two that I made a bad decision. And that is good.'

She nodded to herself and encouraged Rosie to have another sandwich.

'Why is it good?' she asked, puzzled that what seemed so unhappy a decision could have any good about it.

Taking a large bite out of a well-filled sandwich, she realized that supper had been a long time ago and she really was very hungry.

'Once you see you've made a mistake you can try to put it right, but only if you *see* your mistake and accept it. Until you do, there's no way forward.'

'But how can you put this right, Granny? The time has passed. You can't go back to last August and do it the way you now know you needed to.'

'You're quite right. We can never go back, can we? But owning up is the first step. Something might come to help us, now I have.'

She paused and took a good look at her grand-daughter.

'I must say that sherry has done wonders for your complexion. You were so pale when you arrived. Wouldn't it be lovely if we could solve all our problems so easily?'

Rain came in the night, pouring down so heavily that Rosie wakened and lay listening to the drumming on the roof above and the gush of the rainwater flowing into the drain below. Bobby would be pleased. He said the land was too dry, the grass fading, the hay crop meagre. Rain was badly needed to encourage growth and then enough warmth to plump up the crops, especially the potatoes.

She put her hands behind her head and listened to the quiet. Back at the farm, the walls were thin. There was no Uncle Joe to snore next door, but Bobby was a restless sleeper. Even when the room was empty after Uncle Joe died it was never as quiet as this. There were goods trains rattling past in the middle of the night, the long lines of wagons clanking and banging as they went over the level crossing. From the space between the ceiling and the thatch came the scrabblings and scufflings of birds, or mice. Emily never noticed, she slept so soundly. Now she was so far away and Rosie was all alone in their room, the sounds seemed even louder.

Eventually, she fell asleep and woke to a sparkling morning. When she looked out, every bush and tree was threaded with raindrops that shone in the bright light, producing tiny shimmering rainbows until they evaporated in the full warmth of the sun.

'That was a good drop of rain we had last night,' her grandmother said, as she poured tea for them both at breakfast. 'That was what John used to say. I'm going to be very boring, Rosie dear. I'm going to say all the things that he would say. Will you mind?'

'Not if I can say some of them as well,' she responded. 'I often think of what he'd say when I'm at home, especially when I'm in the workshop with Da. It's the smell that does it. Probably all my life I shall cheer up when I smell paraffin oil or hand cleaner, though I'm sure other people absolutely hate it.'

'Yes, you're right. Smells and tastes and tricks of the light and times of the year. They're such an irresistible prompt to memory. Did I ever tell you about the fire at Lenaderg when Sarah rescued the wee lassie from the top floor of the mill? Every time I smell smoke from a bonfire, I see Sarah standing at the door, her hair grey, her eyes black. It must be twenty years or more ago, before she married Hugh, but the smell of the smoke brings it back as if it were last week.'

'You've *never* told me about that, Granny.'

'I was so sure I had. I must have imagined it. They say old people imagine things,' she added, teasing, for Rosie would never allow her to say she was old.

298

'But I've shown you Sarah's albums haven't I? The pictures she took when she was still at school.'

'I *think* perhaps you did, but it seems a long time ago. Perhaps it was when Emily and I used to come for our holidays. I'd so like to see them again. Please.'

They ended up in the dining room, because it was easier to sit side by side at the table than to pass the heavy albums back and forth between the comfortable fireside chairs in the sitting room.

All morning they went through the volumes. Rosie had so many questions to ask and her grandmother so many stories to tell that they went straight back after lunch. The next one was the one that began with the double-page picture of Ashleigh House taken with a special camera whose name Rose couldn't remember.

The picture that really intrigued Rosie followed a few pages later. There stood Auntie Hannah under a rose covered arch with Uncle Teddy, hand in hand. They looked very young and so very much in love.

'She looks so beautiful.'

'Yes, she does, doesn't she? She was always a pretty girl but that summer she was radiant. Love does that to you, they say. She was only eighteen. Lady Anne and I agreed they could be engaged, but we arranged for her to have a year at a finishing school in Switzerland before they were married...'

Rose broke off, somewhat startled by a polite knock at the dining-room door.

'Goodness, who can that be?'

'Mrs Love?'

'No, no, she's in Belfast for the weekend.'

The door opened quietly. Richard P looked from one to the other and began to laugh as he came into the room.

'You realize, don't you, that I'm a burglar? I've just packed up the family silver, your jewels and all the valuables in the house and am now about to drive off.'

Rose stood up laughing.

'Oh Richard, how lovely to see you. *Two* visitors in one weekend,' she said, kissing him. 'I wasn't expecting you.'

'I wasn't expecting to be free, but Father was feeling generous. Either that or he thinks no one is going to be ill this weekend. Mother said you'd be here,' he added, smiling briefly at Rosie.

She smiled back, but could think of nothing to say. It seemed such a very long time since she'd seen him and somehow he was different.

'Have you had lunch, Richard?'

'Yes, I've been well fed today, Auntie Rose. Mother's proper lunch. None of your sandwiches in a paper bag with stewed tea from one of the cottages. You know, they ought to teach you to drink stewed tea at medical school. It's absolutely obligatory for practice as a country doctor.'

Rosie watched as Richard cast his eyes over the volumes of photographs piled up on the table, then turned to ask her grandmother how she was. To Rosie's surprise, her grandmother's answer was so brief and so totally reassuring that

Richard seemed quite taken aback.

'Good, good,' was all he said as he sat down.

There was a moment's pause. Rosie thought he was about to make some important announcement, but the moment passed. He looked towards the window and the bright prospect beyond the shadow of the house.

'Actually, I thought you two ladies might like an outing,' he began. 'I wondered if Auntie Rose would like to go and look at her mountains more closely. Newcastle, perhaps?' he added, looking from one to the other.

'Oh Richard, what a kind thought,' replied his godmother. 'It's such a beautiful day. I really shouldn't keep Rosie shut up in a dim room.'

'You didn't keep me shut up, Granny. If anything, I kept you. We almost forgot to have lunch we were so busy.'

'All right. I agree,' said Rose smiling. 'Six of one and half a dozen of the other. But Richard is quite right and it's a lovely idea.'

She paused for a moment, a strange look on her face that Rosie couldn't quite read.

'What I'd really like, Richard dear, if you don't mind, is to go down to Corbet Lough. We were talking about it this morning and I haven't been there for years. I used to take Sarah and Hannah there to feed the swans when we first had a pony and trap. Dolly. You remember, there was a picture of her looking over the fence in the back field at Ballydown,' she said, turning to Rosie, a slight, wistful look on her face.

'Anywhere you wish, Auntie Rose. Yours to command.'

'Is there any stale bread, Granny? Shall I go and look?'

'Yes, I'm sure there is, the weather has been so warm.'

The lough was shining in the bright sunlight, the merest hint of a breeze flowing across its cool surface as they bumped over the broad grassy area between lough and road. The only other people in sight were a handful of fishermen parked at well-spaced intervals along the western shore.

'I think there's a path runs part of the way round,' Richard said as he helped Rosie out of the rather cramped back seat.

'Yes, I think there is,' agreed Rose, 'where those fishermen are. But I shall sit in the sun. I've brought a book in case I get bored, which isn't really likely.'

She cast her eyes round the small, man-made lake, created a century earlier to supply water to the River Bann should the level fall too low for the many mills dependant upon it. Lying between low, richly green hills, thickly grown with water-loving plants and small trees, it now looked as if it had always been there. Rose settled herself more comfortably in the passenger seat and looked away towards the fishermen.

'Why don't you see where it goes?' she suggested.

'Would you say that was a tactful way of getting rid of us?' Richard asked, as soon as they were out of earshot.

Rosie smiled and nodded vigorously, delighted

at the change in his tone of voice. This was the Richard she remembered, not the rather too bright young man who'd appeared at the dining-room door.

'Yes, I think she wants to be on her own. We talked such a lot this morning, she probably needs a rest.'

'How do you think she is?'

She was just about to reply when he interrupted her.

'And that is both a Richard question and a doctor question.'

Rosie laughed and told him about her arrival, their supper by the fire and the hours they'd spent talking about the pictures in the albums. She paused only when they had to navigate one of the tiny streams that flowed across the path on its way into the lough, though a convenient stepping-stone was usually provided.

He listened carefully to her detailed report and looked at her as often as the narrow path permitted.

'Good news, Rosie. Good news,' he declared, as she finished her account. 'It *was* very unfortunate her being ill in England. She's quite right, she needed to be here. And I think what she's doing now is trying to reconnect. Thank goodness she has you to talk to.'

'And what about you?' she came back at him. 'She says you've been over nearly every week.'

'Yes, I do what I can, but it's not what you're doing. Perhaps it's only a woman can speak to another woman's grief. It's something I need to know much more about, at any rate. There are some good books being published in that area, but I get very little time to read. What about you, Rosie?'

'You mean time to read?'

'No, I mean how are things at home? With your mother? With the family? Auntie Rose told me about this big job of your father's. Sounds extraordinary.'

'Yes, it is quite extraordinary. You know they still haven't got to Richhill and they've been at it four weeks already. But Da seems to be enjoying it. The Boss's son is with them. Work experience, I think they call it, and he's rather nice. Apparently he's a good cook. Da was amazed when he got stuck in the first night and produced something tasty. It means I don't have to carry casseroles on the bar of the bike when Bobby and I go to see him.'

'You mean the two of you go on one bicycle?'

'Yes, of course,' she said, amused by his look of horror. 'Bobby is very strong and we walk up the lane and the steep bits. We've been doing it for years. We're very clever at it now.'

'Well, I suppose you know what you're doing.'

She was surprised to hear so clear a note of anxiety in his voice, so unlike him.

'How long will the job take?' he continued.

'They've no idea. Last week they had to divert a stream so the load could cross a field instead of keeping to the road, because there was other traffic on the road and it's so narrow at that point the load fills it from side to side. And they've had to knock down a garden wall. Da's helping to rebuild it in the evenings when the load's not moving.'

'Does it move at night?'

'Sometimes. Depends on the road engines. They keep overheating and breaking down with the strain. It needs at least two of them to get it moving. Going downhill is the worst. It's so heavy, they have to get a fourth engine and use all four as a brake. Da says you never know what's going to happen next. One of the lads had a very close call. A steel cable snapped and the whip just missed him. It only caught his hand, but he could have been killed. But the kind woman whose wall they'd knocked down used to be a nurse and bandaged him up. Poor Da, it's a huge responsibility.'

'I see what you mean. Though Auntie did say there were other problems as well...'

'Well, we may be about to be made homeless,' she said, surprised at how light her tone was and how easy with him she now felt as they walked along the far lough shore and talked, just as they'd always talked.

'You did say something last August about doing a course in Belfast, Rosie. What happened about that?'

'Overtaken by events, I think the phrase is. Da said he'd consider it, but then when Granda died there was the question of whether Granny could still afford it. Poor Granny was ill in England, so there was no question of asking her. Besides, Da was in a bad way after Granda, though he tried not to show it.'

'So what are your plans now?' he asked, his attention closely focused on a nearby fisherman who was reeling in.

'I haven't any,' she said, taking a deep breath. 'Not till I see what's happening over the farm. If we have to move, I'll have to help Da. Goodness knows where we can go. I'm taking Da's advice on the subject,' she went on, turning to face him. 'He says its vexatious to the spirit to dwell upon uncertainties. It undermines your ability to act when the time comes. I don't know whether that is Da, or one of the Quaker writers. He does have a few books of essays and letters that he reads when he has time. Like you, that's not often.'

'But wise, whichever it is,' he responded, suddenly thoughtful and rather sombre. 'I would be inclined to fidget with a problem when it would be far better left to time to resolve it.'

The flatness in his voice had grown more marked. So different from his lively response to her stories. They walked in silence for some minutes until they found themselves exactly opposite the point where Richard's Morris was parked by the water's edge.

'D'you think Granny can see us across the water?'

By way of answer, he took out a large white handkerchief and waved vigorously.

'Yes. Look, she's waving her scarf.'

'Speaking of across the water,' he began, 'I have some news to share with you. I've been invited to do a year's internship. Mother and Father think I should go. It would be good experience,' he went on, watching her expression to judge how she took the news.

Rosie's heart sank. First Emily. Then her Da.

306

Now Richard. Soon, there'd be no one to help her carry the burden of loneliness she felt, running the house unaided with nothing to look forward to but more months and years of the same wearying jobs.

'Where, across the water?' she managed to say at last.

'London. Guy's Hospital. One of the best teaching hospitals in the country.'

Rosie nodded, but could think of nothing more to say just at that moment. If Dr Stewart and Aunt Elizabeth thought it was a good idea, then it most certainly was, but what filled her mind was the knowledge that Helen was in London and she was sure Helen would make Richard very welcome.

'When would you go?'

'End of the month.'

'So soon?'

From somewhere at the back of her mind, she heard herself saying the same words to someone. That was it. The night the solicitor's letter had come and then, on top of it, her father told her the news about the big load.

'Sometimes things happen so quickly. You go on day after day doing very boring things. Nothing seems to change. Then suddenly, in a month, a week, a day even...'

She broke off. On the path ahead, between the luxuriant waterside vegetation, a swan stood staring at them. As they paused, it puffed up its chest, raised itself to its full height, flapped its great shining wings and emitted strange noises that oscillated between a hiss and a honk.

'That hump of sticks must be the nest,' he said quietly, taking her hand. 'Let's turn back. It's not fair to frighten the poor thing. There may be eggs still hatching.'

'You were saying something about how quickly things can change,' he prompted her as they hurried back along the path.

'Yes. I was thinking about all the sudden changes in the last year,' she replied, looking up at him and shaking her head. 'Not a good idea. Vexatious to the spirit, as Da would say. Sometimes sudden changes are for the best. Like London. You really must go to London if you have the chance. It's not just the hospital work. You could probably do that in several places. But London is special. It's all those theatres and films and art galleries and the British Museum,' she went on, ticking them off on her fingers. 'I'm very envious,' she added. 'I'd so love to go there one day.'

'I'm sure you will. Provided Emily doesn't persuade you to go and join her in America.'

Again she was aware of an unfamiliar note in his voice she could not place.

'She didn't want to leave me behind when it came to parting,' she admitted. 'She knew I couldn't leave just now, even if I had the fare and the obligatory fifty dollars, which I haven't. But she reckons she can save what I need in a year. Faster, if I can get a job myself.'

'Any hope of that?' he asked, a little too casually.

'No, none at the moment.'

They rounded the edge of the lough and saw

308

the small, composed figure turned away from them, gazing out over the water to where a flotilla of swans were sailing leisurely past, a group of grubby-looking cygnets trying hard to keep up with them.

'So, we can take Auntie Rose to the Mournes this time next year, all being well?'

'We'll have to ask her when the time comes, won't we?'

After such an immensity of circumstance as would fill a whole year, she wondered where any of the three of them might be in twelve month's time.

Twenty

Rosie was grateful when the second half of May began to produce the cloudy skies and the rain so much needed on the land. After a week of rain every day, followed by chilly nights, she and Bobby agreed that they'd had quite enough for the time being. Unfortunately, the wet, cool weather continued.

Day by day the skies remained cloudy, the nights unusually cool. There were regular showers and they were heavy. Towards the end of the month the showers gave way to violent rainstorms and one afternoon of bouncing hailstones. The apple blossom had just been coming into bloom on the sunny weekend when Rosie had walked with Richard by Corbet Lough. Tossed by brisk winds, the blossom began to fall before it was fully open. After the hailstorm, the long grass in the orchard was white with the fallen petals. It remained to be seen whether or not there'd been adequate pollination in the very short period when the blossom was still intact, but the outlook for the Bramleys was certainly not good.

A few hundred yards beyond the point where Rosie and Bobby had visited their father in the middle of the month, the big load stuck, bogged

310

down in a hollow. Not even a battalion of road engines could shift it from its position in a sea of mud. For two weeks, no progress could be made, so the four-man team turned to dismantling predictable obstacles along the route that had been agreed. The road engines were so well looked after even the working parts shone. Mrs Braithwaite's garden wall was completed and pronounced much superior to its predecessor, one the team had been forced to demolish.

In those two weeks of standstill the lady herself, a kindly widow in her forties, became a neighbour and a good friend to the haulage team. A mere fifty yards away from the site caravan, she offered the use of her kitchen to young Mr Charles who'd developed his cooking skills and had now outgrown the paraffin stoves provided. Her small sitting room was available to Sam Hamilton and the visiting surveyor when they had to consult over maps and plans and her kitchen stove provided warmth and dry clothes for everyone.

Rosie and Bobby braved the weather to visit their father and took an instant liking to Mary Braithwaite. A small, bright-eyed woman, she hurried out of her front door as soon as they appeared, carrying a batch of scones under a large umbrella. While tea was being made and the rain continued to pour down outside, she entertained the two of them with an account of the trials and tribulations of the team, who sat back and enjoyed the stories every bit as much as they did.

At the end of this turbulent month, between

one day and the next, the weather changed. The barometer went up and fine dry weather settled in again. Rosie enjoyed the first fine days of sunshine, but, after the first full week without the smallest shower, the effects of May's deluges had been completely erased. With long hours of hot sun and a small, warm breeze, the cart ruts grew dusty and the ground brick hard again. When Bobby dug the first spadefull of potatoes, it was obvious the crop would be poor.

For a week or two Rosie found the hot weather simply tiring, the nights hot enough to prevent the best of sleep, but the actual daily chores were easier. The freshly scrubbed kitchen floor was so quick to dry, she'd no need to fear someone would undo her work by tramping across its damp surface. The washing, hung out by mid-morning, was ready to take in as soon as lunch was cleared away.

Only the milk going sour and the butter melting as soon as it was brought in from the dairy, created extra work. The wet cloths hung over the milk jugs to keep them cool dried out in such a short time. Even the pieces of slate on which they sat in bowls of water in the coolest part of the dairy began to feel less than chill to the touch. Whenever she finished a job and wondered what came next, she would remember the milk jugs, hurry across the yard and soak the cloths yet again.

Halfway through June, the water tank her father had installed on the roof of the barn ran empty. The rainwater barrels normally used for washing and cleaning had long since been

312

exhausted. Now the only water supply was the well at the far end of the orchard. Even in the longest drought, it had never run dry, but it was a long walk from the house and the galvanized buckets were heavy even before they were filled.

'Hallo, Bobby. Do you come here often?'

Rosie put her buckets down and waited while Bobby finished filling his. Even from a distance she'd guessed by the set of his body that he was weary and dispirited. His lack of response to her small attempt at lightness told her all she needed to know.

'How many buckets do the cows need?' she went on, as he straightened up and wiped his forehead with the back of his hand.

'Twelve,' he said shortly. 'Morning and evening both.'

'Goodness, Bobby, I'd no idea they drank so much. I thought I was bad enough having to carry four buckets a day unless Ma's in a good mood.'

'And that means eight journeys for you,' he replied, his tone softening slightly.

'How did you know that?'

'Saw you pouring one into the other up at the house. You've not got the Hamilton shoulders,' he declared grinning. 'Just as well, seeing you're a girl.'

'Why's that?'

'Men don't like strong women.'

Rosie burst out laughing and sat down on the trunk of an old apple tree fallen alongside the well a very long time ago.

'What else don't men like?'

Always the quietest of her brothers and not yet sixteen, Bobby had never yet asked a girl to go for a walk or to the dance in the Orange Hall on a Saturday night.

To her surprise, he came and sat down beside her, his overflowing buckets left sitting in the sun, the strong light reflecting from their oscillating surface.

'They don't like being told what to do all the time when they know rightly what to do.'

'Does Ma tell you what to do?'

'Oh aye.'

'That *is* awful. I didn't know that. She used to do it with me in the house, but she hardly ever even speaks to me now. But *you* don't need to be told what to do, surely. You know just as much about the job as she does. After all you've worked the farm for three years now.'

'Three years too many,' he retorted, his tone bitter and bleak.

She had never heard Bobby speak like this before. But then, their paths seldom crossed in the course of the working day and when the family were together, he seldom said anything. As soon as he'd eaten his supper, he'd go off to the barn with Charlie. Sometimes she heard hammering from the workshop, but mostly all was quiet and she knew they were listening in and exploring the new wireless stations on the equipment Granda had bought for them.

'It's all right for you Rosie. You're good-lookin'. You could marry one of them men at Granda's funeral, the posh ones from England, like our Aunt Hannah did. But I could be workin' here the rest of my life. Even if there were any jobs goin', Ma'd never let me go. The only thing she likes is babies and cows.'

Rosie smiled to herself and tried not to laugh. It was so unlike Bobby to comment, but he wasn't far wrong. There'd been no trouble with her mother when they were very small. She herself could remember Jack and Dolly as toddlers. They were always well cared for, petted in fact. But she'd had enough of them by the time they were five, as Emily had once concluded.

'But Bobby, if a job came up you'd *have* to go. It's *your* life. She can't keep you here like a hired man.'

'And what about you?'

'What do you mean?'

He shook his head and looked at her gravely.

'I know Da's been great an' given us a bit of money, but you're just the same as me, as far as Ma goes, a hired girl. How are you goin' to get away unless you follow Emily when she's saved up for your ticket?'

'I don't know, Bobby. To be honest I haven't thought about it very much. There's been so much else on my mind since Granda died. But you're right. I couldn't go on living at home, year after year, any more than you.'

She stood up and smiled encouragingly at him.

'Why don't we go and see Da again? Tomorrow say.'

'Aye. That would be great. This weather is just the best for them. They'll be halfway to Armagh,' he said with a grin.

'Yes. And if they're doing that well you might

find Da could let you try your hand on one of the road engines.'

A smile lit up his face Rosie felt she would never forget. Like the sun coming out from behind a cloud and lighting up the whole landscape, so the set of both his face and his body was transformed. He nodded as he picked up his buckets and set off through the orchard, a visible lightness in his step, as if the weight of the buckets was a matter of complete indifference to him.

Bobby was quite right about progress of the big load. After all the problems and setbacks, conditions were now ideal. By the fourth week in June they were cycling as far as Armagh itself. On a route that skirted the city, an old, broad track, rock hard in the dry heat, the whole encampment was moving steadily.

Sitting in the barn a few days later, painting a spray of wild rose in the small area of workbench which Bobby kept free for her, she found herself thinking back over the long, slow progress of the big load. The weather had been fine and dry in the first weeks, but every day something had happened to bring them to a halt. Sometimes they couldn't even get started. It had been an anxious and dispiriting time, whereas now everything was going forward, the day's journey almost predictable, the team so well used to each other's ways of working that when she and Bobby had stood and watched them, it looked as if they'd been doing the job all their lives.

She ought to try and remember the big load

whenever she found herself beset by problems, struggling, or even completely bogged down as they'd been for those weeks almost outside Mary Braithwaite's house.

'No, that won't do either,' she said to herself, as she washed her brush and tried again to mix a shade of pink pale enough for the fully open bloom sitting in a jam pot in front of her.

She'd made her first attempts at watercolour when Miss Wilson insisted all her girls try either paint or pencil. She'd always loved colour, so she chose paint and had tried to work from the collection of picture postcards they'd been offered for inspiration, but nothing ever seemed to come out the way she'd imagined it. Only in Kerry had she first produced anything that began to please her, working directly from the flowers in the hotel garden.

She tried the pink on a spare sheet of paper. Still too dark, but better than it was.

She smiled to herself. If she were a writer, she could use the big load to write a fable. Like *Pilgrim's Progress*. Or *The Tortoise and the Fox*. It would have something of the quality of those wonderful tales where the youngest son overcomes all obstacles and by hard work, patience and courage, rescues the princess and carries her off to live happily ever after.

Quite suddenly she thought of Patrick Walsh. That was probably what Patrick thought he wanted to do. He'd virtually said so in more than one of his letters. Descend upon the farm, preferably on a white horse. No mode of transport as prosaic as the train from Portadown would serve *his* turn.

The thought of him arriving on the doorstep, every inch the Fenian of Uncle Joe's warped imaginings, and her mother's likely reaction made her laugh.

'Poor dear, Patrick,' she said aloud.

It had taken Rosie some time to realize that Patrick didn't live in the same world as herself, at least as far as matters like relating to someone you said you really cared about. In his second letter, written in reply to her account of her grandfather's death, he did manage to say how sorry he was and how grateful he'd always be for his help in escaping from Currane Lodge, but even on that occasion he'd gone on to speculate on the nature of mortality, quoting a couple of lines from St Augustine and Joyce and then some verses in Irish.

She'd reminded him that she didn't read Irish each time she wrote, but he never remembered to send the translations she'd asked for. When he wrote about her, he always used the high-flown, decorative phrases, the quotations from Irish poetry he'd used in his very first letter.

It was weeks now since she'd heard from him. The young postman who'd been so interested in the arrival of his letters had found himself a girl-friend and no longer looked out for the Dublin postmark and the elaborated swirls and curls of his script. Without quite meaning to, with a sudden shock, she realized she no longer looked out for the Dublin postmark either.

So was it no more than what Lizzie would call 'a holiday romance'? Maybe she would have to accept that was all it was. Nevertheless, she had to admit every time she looked at small flowers blooming in rocky places, she would remember the drive from Waterville to Tralee with a boy who had kissed her twice.

Two days before the end of June, as her mother sat by the stove reading the Sunday paper and she herself was about to start peeling potatoes for the evening meal, Rosie heard a motor stop on the lane. There was a brief exchange between two men, the tramp of boots across the yard and a moment later her father stood in the doorway.

'Da!' she cried. 'Have you got there?'

'No, not quite. But we're so near, the managers at Milford are providing the security tonight to give us a few hours off.'

He looked across at Martha, who remained hidden behind her newspaper and made no gesture of welcome.

'Are any of your brothers here today?'

'Yes, Sammy's home. He's with Bobby and Charlie in the barn. Jack and Dolly are down at Loneys.'

As she spoke, three figures crowded the doorway, one behind the other, as delighted to see their father as she'd been herself.

'I read a bit about the big load in the Armagh papers. When'll you be done, Da?' asked Sammy, as all three shook hands with their father.

They pulled out chairs from under the table and sat down together. For some time, her father answered their questions in his customary precise and accurate manner, describing the present position and situation of the load. Before they had time to share their own successes with the wireless in the barn, Rosie saw him put his hand up to his jacket and take out an envelope from his inside pocket.

Instantly she knew what it was, for she and Bobby had delivered three similar envelopes in the course of the last months.

'Here you are, Martha. You might like to read that,' he said politely, as he handed the letter to her.

She threw him a tight, disagreeable look, grabbed the spectacles Rosie handed her without a word of thanks and pulled out the single folded sheet of paper from the open envelope.

'I don't believe it,' she said shortly. 'Sure where would you get that amount o' money an' you always sayin' ye have none.'

'I've never said I had *no* money, Martha. Rather that I regretted I had not *enough* money to provide for so large a family. Despite that, what I *had* saved, along with the help of this big job and some small assistance from my boss, was enough to meet the figure the solicitors had agreed with the American Loneys. This house is now ours.'

'Yours, ye mean. I'm sure you've not put *my* name on the deeds.'

'In the event of my death, the house *is* yours for your lifetime. After that, our children will benefit according to their needs.'

'What d'ye mean? Whose goin' to get the farm when I'm gone?'

'There will be no farm, Martha. What I've

bought is the house and outbuildings, the orchard and the small field beyond. The rest of the land will be let in the autumn. The income from that will repay the small loan the company have made me to make up the purchase money.'

'An' what about my cows?'

Rosie could hardly believe her ears. Her father had managed to buy their home and all she could think about were the cows.

'I thought that securing our home for our children would be more important than providing for the cows. You could keep one in the orchard, could you not?'

'Sure, what use is one? The milk float isn't going to collect the milk of one cow. An' then I'll have no milk money either. An' what's Bobby gonna do? Kick his heels in the barn all day, listenin' to the wireless?'

Bobby looked up quickly, his face pale. Sammy and Charlie shifted uncomfortably.

'I have some news for Bobby. Young Jack Withers has done so well on the big job that Mr Lamb is letting him go to our associate company, Irish Road Motors. He's suggested to me that Bobby might take Jack's place. That's if Bobby doesn't mind being his da's helper.'

Bobby's face lit up, relief and pleasure mixed together.

'That'd be great, Da, I'd like that fine.'

Charlie and Sammy clapped their brother on the back.

'Good man, Bobby. You'll be drivin' engines yet.'

Rosie watched her father carefully and waited

321

for what he would say next. She knew he'd written to the solicitors, gone to see them and had the farm valued, but she was amazed it had all happened so quickly. Then she remembered Emily's first letter from New York had taken a mere five days to come so speedy were the new transatlantic liners. She'd have to get used to the idea America was no longer as far away as it had once seemed.

'What about Rosie?'

She was quite startled when she realized it was Bobby who spoke. Her mother twisted round in her armchair to stare at him. Bobby ignored her sour look and waited patiently for an answer.

'Well, there'll be much less work without animals, as you well know, Bobby. Rosie has worked hard too, especially since Uncle Joe began to fail, but it's time now she found something that suited her better. We'll just have to see what opportunities come up. You've been lucky, I'll not deny that, but I don't see why Rosie here shouldn't be just as fortunate, even if it takes a wee bit of time.'

Sunday, 28th June, 1925
Richhill

My dear Emily,

It is late and I'm half asleep, but I really must tell you the good news before I shut my eyes. Da came this afternoon and he's bought the house. So we don't have to think about moving. When you are rich and want to come home

322

to visit, you will now have your own old home to come to. Needless to say, Ma couldn't find a good word for Da after all his hard work. To make up the last bit of the money he needed, he's let out our twenty acres to his boss. When she said, 'What about my cows?' I couldn't believe my ears.

The next wonderful news is that Bobby is going to Pearson Haulage to be Da's helper. Jack Withers has got promoted to the sister company, which is good news for him. Maybe now he and your friend Susie at Fruitfield will be able to get married. Oh Emily, how I wish you could have seen Bobby's face when Da told him. He is just delighted.

Of course, this means that if Ma has no cows, she can look after the house herself. Da made it clear that I'm now free to find a job. I've no idea where I can even look for one, but never mind. Something will turn up. At least I can tell Miss Wilson and Lizzie's parents and they'll keep an ear open for me. I went through all this week's newspapers this evening and as usual there is nothing except 'Smart boy wanted'. It makes me furious.

We still don't know what's happening over Ma's cows, but at one point she did announce that 'she had money' and would rent a couple of fields herself. Da never said a word. Just imagine, Emily, if she *has* money then she's saved it from what Da gives her and what she got from you and the boys for your keep. She's already told Bobby he'll have to pay her half what he earns the same as his brothers did!

Rosie paused and re-read what she'd written. She smiled to herself. She was on the fourth page already. But it didn't matter how much she wrote, Emily would be glad to have it.

Before she went they'd talked about the fact that Emily hated writing letters. She'd said if she managed two small pages it would be the height of it, but she'd promised faithfully to do her best. What neither of them realized was that Emily could write perfectly well if she had a list of questions to answer.

It had happened by accident. Rosie wanted to know what Macy's was like, who the girls were with whom she was sharing an apartment and what she wore to work. Emily had written straight back. A big, long letter. At the end of it she admitted the whole problem was thinking up what to write.

She sighed. Even with the all the news she'd had and knowing that Emily was happy, she still missed her desperately. Especially at night, getting ready for bed, for that was when they had always talked things over that they'd rather not have overheard.

She still found it hard to imagine Emily in New York, working in Accounts at Macy's. It was a big department store, she'd said, far bigger than anything in Belfast. She'd known its name before she went because the eldest of Great-Uncle Sam's sons had started off there before he went into business on his own. It had been an easy matter for him to arrange an interview for her. In her first letter she said she was earning so much money she couldn't believe it. Rosie was not surprised. Wages were so pitifully low in Ireland anything reasonable would seem like a fortune.

She took up her pen again, found the ink had dried on the nib and had to get out of bed to clean it on an old handkerchief. At least sitting up in bed these nights presented no difficulty. Even in her oldest and thinnest of nightdresses, she was still too warm.

I should have said that the big load hasn't got to Milford yet, but they are very near. A week should do it, says Da, and he's arranged for Bobby to go and give them a hand for the last stretch. Charlie has been very good and asked me if I'd like to come and listen in on Bobby's headphones while he's away, so next time I write I'll be able to tell you the news from all round the world as well as what's happening here at home.

Lizzie and I went for a walk yesterday afternoon and she was asking for you. She sends her love. She was telling me Hugh has tried for another job. Needless to say he didn't get it. But Lizzie never seems to mind. She has her date now for starting in Belfast. Monday 24th August. Just like school, she says, only the holidays are shorter. She's going to stay Monday to Friday with a friend of her mother's who has a boarding house and come home to Hugh at weekends.

You would have laughed at the way she told the story of Hugh's interview at McGredy's.

Apparently, they'd set up a number of things he had to do, like prune a rosebush after he'd been told how to do it, select blooms for a display, write indentification labels and so on. Needless to say he made a mess of all of them. The funniest bit was when she told me about something called 'budding'. It seems he kept dropping the bud. In the end, he lost it so he couldn't do whatever it was he was supposed to do with it, but he ended up covered in scratches. Poor dear Hugh, he really is one of the nicest boys I've met and I'm not surprised Lizzie is mad about him, but I doubt if he'll come to much without her help.

I think my eyes really are about to close so I must stop, but I will write again soon and ask you lots of questions.

She added love and kisses, wiped her pen, screwed the top firmly on the ink bottle, parked it on top of the closely written sheets and slid down under the bedclothes.

She was asleep in moments and slept blissfully all through the night. She woke up in the morning thinking of roses.

Twenty-One

By the time Rosie had hung out the washing next morning, she'd made up her mind what she was going to do. She'd gone through the week's newspapers, found the advertisement for the job at McGredy's and read it again. Naturally, it asked for the usual: Smart boy. Application in own handwriting.

Pedalling along the Portadown Road on Emily's bicycle, the fullness of the better of her two dark skirts hooked carefully out of the way of the spokes, she told herself there could be no harm in trying. The worst that could happen was someone asking her if she was unable to read.

Finding the new rose field was certainly not difficult. Turning a corner on the main road, the sudden sweep of vibrant colour amid the green fields and tawny shapes of cut hayfields was quite startling in its brilliance. A small notice mounted on a white post pointed along a lane which skirted the lower borders of the rose-field's sloping site. It said simply: *McGredy's*.

A short distance along the lane, she found an open five-barred gate and a rough track leading to a large wooden shed, its doors and windows wide open in the heat of the afternoon. Apart from the high-pitched hum of insects fumbling in the opening blooms, there was no sign of activity in any part of the field. She wheeled her bicycle up the dusty rutted track and parked it carefully to one side of the open door.

'Yes?'

A small, wiry-looking man in blue dungarees sorting papers at a high desk under the window slid down from his stool and regarded her irritably.

'I've come about the job.'

She smiled and tried to sound as if his reply were perfectly unexceptionable, though the signs were distinctly discouraging.

'It's not an office job, you know,' he shot out, as he looked her up and down.

She wondered if it had been a mistake to put her hair up. It always made her look older and smarter. Or perhaps it was her better skirt with her favourite red blouse with its hint of orange that appeared to annoy him so much.

She assured him she hadn't been expecting an office job. That she'd prefer to work with plants.

'Have you ever pruned a rose?'

'Yes, I have.'

'Bush or rambler?'

'Both.'

'Autumn or spring?' he snapped.

'Both.'

He turned away and looked into the distance as if he were thoroughly disgusted with her answers.

'And which was most successful?'

'Neither, to be honest. If you pruned in the autumn to avoid wind shake you could be sure there'd be a quiet winter. On the other hand, if you left them to the spring and the season was early there was all that wasted growth.'

He put his hand to his belt and pulled out a pair of secateurs, rather like the good cowboy in a comic drawing on the baddie. He dropped them noisily on the desk.

'Bring me in a long stemmed rose, about nine inches, that'll bloom tomorrow.'

'Colour?'

'Same as your blouse,' he snapped, turning back to his papers.

She took up the secateurs and stepped gratefully out of the wooden shed which had grown unbearably hot. A slight breeze just stirred the blooms, wafting the most intoxicating perfume on the air.

'Oh well, it's worth it for this,' she announced to the nodding heads.

She walked across the field below the shed moving steadily from whites to yellows, fondant orange to cream, shades of pink to dark toned reds, strong flame reds and orange reds. Once or twice she recognized an old friend from Granny's garden, but there were no climbers here and none of the old-fashioned florabunda roses she'd brought from her home at Salter's Grange all those years ago.

Thinking of Granny encouraged her. She'd love this field, the colour, the smell. Only the regular rows would displease her, but that couldn't be helped if you were growing roses for a living. Granny's roses were her pleasure and a part of her history. There wasn't a rose in her garden that hadn't a story behind it. Whenever Rosie had helped her with her pruning, she'd told her where each plant had come from, when it had been bought and often what the buying had celebrated.

She paused, having found just the colour she needed, a wonderful orange red she'd never seen before. She touched the petals gently, as delighted by the rich colour as she'd been when she and Granny had found the fabric for her blouse. Margaret McGredy, it said, on the large painted post that marked each row. How lovely to have a rose named after you, something that would give pleasure to everyone who laid eyes on it. A celebration or a memorial perhaps for the wife, or mother of the rose grower himself. Like having a book dedicated to you.

She moved along the row looking for what she wanted. With the heat and the dryness the roses had bloomed early, showers of petals already lying on the dry earth shrivelled in the heat. Some of the best buds were on shorter stems and many glorious blooms were already past their best. She spread out the fingers of her left hand. From the tip of her thumb to the tip of her first finger was exactly five inches.

'Rule of thumb,' her father had said to each of them, when he'd measured their spans. 'Useful when you've nothing better.'

At last, she found the bloom she wanted and measured its length. Ten inches. One finger joint's length above where it sprang from the main stem of the bush, she cut it crisply and stood gazing at it in her hand, the outer petals just beginning to unfurl, the centre still tight rolled.

She walked back to the shed, and handed it to him silently. She watched him run his eyes along its length and inspected the diagonal cut she had made taking it from the bush. To her surprise, he'd provided a jam pot full of water on his desk. He placed the rose in it and screwed up his face.

'Ever budded?'

'No, not yet.'

He pushed past her and headed for the top corner of the field, the one area that lay in the heavy shadow of trees. Here, there were rows of spiky-looking briars, most of them tagged with what looked like tiny pieces of paper.

He dropped down on one knee, took a small box from his pocket, chose a long runner from the nearest plant, cut a notch and inserted a small fragment of green. With a deft movement, almost too fast for her to follow, he bound the join with a small strip of white fabric just like all the others.

She thought of Hugh and gave thanks for Lizzie's account of his disaster. The secret was to get the living bud into the notch in such a way that it would bond. The tiny bandage was to hold it in place until it did.

He left the knife and the little box on the ground and stood up, signalling to her brusquely to do what he'd just done.

The box was filled with wet paper. There were three more buds. She dropped to her knees, sat back on her heels, examined the bud he'd inserted and picked up another of the long trailers.

She looked carefully at the position on the briar he'd chosen, then made her own cut. She pushed in the first bud as quickly as she could before it dried out in the hot sun, but it seemed to wobble a little when she wrapped it in its bandage. The second was better. The third cut she made deeper still and that bud was quite steady when she bound it.

'Let's see yer hands.'

She stood up and held out her hands obediently, wondering what further strange tests he might devise for her.

'Not a mark,' he declared, as if he could not quite believe it. 'But look at yer skirt.'

'Its only dry soil,' she responded. 'It'll brush.'

'Ye don't scrub many floors or carry many buckets with those hands.'

'Depends what you call many,' she came back at him. 'It's eight buckets a day in this weather. The floor's only twice a week now, but it's four or five in bad weather.'

He shook his head.

'Women are no good at budding. They bend over and give themselves bad backs.'

He stared at her with a peculiar look she could not read. Either he was making a deliberately provocative statement, in which case she would have to disagree, or it was the next step in her trial.

She was just about to speak when he turned his back on her and waved at a young man wearing dusty trousers and an open-necked shirt. He'd just entered the field and was already striding towards them. To her amazement, when the newcomer stopped beside them her taskmaster greeted him with a broad smile.

'Them three,' he said, as the younger man bent down and examined her work.

'Good,' the man said promptly. 'Very good. Is this the smart boy, Billy?' he asked, laughing as he stood up again and offered her his hand.

'I'm Sam McGredy,' he announced. 'Pleased to meet you. And you are?'

'Rose Hamilton,' she replied politely. 'But everyone calls me Rosie.'

He eyed Billy who was now scratching his head and grinning to himself.

'I suppose Billy here has been giving you a bad time,' he said, laughing again as he released her hand.

'That's all very well, Mr Sam. But if you'd had as many damn fools in here as I've had in the last week, you'd be pretty fed up yourself. Sure, there was a lad here on Friday last who lost the bud before ever he got it anywhere near the briar. An' I thought I was gonna hafta bandage him up, he had that many scratches. Forby the one that was colour blind and the one that didn't know what an inch was.'

'And Rosie here has passed muster?'

'Aye. She has an eye in her head, an' great hands,' he declared with ungrudging admiration.

Rosie could hardly believe her good fortune. Not only had she survived Billy's obstacle course, but because of the happy chance of Mr Sam himself appearing unexpectedly, she'd been offered the job on the spot. She'd accepted immediately and said she'd be happy to begin the following Monday. Although it would be temporary for three months and the wages were somewhat less than Emily's when she'd first started at Fruitfield two years ago, she cycled back towards Richhill feeling as if she'd just been left a very large legacy.

She thought of all the people who would be delighted by her good news. She could ride over to Milford tomorrow and tell Da and Bobby, Miss Wilson on Thursday and Granny at the weekend.

A woman should always look after her hands, Miss Wilson had impressed on all her charges.

She'd taught all her girls that they could still have the hands of a lady however hard they worked physically, so long as they took a little care. It wasn't a question of vanity, she insisted. If you were caring for a child, or a sick person, or if you wanted to do fine embroidery, it made such a difference. But knowing the actual vanity of some of her girls, she'd added, 'and if you want to wear silk stockings'. Rosie smiled to herself, knowing how pleased her friend would be when she heard that Billy thought she'd never carried a bucket or scrubbed a floor.

Her grandmother had agreed thoroughly with Miss Wilson's advice about hand care.

'Oh yes, Rosie, dear, she's quite right. When times were very hard and I was sewing babies' dresses, I couldn't buy creams at the chemists, but there was always goose grease and oatmeal. They didn't smell very nice, but they did the job. A far cry from these pretty bottles Hannah sends me, aren't they?'

Thinking of Granny and the pretty bottles which now found their way to her own bedroom, Rosie almost missed seeing a small, compact figure with a watering can waving to her from the roadside.

'Mrs Braithwaite,' she called, slowing down and cycling across the empty road. 'I'm sorry, I was miles away.'

'Yes, I know,' she replied, laughing merrily. 'Who's the lucky man?'

Rosie laughed too and shook her head as she parked her bicycle carefully against the new wall and stood beside it.

'I've just got my first job.'

'Oh Rosie, how marvellous. Oh, your da will be pleased,' she said, dropping her empty watering can and hugging her. 'I know he's been concerned about you and Bobby. Well, about all of you, of course, but particularly you and Bobby.'

'I've got more good news for you.'

'What?'

'Bobby's going to be Da's helper. Jack's had promotion.'

'O ... hhh.'

Mary Braithwaite clasped her hands together, her dark brown eyes sparkling, her mouth open.

'Isn't that just lovely news? I was feeling a little bit sad today. It's my husband's anniversary, you see. I know one mustn't look back, but *this* is a real gift. *Both* of you. Sam will be *so* delighted. I might even cycle over to Milford and congratulate Bobby and Jack. I haven't been just recently. It does seem to be going so well now,

335

doesn't it?'

They sat down together on the wall and talked as if they'd been friends for a long time, the conversation moving from the big load to the plants now occupying the niches left for them in the garden wall, to the colour of Rosie's blouse and the tasks she'd been set by Billy at the rose field.

Rosie went to her bicycle basket and took out the single bloom of Margaret McGredy Billy had presented to her when she was leaving. He'd wrapped it carefully in wet cloth and laid it gently across the width of the woven carrier. The older woman examined it carefully and held it against the sleeve of her blouse, agreeing it was an extraordinarily good match.

Still talking, long after Rosie had said she didn't have time for a cup of tea, they admitted they could have had a cup of tea three times over.

'You'll be passing every day on your way home from work now. Come in for a chat if you feel like it. I'm seldom far away. And I'd love to see you.'

If it hadn't been for Mary remembering to ask how Emily was settling in, Rosie would have been pedalling up the slope of the hill well before they heard the sound of the oncoming motor, but once they heard it, it made sense to wait and let it pass by. It came over the brow of the hill, slowed as it came towards them and stopped.

It was Uncle Henry. Rosie's heart sank as he got out of his recently-acquired model T Ford and came towards them, beaming graciously.

'Hallo, Rosie. Has the bike packed up?'

'Mrs Braithwaite, this is Uncle Henry who lives in Richhill,' she began, wishing that she could dissolve into thin air. 'Uncle Henry, this is Mrs Braithwaite, who was so kind to all the people on the big load, when it got stuck over there,' she continued, waving a hand towards the hollow beyond the bonnet of the car.

'How *do* you *do*, Mrs Braithwaite,' he said, in his most ingratiating tones. 'I've heard so much about the big load from Rosie and my sister Martha. My goodness, what adventures there have been,' he went on, throwing out his hands and oozing charm.

It was Uncle Henry at his memorable worst. She watched him deploy what he considered his most irresistible manner to cover his minute observation of Mrs Braithwaite herself.

He made a number of comments about the weather, the prettiness of the garden, his journey to Portadown to collect provisions and the un-reliability of the young man he had left in charge of his shop, before he finally decided he'd no excuse to remain longer, by which time, no doubt, he'd stored away as much as there was to be gained from the happy chance of his en-counter.

He disappeared down the hill in a cloud of unpleasant exhaust fumes.

'I'm sorry, Mrs Braithwaite, Uncle Henry is the most dreadful gossip in all of Richhill.'

'Yes,' she said slowly. 'Not a nice man at all, even if he is a relative of yours. He has a way of looking at a woman, that is not appropriate.'

Rosie nodded, grateful to find her friend's warm and lively manner was not simply her habitual way of dealing with everyone.

'I make sure I'm never left alone with him.'

'A bachelor?'

'Yes.'

She nodded crisply and then smiled.

'He has a very good opinion of himself, Rosie, but it doesn't take much to see through him. Don't worry about him gossiping. I've known worse than him and I've nothing to be ashamed of, if you understand me.'

Rosie did understand. It wasn't just the letting slip of her father's name, or the fact that she'd been to visit him, it was her warmth towards herself, the uncomplicated easiness of their talk. Surprised at herself, she concluded that this woman loved her father and she'd be very surprised if her father didn't love her.

'Mrs Braithwaite, I would like to come and see you sometimes...'

'Rosie dear, please don't call me Mrs Braithwaite. Call me Mary. Unless your Uncle Henry's around. We'll both know exactly what we're thinking if you call me Mrs Braithwaite then.'

'I've so enjoyed our talk ... Mary. Goodness knows what time it is. I'm not sure there'll be any supper tonight until I get home and make it, but there'll have to be some changes before I start work next Monday.'

'Good luck, Rosie. Can I tell your Da the good news if I happen to get over before you do?'

Rosie nodded as she wheeled her bicycle to the side of the road and hitched up her skirt.

'He'll be glad to see you, Mary,' she said, smiling at her new friend, as she pushed off across the empty road to cycle the two miles home. 'He really will.'

When she arrived back at the farm a little after five, the kitchen was empty and the stove almost out. Hastily, she did her best to revive it. No doubt the cows did need milking, but couldn't her mother give a little thought to the family and at least keep up enough fire for cooking supper, even though she had no intention of doing it herself. She knew Jack and Dolly needed their meal and Charlie would come in ravenous after a long day having had only his sandwich for lunch.

She'd just persuaded the fire not to go out and was putting small pieces of coal on top of the crackling sticks when she heard a step behind her.

'Hallo, Charlie,' she said without looking up.

When there was no reply she turned round. Her mother was standing staring at her, her hands on her hips.

'So, ye did come back after all?'

Rosie's heart sank as she registered the familiar phrase.

'The Mackay's must be well sick of you up there every day, running after Lizzie. Has she no work to do either?'

'I wasn't up at Lizzie's,' she replied doing her best to remain calm. 'What would you like me to cook for supper?'

'Suit yerself.'

Rosie collected a bowl full of potatoes from the sack in the corner of the room, put on her apron, poured water from the bucket into the tin basin and proceeded to wash them.

'I suppose it was yer idea to get yer father to sell my cows.'

'The idea never occurred to me. If Da had to raise a lot of money then the cows wouldn't make much.'

'Hello, Ma. Hello, Rosie.'

Charlie appeared in the doorway and cast a glance round the kitchen. With no sign of a table-cloth and not even a pot on the stove, he knew supper was some time away.

'Can I give you a hand to drive the cows up into the orchard, Ma, seeing Bobby's not here?'

She looked at him as if he had suddenly lost hold of his senses.

'Sure what would I want them in the orchard for?'

'Tomorrow's the last day of the month, Ma. The lease runs from July the first, that's Wednesday. It'll be Mr Lamb's land then.'

'We'll see about that,' she said angrily. 'I wasn't consulted about my cows, nor the land they graze on. Your father needn't think he can sell them over my head. I won't have it. I'm goin' to see my brother Henry an' ask his advice. Ye can help yer sister make the supper if yer so keen to be useful.'

She turn on her heel and marched out, every line of her body rigid with fury. Rosie looked after her, then across at her brother.

'What *are* we going to do, Charlie? Da's done his best. He said she could keep one cow in the orchard if she wanted to, but the land *had* to go.

She knows that.'

'Aye, but she'll not admit it,' he said, shaking his head. 'We'll have to leave it to Da. Don't worry, Rosie. He'll be back soon an' he'll have an answer.'

She knew he meant to comfort her, but she was far too worried to be comforted. Faced with her mother's behaviour the wonderful sense of delight she'd shared with Mary Braithwaite simply evaporated. It was as if her father had said not a word about the land having to go nor about herself and Bobby being free to find jobs for themselves.

In her present mood, she felt there was no point telling her about her job at McGredy's. At best, she'd ignore her and then accuse her of never having told her. At worst, she'd fly off at her. Rosie felt she couldn't sustain yet one more outburst of violent temper.

At the same time, the matter of the cows was becoming more serious. If the animals were not moved, her father would be in breach of the lease. Mr Lamb would certainly not make difficulties while her father was still away, but if Martha went on tending them without Bobby to help, who was going to run the house and put food on the table after next Monday? For the moment, the only thing she could do was carry on as best she could. It wasn't something she could discuss with Miss Wilson and sadly, just when she most needed her, Lizzie had gone with her mother for a week's holiday in Newcastle.

The only good moments in the very unpleasant

week that followed she spent in the barn painting a sequence of pictures to record, day by day, the unfurling of her precious rosebud. Margaret McGredy took two days to open fully, putting out a mass of orange-red petals whose richness and texture delighted her. On the fourth day, stepping into the barn after her visit to Miss Wilson, she found a heap of soft petals lying on the workbench. They were just beginning to shrivel in the continuing heat, their fragrance scenting the warm air.

Tomorrow, she'd be going over to Rathdrum for the last of her two-night visits. Once a working girl, she'd only be able to go when she had a half day on Saturday, just like Sammy coming home from Armagh. She could wait on longer. She'd got to tell her mother tonight that she'd be at work from Monday morning, leaving with her father, Charlie and Bobby somewhere after seven.

She managed to get out her story uninterrupted, despite the sour look on her mother's face.

'Oh, that's news indeed. Well, at least you'll be able to pay somethin' towards your keep. You'll find it a queer change not being able to run around with your cronies and go visitin' up in Richhill.'

'Yes, it will be a change, Ma. I'll not be here to do the washing and cleaning and cooking.'

'Sure ye can cook when ye get home. Doesn't many a girl do that? Ye know I've the milking to do. I haven't time for that.'

'And what about the washing and cleaning?'

'What about it? Can't ye do the washing Sunday instead of Monday. I have to work seven days a week. Who do you think you are to come home and be waited on?'

'What about Emily? You didn't expect her to do housework in the evenings?'

'Emily paid her way from the day she left school. You've never earned a penny. Just remember what you cost me when you were runnin' up to Miss Wilson, readin' poetry and paintin' wee pictures. Maybe ye fancy getting' a man wi' money like your aunts did. Well, let me tell you, I'm not such a fool as you think. An' while you're in this house, you'll work for your keep.'

'As well as paying for it, Ma?'

'An' why shoulden you? You've lived off my back an' outa my purse since you left school...'

'Out of whose purse, Martha?'

Rosie could hardly believe her eyes. Her father and Bobby stood in the doorway, blocking the light, before they came into the room and sat down. Martha had been shouting so loudly she'd had been totally oblivious to the usual sounds in the yard.

'Out of whose purse, Martha?'

He repeated his question quietly and without emphasis.

'Out of my purse,' she shot back at him, her tone only barely modified.

'Judging by what you said on Sunday, Martha, about leasing some land for your cows, it would seem that your purse has been fuller than the needs of our family. You've saved quite a bit from what I give you and from what you've taken from our children. Even from Bobby and now Rosie, were I to permit it.'

'And why shouldn't they pay for their keep?'

'Because, Martha, I have always provided for their keep, as your savings demonstrate. Our children have been very generous with you, paying you out of the little they earn, or, working without any payment and very little thanks.'

Martha opened her mouth to interrupt, her face screwed up with fury, but Rosie saw her father lift his hand.

'I haven't finished, Martha. I have something to say to you and you will oblige me by listening. It is then for you to decide what you want to do.'

Rosie decided her legs might give way if she didn't sit down. She pulled out a chair and placed herself beside Bobby.

'You have a choice to make. You can sell the cattle, add the money to your savings and take over the proper running of this house. Alternatively, you can rent land, hire a man to help you and keep your milk money for your own use as you've done since Uncle Joe died. In that case, I will ask our neighbours to find our family a pleasant, cheerful woman as a housekeeper. I shall have to deduct her wages from what you normally get for your purse. The money for groceries you will receive as usual.'

He stood up.

'I hope I've made myself plain, Martha. We did agree some eleven years ago that we had a family to raise. That you would do your work and I would do mine. I told you then that if we couldn't agree, I would have to make other arrangements for the well-being of our sons and daughters. That decision still holds good.'

He stood up and glanced across at Bobby who was as distressed as she was herself by their mother's hostile expression.

'Bobby and I will go and bring the cattle into the orchard. That will give you time to make up your mind what you want to do.'

He paused and then continued.

'As for expecting Rosie to cook and clean after a day's work at her new job, I think you owe her an apology.'

He turned and went out into the yard without another word, gratefully followed by Bobby. A moment later, her mother stumped out after them and left Rosie to herself.

She had a headache and felt slightly sick as she pulled out the casserole to stir it and add a little seasoning and get the vegetables going.

Suddenly she had an image of herself on the loveliest of August mornings, the day after Granda's funeral, spinning along the road from Banbridge and hearing her Auntie Sarah saying how her da would act when the right moment for action arrived. She'd also said that when he made up his mind he would be absolutely clear about what had to happen and he would be un-shifting in his resolve.

Twenty-Two

After the unusually hot summer, autumn came more quickly than usual, the trees, parched and already weary of growth, dropped their leaves at the first hint of frost and the slightest gust of wind. November mists arrived as early as October and by December the land was already sunk deeply into winter rest.

For Rosie, the months passed with unbelievable speed. Every week brought new experiences. So absorbed was she by skills to be learned, people to meet and the whole exotic world of rose breeding opening before her, she began to think she might be forever spared from the dreary burden of repetition. However often she made up an order for blooms, or wrapped the root balls of spiky bushes for despatch, however often she pruned or budded, she marvelled that she never got tired of handling the material she worked with every day.

There were indeed times when she felt the chill of damp earth, days too when the sadness of dying blooms called up a strange longing she couldn't quite put a name to. But, for the most part, she was happy. Whatever the tensions at home, she could be sure of friendliness at work and often laughter.

346

Billy McWilliams, the overseer, the man who had given her such a bad time when he'd interviewed her for the job, became a good friend. He also turned out to be the brother-in-law of the young man who'd been her father's helper on a memorable delivery from Fruitfield to Jacob's Biscuit Factory in Dublin at the time of the Easter Rising. Having confessed to her how much he hated summer and how much more he hated people who had no feel for his beloved roses, he set about teaching Rosie all he knew and the range and scope of his knowledge was extraordinary.

For a man who could barely read and write and was heartily glad to have someone who would sort his invoices in a fraction of the time it took him to do it himself, he was able to quote the genealogy of a rose all the way back through its ancestors, naming the breeding stock used and the rose-breeders responsible. He talked about roses like Margaret McGredy or Norman Lambert as if they were personal friends and loved speculating as to what might happen if they were cross-bred.

'You can never tell, Rosie, that's the joy of it. Cross a red with a white and you'll not get pink. Its not like mixin' paint. Far more interestin'. You might get half a dozen sports an' maybe only one of them will be robust. You have to learn to throw away. To move on, try somethin' new. An' in time, when you've made enough bad choices and have a whole lot of poor, wee spindly things about the place, you'll know a good grower when its less than the size o' your thumb.'

She listened and watched what he did, the thick fingers with the dirty, chipped nails, moving faster than a woman knitting or using a type-writing machine.

In the very short days of December, Mr Sam gave his staff extra time off to compensate for the long hours they worked in summer and to celebrate the prize the nursery had recently been awarded. If Billy McWilliams had won ten thousand pounds in the Irish Sweepstake, he wouldn't have worn a bigger smile than the day the telephone call came from Mr Sam in London telling him Margaret McGredy had won the National Rose Society Award for a hybrid tea.

Billy was ecstatic. He tramped round the large shed that provided both office and despatch department, muttering to himself. In their tea break he reminded her she'd worn a blouse that very colour the day she'd come about the job. Cycling down the lane that night, her flash-lamp catching the glitter of frost on the road ahead, she remembered the sequence of pictures she'd made, one for each day of the opening and falling of the bloom he'd given her to take home with her. She thought perhaps he'd like to see them, a reminder of a day they joked about like the friends they'd become.

Meantime, she had the opportunity to go to Rathdrum for three whole days. She'd been looking forward to it for weeks. Going on a Saturday afternoon and having to return on Sunday evening made it seem such a very short time. It felt as if they'd just got started to talk when she had to put her nightdress back in her suitcase and walk down to Emily and Alex's, so he could run her to the station in Banbridge.

'Oh Granny, it is lovely to be here. I feel as if we haven't had proper talk since I got my job. By the time we got through all the news of how everyone is and what they're all doing we haven't any left to put the world to rights, as Da calls it.'

'Well, we'd better get started right away then, hadn't we? Let's hear your news first. I've got a lovely tray of sandwiches out in the kitchen and some of the sherry you like best. The first sherry you ever had. Do you remember?'

Rosie nodded happily and drew in a deep breath.

'Da is well and seems in very good spirits. I think he's terribly pleased with how well Bobby is doing and Bobby is saving up for a motorbike like Charlie's. Sammy has fallen in love. Her name is Marjorie and she lives in Portadown, but that's all he'll tell us. Billy has finished his training and has his new uniform. I must admit he looks well in it, but he's very full of himself. Ma thinks he's just great.'

'And Ma herself?'

Rosie smiled wryly.

'Well, I have to say, Da won the battle outright, but she still tries to put him in the wrong. Every time she sets a jug of milk on the table she says if it hadn't been for her fighting to keep Daisy we'd have no milk.'

'What does he say to that?'

'Guess.'

Rose raised an eyebrow and smiled.

'Nothing?'

'Absolutely right. Sometimes he even manages to behave as if she hadn't spoken, but quite often now Jack or Dolly will pipe up and say, "But we could get milk from Mrs Loney like the Mackays do." That makes her very cross. But she *is* better than she was. She reads a lot and goes to see her friends. She might even be glad she's not having to spend long hours milking in a freezing cold byre these evenings.'

Rosie stretched out in front of the blazing fire and sniffed appreciatively at the perfume of the well-seasoned logs.

'What are you burning, Granny?'

'Apple wood. Isn't it lovely? Mr Lavery had to take out some dead trees a couple of years ago and John bought it all for me and stacked it at the back of the workshop. Aunt Elizabeth used to burn apple wood years ago when I first came up to Rathdrum to see her and we made quilts together. Though she got hers from over your way. Fruit Hill, I think. She had relatives there.'

'How is Aunt Elizabeth?'

'Better. You can't get rid of arthritis but these new tablets have helped and the wax treatment is a great comfort. She's able to sew again, but it's her encouragement that achieves so much for the co-operative, as I keep telling her. Some women, Rosie, think so little of themselves that it's heart-breaking. Then Elizabeth gets them working, sewing or knitting and they see just what they *can* do. It's not just the money they earn, it's the fact that they can do it.'

'I understand that better now than I did a year ago. There's more to earning money than the money itself, though the money's important enough.'

'Exactly. Once a woman has money in her purse she can make decisions, whether it's food for her family or better clothes and then she begins to feel she has some control over her life, however small.'

'Are you still enjoying it?'

'The co-operative? Oh yes. The first time I made a pattern for a baby's dress and showed a very poor young woman how to make a few shillings for herself, I knew I'd found what I needed. Elizabeth says I perked up visibly that very day.'

She paused and looked very thoughtful as if she'd suddenly remembered something very precious.

'D'you know, Rosie, years and years ago when I was not much older than you, I asked my mother about the loss of my father and how she felt about it. She said she thought of him every time she put food on the table and how pleased he'd be that his children had enough to eat. Then I thought of John. He'd be so pleased I'm doing something I used to be very good at and helping those women, who're as poor as he and I once were.'

Rosie nodded and watched her grandmother as she took her time placing a new log on the fire, using the long brass tongs so she didn't have to bend over. It was clear to her that she was a lot happier now than she'd been even a few months ago.

'Have you heard from Richard P at all?' she asked, as she straightened up.

The mention of Richard was only to be expected when they'd been talking about his mother, but to Rosie's dismay she found herself blushing.

'I did have a birthday card in July,' she said awkwardly. 'I don't know how he knew my birthday. Unless he asked you,' she added, recovering herself somewhat.

'Yes, he did ask me,' Rose admitted. 'But I wondered if he might have written.'

Rosie shook her head.

There was a moment's silence in which Rosie looked into the fire and her grandmother considered what it might be best to say.

'I thought you and Richard seemed very easy with each other when we went to Corbet Lough. You looked so right together.'

'Yes, I always feel right with Richard. I like talking to him. He never treats me as if I were years younger.'

'Yet he's aware that you're still only seventeen and he's twenty-four. Richard has been away, has studied, qualified and begun a career whereas you're only just setting out. Richard would be very sensitive to the difference.'

'Whatever do you mean, Granny?'

Rosie looked at her grandmother quite baffled by what she had said.

'Well, I don't know how Richard feels about you, though perhaps I might guess ... but there's something I think you should know. If as

352

thoughtful a man as Richard *does* care about a young woman, a "young" young woman, that is, like yourself, he may be reluctant to stand in her way. He might decide to be patient and wait till she has more experience of the world before making it in any way clear what he might feel.'

'Isn't that what happened with Auntie Sarah and Uncle Hugh that died. Wasn't she only eighteen?'

'Yes, you're quite right. I think Hugh had loved her all her life, though she was only six when they first met.'

She paused a light smile playing about her lips.

Rosie waited. By now she knew the expression well. Granny was seeing scenes from past life that called up memories, she might, or might not, feel she should share with her.

'John and I never did work out who proposed to whom. It might well have been Sarah, knowing her, but Hugh waited till Sarah had made her own life. He wanted her to have a real choice. He didn't want her to marry him just because there was nothing else to do, like these young women we read about, the debutantes, marrying from the ballroom.'

'And you think Richard may be waiting, like Hugh did?'

'What do you think, Rosie?'

'I think he's probably in love with Helen.'

'Now what makes you think that?'

'Well, she *is* so lovely and so lively...'

'Indeed she is. But so my dear Rosie, are you.'

'But...'

'I think you *are* fond of Richard, but we'll just

have to see what happens. Two people can change a lot in a year when they both find themselves in quite new circumstances. You're certainly a very different young woman from the pretty girl John and I took to Kerry a mere eighteen months ago.'

Rosie had barely walked into the section of shed Billy used as an office, when he hailed her, his face grim. He'd drawn himself up to his full height, which was little more than a few inches taller than she was herself. He now sat down soberly on his stool.

'The boss wants to see you right away. He's over in the Portadown showroom and he's expectin' you.'

For one awful moment, Rosie thought something dreadful had happened. Then she saw the tiny glint in Billy's eye and knew he was teasing her.

'So, I'm for the sack, am I? Who'll make your tea then, Billy? And who'll sort your invoices when you drop them on the floor?'

His face cracked into a broad grin.

'He still wants t' see you.'

'What about, Billy?'

'Well, it's not for me to say, but I showed him them paintin's you brought in for me before ye went to see Granny. My goodness, he was pleased with them. Delighted. Told me to send you in as soon as you were back, *if* I could spare you,' he added, teasing her again.

'And can you, Billy?'

'Well, I can try. For the good of the business.'

He winked. 'Away on wi' ye. An' good luck,' he added laughing.

It was a strange experience to see one's work in the hands of another person. Brothers and sisters and friends were one thing, but someone like Mr Sam was quite a different matter. Although he was the most approachable of men and she'd never been in the least shy of him, she felt quite overwhelmed to find herself sitting in his small, overcrowded office, her watercolours of Margaret McGredy in his hands, as he stood by the window studying them again in the best of the dim December light.

When she first arrived, he'd told her about the forthcoming Northern Ireland Trade Fair, which was to be held in June in the City Hall in Belfast. Then he'd shown her the brochures and plant guides from previous events, collected by Billy, carefully tied up in bundles with green string, labelled and stacked. Then he said he wanted her to join the small team who would be mounting the display and presenting the company to home and foreign buyers.

Fortunately he hadn't noticed how utterly amazed she was and had simply gone on to explain he wanted her to design the layout of the stand. What really mattered, he said, was the overall balance of colour. The stand and the roses had to be in perfect harmony, so those responsible for the construction of the stand and the provision of blooms were to do whatever she thought best.

'Billy will keep you right about which varieties will be ready and you may have to change some of the details at the very last minute, but I want the overall design based on our newest roses. I want you to paint watercolours of *all* of the roses we use so that we can provide colour postcards for our customers. If I may, I'd like to hold on to these you've done already to let the printers see what I have in mind. They remain your copyright, of course, and there will be a fee. Will you leave it to me to work out an appropriate figure? Meantime, as designer to the team your salary will be doubled. What do you say to the general idea?'

'Yes, please.'

He laughed and shook his head.

'Good. That's great. That's what I like. A woman who knows her own mind.'

'Now let me fill you in on the time scale of the whole operation. The snow might be falling down next week, but what we'll be looking at is June the fourteenth. That's the second Monday in June and the trade fair runs for six days. We start in February with publicity and invitations and I'll need a lot of your work as early as that...'

It was the middle of January before Rosie quite caught up with what her new job would entail. Initially, the main difference was that she now spent half her working week painting. Sometimes she stayed at home for a whole day, so that she could use her own workbench in the barn. At other times, it was more convenient to work in a small room at the back of the Portadown showroom where blooms from the greenhouses could be brought fresh to her each morning. It was entirely up to her to decide what suited her work best.

When she set out in the New Year she was anxious lest she wouldn't be able to turn out watercolours as good as those of Margaret McGredy, for she'd always thought that those were the best she'd ever done. But soon she discovered she need not have been anxious. The more she worked, the easier it seemed to be and she was enjoying painting even more than before.

She had to keep reminding herself she could now afford to buy all the tubes of paint she needed. Instead of managing with just a few brushes, she could add to her range, acquiring larger brushes for background washes and a number of very fine ones, one in particular so minute it made shading much easier. And then, as if that were not pleasure enough, she had a polite request from Mr Sam's secretary for a note of the cost of her art materials. Whatever she spent, the secretary explained, she'd be reimbursed at the end of each month.

'And now ladies and gentlemen we approach the main staircase that leads to the circular gallery from which you will be able to examine the classical paintings more closely and also to look down upon the impressive entrance hall...'

The voice of the guide echoed through the high-domed space as they followed him up the shallow carpeted treads of the staircase. It was late March and bitterly cold. The first daffodils had just managed to make an appearance in the half barrels outside the front door at home, but a stiff breeze blew dust whirling round the farmyard and the trees showed not a sign of leafing.

Here in Belfast, in the huge interior of the City Hall, there was no wind, but the chill of acres of marble seemed to intensify the cold, so that it penetrated even her heavy winter coat. Rosie was grateful now for the welcome warmth of the silk scarf she'd set inside the collar, although all that was in her mind when she dressed was the patterning of its delicate colours.

Other members of the large group of owners and exhibitors looked even more pinched and chilly than she did, their eyes focused on the tall pillars, the echoing spaces, the fall of light. She tried to concentrate on what the guide was saying but gave up after a short while. An account of the classical paintings, the sources of the marble, the time taken to build this impressive edifice, its cost, or even an outline of its recent function as the seat of parliament for the recently established state was not actually going to help her very much when it came to displaying the very best that McGredy's could produce. What mattered was her getting a feel for the actual place where the McGredy stand was to be located.

They tramped the circuit of the marble gallery in one direction, returned to their starting point and then set off in the opposite direction. Not an entirely helpful itinerary, she thought, remembering the sketch plan she'd been provided with. As far as she was concerned everything would happen on the ground floor. The area designated for McGredy's was clearly marked and it wasn't even visible from the circular gallery.

'We are now approaching the Banqueting Hall...'

The voice boomed on relentlessly.

'Not much point, is there, if we're not being given a banquet,' her colleague, Brian Singleton, whispered in her ear.

Rosie nodded and smiled encouragingly at the smartly dressed young man who had long since put away the notebook he was rarely seen without.

'Can't go on *much* longer.'

She was beginning to wonder if she had mis-read the itinerary they'd been given. She'd been quite certain that somewhere it had said 'Tea'.

Fifteen minutes later, the Banqueting Hall having proved to be as impressive, bleak and empty as the entrance hall below, they were shepherded into a smaller room where tall, metal urns hissed out clouds of steam into the cold air and created the smell of warmth if nothing of the feeling.

'Ladies and gentlemen, on behalf of the Mayor and Corporation I welcome you to the City Hall...'

'Oh, not more talk...'

Brian was beginning to sound quite desperate.

'...the minister for Trade and Industry, the Secretary for Industrial Development, the Prime Minister's secretary and members of the City Council, all of whom will be moving among you and be able to answer any questions you may have.'

'Here you are, Rosie. Nice cup of tea. Let's bag one of those little tables. Billy and Trevor must have got separated. Mr Sam is talking to one of the ministers.'

The tea was hot, the scones and cake home-made. Gradually, given a large party and the relatively small room, a little warmth was generated and Rosie and her three colleagues began to feel warm again.

'I need to go downstairs again,' she announced, 'but don't let me spoil your tea. I'll be back shortly.'

'Don't get lost,' said Billy, winking at her.

She smiled across at him, the sight of him in a suit and a stiff collar still something she couldn't quite get used to.

'Are you sure you don't want one of us to come?'

'No, I'll be fine, thanks.'

The buzz of noise receded almost immediately as she stepped out into the circular balcony where one or two small groups of people had come to have more private conversations.

As she descended, she was the only person on the wide, shallow staircase leading down to the entrance hall.

Bit like Cinderella, she thought to herself, as she paused for a moment to look up at the immensity of space above her, the inside of the great green dome she'd only ever seen on picture postcards.

She continued to walk downstairs very slowly, trying to visualize the place filled with stands and crowds of people. She stopped a moment and took the ground plan of the layout from her pocket, so absorbed she didn't notice a tall, dark-coated figure glance over the balcony, walk slowly down the staircase behind her and wait patiently till she'd finished.

'Can I be of any assistance?'

He held out his hand and said something so quickly the only bit she caught was 'Trade and Industry'.

'Thank you. I'm just trying to imagine what it will be like in June.'

'Warmer, I should think.'

Rosie laughed.

'Not *too* warm, please. Roses don't much like heat, not when cut at any rate.'

'McGredy's, I presume.'

She nodded and decided from the handsome cut of his heavy winter coat and his practised manner that he must be one of the important people who'd been announced upstairs before tea. She'd a feeling she'd seen him somewhere before, but couldn't think where it might have been. He was quite tall and slim, rather broad in the shoulders, with reddish hair beginning to recede. Alone among the pale, winter faces, he looked tanned and very fit as if he'd spent a long time abroad.

'Do you live in the Portadown area?

'Richhill, actually. Down by Richhill Station. Do you know Richhill?'

He smiled and bowed his head slightly.

'My job is to know everything,' he said pleasantly.

He ran through a list of local Richhill firms. She was surprised and impressed it included businesses as small as that of Lizzie's father.

361

'My father worked at Fruitfield,' she offered. 'But he's now with Pearson's Haulage. My younger brother's there too. And Charlie's with Irish Road Motors.'

'And your father is...?'

'Sam Hamilton.'

'And you are?'

'Rose.'

As she told him her name, the one all her friends and colleagues at McGredy's used, her mind filled with a totally unexpected image, the young man with creamy skin and red hair who had kissed her in an empty room in Kerry when she was barely sixteen.

What a long, long time ago it seemed. Wherever he was, she hoped Patrick Walsh was safe and well. Not entirely adjusted to the real world, she decided, looking back, remembering the girl she was then and his letters, full of literary references, artistic flourishes and phrases in Irish.

'You'll be a rose when you've grown up just a little bit more.'

She smiled to herself. It looked as if he'd got *that* right after all.

'Rose,' her companion repeated. 'How very appropriate.'

He turned away and glanced up the wide staircase as if he were expecting someone to come and join him.

'When you come up in June, will you be staying in town or travelling home each evening?'

'Oh, I shall stay. We have to be here *very* early in the morning. I have a friend in digs I can stay with for the week.'

'I suspect you're going to be very busy in the next two months. If you have any difficulties with arrangements for the stand I may be able to help. I have an office here.'

He reached into an inside pocket, took out a notecase and handed her his card.

'J. Slater Hamilton,' she read. 'Hamilton,' she repeated, beaming at him. 'As my grandfather always used to say: "A good Ulster name and there's a lot of us about."'

'Used to say ?'

'He died a year and a half ago.'

'Sad for you. And for your grandmother. Is *she* still alive?'

'Oh yes, very much so.'

He held out his hand.

'It's been nice meeting you, Miss Hamilton. Let me know if I can be of service.'

With which, he turned away and strode up the shallow stairs two at a time.

Twenty-Three

'Oh Lizzie, what a lovely big room.'

'Aye, it's nice isn't it? Bit of luck I had there. It's really for two, but Auntie Maggie is gettin' fed up with boarders, so I'm the last. She's goin' to make this a sittin' room when I finish.'

Rosie put down her suitcase and hurried across to the tall bay windows that looked out upon the quiet, tree-lined avenue. A short walk from Queens University, the elms that gave their name to Lizzie's address were in full leaf, but still kept the softness of early June before the month's growth strengthened the leaves and took away their delicate translucence.

'I thought of stayin' up this weekend to keep ye company, but Hugh would go baldy if I diden come home on Friday night. He misses me terribly. Mind you, I miss him too, but it's not as bad when you're busy an' we've these exams at the end of the month. Not that they matter all that much. I don't need the bit of paper, I just need what they taught me.'

'Any progress on the shop?'

'Aye, Da's been great. He's bought a house in Richhill that's in a bad way and has started doin' it up. He's going to rent it to us for the shop. He says we can use the upstairs for storage, but I'm thinkin' if we got married we could live up there. Ye couldn't swing a cat the bedrooms are so small, but we could manage. It's just across the square from yer Uncle Henry...'

She stopped, a wicked smile on her face.

'He knows there's to be a shop but we didn't let on what kind an' he thought maybe there'll be competition. He's been tryin' every way to find out what we're planning. But it was *him* give us the idea.'

'What idea, Lizzie? I can't imagine Uncle Henry giving anybody anything for free.'

Lizzie laughed and threw herself down on the large sofa fitted comfortably into the width of the bay window.

'We were helpin' Da the weekend before last an' we sees the Ford go off. An' a while later he comes back with a pile of newspapers under his arm. "That's it," says I. "Newspapers, magazines, confectionery and bits and pieces you can't get over the road at yer man's, like buttons and elastic." Imagine goin' to Armagh or Portadown for a bit of knicker elastic.'

Rosie laughed and hugged her friend.

'Oh Lizzie dear, I'm so glad it's all going so well. I saw your ma and da out for a walk the other evening when I was coming home and your ma was looking just great. I got a big smile, but I didn't stop because it was nearly eight o'clock and I was starving.'

'Did ye get any supper?'

'Would you believe it, I did? And not dried out in the oven either. A soup plate over a saucepan of water and a lid over that. I don't know what's

365

been going on, but something's brought her round. Long may it last,' she added, dropping down on the sofa beside her.

'So what's happenin' tomorrow?' Lizzie asked.

Rosie laughed, opened her handbag and took out a small sheaf of papers held together with a large clip. She read the first few items from the list on top of the pile.

'Collect postcards from the printers. Collect the blouse that had to be altered. Go to the newspaper offices with details for their feature page...' Rosie then stopped and explained, 'We can't get in to the City Hall till seven on Sunday morning, but we have to have everything else done by then, for it'll take the whole of Sunday to set up the stand. It has to be absolutely perfect for the roses arriving at seven on Monday. We open at nine thirty.'

'That'll keep you outa mischief. Has Brian Singleton asked you out again?'

'Yes, he has.'

'An' why don't you go? He's nice lookin'. D'ye not fancy him?'

'I like him as a friend.'

'What ye mean is ye don't fancy him.'

The weekend was warm and dry. Rosie was grateful that Lizzie had gone home as usual on Friday evening leaving her the large, quiet room. She had so much on her mind, she was finding it difficult to sleep, but a telephone call to Billy late on Saturday afternoon was reassuring. All the bushes they'd earmarked together would have blooms at the stage they needed for picking in the very early hours of Monday morning, plus enough buds coming on to provide replacements for later in the week.

Billy was not much impressed with the BBC's new weather forecasting service which Mr Sam's secretary posted on the information board each day, but his mother's corns were grand. They'd never let him down yet. They always gave trouble before rain and heavy rain was the last thing they needed.

By early evening on Sunday the work of constructing and furnishing the stand was finished and the City Hall's own staff were wanting to lock up and go home. It had been a long, long day from a very early start. There'd been wearing hours when they could do little but watch while carpenters, carpet layers, or electricians finished their section of the work, making sure it was exactly as planned, but it had been worth it. The finished result was just what they wanted.

'It really does look good,' declared Brian Singleton, stepping back and narrowing his eyes.

Everyone agreed, collected their belongings and headed towards the back exit.

'Can I give you a lift home, Rosie?'

'Thanks, Brian, that's very kind, but I'm staying in Belfast with a friend tonight, so I can be down on time in the morning.'

'I could drop you there,' he persisted.

'Actually, I need the walk. I've had a bit too much of sawdust and the smell of glue and paint all day.'

Sitting alone in Lizzie's room some time later, a large pot of tea on a tray beside her, she did wonder quite why she was continuing to say no to such a nice young man as Brian. It wasn't as if she didn't like him. She did. He was a reliable colleague on the job and good company when the job was done. As she emptied the second mug of tea, she decided that she'd think about Brian seriously when the trade fair was over and she felt her mind was her own again.

After all these busy weeks, it was strange to find herself on her own in Belfast on a pleasant summer evening with no work to do. She was too tired to go for a walk and certainly too tired to paint, even if she'd had her box and brushes with her. She lay on the sofa and fell asleep briefly. Waking up, she was so comfortable, and so reluctant to move, she lay and watched the light fade as the sun moved west. Voices of couples walking past below floated in through the open windows.

In a week, it would all be over. Mr Sam's secretary had reminded her she was now entitled to a week's annual holiday with pay, plus some extra days in lieu of overtime. After all the intense work and effort, it would be so good to have time to herself again. She'd go and see Granny.

Since those winter days just before Christmas her visits had all been too short. In the last couple of weeks, she'd not been able to go at all, though she *had* spoken to her on the telephone, a strange and frustrating experience. The connection was so perfect they might as well have been in the same room, but the context of the general office in the Portadown showroom meant her call could only be brief and rather impersonal.

Suddenly and unexpectedly Rosie found herself thinking of J. Slater Hamilton, the tall man she'd met on her first visit to the City Hall. Mr Sam had been most impressed when she'd produced his card and relayed his offer of help should it be needed. 'Secretary to the Minister for Trade and Industry. A Cabinet Minister, no less,' he'd said. 'A very useful contact.'

They'd had no need to take up his offer of help, as it turned out, but she'd found herself puzzling over their conversation more than once. In fact, she'd been so puzzled she'd mentioned it to her grandmother on one of her visits back in April.

'We don't have a distant relative called Slater Hamilton, do we, Granny?

'Why, dear? Have you met a possible one?'

'Hmm. Nice man. He was at the City Hall, one of the government people sponsoring the whole thing. He knew Richhill and Pearson's and Fruitfield and Rountree's. Though, of course, he said it was his job to know everything like that.'

'Well, you'd have to be pretty knowledgeable these days with the state of business so depressed. The new government has no money to invest and neither has Westminster. Uncle Alex says we're heading for real depression if something doesn't change soon.'

She paused and thought for a moment.

'What did your Slater Hamilton look like?'

Rosie described him as best she could. She'd even mentioned that he'd looked familiar, but she couldn't think where she'd seen him before, especially as she thought he'd been abroad.

'He certainly didn't get that suntan in Belfast last winter.'

'Red hair?'

'Well, yes, but it was a bit thin on top. And it was receding, like Da. He was quite old, probably forty or more. Maybe even fifty.'

Rose laughed heartily and shook her head.

'Oh Rosie, my love, you do make me laugh sometimes. Not *at* you. At myself. Forty seems so *young* when one gets to seventy. But it must seem so ancient when you're just about to be eighteen.'

They hadn't said any more about him, but in May, Rosie remembered to bring his business card to show to her. She'd put her spectacles on, looked at it closely and asked if she thought she would see him again in the week of the trade fair. She'd said she probably would and put the card back in her handbag.

Rosie sat up and decided she was hungry after all. The idea of scrambling some eggs in Lizzie's little kitchen was suddenly very appealing.

Although the trams were already running, the city itself was still quiet when she set out for the City Hall on a lovely summer morning, the sky almost a perfect blue except for little white clouds over the Cave Hill and Black Mountain. The hill slopes were ablaze with gorse, reminding her of the rather different blaze of colour she was hoping to create when the lorry arrived from the rose field. Part of her felt anxious, another part felt confident they'd taken account of every eventuality, but she knew she wouldn't feel

370

better till she had buckets of roses at her feet and blooms in her hands and knew neither the pickers nor the weather had let her and Billy down.

Everything went exactly to plan, down to the last printed label, the name of each rose encircled by garlands made up of tiny, painted portraits of the rose itself. To her great delight the blouses worn by the girls who would be at work on the stand all through the week looked quite stunning.

When she'd discussed the question of dress for the week with them, their response was immediate.

'Sure we always wear the same, black skirts and white blouses.'

She'd been horrified at the though of *white* blouses, almost the worst colour for any girl to wear next to her face, especially as these girls were not professional models, skilled at make-up, but the girls who ordinarily worked in the fields, or the showroom and therefore knew something about roses.

She'd argued for colour and it had been accepted. When she met the girls chosen for the trade fair, she'd put forward the idea that each girl should chose a rose and match her blouse to it.

Not surprisingly, there'd been problems, even before a suitable dressmaker had been found. Some girls had chosen colours that didn't suit their complexions and she'd discovered how tactful she could be. In the end, they'd worked out a colour for each girl, the blouses echoed the blooms against which the girls would move. As for the skirts, there was nothing wrong with black, because the outfit was completed by a moss green overall embroidered with the Mc-Gredy crest. Some of the men had been uneasy about wearing pale pink shirts instead of white, but again, worn with black trousers and moss green blazers the same shade as the girls' overalls, they'd had to admit they did look very smart.

A few minutes after nine o'clock, staring at the finished effect of staff and blooms and wondering if there was anything more she needed to do before the doors opened in half an hour's time, she turned to find Slater Hamilton on his way to work, a bulging briefcase in his hand.

'Well, are you pleased? You ought to be.'

'Yes, truly I am. Though I think I'm more relieved than pleased at the moment. When I'll be really pleased is when I see full order books after all the hard work.'

'Some American buyers are scheduled for today. I may see you again later,' he said, turning away.

'Just a moment. Mary, would you bring me Patience, please.'

He stopped, somewhat taken aback, as she spoke to a rather plump, round-faced country girl wearing a pale, pastel-pink blouse under her green overall.

'You are our first visitor,' Rosie explained.

She took the rose Mary passed over to her, a small spray of foliage already in place and handed it to him.

'It may fit your lapel. If not, I have a pocketful

of pins.'

'Thank you,' he said, tucking it into the lapel of his elegant grey suit. 'That will be most helpful for my day's work.'

Within minutes of the doors opening, the vast marble hall was full of people. She was kept busy answering questions, providing buttonholes for the gentlemen and postcards for purchasers. A glance across at Brian Singleton, his head bent over a clipboard suggested that orders were flowing in already.

There was little respite from the stream of interested viewers until halfway through the afternoon. A member of the City Hall staff appeared suddenly and cordoned off the stand with dazzling white ropes suspended from highly-polished brass supports. Moments later, the Americans, including a very influential rose-breeder from California, appeared, escorted by Slater Hamilton and two of his dark-suited colleagues.

When they were followed by three photographers, who grouped and regrouped the Americans, their hosts and Mr Sam, Rosie moved behind one of the display stands and slipped off her shoes for a blissful ten minutes. Fortunately, she'd just put them on again when Mr Sam asked for her. He wanted a photograph with all his staff and he insisted she stand beside him.

'Your boss obviously thinks very highly of you,' Slater Hamilton observed, as he and his colleagues waited politely for the Americans to finish their conversation with Brian Singleton and Mr Sam.

'He's given me a wonderful opportunity. A year ago, I was keeping house for my family with no prospect at all of a job.'

'And you found this job yourself?'

'Well, not *this* job exactly. I started in the rose fields...'

There was a movement in the small knot of people to their right and visitors surged towards them as the cordon of white rope was removed.

'We must continue this conversation...'

He strode off to catch up with the small party as it continued on its way to the next point on their itinerary.

An hour later, a stiff white envelope was delivered to Rosie containing a single sheet. She read the brief message twice.

If you are free for dinner tonight at 7.30, Grand Central Hotel, Royal Avenue, or one other evening this week, I should like to continue our conversation. I must also confess I have a matter of some importance to me upon which I should value your comments. Please reply by the messenger. I should be most grateful for your assistance.

She didn't need to study the signature, she simply looked at the piece of paper and the messenger who stood waiting. She *was* free tonight. She might be free every night, but she couldn't be sure. If a problem occurred she might need to go up to the rose fields herself so that she and Billy could sort it out together.

She took a pencil from her pocket, turned over the sheet of paper and scribbled a message. As Granda would have said, 'Sure there's no time like the present'.

'It *was* good of you to come. From what I could see you were on your feet all day. I'm surprised you're able to look so fresh.'

Rosie smiled at him and sat down gratefully, her back aching gently. She hadn't looked fresh when she'd arrived back in Lizzie's lovely room, but a bath and a whole pot of tea had done wonders. So had Granda's dress, the red one he'd bought for her in Kerry. She'd brought it with her, just in case, as she'd had no opportunity to wear it again since his funeral.

'When I first started in the rose fields, I was exhausted by lunch-time, but I got used to it quite quickly. And the last weeks have been so busy, I think I must be getting fitter. Actually, I did have an hour's rest this evening. When we closed, there was nothing that needed to be done. Later in the week, there'll have to be replacements.'

'You mean in your arrangements?'

'Yes, the centre of the big side panels are done with rosebuds set in damp moss. They'll start to bloom with the heat and spoil the design.'

'And can you just put fresh ones in?'

'Yes, that bit's quite easy. The difficult bit is picking buds at the right moment back in the fields, so they'll be ready for me next day, but my friend Billy has been doing this many, many years.'

'How long will this one last?'

He nodded down at the buttonhole she had given him that morning.

'You've had that in water?'

'Yes, while I was working in my office, but I wore it for several hours when I was conducting visitors.'

'Two, maybe three days, if you keep resting it. I'll give you a new one when it fades.'

He paused, scanned the menu rapidly, consulted her and ordered their main course.

'You chose Patience. Was that significant?'

She laughed.

'We have great hopes for Patience at the National Rose Show, but I picked it to go with your suit.'

The large dining room was quiet on a Monday evening, the sound of cutlery and china absorbed by the heavy velvet curtains and the thick carpet. The meal was served promptly and Rosie discovered how hungry she was. They ate in companionable silence, until coffee arrived and he poured for them both.

'To continue where we left off...'

He asked most carefully about her job, how exactly she'd found it, how her brothers and sisters and friends had tried to find employment. She answered his questions freely and told him as much as she could, especially about each member of her own family, and about Lizzie and Hugh and their plan to open a shop in Richhill.

'You've been most helpful, Rose, if I may call you Rose.'

She nodded and smiled.

'We have some very difficult problems ahead of us. Young people like yourself not able to get further training or apprenticeships. Talented ones like your sister Emily leaving, because wages are so very low. What you've provided me with is a case study, if you like, but I suspect when I make further enquiries I shall find what you've told me repeated all over the province. I've no idea what's to be done, but finding out the existing situation is a good place to start, don't you agree?'

'Yes, yes, I do.'

She paused and then ventured to ask him about his own family and whether or not they'd been able to help him with his research.

'I've just one son, at university in England,' he replied, as openly as she had done to his own questions. *'His* future is quite secure. He wants to do engineering and fortunately I can afford to support him till he's qualified.'

He paused, looking round the almost empty dining room as if looking for someone he knew. As her own mind filled with questions, she wondered if he was going to say something more.

'I'm out of touch in some ways, because I've been abroad for many years. In Australia. I've followed the political situation here, but I only came back last year when the new government began to find its feet. I have one or two friends in office now who think my experience overseas in various industries might be useful here.'

'So you came back because of the job?'

'That's what I've been telling myself.'

She waited, a sense of tension growing as she

sipped her coffee and tried to be patient.

'Have you ever heard of Annacramp?'

She laughed.

'Of course, I've heard of Annacramp. When I was little I thought everyone in the world knew about Annacramp because Uncle Alex met Great-Uncle Sam in Canada, in some strange place called German Township, and that's what they started to talk about. That was why Uncle Alex came to Ireland to look for his family. He was an orphan, you see, but when Great-Uncle Sam mentioned the name, it must have rung a bell. So he set out to find the Hamiltons with nothing but the name of a townland and his own name.'

'And what was his name?'

'Why, Hamilton, of course. Alex Hamilton,' she went on, laughing at herself for not making it plain to him. 'I'm sorry, it's one of those family stories you hear so often you forget to put in the details. Uncle Alex was an orphan, sent to Canada when he was only a little boy. He worked on farms from the time he was nine. He met Sam at some sort of trade-union meeting. Sam was like Aunt Sarah, always thinking what could be done to help working people. Anyway, the two of them got talking, Sam made some remark about Alex's good Ulster name and the next thing Alex was saving up to come to Annacramp.'

'And did he come?'

'Oh yes, he did. Someone in Annacramp sent him to Thomas Scott's forge in Salter's Grange, and Thomas sent him on to Granda and Granny at Ballydown to see if Granda could get him a job in one of the mills. When Granda saw him he said he was the very image of *his* father and that was that. He's been Uncle Alex as long as I remember. He and Granda worked together. And last year, when he and Emily had their little boy, they called him John. So there's still a John Hamilton at Ballydown.'

He'd listened to the story with a smile on his face, but at the mention of Ballydown the smile faded. He dropped his eyes and studied the pattern on the damask tablecloth as if trying to memorize it.

'Would that all such family stories ended so happily.'

'Do you know Ballydown?

'Yes.'

'And Annacramp?'

'Yes.'

'And J is for James?'

'Yes.'

There was a moment of complete silence.

'Would you like some more coffee?' he asked politely.

She took a deep breath as if the decision was more than she could manage.

'Yes, please.'

'How did you guess?'

'Last year when Bobby and I were carrying buckets of water for the cows, he told me I didn't have the Hamilton shoulders. He said it was lucky because I was a girl. And when I told you just now about Alex I suddenly remembered what Bobby had said. *You* have the Hamilton shoulders and your forehead is just like Da's, if

379

it wasn't for the colour of your hair.'

'Great-Uncle Sam,' he said matter-of-factly. 'Granny's red-headed little brother. Is he still with us?'

She shook her head.

'He was killed by a stray bullet in Dublin in 1916. He was trying to help one of our cousins escape from the College of Surgeons.'

'And the cousin?'

'Brendan Doherty,' she nodded. 'He survived. Went to America. He and *his* cousin, Sean McGinley, have both been very kind to Emily.'

'I had no idea how I was going to tell you, but you've saved me the trouble. The question now is what to do. Would that I could arrive like Alex and be welcomed, but I don't deserve that. I behaved appallingly. I turned my back on my family for the most selfish of reasons when my parents had been extremely generous to me. Unlike *your* brothers, I had an apprenticeship and went into management. I was rather success-ful in business. Less successful in my private life. My wife died soon after our son was born, but by then any feeling we'd had for each other had gone. My son was brought up by her family, the Slaters, with whom I went into business for a time, hence my name. I'm about to resume James, regardless of what might happen here.'

'What age were you then?'

'When?'

'When you rejected your family?'

'Nineteen. Twenty, perhaps.'

'But that is a long time ago, isn't it?'

For some reason, the only thing Rosie could

think of was seedlings. Billy said that after you'd grown enough spindly ones that had to be thrown away, you'd be able to spot a grower when it was no bigger than your thumb. She pushed the thought out of mind, because she couldn't see what on earth it had to do with the matter in hand.

'Yes, it is a long time ago. But surely that makes matters worse and not better?'

She wondered what he could have been like in his twenties, but she could make no connection between the confident and considerate man that sat opposite her and the young man who'd rejected his family.

'But why? I think Da would be delighted to have you back.'

'And could forgive me for the hurt I caused? Especially to your granny, whom he always loved so dearly.'

'Da's a Quaker now. They're very good on forgiveness.'

A small smile touched his lips.

'And your grandmother?'

For a few moments she hesitated. She went back over the evening she'd shown Granny James's business card. At the time, she'd said nothing, but there'd been a sudden moment of quiet before they moved on to speak of other things. That was what was significant now.

'Uncle James, I showed Granny your business card early last month. I think she's worked it out already. She's just waiting till the time seems right.'

381

Twenty-Four

There was heavy rain in Belfast on Monday night. Rosie woke, heard it drumming on the roof but was so tired she fell asleep again without having time to worry about any consequences it might have. All it did was freshen the streets of the city. Next morning, the air was clear and bright and when her colleagues arrived from Portadown they replied to her anxious questions about the rain with laughter. They'd had no rain at all.

The dry, settled weather seemed like a good omen and the days that followed were rewarding and enjoyable. On Tuesday, a busload of ladies from the Armagh Group of Women's Institutes arrived to visit the fair, among them Miss Wilson, Mrs Mackay and Mary Braithwaite. They were tremendously impressed with the stand and what the staff were wearing and delighted by the colour postcards of roses they were invited to choose. On Wednesday, Dr Stewart arrived with Aunt Elizabeth and her grandmother. They confessed they'd kept their visit a surprise because they didn't want to upset any plans she might have made.

'Norman Lambert, perhaps? What do you think, Rosie?

She nodded at Mary, a shy country girl, who in the short space of time since Monday was now cheerfully choosing buttonholes for the gentlemen visitors as if she'd been doing it for years. She watched, delighted, as Mary carefully pinned the rose on Dr Stewart's lapel.

'That smells wonderful, Mary. Do I have to buy a whole bushfull now?'

'No, sir, just tell everyone where you got it, please.'

'I will do that with great pleasure, my dear. Thank you *very* much.'

'And ladies can choose colour postcards,' Rosie said, giving both her aunt and her grandmother a quick hug.

'Rosie, these are really lovely,' said Elizabeth, casting her eye over the selection spread out before her. 'Will your father manage to get up to Belfast this week?'

'Yes. Friday afternoon. Bobby and Charlie too. They've all managed a half day off.'

'Richard is hoping to come up tomorrow. He arrived home this morning looking ghastly. Apparently it was a rough crossing and after that they lost his luggage,' she went on, raising her eyebrows.

'But I thought it was to be the *end* of June.'

'So did I, but we all forgot there's a fortnight's holiday included in his year's contract.'

Elizabeth moved away and crossed the stand to join her husband, Dr Stewart, who was deep in conversation with Brian Singleton and at the same time casting his eye down his lists very intently.

Rosie turned to her grandmother and found her gazing at the publicity photographs taken on Monday.

'This is a splendid photograph, Rosie. Pity it's not in colour. Were these the Americans we've heard about?' she asked, examining the other images in the display Brian had added to the stand the previous day. 'Very good of Mr Sam. Good of Slater Hamilton too,' she said thoughtfully, running her finger along the large black and white print and pausing at his tall figure.

'I had dinner with him on Monday.'

'Oh, you did, did you?'

She could see her grandmother was pleased and would have said more, but as another group of visitors began to swirl around them there was no opportunity.

'Would you have a pencil and an envelope?' her grandmother asked.

Rosie produced a pencil from her pocket and gave it to her, but an envelope was more difficult. She left her choosing a postcard and went across to ask Brian if he had one. All he could offer was one that bore the address of the Portadown showroom printed on it, but she took it and thanked him. She knew it wouldn't matter.

'I've just written a short message,' her grandmother said, as she slipped the postcard into the envelope and sealed it. 'But it may make it easier.'

'I'll see he gets it.'

'Oh, I mustn't forget what I have to tell you. Helen is engaged.'

For one long, distressing moment, Rosie felt

herself go rigid with anxiety.

'I've forgotten the young man's name, but Richard P says he's a good chap. Another doctor, I gather.'

She gave Rosie a small, secret smile, squeezed her arm and said they must see each other soon, they had rather a lot to talk about. Then with a wave, she went to join Elizabeth and Richard, who had just finished ordering some new roses for their front garden.

An hour later, Rosie turned to find a familiar, tall figure smiling down at her.

'Mr Hamilton,' she said politely, the stand still crowded with colleagues and visitors.

'I can see how busy you are, but I thought you'd like to see this. We can make arrangements another time.'

He handed her the reply-paid envelope on which she'd written his name and waited patiently while she read the short message several times over.

Dear James,
   Welcome home! I look forward to seeing you when time and occasion permits. Rosie has my telephone number, so new I keep forgetting it. With love, Ma.

'Lizzie, I have such wonderful news,' Rosie said, as she pushed open the door of their room sometime after six, her arms full of roses, still lovely and full of fragrance, but already beginning to be overblown.

Lizzie was lying on the sofa, a hot-water bottle

clutched to her stomach. She was very pale and looked as if she might have been crying.

'Oh my poor dear, what's wrong?'

She dropped the roses on the nearest single bed, came over and took her friend's hand.

'I feel awful.'

'Is it your monthly? Has it just started?'

Lizzie nodded, bending over, clutching the hot-water bottle fiercely against her stomach.

'You don't normally have much trouble, do you?'

Rosie bit her lip. It was perfectly obvious something was not right, but Lizzie wasn't doing much to tell her how she felt. While she was still thinking what to do next, Lizzie gave a little cry.

'I think I've wet myself.'

She attempted to stand up, but had to sit down again, crying out in horror as she saw blood trickle down her bare legs and make small puddles on the worn carpet.

'I'm goin' to die,' she moaned. 'Somethin' awful's happenin' to me. An' what's poor Hugh going to do without me?'

She burst into tears and sobbed as if her heart would break.

'No, you're not. No one dies of a heavy period. Here, stick this between your legs and we'll get you sorted out.'

Rosie picked up the neatly folded hand towel beside her own bed, put her arm round her and helped her remove her saturated knickers. There was indeed an awful lot of blood. She was concerned at the amount and its appearance.

'What was last month's like? Was it very

light?'

She shook her head.

'It didn't come at all last month.'

'Does that often happen?

'No. It's never happened before. Rosie, I'm goin' to bleed to death. I know I am.'

'No you *are* not.'

Rosie racked her brains trying to think of what might help. She knew perfectly well what a missing period meant. If Lizzie and Hugh were married, there'd be no puzzle at all, but she was certain Lizzie had never made love with Hugh. This was the girl who had never even seen a boy peeing in a hedge until the day she'd met him in the strawberry field.

'Sure them one's could pick it up off the grass.'

Suddenly, she remembered overhearing her mother and one of her neighbours fulminating about some girls who were 'always falling pregnant'. From what she'd been able to grasp, it seemed they were so fertile that even a kiss and cuddle behind a haystack could have an unfortunate outcome.

'Lizzie dear, now I don't want you to be upset with me, but I need to know. Have you and Hugh been cuddling together without your clothes on?'

'An what if we have?' she replied crossly, a little colour mitigating the ghastly pallor of her face. 'I've never done what you're not supposed to do. I know better than that.'

Rosie took a deep breath.

'But have you ever got damp?'

'Yes, well,' she said, tossing her head. 'But sure what does that matter? I told you we've never done anythin' wrong. Hugh knows all about that. He's explained it all to me, but he'd never do that. It would be trouble for me and he loves me far too much for that.'

Rosie gave a sigh of relief. She'd no idea what she was going to do next, but at least she could reassure Lizzie she wasn't going to bleed to death.

'Lizzie dear, I know you've done nothing *wrong*, but I think there may have been an accident.'

'You mean I'm in the family way?' she demanded, her eyes wide, a look of absolute horror on her face.

'Well, you were, at least I think you were, but you're certainly not now. That's what the bleeding's about. That's why you're going to have to see a doctor.'

She shook her head vigorously.

'If I see a doctor then Auntie will know and she'll tell Da. He'll go mad. I can't do that.'

'I suppose you'd rather die?'

'Ach, Rosie, don't be cross with me,' she said, bursting into tears again.

Rosie put her arms round her and comforted her.

'I do know *one* doctor who wouldn't tell anyone. If I can get him to come, would that be all right?'

'That nice old man, the one you call Uncle Richard?'

Rosie nodded. That nice old man, as Lizzie called him, had driven to Belfast this morning, spent the day tramping round the trade fair and was probably now having a well-earned nap after his supper, but at least she could talk to him, or Aunt Elizabeth, and they would know what it was best to do. Granny would know too, but the chances were she was still with them at Dromore. She often stayed the night if they'd been out together all day.

'I can't telephone from here, can I? Your aunt might hear.'

'You're in luck. She's away over t' see m' cousin and won't be back till after nine.'

'Right. Now you promise not to frighten yourself while I'm gone. You're *not* going to die. Got that? Here's another towel. You might need it. I'll clean you up when I come back.'

She picked up the phone and a crisp voice said, 'Number please?'

'Dromore 6.'

'I'm trying to connect you.'

At least she had no difficulty remembering the Stewart's number, it was one of the first telephones in Dromore. She listened to the small noises coming through the earpiece on the heavy handset and wondered if she might have been cut off. Then she heard the fierce ring of a bell at the other end.

'Doctor Stewart's practice. Can I help you?'

For a moment, she was so taken aback at the sound of Richard P's voice that she completely forgot what she was going to say. She listened helplessly as he patiently repeated what he'd said.

'Richard, I'm so sorry ... it's Rosie. I wasn't expecting to hear you.'

389

'Rosie!'

His tone was a mixture of surprise and joy.

'Rosie, is everything all right. Are *you* all right?'

'Yes, yes. I'm fine.'

There was no missing either the concern or the tenderness in his voice.

'I was hoping to see you tomorrow, even if just briefly,' he went on quickly. 'Mother says you're very busy, but I thought we might meet at the weekend.'

'Richard that would be lovely, but I need to ask you some urgent doctor questions right now. I'm staying with Lizzie and she's bleeding. I need to know what to do.'

'Right. Tell me what you can.'

His tone of voice had changed instantly.

She told him about what had happened so far, explained about the missing period and Lizzie's innocence about the possibility of her having conceived.

'Yes, it certainly sounds like a miscarriage,' he agreed. 'I'll come right away, but I'd better tell you what happens next in case I'm delayed. I know where you are. What's the number of the house?'

She gave him the number, then listened carefully as he explained about the release of the conception sac which was bulbous and could be painful.

'Richard, we might have Lizzie's aunt to deal with. Could we say it's appendicitis, or we think it is?'

'Yes, of course. One often gets false alarms

with appendicitis. Don't worry if there's a lot more blood. It always looks far more than it really is. I'll be as quick as I can.'

Even allowing for the empty roads and the fact that Richard had borrowed his father's more powerful motor, Rosie was amazed at how quickly he managed the journey from Dromore. Less than an hour after her telephone call, she heard a motor stop outside. Looking down from the bay window, she saw him jump out, snatch his bag out of the back seat and stride towards the front door. She ran down to let him in.

'How is she?'

'She seems in good spirits. I think it's me that's flagging.'

'What about the conception sac?'

'About half an hour ago. It *was* painful, but I told her it was good practice for having a baby. It didn't go on for terribly long.'

'Hello Lizzie. I'm Richard,' he said holding out his hand. 'How are you feeling?'

'Awful. But I don't think I'm dyin' anymore.'

'No, we're not having that,' he said briskly.

He took her pulse and looked around, fixing his eyes on a clean towel that covered a pile of stained cloths. He raised an eyebrow at Rosie who nodded and brought the relevant one for him to examine.

'You've been lucky that you had Rosie here. There's no harm done and you'll be all right in a day or two. The only thing we need is to avoid infection. A bath tonight when you're feeling a little better. Regular washing and clean linen. I've brought some antiseptic you can use and if

391

you're in any doubt at all you can ring me.'

Lizzie looked up at him and smiled.

'Neither Rosie nor me's had any supper. All that blood would put ye off. But I'm starvin'. D'ye think the pair of ye could make some scrambled egg and toast? There's always plenty of eggs in the kitchen, but not much else. I'll be all right for a while now,' she added firmly, looking from one to the other. 'I'll maybe go to sleep for a bit,' she added, dipping her eyelids.

The boarder's kitchen was clean and bare, but rather dim and miserable. Even at midsummer, little sunlight ever penetrated it's north-facing window and when it did, it was absorbed immediately by the dark wood of the cupboards and by the brown and cream linoleum on the floor. There was a permanent smell of Jeyes Fluid and unburnt gas.

Rosie fetched a clean towel from the linen cupboard and together they washed their hands in the icy cold water that gushed fiercely from the single tap over the large, square Belfast sink.

'You've done very well, Rosie, especially when you had to work out what was happening. I wish some of the nurses I worked with in London could keep so calm.'

'I didn't feel calm. I was really upset I didn't know what was going to happen next, till you told me.'

'It's not what you feel, Rosie. It's what you *do*. But it's sad poor Lizzie had such a fright, because she was so ill-informed. Didn't you do any biology at Miss Wilson's?'

Rosie burst out laughing as they shared the

towel to dry their hands.

'The life cycle of the butterfly, the circulation of the blood and the germination of sunflower seeds.'

'You're joking! No, you're not. You're serious.'

'Dear Miss Wilson, she is lovely and kind and full of wisdom about how one copes with the difficulties of living and growing up, but she never married and she thinks such things are not to be spoken of.'

'It could have been *very* unhappy for Lizzie.'

She nodded and opened the cupboard door to see whether there really were eggs or not.

'Rosie, there's something I want to ask you.'

'Mmm,' she said, her back to him, as she found a whole rack of eggs, began to pick them up and count them into a bowl.

'I can think of no more unsuitable place than our present surroundings. I had quite other plans, but after being patient a whole year, I cannot wait a minute longer. Rosie, will you marry me? As soon as possible. Please.'

She put the bowl of eggs down on the table as if it were very fragile, turned round and looked at him. He stood leaning against the sink, the one place where he wouldn't get in her way if she moved between the cupboard and the stove. She could not quite make out the look in his eyes. Excitement. Anxiety, perhaps. Some mixture of both.

'Yes, Richard I will. As soon as you want, but just suddenly I think I need to sit down.'

* * *

It was seven o'clock on Saturday evening when the very last rose petal was picked up from the marble floor of the City Hall. Dismantling the stand seemed to take no time at all in comparison with the long hours of putting it together the previous Sunday, working behind closed doors, aware of the empty streets of the city and the echoing peal of church bells.

The Northern Ireland Trade Fair had been a huge success. Not only for McGredy's, whose order books were full, but for most of the other companies who had put their goods on show or advertised their services. Mr Sam had been delighted, had given them all a bonus and said that all those who had worked so hard in Belfast should take Monday and Tuesday off.

As she drove back home to Portadown in the company's van, squeezed into the front seat between Billy and Mary, the van full of the paraphernalia of the display, she looked back on the week just past as over a huge landscape viewed from the top of a hill.

So many successes and such unexpected joy.

Apart from Lizzie, no one yet knew of her engagement to Richard. Tomorrow he would be coming over to meet her parents and to take her back to Rathdrum for her promised visit to her grandmother. She'd no idea what her mother would say to Richard, or whether she would even be there to greet him, but of her father's response she had little doubt. Granny had spoken often enough of the qualities of her godson and Da knew how good her judgement was.

She could see his face and that slow smile, so

much more frequent these days. It reminded her of a particular smile she would never forget. It was a genuine coincidence that Uncle James, as she now called him, had come back from a visit to the new government building at Stormont on Friday afternoon and paused by the stand merely to say a friendly word and ask her how the day was going.

Her father was studying the postcards she'd painted in the barn throughout the winter and spring. Bobby and Charlie were standing beside him, blocking him from view. Sam had already been introduced to Mary, who was fixing a fragment of foliage behind a rosebud to give to him, when he turned round unexpectedly and found himself face to face with the man she'd first known as Slater Hamilton.

'Hallo, Sam.'

'Hallo, James.'

Neither had the slightest doubt about who the other was, nor was there the slightest awkwardness between them. Rosie did wonder if Granny had been in touch with them both. But what really held her was that slow smile of her father's, the enthusiasm with which he introduced Bobby and Charlie to 'Uncle James' and the way they all stood and talked together before Uncle James had to go back up to his office for the final meeting of his day.

'There ye are Mary. Home James. An' I won't see you till Wednesday.'

Billy drew up at the end of the long lane that ran up to the farm where Mary lived with her family. Rosie watched her go, still wearing her pale pink blouse and her moss green overall, a girl for whom the week in Belfast had been a visit to a different world.

'My goodness, she's come on,' said Billy, as he put the van back in gear. 'She wouldn't have said boo to a goose a week ago and I heard her doing Brian's job the day when he was out for his lunch. An' doin' it as well as he would. She's no dozer, Mary.'

'There's more to us girls than meets the eye, Billy,' she said, teasing him.

'Well, I foun' that out when you turned up a year ago.'

They fell silent, weary after such a tremendous effort, the shadows lengthening as they drove along the familiar road. They moved gently down the dip where the big load had got stuck, passed the new garden wall where Mary Braithwaite's plants were now a mass of bloom. Two miles on Billy turned down the lane to Richhill Station and swung into the yard.

'That's you now, Rosie. Enjoy your wee holiday. I'll see you Wednesday. Have you roses in the back?'

She collected a last armful of roses, fresh yesterday and likely to last four or five days more, and stood waiting as he turned in the yard and drove back out on to the lane. She waved him goodbye and walked slowly towards the open door of the house. Her father's bicycle was parked in its usual place against the wall of the barn and smoke rose from a fresh fire.

It seemed a long, long way from the night her grandfather had been taken ill and she'd spent the week of his dying getting to know the man she loved and soon would marry.

Sure a good thing's worth waiting for.

Her grandfather's words came back to her as his words so often did. She remembered too what her grandmother had said back in the winter when they'd talked about Richard.

Granny had been right. He *had* been waiting. And Granda was right too. Richard's waiting had given her time to make a life of her own and at this moment she was quite sure their future together would be the all the richer for it.